FORGE BOOKS BY NICHOLAS GUILD

Blood Ties

THE
IRONSMITH

NICHOLAS GUILD

A TOM DOHERTY ASSOCIATES BOOK

NEW YORK

THE IRONSMITH

Copyright © 2016 by Nicholas Guild

A Forge Book
Published by Tom Doherty Associates, LLC
175 Fifth Avenue
New York, NY 10010

www.tor-forge.com

Forge® is a registered trademark of Tom Doherty Associates, LLC.

The Library of Congress Cataloging-in-Publication Data is available upon request.

ISBN 978-0-7653-8226-9 (hardcover)
ISBN 978-1-4668-8659-9 (e-book)

Our books may be purchased in bulk for promotional, educational, or business use.
Please contact your local bookseller or the Macmillan Corporate and Premium
Sales Department at 1-800-221-7945, extension 5442, or by e-mail at
MacmillanSpecialMarkets@macmillan.com.

First Edition: February 2016

Printed in the United States of America

0 9 8 7 6 5 4 3 2 1

For my dear son Michael

ὦ παῖ, γένοιο πατρὸς εὐτυχέστερος
Sophocles, Αιας, 550

THE
IRONSMITH

PROLOGUE

The horsemen appeared without warning. There were eight of them and they wore the chain mail corselets of the Tetrarch's soldiers. With the sun behind them, they lined the bluff above the riverbank, implying that both resistance and escape were impossible.

It was just after dawn, and cold. The only sound was the whisper of the Jordan as it passed over its rocky bed.

"They must have ridden half the night," the Baptist said. He knew, of course, that they had come to arrest him. He felt no fear, which surprised and pleased him. The end was always worse in expectation than as an actual presence.

"We can escape across the river. It isn't more than a few feet deep, and on the other side we'll be in Judea."

The Baptist shook his head and tried not to smile. Only Joshua could imagine they would have a chance.

"A horse can move through the water faster than a man. They would ride us down before we were halfway. Besides, even if we reached the other shore, why would they hesitate to kill us in Judea?"

He glanced around at his other disciples and saw their fear. They were crowded together under an acacia tree and seemed to be trying to disappear into its shade. There were ten of them altogether, and they were his only legacy.

Joshua alone stood with him. Joshua alone seemed afraid for something beyond his own life. Perhaps the legacy had dwindled down to only one.

"I don't suppose they plan to arrest us all," the Baptist went on, giving the impression that he thought of it as an abstract question of tactics. "They didn't bring enough men. Still, they look as if they are waiting for us to take flight so they can have a little sport. I had best go to them."

"You can't simply let them have you," Joshua murmured tensely, his hand closing around the Baptist's wrist. "John, the Tetrarch will have you killed."

The Baptist merely shrugged.

"You can't let him."

Gently, the Baptist freed himself from Joshua's grip.

"We've talked about this," he answered, smiling with apparent serenity. "We knew it was coming. My life isn't important. Only the ministry is important, and if the rest of you die with me, the ministry is over. Now, trust in God, as I do, and let me meet the destiny He has prepared for me."

That was the last his followers saw of him, walking slowly toward the bluff where the soldiers waited.

1

Noah, an ironsmith and a resident of Sepphoris, the old capital of Galilee, was at the forge when Hiram, his senior apprentice, came to tell
him he had a visitor.

"He says he is your cousin. He's waiting outside."

The ironsmith set down his hammer and wiped his face with his
right hand. He was wearing nothing but a loincloth and sandals, since
at the forge, clothing had an annoying tendency to catch fire. The muscles of his arms and powerful chest gleamed with sweat. He did not
seem pleased by the news.

Except for his sister, who lived with him, Noah had no relatives in
the city. He had a distant cousin in Jerusalem and, for the rest, everyone
who could claim kinship lived in a village an hour's walk to the south.
So family visits usually meant bad news.

He looked at the bar of metal he was holding with a pair of tongs and
buried it in the hot coals. It would have to wait. He reached down and
dipped his hands into a bucket of water he kept for the purpose, scoop-
ing up enough to rinse his face and rub a little over his chest.

"Let's go see," he said.

Hiram followed him to the workshop door, which stood open. There
was a man crouched outside. He was covered with dust and appeared
utterly spent. With what seemed great effort, he looked up and smiled
weakly at Noah, who recognized him at once.

"Go bank my fire," Noah told his apprentice, never taking his eyes from the visitor. "When you're finished, we'll be in the scrub room."

He waited until Hiram was gone, and then he reached down to help his cousin to his feet. It pained Noah to see him in such a condition.

"They arrested the Baptist," Joshua said, as soon as he was standing. "Soldiers came and he gave himself up. He didn't even try to get away."

Noah could only shake his head. John was a distant figure, someone he had heard spoken of, but no more. It was the narrowness of Joshua's escape that filled him with dread.

"Are they hunting you?"

"I don't know." Joshua raised his hands in a helpless gesture.

"Come with me."

Noah put his arm around his cousin's waist, partly out of affection, for they had been close friends since childhood, and partly to make sure Joshua kept his feet. The contrast between them could not have been more pointed—Joshua tall and slender and Noah a solid block of muscle not quite reaching his cousin's shoulder.

Noah led him into a small room with benches against three of its stone walls and a tub of cold water in the center of the floor. It was where he and his apprentices cleaned up after a day in the heat and smoke.

When Hiram came, Noah already had Joshua stripped and was washing him, since he seemed too weak to do it for himself. He sent Hiram across an alley to his house to fetch some food and wine.

"How long have you been on the road?" he asked.

"Two weeks and more. I've lost count of the days."

"How have you lived?"

It seemed a reasonable question since, as a disciple of the Baptist, Joshua wouldn't have had any money.

"People along the way took me in and fed me, sometimes."

"How long since you've eaten?"

"Three days—no, two. The day before yesterday an old woman gave me a fig." Joshua smiled. The recollection seemed to amuse him. Then, quite suddenly, the smile disappeared. "If I can stay here the night, tomorrow I'll be on my way again."

"Where are you going?"

"To a place called Capernaum. It's a fishing village on the Sea of Kinneret. I have a friend there."

"What will you do?"

"Carry John's message. What else is there to do?" Joshua shrugged, but there was something of defiance in the gesture. Noah understood and reached across to pat him on the knee.

"Well, you won't be leaving for Capernaum tomorrow," he said. "You'll need at least three or four days to gather your strength. In four days it will be the Sabbath and you can come back to Nazareth with me and see your family."

"No. I'll keep the Sabbath here, if it's all right." Joshua made a weak gesture with his right hand, as if warding off a blow. "You know what my father is like. At least here no one will tell me that I'm a fool and ought to go back to being a carpenter."

"You're a fool and ought to go back to being a carpenter."

They both laughed.

When the food came, Joshua was too weary to eat, so Noah took him to his house and made up a bed for him. Once Joshua was asleep, which was almost instantly, Noah went downstairs to the kitchen and poured himself a cup of wine.

It was early afternoon and his sister, Sarah, would soon return from her errands. He needed to consider what to tell her—and, more importantly, what to do.

With the Baptist under arrest, the question became whether his disciples would then attract the Tetrarch's interest. It seemed wisest to assume that Joshua's name was on their lists.

It did not fail to occur to Noah that Joshua's presence in Sepphoris involved certain risks for him as well. If Joshua really was a fugitive and he should be found in this house . . .

The thought made him feel ashamed. Joshua needed time to rest and recover. The risks would have to be borne.

But it was also true that the danger was greatest in the cities, where the Tetrarch concentrated his power, so Joshua's plan of seeking refuge in some obscure fishing village had a certain merit. If he had friends there he would probably be safe enough. In the countryside, Herod's tax gatherers and soldiers were regarded as an invading force and were hated accordingly.

They would not have arrested the Baptist unless they meant to execute him and, once he was dead, perhaps in a few months, the Tetrarch would grow forgetful.

The problem thus became getting Joshua safely to his place of hiding.

Noah saw no point in keeping any of this from Sarah. She would have to know that Joshua's presence in their house had to be kept a secret, and therefore she would have to know why. She was neither foolish nor hysterical, and she could even be of use.

As for Hiram, he did not even know the stranger's name, and he was a good sort. A word would keep him silent.

While Noah sat alone in his kitchen, his fingers touching the rim of a cup of wine he had not yet tasted, his thoughts were the prey of recollection. He had spent his childhood in Nazareth, but he had been born in Sepphoris, in this very house, where his mother had died giving birth to Sarah, early enough that his mind held no memory of her. His father had remarried a year later. Then his father had died and, as his stepmother had not wished to be encumbered with children not her own, brother and sister had been given over to the care of their grandparents in Nazareth.

Thus, he had known Joshua all his life. As children they had learned their letters together, had played together, had sometimes quarreled, and then missed each other bitterly during their short estrangements. Each had stood as the other's friend when each took a wife, and when, only a few months apart, each had watched helplessly as his wife suffered and died, they had grieved together. What had they not shared?

And now Joshua had come with a new trouble. Well, to whom else should he have come?

Noah did not endorse the life his cousin had chosen. For all that he thought the Baptist was a good man and a true servant of God—perhaps even a prophet—it would not have occurred to Noah to go off and be his disciple, living on nuts and berries beside the Jordan River. His piety simply did not take that form. Yet he did see why it had occurred to Joshua. Even in childhood they had differed widely in temperament, but they had always understood each other.

And now Joshua wanted to go off to some fishing village in the north to preach the Baptist's message of repentance, and Noah had no trouble grasping why, for Joshua, that might be the inevitable choice. Thus it was also inevitable that Noah would help him to do it.

The only question was how.

The first step was to restore Joshua's strength.

It had been a shock to see him in such a condition. They had not met since the Passover, two months before, and he had looked wild enough then, with his torn, faded cloak and his tangled beard down to his breastbone, but now he appeared spent, as if the life he had been leading had at last used him up.

He needed rest and quiet and safety, and these things, at least, Noah could provide.

When Sarah came home, Noah told her that Joshua was asleep upstairs. Then he told her that the Baptist had been arrested. She seemed to guess the rest.

Sarah was tall and thin, which made her arms appear even longer than they were. When she grew nervous or excited she seemed to lose control of her movements and was always knocking things over, which explained why she wrapped one long hand around the other and held them both against her modest bosom as she asked the inevitable question.

"Is Joshua a fugitive?"

"He doesn't know. They didn't try to take him with the Baptist, but they could easily change their minds. I think it best we assume they will."

"What can we do?"

"Hide him until he is fit to travel and then help him escape to the north."

"Is he ill?"

"No. Just worn out."

"I bought fish," she said, smiling as if everything had worked out perfectly. "It is strengthening and easy on the stomach."

Noah kissed his sister on the cheek.

It was only the middle of the afternoon, so Noah returned to his forge.

As soon as he was gone Sarah went upstairs to the spare bedroom, where Joshua was asleep. The door was slightly ajar and she could tell from the sound of his breathing that he would not wake up for some hours. She returned to the kitchen, where she had to make decisions about dinner.

Half a carp, split down the backbone, dried and salted, was wrapped in palm fronds and lying on the table. Careful planning was essential when one cooked for only two people, and Sarah had been hesitant about buying a fish—even half a fish—that was nearly a cubit in length, but with Joshua there it would be just enough. She would soak it in unmixed wine and then add some water, a few herbs, and a little flour and let it all simmer in an iron pot until sunset.

It would be pleasant to have Joshua in the house for a few days. Like Noah, Sarah had grown up with her cousins, the sons and daughters of Joseph and Miriam, who lived in a house separated from her grandfather's by little more than a few paces of open ground. Joshua was not her particular favorite, but he was family, and Sarah had been a close friend of his wife. She had played with Rachel when they were children. As young women, hardly out of girlhood, they had shared many secrets, and Rachel, her womb torn open trying to give birth to Joshua's dead son, had died in Sarah's arms.

It was another bond with Joshua, the grief he and Sarah had each endured when Rachel was lowered into her grave. She could not look at Joshua without remembering his wife.

Still, she had always thought Joshua odd, and he had grown even odder since Rachel's death.

For one thing, she did not understand his piety. He had always been pious, but in recent years his feeling for God had grown into something that Sarah could hardly put a name to. It was odd. That was the only word for it.

The Baptist was a prophet, and that was a whole other thing, but ordinary men were not prophets. Joshua, she felt quite sure, was not a prophet. He was a carpenter who had lost his wife. It was the duty of ordinary men to live in the world according to God's law. God bid us to say prayers at the proper times, to honor the holy days, and to keep His commandments. That was enough. That was righteousness. Joshua should go back to his trade and marry again.

For that matter, Noah should marry again. In Noah's case, his sister had particular reasons for thinking so.

Just as the sun was going down, Sarah removed the iron pot from its hook in the fireplace and set it aside. By the time Noah entered the kitchen, dinner was ready.

"Is Joshua still asleep?" he asked, after he had sat down at the kitchen table.

"Yes. I looked in on him just a few minutes ago."

Her brother nodded, and then his face became shadowed with anxiety.

"Eat your stew," Sarah ordered, in a voice that perfectly mimicked their grandmother's.

This made Noah laugh and the shadows disappeared. He picked up a piece of bread and tore it in half. He began using it to scoop up pieces of fish.

Sarah, who had not touched her food, sat with her hands folded together. She seemed to be trying to take up as little space as possible.

"Will Joshua go back to Nazareth?" she asked.

Without looking up, her brother shook his head.

"If they want to arrest him, that will be the first place they look. He has it in mind to go north, to some fishing village where he has friends."

"What will he do there?"

"Preach, I assume. He wants to carry on John's teaching."

There followed a silence, which Noah understood to be his sister's way of expressing her disapproval. He looked up at her and smiled.

"Did you think that he would go back to being a carpenter?"

Sarah didn't answer immediately. Instead, she looked down at her stew, then tore the corner off a piece of bread and began eating.

This indicated, as clearly as any words, that she was upset.

"What do you think they will do to the Baptist?" she asked finally.

"Given that the Tetrarch is Old Herod's son, I think they will kill him."

"Why would they do that? He is a holy man."

"Why then would they arrest him? The Tetrarch is no David. He will not suffer even a prophet's rebuke."

With a shade too much haste, Sarah reached for her wine. A drop spilled out and ran sluggishly down the side of the cup. She instantly put the cup down again.

"Perhaps this village in the north could use a carpenter," she said, almost defiantly. "Joshua needs to settle down somewhere and begin his life again."

Even as she was speaking the words, she knew they implied more than she intended. She had merely to look at her brother's face to know that he understood what was in her heart.

You want him to marry again, his expression said. *As you want me to marry again, so that then you can marry Abijah.*

Instantly she felt ashamed. It was not Noah's fault. He had told her, many times, *"I will not perish because you are not here to cook my meals. I can hire a servant. Abijah is a good man. You should marry him and be happy. The very last thing I want is to deny you this."*

And she did love Abijah. He was so handsome. And he loved her—skinny, awkward creature that she was. Every girl in the district was half mad in love with him, yet he wanted only her.

But her brother—her good, kind, pious, learned brother, the best of men—how could she leave him? She remembered how crushed with sorrow he had been when Ruth died, how his heart had bled with mourning. Sarah had come to stay with him after that, to keep him company and see that he remembered to eat his meals, and she had never left.

She could never leave her brother alone. Never. Abijah, she could only hope, would be patient.

Secretly she blamed Ruth. Sarah could not have brought herself to say such a thing, or perhaps even to think it, yet she felt it. Ruth had been a good enough sort of woman, but nothing beyond the ordinary. Why did her memory hold Noah in such bondage?

And there were certainly plenty of women who would have been prepared to take her place. One was Sarah's friend Huldah, who showed a lively enough interest that Sarah persuaded her brother to invite Huldah and her father to dinner.

Noah had spent most of the evening in conversation with the father about some question concerning the calendar. He was perfectly gracious to his sister's friend, but that was all.

For three days Sarah heard nothing from Huldah, and then they met at the house of a mutual friend. With some hesitation, Sarah brought up the subject of the dinner party.

"Your brother looks at me with no more interest than if I were a cooking pot," Huldah said. She was right, of course, and that ended Sarah's efforts as a matchmaker.

"This stew is very good," Noah said, smiling. He meant to distract her, she knew. She had the feeling sometimes that he could peer straight into her mind. "The broth is delicious."

About two hours after sunset, Joshua woke up. Noah had been sitting in the dark, waiting.

"Are you hungry?" he asked.

"Yes. And very thirsty."

Sarah had kept the stew warm. There was also fresh bread, and Noah watered the wine eight parts to three. It was a meal for an invalid.

Nevertheless, Joshua seemed to enjoy it.

"John cared nothing about food," he said. "Sometimes it would be days before he would remember to eat. If Simon hadn't brought his fishing net, the rest of us might have starved."

"Is he your friend in Capernaum? You said it was a fishing village."

"Yes. That's him. Simon went home to visit his wife about a week before John was arrested, but he left his net."

"What was John like?"

"You never heard him preach?"

"No."

Joshua shrugged, as if he had decided to forgive the oversight, and then he said, "John was the purest soul I ever knew."

"In what way?"

"In every way. He cared nothing about pleasure or comfort. For John, there was only God. He was God's prophet."

"So naturally the Tetrarch arrested him."

"Of course. John expected it."

"Did he?"

"Yes." Joshua smiled tightly, giving the impression that its very obviousness was painful to him. "I remember how he walked over to meet the Tetrarch's soldiers. It was as if he welcomed them as friends."

"Did he wish to die, then?"

"I don't think it made any difference to him. 'Let me meet the destiny God has prepared for me,' he said. What mattered was the will of God."

"What matters to you?"

"To carry on John's teaching. To make myself worthy to be called his disciple." Joshua smiled, as if he had just said something amusing. "Did you ever think that I, of all people, would end as a messenger of God?"

"Perhaps not, but somehow it fails to surprise me."

On the evening following the Sabbath, after Noah had returned from Nazareth, Joshua was waiting for him.

"Did you see my family?" he asked.

Noah shook his head. "Only at the prayer house."

Joshua seemed disappointed, and let the subject drop.

"I think it is time I was on my way," he said, finally. "I have my strength back."

"Are you sure?"

"Yes."

"Then I would like to offer a suggestion. Take the road to Tiberias, which is well traveled and safe. Then journey to Capernaum by boat."

"And if they are looking for me?"

Noah crossed his arms over his chest and smiled, visibly pleased with himself.

"Who will they be looking for?" he asked. "A follower of John. A beggar. An ascetic with a long, ragged beard." He reached out and playfully pulled on Joshua's chin whiskers. "While they are searching for this man, they will not see you."

"How will you manage it?"

"Leave it to me."

The next morning, early, Noah sent his sister off to the marketplace. Sarah knew what was required and would make a better selection than he could himself.

She came back two hours later with an embroidered tunic of Egyptian cotton and a wool cloak dyed blue. She had also brought back new sandals and a small vial of scented oil.

"You did very well," her brother told her. "Now, can you manage something about his hair and beard?"

"All I need are scissors and a comb."

An hour later, a different person stood before them. Joshua's hair, glistening with oil, was swept back from his forehead and ended just at the collar of his robe, and his beard was cut short and to a fashionable point. Sarah, with a woman's attention to detail, had even trimmed his fingernails.

Joshua, who seemed amused by his transformation, raised his arms and turned slowly in a full circle for their inspection.

"There is still something missing."

Noah shook his head and then disappeared upstairs. When he came back he showed them a silver ring with a small red stone.

"Put it on," he said to Joshua. "I think a bit of jewelry is necessary to complete the impression."

Joshua held up his hand, turning it this way and that so the ring caught the light.

"Where did you get this?" he asked, making the question sound like an accusation.

"It was in a trunk in the cellar when I moved back into this house. I can only assume it must have been my father's."

"Then someday you will want it returned." Joshua smiled, with just a hint of mischief. "I promise I won't give it away."

Joshua had to be dissuaded from leaving immediately, but Noah pointed out that it was an eight-hour walk to Tiberias and thus he could not hope to reach there before sunset. But if he left at first light, he would be in Tiberias by the early afternoon and might still catch a boat to Capernaum.

"Besides, you want to be on the road with the crowds. It will be safer and less conspicuous."

"I will feel conspicuous enough dressed like this," Joshua said, with a laugh. "I hardly know myself."

"Neither will anyone else."

The next morning, Noah accompanied him as far as the eastern gate and, at the last moment, pressed a small purse of silver coins into his hand.

"It completes the disguise, and you will need money on the journey."

"I hardly know what to do with money anymore."

"Believe me, there isn't enough to allow you much practice."

They embraced, and Joshua disappeared into the mob of travelers.

Where would this journey take him? Noah could not conceal from himself a sense of foreboding. "May God be merciful to His servant Joshua," he whispered, and turned back reluctantly to his accustomed life.

2

The Baptist was taken to Machaerus, a hilltop fortress in the middle of the Perean desert, just east of the Dead Sea. From the valley all one could see were its stone outer walls, gray and forbidding.

Such a stronghold, miles from the nearest city, was a monument to fear. It was intended as a refuge for Herod Antipas, Tetrarch of Galilee and Perea, a place where he might wait to be rescued by his Roman masters, should his own people rise against him.

Caleb bar Jacob, the Tetrarch's watchful servant, was mindful of that fear as he too traveled to Machaerus. Fear was the condition upon which power was granted and held.

The Baptist preached that men should repent of their sins, for God was about to redeem his creation. Redeem it from what, if not from Antipas? Was it at all surprising that the Tetrarch feared him? He had good reason. John was loved, while Antipas was an object of hatred. Antipas built cities of marble while there was famine in the villages. Only the patronage of Rome kept him from being torn apart.

So what more apt place than Machaerus to serve as the Baptist's prison? To be sent to Machaerus was almost to be removed from the earth.

Dawn was just breaking as Caleb set out from Beth Haram on the last leg of his journey. It was nearly thirty miles and no one traveled fast in the desert. His party was small, comprising an escort of only ten mounted soldiers. Caleb rode in the lead, to stay out of the dust as much as possible. There was also a single wagon, kept tightly covered, for its occupant hated and feared the daylight.

It had been quite cold when they left Beth Haram, but by midmorning the sun was ferocious.

The desert had a kind of pitiless beauty. The wind had worn its rocky hills into strange shapes, exposing bands of color—dull red, black, and iron gray, with here and there a streak of sulfurous yellow. In the middle of the day there was no sound, for not a breath of air moved and no living thing stirred. Yet the sun danced. You could see it shimmer on the flat, stony landscape.

For the last two hours, Caleb had been within sight of Machaerus atop its hill. Doubtless he was being watched from the fortress ramparts, and probably the soldiers had guessed that this visit had something to do with their celebrated prisoner.

For John was famous—famous and revered by many as God's prophet. To arrest him and, certainly, when it came to that, to execute him, involved risks.

But it also presented opportunities. John was a man like other men. Like all men he must fear pain and, most of all, death. Like all men he could be broken, and a broken, repentant John, begging the Tetrarch's forgiveness, could have his uses. First, it would discourage John's followers. Second, and perhaps more important, it would appeal to the Tetrarch's vanity. Either way, Caleb advanced in his master's confidence.

And John had smoothed the way for him by besmirching the Tetrarch's marriage. He had said that for Antipas to marry his half brother's wife, who was also his niece, was in the sight of God an unclean thing.

The Lord Eleazar, the First Minister of Galilee, had advised Antipas to put the matter from his mind. Perhaps he was even right, for the Lord Eleazar was a clever man who knew when to strike and when to stay his hand. He it was who had brought Caleb into the Tetrarch's service.

Some events are like a flash of light in the darkness. Caleb had not been present during the discussion, but he heard the details from his wife. Michal was the confidante of the Lady Herodias, the Tetrarch's wife, who had little enough reason to love either the Baptist or the Lord Eleazar.

And Antipas, it seemed, had not found the First Minister's advice congenial. He had complained that the dignity of his name seemed to count for nothing. He hinted darkly that the Lord Eleazar had grown timid, that he was more interested in protecting his own vast wealth than in upholding the honor of his master.

So was the First Minister falling from favor? Or was the Tetrarch merely giving vent to his frustration over advice he did not quite have the courage to ignore?

It was a question that required the nicest judgment. Caleb owed his position to the Lord Eleazar. He was his disciple, his chosen instrument, almost his second self. But if the lord was heading to his ruin—a course that would most likely end with his head on the executioner's block—Caleb might be lucky to escape alive himself. In any case, his career in the Tetrarch's service would be finished.

Unless, of course, he had by then distanced himself from the First Minister. Unless he had positioned himself as the logical successor.

On the other hand, such a move could be a terrible mistake. If the Tetrarch's anger was no more than a mood, and the Lord Eleazar remained in power, Caleb's betrayal would never be forgiven.

In the end the Tetrarch himself settled the matter. He invited Caleb and his wife to a banquet and seated them on couches very near his own. The entertainment was a performance of a comedy by Menander, and after it and a dinner that went on for half the night, Antipas wanted to gamble. He liked to win, so of course the dice were crooked, and Caleb cheerfully lost over a thousand silver shekels.

Then at last they rose from the table, and Antipas threw his arm across Caleb's shoulders and took him out onto the terrace to admire the sunrise. The Tetrarch was in rare good spirits, laughing and quoting lines from the play, which he seemed to know almost by heart, and then suddenly his mood darkened.

"Tell me, my boy, what do you think of this business with the Baptist," he asked, absolutely without preamble. "Do you agree with the First Minister that we should leave him alone?"

"The Lord Eleazar is a wise and careful man."

Caleb was afraid to say more.

"Then you do agree."

Antipas lifted his arm from Caleb's shoulder and seemed to withdraw into himself. He stared at the light streaming over the eastern hills, as if facing the last great disappointment of his life.

"I did not say that I agree, Lord," Caleb answered, searching his mind for everything in the reports about John that could be made to seem incriminating. "But perhaps it is not my place to agree or disagree."

"Your loyalty to the Lord Eleazar is commendable, but I would have you speak your mind. Do you think such an insult to the Lady Herodias is to be borne?"

"I am sure any such discourtesy was far from John's mind, sire. I truly believe he intended to insult only you."

This made the Tetrarch laugh, and he put his hand back on Caleb's shoulder.

Today he loves me, Caleb thought, feeling the weight of that hand. *Today I am a great favorite. And tomorrow?*

It is like keeping company with a wild boar. He watches you through fierce, greedy eyes, and the next instant he may run you down and tear you to pieces, spilling your guts on the ground with his tusks.

But for now he laughs.

"However, his attitude toward the Lady Herodias is not the main point," Caleb went on, when the laughter had subsided. "If it were merely that, I would have agreed with the lord that the wisest course was simply to ignore him. He would be beneath Your Highness's notice."

The Tetrarch seemed to consider this, perhaps trying to decide if his servant was being disrespectful. Apparently he decided not.

"Then what is the main point? His influence with the mob?"

"The mob, yes," Caleb answered. He felt himself sweating and hoped it didn't show. "The mob is always dangerous. The question is, what has John been telling the mob? He preaches that God will soon come to restore the world, presumably to its Edenic purity. Were there any kings in Eden?"

He did not wait for the Tetrarch to answer.

"We live in a fallen world, sire. This Scripture tells us, that through our own sinful nature we have lost Paradise. And without kings to rule us, we would tear each other apart. That is why Your Highness rules in Galilee, because it is the will of God. It is the *mercy* of God. The Baptist in his vast arrogance would set that aside. He conspires—"

"Conspires?"

There were certain words, Caleb had learned, that sent a thrill of horror though the Tetrarch's heart.

"Yes, sire. John has disciples."

The officer in charge was a man named Zev, and he would probably never leave this place alive. He was over fifty and had been posted to Machaerus about ten years before, doubtless for some obscure offense. He did not give the impression he would last another ten years in the desert. Machaerus was not easy duty.

But the officer managed to assemble a passable guard of honor when he opened the gates. Caleb followed him to the garrison office, where he was offered some indifferent wine.

Zev smiled as he poured it, and Caleb experienced a twinge of injured pride. Was this rude soldier, who was old enough to be his father, patronizing him?

Some men, even in youth, were blessed with commanding presences, but Caleb knew that he was not one of them. He was of no more than average height, and slender enough to give the appearance of weakness. Worse yet, even at thirty his face was unmarked by time and suggested a boyish inexperience. His beard had never grown in beyond a few ugly little tufts, which he kept trimmed so short that he almost looked clean shaven, after the Greek fashion. Sometimes, as in his dealing with the Tetrarch, who seemed to look upon him as a son, his apparent youthfulness was an advantage, but on occasions such as this it felt like a curse.

Thus, before even tasting the wine, before even sitting down, Caleb took from his pocket the scroll that contained the Tetrarch's warrant and opened it on the table for the commander's inspection. Let him know that "the prisoner John, called 'the Baptist'" was now under the authority of "my servant, Caleb bar Jacob, who is in possession of my perfect confidence." For the convenience of his master, Caleb had written it all out in Greek, the only language the Tetrarch understood with any fluency, but the words did not matter. All that mattered was the seal and the signature.

Zev's examination of the document was no more than a glance. It was likely his literacy did not go beyond a stumbling acquaintance with the Hebrew characters, but again it didn't matter. He knew who was in command.

"Will you be taking John back with you?" The question was asked almost humbly.

Caleb shook his head, and it was just possible to detect a certain darkening of the commander's expression, suggesting he would have liked to be relieved of this burden.

"No. He is safest here. He is a popular figure, and his popularity renders him dangerous. We don't want him near the cities."

"Then you plan to execute him?"

"That has not been settled. We must see how he responds to interrogation."

"Interrogation?"

"Yes." Caleb allowed himself a tight smile. "That is the polite word for it."

This answer seemed to perplex the commander. It was possible that, in the isolation of Machaerus, he had never heard of John's insulting references to the Tetrarch's marriage, but did the precise nature of the charge matter? The Tetrarch's will was a law unto itself.

"It may be a problem," Zev announced, with perceptible reluctance. "He has only been here a fortnight, and already the men are grumbling. They say he is a prophet and beloved of God. They say it is a sin to keep him in prison."

"John is not a prophet. The age of prophecy is over. God has not sent us a true prophet in four hundred years. John preaches to the rabble and infects them with treason."

The commander did not react, and Caleb suddenly discovered that he was angry.

"I don't care what your men think," he went on. "I look to you to keep them in order—unless you feel this is beyond your capacities."

"I will keep my men in order," Zev answered sharply.

"Then where lies your problem?"

"I only think it will be difficult to find one of them willing to assist in the 'interrogation.'"

He seemed a little ashamed of the admission, and rightly so.

"You needn't fear," Caleb answered, after a pause just long enough to make his contempt felt. "I have provided for that contingency."

———

His interview with the commander finished, Caleb supplied himself
with a jar of beer and brought it to the covered wagon that had accompanied him all the way from Galilee. Inside was Uriah, huddled in a
corner, clutching his knees and rocking back and forth like a frightened
child.

He was terrified of the open sky.

In the dungeons of the Tetrarch's palace in Sepphoris, the old capital
of Galilee, Uriah was more feared than death. The dungeons were his
home, and his duties there his consuming pleasure. He hardly seemed
to know that there was a world beyond the cold, damp walls within
which he exercised his authority.

But now he was in a pitiable condition. Caleb knelt beside him and
put the jar of beer into his hands.

"Drink," he said quietly. "It will be dark in a few hours, and then I
myself will take you down to the prison."

Uriah finished off about half of the beer in what seemed like one
swallow. He really was quite loathsome. His torso was short, but he had
the long limbs of an ape. He seemed utterly hairless, and his skin was as
pale as bread dough.

"I want walls around me, Master. Even in this wagon I feel as if a
breath of wind will carry me away into the empty air."

"I understand. I will see you safe."

And he would. Very soon Caleb would have need of Uriah.

That evening, having endured the company of soldiers all through dinner, Caleb took a stroll around the fortress walls. Below him the valley
was covered in impenetrable shadow, but Machaerus was high enough
that the blood-red sun had not yet completely disappeared behind the
horizon, and the gathering darkness allowed for a comfortable feeling
of solitude.

Where was this place? Caleb had never before traveled to Perea and
had only the dimmest notion of its geography, but somewhere out there
to the west was the Dead Sea. He had seen it once as a child, on an
excursion with his family, and he remembered how still and gray the
water had seemed, like slate.

That had been a day's journey from Jerusalem, his home.

Jerusalem. He had not been inside its walls in eight years, not even for the holy days. He might die and never see it again. He did not even know if his parents were still alive.

And all because of Michal.

"Go. And take that sinful woman with you," his father had said, the anger in him as cold as snow. "Live among the gentiles if it pleases you. You are almost one yourself."

His father, who was rigid even for a Levite, cursed him. His father, Caleb was quite sure, had never loved him. This was simply the last episode in a long history of rejection. And from that moment he had no father.

That sinful woman. A fair description, if one was honest. Michal had been seventeen when they met, a married woman bored with her husband. They were lovers within days, and perhaps, Caleb could reasonably surmise after eight years with her, he had not been the first.

Her husband had made no difficulties, agreeing to divorce her on payment of a trifling sum. Perhaps he was one of those who thought all women were as interchangeable as loincloths. Or perhaps he had been glad to escape.

But Caleb knew, even after the eight wretched years of their marriage, that he would never give her up. He would as soon surrender the breath under his ribs.

She was mostly in Tiberias now, an intimate friend of the Tetrarch's wife. It was agony to be away from her.

She teased and tormented him. Perhaps she had another lover.

But the day would come, Caleb comforted himself, when all Galilee would fear him, when no man living would dare to take his place in her bed. And then she would have to behave and be his alone.

What was he now? Very little more than one of the Lord Eleazar's senior clerks. He had an office in the old palace in Sepphoris and a handful of scribes to deal with the more obvious tasks. He was in charge of the prison, although he did not administer it, and unofficially, by virtue of the fact that he had recommended the appointment of the commander, who was his creature, he controlled the palace garrison.

But the source of his real power lay in the network of spies he had painstakingly created and which reached into every corner of Galilee. He knew what went on in the houses of the great and in the merest village. He knew what was said and done and, sometimes, even thought. He was the Tetrarch's snarling watchdog, and for this he was feared.

And that fear made him powerful, the rewards of which were not contemptible.

The one check on his power was the Lord Eleazar, who was already vastly rich and therefore could afford the luxury of scruples.

Power was magical. It settled every grievance and put all doubts to sleep. It could even dull his own fear, which nothing ever banished entirely.

And, once he had used John to undermine the Lord Eleazar, he would have power that was almost limitless. He could see the future opening before him like the dawn.

The last sliver of the sun was gone, and the light over the western hills was collapsing as if of its own weight. The oil lamp Caleb had brought out with him hardly allowed him to see his feet. He decided he would go back to his room, drink a few cups of wine, and go to bed.

Tomorrow would bring John.

Caleb had no idea what to expect from this desert preacher.

At their first interview, the Baptist was naked except for his chains. He seemed exhausted. He was bleeding from cuts on his knees and the tops of his feet, which suggested that he had had to be dragged from his cell.

Without even glancing at Caleb, who was seated behind a table, John collapsed to the floor, where, in the most dispassionate way imaginable, he sat examining the various wounds and abrasions on his feet.

Under more promising circumstances he would have been an impressive figure, for he was tall and there was an immense dignity about him. The bones were visible beneath his skin, so the stories of his ascetic manner of life were doubtless true.

Finally he did look up. Yes, he had the face of a prophet. He seemed ageless but was probably somewhere between thirty and forty. His eyes were large and black, and there was in them a complete absence of fear.

"You are John, called the Baptist?"

"You know who I am."

"Do you know who *I* am?"

"No."

"I am Caleb bar Jacob. I am here by authority of the Tetrarch."

John's face registered no reaction, and he returned to the contemplation of his injured feet.

"Are you in pain?" Caleb asked, leaning forward a little. "Would you like me to send for a physician?"

"No." John raised his head, but not to look at his interrogator. He seemed merely to have lost interest. "It is of no consequence. I don't imagine I will be left to suffer long."

"Nothing has been decided," Caleb replied quietly. "You are in my hands now."

"I am not in your hands, but God's."

And John had smiled at him, as if he were humoring a child. In that instant he made Caleb hate him.

The next day, during their second interview, John suddenly lapsed into silence, as if he had just noticed something of interest.

"From your robes I conclude you are a Levite," he said at last.

"Yes. I was trained as a musician."

"A Temple servant and a jailer." John smiled in amusement. "That is an interesting combination of employments."

"The service of God takes many forms."

"Is that what you call it? 'The service of God'?"

"Yes, because I protect the proper order of things, the order which God Himself has ordained. I serve those whom God favors and in so doing find favor myself."

"Favor with whom? With God or the Tetrarch?"

"With both, I hope. But more importantly with God."

John appeared to consider this. For perhaps a quarter of a minute he merely stared at the floor, and then he sighed heavily. A great sadness seemed to take possession of him.

"Are you so blind, Caleb bar Jacob, son of the Temple, that you imagine you can serve God by doing evil? Does not your conscience cry out against it? I implore you to listen to that inner voice which laments your sins, because God will one day reclaim His creation and you will be called to answer for all that you have done."

"I answer now, John. As you do. God rewards the good and punishes the bad—not in the future but now, in every hour of every day." Caleb allowed himself a pleasant smile. "I sit here with your life in my hands and you are huddled on the floor in chains. Has not God shown His favor to me and turned His face from you? How can you imagine this is not His judgment on us both?"

The logic of the thing seemed so obvious that he was almost moved to compassion for his prisoner.

"You have sinned, John. You have turned the rabble against those whom it has pleased God to raise to authority, and He has visited your sin upon your head."

"I see. You have power and therefore whatever you do has God's blessing. Every wicked king since the beginning of the world has used that argument. It is how a robber thinks when he breaks into another man's house: 'I have his treasure in my hands, so let me use it as I will.'"

"Do you compare the Tetrarch to a robber? He has what he has from God."

"Did he not steal his own brother's wife? And shall he not be rebuked for that, as Nathan rebuked David over Bathsheba?"

"Nathan was a prophet."

"And what is a prophet except one who speaks God's truth and is not silenced by fear of the mighty?"

Then Caleb surprised himself by asking the obvious question.

"Are you not afraid?"

And, without even looking at him, John answered, "No. It is you who should be afraid, Caleb bar Jacob, for the ax is even now laid to the root of the tree. When God sends His messenger to judge the world, the unrighteous will be consigned to death and the righteous will live forever. I will have but a little time to sleep."

As it happened, there was another occupant of the prison at Machaerus, a soldier waiting to be crucified for desertion. His presence occasioned another conversation with the commandant.

"Carry out the sentence today," Caleb told him. He wanted no witnesses to what was planned for John and he did not feel it necessary to explain.

Zev again looked uncomfortable.

"Two of the men we usually use for executions are on extended patrol. They won't be back until the day after tomorrow."

"Then take your deserter out and cut his throat, after which you can crucify him at your leisure." Caleb smiled unpleasantly. "You might call this his lucky day."

When they had the prison to themselves, Caleb and Uriah discussed what to do with John.

"It is necessary to break him," Caleb said. "I would prefer some method that left no marks on his body. What would you suggest?"

Uriah seemed to consider the problem for a moment.

"Hang him in chains," he said, and then he laughed quietly. "I'll wrap his wrists and ankles in rags and then, when his arms are secure, I'll pull up the leg chains behind his back until he's well off the floor. An hour of that and he'll think his spine is about to snap. Three hours and he'll be begging for mercy."

Caleb nodded approvingly.

"We'll allow him six hours to consider his situation," he said. "Then I'll have another talk with him."

Since he did not care to involve himself in the specifics of the thing, Caleb went up to his room and took a nap.

When he returned, a little over six hours later, he tapped lightly on the prison door and it was opened for him by Uriah.

"Well?"

Uriah looked unhappy.

John was hanging belly down from iron rings bolted to the ceiling. His feet were about on a level with his shoulder blades and his back was bent at a fearful angle.

Caleb took a stool and sat down in front of him. They were at eye level and separated by less than the length of one's arm. John's face was drenched in sweat.

"How do you feel?" Caleb asked pleasantly.

"Numb."

It was not the answer Caleb had expected.

"Numb?"

"Yes. God has taken away the pain. One has merely to be patient. My body feels dead."

"Shall I tell Uriah to begin cutting your toes off?"

"Is that his name?" John managed a weak smile. "He didn't introduce himself."

"Shall I?" Caleb repeated. He was angry, but he realized it would be a

mistake to let his anger show. "Perhaps he could trim your feet right
back to the instep."

"I doubt if I would feel it. Besides, it would only bring me that much
closer to death."

John closed his eyes, as if weary of the subject.

Caleb suddenly felt as if he had been dismissed like a servant. He
stood up and walked away. He did not want John to see his face.

He went over to where Uriah was waiting.

"When I am gone, take him down," he said, almost between his
teeth. "Give him an hour to recover and then put him in a cell. No light,
no food. Give him a bucket with a few cups of water in it. Once he is
inside, don't go near the door. I don't want him to hear a sound."

The sense of having been utterly abandoned was the most terrible
thing most people could imagine. A few days of isolation in a dark room,
never knowing if you were being left to starve, or if you would ever
see the light again, must dissolve any man's courage. Caleb had never
known it to fail.

Of course there was always the risk that John would simply go mad.

"How long shall you wait, Master?"

"I haven't decided."

In the event, he waited five days.

"What do you hear of him?" he asked.

Uriah shook his head. It was a gesture of perplexity—and fear.

"I hear his voice sometimes, as if he is speaking quietly to someone.

"Perhaps he's out of his head."

"No. I crouched by the door and listened. He prays to God."

"For what? For deliverance?"

"No. He praises God for filling his soul with light."

It was obvious that all this had made its impression on Uriah, as well
it might. One expected screams and curses, and in the end merely sobbing, but not a benediction.

"I hate him, Master."

Caleb smiled, pretending he understood and sympathized. Of course
he did not. The workings of Uriah's twisted spirit were a mystery to
him, one he did not want to understand.

"Open the door."

Caleb entered the cell, carrying an oil lamp, and John merely turned
his face away from the light.

There was still water in the bucket that rested beside John's right hand—it caught the light. Most men would have drained it dry within the first day.

In that instant, when he saw the water shimmering, Caleb knew he had lost.

"So it was just another trick," John said, his voice cracked like old leather. "I thought you might really have left me to die. I am disappointed in you."

"Do you wish to die?"

It was a question Caleb had not expected to hear himself asking.

"No." John shook his head, slowly, as if the joints in his neck ached. "I wish only to be the servant of God."

"Then you fear death?"

"No."

He raised his face toward Caleb, careful to avoid looking directly at the lamp. He smiled.

"Why should I fear death? It is simply the gateway to eternal life."

Caleb turned on his heel and almost ran out of the cell.

It had become clear that no one was going to force the Baptist to his knees. There would be no abject surrender, no groveling at the Tetrarch's feet. A man who is not afraid of death has nothing else to fear.

Antipas would be disappointed. He enjoyed inspiring fear in others, perhaps because he was so afraid himself. And he was not a man who accepted disappointment easily.

But at least there were still the disciples. Caleb would begin making inquiries. The inquiries would lead to arrests. The very scale of the purge would demonstrate its necessity—and his own indispensability.

In the meantime, there was little more to be gained in this place. Caleb's notes on their conversations, suitably annotated, would be enough to convince the Tetrarch that John was dangerous and needed to be put to death.

He went back down to the prison and gave the order.

"Will you stay to see it done, Master?"

"No. I will come back in half an hour and examine the body."

He spent the interval in the room that had been assigned to him, drinking perhaps more wine than was quite prudent. Caleb did not consider himself cruel. He simply didn't care. But he was still smarting under his defeat.

When he returned to the prison, the Baptist's corpse had been dragged out into the middle of the floor and was lying on its chest, with the head resting just next to the right shoulder. He clearly had not died where he lay, because there was very little blood. His chains had been removed.

Uriah was sitting on a bench, his head lowered and his elbows resting on his knees. His hands were caked with dried gore.

Caleb knelt down for a look. John's eyes were open and were still moist. The frayed condition of the wounds around the stump of the neck suggested that Uriah had used a knife and had cut from back to front.

Sever a man's throat and he dies within seconds. The Baptist had probably suffered for several minutes.

"Did you want to hear him scream?" Caleb asked, trying to keep the disgust out of his voice.

The executioner raised his head.

"I gave him ample time to know that he was dying." Uriah lifted up his hands and stared at them, as if they had somehow failed him. His face reflected sullen disappointment. "He made no sound."

3

Tiberias was a city of stone and brick, but the mortar that held it together was pride. Herod Antipas, Tetrarch of Galilee and Perea and son of the Great Herod, wanted for his capital a magnificent new city after the style of the Greeks, a city of columns, of porticos and statues, a city of marble, white as sea foam. He found a site by the Sea of Kinneret that ravished the eye, and so he razed the village that stood there and drove its people away. Then his builders set to work.

But when they began to dig, their spades and pickaxes brought up human bones. The place where Antipas intended his city to stand was revealed to be a graveyard.

Still, the Tetrarch would not be turned from his purpose. He built his city and named it for his patron, the emperor in Rome. And when pious men refused to live there—for how could those who feared God abide in a place made forever impure by the presence of the dead?—Antipas peopled Tiberias with foreigners and the poor, rounded up from the countryside like cattle and compelled to labor on the terraced waterfronts and the palaces of the great. Others, men of substance, were in the end given no choice but to move their homes and their families there. He would have all of Galilee bend to his will. The son of the Great Herod could do no less.

Eleazar bar Zadok, a priest of ancient lineage and the Tetrarch's First Minister, hated the city. He lived in Sepphoris, the old capital, a place of

rough stone walls and narrow streets, where he had been born and
where, like his father before him, he was warden. He traveled to Tiberias only when his duties required it, and always, when he returned
home, his first act was to immerse himself in living water and thus be
purified. Torah, he knew, did not require this of him. Rather, it was an
expression of contempt, both for Tiberias and for the Tetrarch, whom in
the privacy of his heart he despised.

Yet his attendance upon the Tetrarch required Eleazar to maintain a
house in Tiberias. He had arrived there the afternoon before and had
been pleased to discover that his son was in the city, having preceded
him by only a few hours.

The lad was fifteen and, aside from a worthless nephew who lived in
Sepphoris, was the last of Eleazar's blood. He had come up from Jerusalem, where he lived with his aunt, his late mother's sister, while he
pursued his studies. Zadok, named for his father's father, would be home
for a month. The prospect gave Eleazar much pleasure, as he dearly
loved his son.

At dinner they carefully avoided any discussion of state affairs because knowledge of such matters was dangerous. This was why Zadok
lived in Jerusalem—to keep him beyond the Tetrarch's reach.

But in the end they stumbled, over a piece of gossip.

"I heard before I left that they've arrested John the Baptist," Zadok
said casually. His father's silence made him glance up, and something
unpleasant occurred to him.

"Did you know?" he asked, his tone just hinting at an accusation.

"No. I did not know. Who arrested him?"

"Well, if you didn't, it must have been the Romans."

"I think not. John stayed away from the cities. The Romans wouldn't
interest themselves in a desert preacher."

Simply to distract himself, Eleazar picked up a piece of bread and
began using it to stir his food around. Then he decided he had lost his
appetite.

"Was there anything else?" he asked finally, pushing his plate away.
"Is it known where he's being held?"

"No—nothing."

Zadok seemed surprised and, indeed, a little frightened by his father's
reaction. Eleazar smiled, trying to create the impression that this bit of
news was interesting but no more.

"When did you hear about it?"

"I'm not sure. Four or five days ago, perhaps. I think."

Eleazar changed the subject. He inquired after his son's studies and was favored with a disquisition on allegorical interpretations of the Psalms. He smiled and nodded, but in his mind he was making calculations.

Little more than a month ago, the Baptist had been the subject of discussion between Antipas and his First Minister. John had publicly declared the Tetrarch's marriage unclean in the sight of God—a proposition difficult to refute—and the Tetrarch had wanted to arrest him. Eleazar had warned against such a step, arguing that John would be more dangerous in prison, or dead, than alive and at liberty. When he bowed his way out of the audience, it was Eleazar's impression that he had carried his point.

Apparently not.

Why had he heard nothing of the Baptist's arrest? His subordinate Caleb maintained an excellent network of spies, so why had this information not reached him? Obviously because Caleb had not chosen to inform him.

Where *was* Caleb? Eleazar had neither seen nor heard from him in two weeks.

Assume that Zadok had heard about the arrest five days ago. How long would be the interval between that arrest and its being generally known in Jerusalem? A week? Less? So John had probably been in prison from ten days to perhaps two weeks.

Or, put another way, about the length of time that Caleb had been on his travels.

Eleazar could see quite clearly what must have happened. Without first seeking his consent, which would have been refused, Caleb had gained an audience with the Tetrarch, played upon his vanity and his fears, and obtained a warrant for the Baptist. Then he had disappeared to wherever John was being held.

Well, what else should he have expected? Treachery and cunning, along with a complete lack of shame, made up almost the whole of the man's character. They were what had first recommended him to the First Minister's service.

Eleazar could not help but recall the day he had found him, this child of the Levites, servants in the Temple for a thousand years, this outcast of a prominent family who had washed up in Tiberias like the tangles of wood and useless pieces of fishnet one found along the shore of the Sea of Kinneret. Truly Caleb had been adrift in those days, in debt and friendless. He had come to Eleazar's home in hopes that the Tetrarch's First Minister would intervene for him with his family. He had plainly admitted that he was desperate and, indeed, it was his very brashness in the face of ruin that had led Eleazar to believe he might be useful.

"Do you think that my intervention will be of use?" Eleazar had asked.

And Caleb had merely grinned and said, "No."

"Then I will offer you something better."

It was a simple enough assignment. One expected to be robbed a little by one's servants, but Eleazar had a clerk who seemed to be stealing more money than was quite decent. "Find out for me where he is spending it, and I will give you his place."

Caleb had more than lived up to his expectations. Eight days later, when Eleazar had returned to Sepphoris, Caleb appeared at his door. He had it all. The clerk, it turned out, had a mistress with dreams of a luxurious retirement.

"It was a simple enough matter to track the clerk to his mistress—a prostitute, although the clerk appears not to know it. A few questions revealed that she was indeed expensive, and a few more revealed the name of the merchant with whom she deposited her earnings. I apologize, my lord, but I was obliged to use your name to bring the merchant to reason. He agreed to hold back the prostitute's money until he hears from me.

"I then went to that lady, explained the situation to her, and made her understand that she would never see a single coin of her money unless I had all the particulars. Fortunately she is of a businesslike disposition and keeps excellent records. Here is an accounting of everything she has received from your clerk."

That afternoon Eleazar confronted his clerk, who tearfully admitted his indiscretions and begged for mercy. Eleazar contented himself with merely dismissing the man.

The next morning Caleb assumed his new position. His first advice was that the merchant be instructed to release all of the prostitute's money to her, including everything she had received from Eleazar's former clerk.

"It is in the nature of things, my lord, that many secrets worth knowing come in the way of such a lady. I suspect she will prove well worth every shekel."

And thus Caleb began to assemble his network of agents and spies, through which he seemed, after a time, to know everything worth knowing about the undercurrents of affairs in Galilee. He quickly ceased to be merely a clerk and took over those aspects of rule which are distasteful but necessary, but that was how it had begun.

"What do you think, Father?"

Eleazar had just presence of mind enough to recall what his son had been saying. He smiled, and sensations of pleasure and sadness mingled in his heart. The boy was just at the threshold of manhood and already his ideas were marked with maturity and clarity of mind. He was the single blessing that had emerged from the marriage of two people destined in every other way to bring misery to each other.

"There is a general problem with allegory," he began. "It is too flexible. That way the Scriptures can be made to mean whatever you like. Interpretation becomes a kind of game, requiring little beyond intellectual agility."

Zadok seemed disappointed. His father reached across the table and touched him on the shoulder.

"God does not speak in riddles, my son. Yet if He did, I think you would be the one to solve them."

Father and son would return home to Sepphoris together. They would travel by cart and Zadok would manage the horses, which would please him and make him feel that his father accepted him as a man.

But first Eleazar had to complete his business with Antipas, made now more urgent and more complicated by this affair of the Baptist.

Thus, after breakfast, the First Minister walked the hundred or so paces from his house to the Tetrarch's palace.

The palace was huge and had cost vast sums of money. Building seemed to be a passion with the Herodians, both father and son, but the Great Herod had built, in addition to bathhouses, theaters, and palaces, the Temple in Jerusalem, which might stand for all eternity as a tribute to God's glory. What had Antipas built besides cities in which no one wanted to live and palaces that were like gigantic toy boxes?

Yet a ruler must occupy himself somehow. A ruler's function was less to do anything than simply to be, to possess power, which was, thankfully, rarely used. A ruler collected taxes and quelled any opposition, for which purposes he had a few servants like Eleazar and, more importantly, an army. A ruler existed to be feared.

And, for the rest, Galilee could be trusted to look after itself. The villages were governed by ancient custom, and in Sepphoris Eleazar's father had organized committees of the leading citizens, who attended to necessary public services. They looked to Eleazar, as the city's warden, for patronage and direction, but for the most part they operated quite well on their own. There was little enough for the Tetrarch or his First Minister to do.

So it was probably best that Antipas concerned himself with domestic architecture, no matter how vulgar. It kept him out of mischief.

The chamberlain bowed to him and then disappeared to announce his arrival, and Eleazar was left alone to wait.

As he stood in the great reception hall, he had only to look about him, at the murals on the walls, scenes from pagan stories, full of wantonness and naked flesh, and at the white Greek columns and the polished marble floor, to feel himself in a foreign place, a dwelling unfit for men who feared God.

But what could one expect from a man whose mother had been a Nabatean and whose great-grandfather—an Idumean, of all things—had probably been forced at sword point to accept Torah? Antipas himself had grown up in Rome.

The Tetrarch's family had risen to power in a mere three generations. They were, it seemed, the destiny Eleazar's forebears had embraced for him. His grandfather, who had been a worldly man and saw no hope of prospering in Jerusalem, had accepted an offer of service from the Great Herod, who was then governor of Galilee. After the Roman senate had declared him king of the Jews, Herod showed favor to the family, who received land and honors. Eleazar's father eventually came to lead the city administration of Sepphoris, the rewards for which were not contemptible.

But then Herod, worn down by his years and his many crimes, had at last died. He left a will dividing his kingdom among his three surviving sons. Archelaus was to be king and to rule over Judea, Samaria, and Idumea. Antipas would have Galilee and Perea, and Philip the lands east of the Jordan. The emperor in Rome, however, refused Archelaus the title of king and named him "ethnarch," ruler of the people. Antipas and Philip, since each was to receive a quarter of their father's domain, would each be styled "Tetrarch."

Inevitably, the Great Herod's death was followed by a rebellion—a feeble thing, restricted mainly to the countryside—but the Romans, acting on behalf of Herod's sons, crushed it with astonishing ferocity, and Eleazar learned a lesson he was never to forget: resistance to authority led to chaos and death. God, for whatever reason, had made the Romans masters of the world, and the Romans had appointed Antipas, Herod's son, master of Galilee. To defend this order of things was to do the will of God.

But the order could be broken. The emperor could remove Antipas, as he had removed Antipas's elder brother, Archelaus, who was judged too cruel and therefore a threat to good order and so, at a word from Rome, had been exiled to the wilderness of Europe. Judea, Samaria, and Idumea then became the Roman province of Palestine, governed from Caesarea by a prefect. No one ever heard from Archelaus again.

Thus, like his father before him, Antipas owed all that he had, even his life, to the patronage of the Caesars. One mistake, one reason for the Romans to decide he was a liability, and he would join his brother, who had probably had his throat cut as soon as he arrived in Gaul.

This Antipas understood quite well. He lived with the fear of it every moment of this life, and his fear made him cruel.

So Eleazar served the Great Herod's son because his father had served both father and son and because the alternative was rule by foreigners even more cruel than Antipas.

In the world he knew, power was in a state of precarious balance, and it was his function to restrain Antipas from doing anything that might disturb that balance, lest Antipas destroy himself and surrender Galilee to the Romans.

But Eleazar had no illusions. He was thin and careworn and already past forty. And his duty in life was to protect a monster.

And now, after waiting for more than two hours, he found himself bowing stiffly to the Lady Herodias, the Tetrarch's wife, formerly the wife of her uncle, Herod Boethus, who was, incidentally, the Tetrarch's still-living brother.

She had come out at last to receive him, surrounded by perhaps a score of her women, among whom, standing behind and a little to the right of her mistress, smiling slyly at him, was Michal, the lady's close friend and confidante and Caleb's wife.

In her youth Herodias had been a famous beauty, and even now, in her middle forties, she was handsome. Her hair had grown streaked with gray, but her eyes were large, lustrous and black and her full mouth suggested a sensuous nature. She was accustomed to fawning admiration from men, and even Eleazar, who loathed her, was forced to recognize her power to charm.

Today she was even modestly dressed, with her arms covered. Her garment was of green silk, and a long white scarf covered her hair. The only touch of the harlot was her belt, which was of gold to catch the eye and was drawn tight to accentuate her narrow waist.

"Lady," he said, taking her hand and, at the deepest part of his bow, placing it against his forehead. "You honor me."

"Yet you did not always deem it so," she answered, accepting his salute with a catlike smile.

"Time is a great teacher, Lady, and has obliged me to acknowledge my error. I have prayed and made sacrifice in hopes of God's pardon, and yours."

This made her laugh, a sound like music. They understood each other perfectly and no pardon was possible, only a wary truce.

Eleazar had counseled his master against the marriage, suggesting, with perhaps more force than was politic, that such a union would be regarded as an abomination by the Tetrarch's more pious subjects, among whom, he implied, he himself would be numbered.

The Tetrarch, of course, married her anyway. And, of course, he had told his wife of his minister's opposition.

"The Tetrarch is taking his massage," she said. "Shall I have someone conduct you?"

"I know the way, Lady. I thank you."

She offered her hand again, and again he bowed and touched it to his forehead.

To Michal he also made a slight bow. She smiled her teasing smile, to which Eleazar had long since grown immune. There was a scandal behind that marriage as well, which was perhaps what recommended her to Herodias.

As Eleazar made his solitary way along the palace corridors, the

Tetrarch's minister tried to clear his mind. Today he wished only to be the faithful servant of his master—faithful even to the extent of giving him advice he did not wish to hear. For he knew the Tetrarch was on the verge of making a dangerous mistake.

Antipas, like his father, tended to corpulence, and at fifty, having reached an unwieldy girth and showing no inclination to place a check on his appetites, had adopted a regimen of steam baths and massage. Twice a day he subjected himself to the pummeling of a Greek slave, followed by half an hour of steam, a swim in a pool of warm water and, at the end, a cold plunge. He had been enduring this program for over a year with no detectable result. Every month he grew visibly heavier, and lately his breathing had acquired a squeaking sound, as if he were being throttled by his own flesh.

Eleazar found him lying on his belly, a great expanse of pink flesh on a block of white marble, having his buttocks kneaded. His face happened to be turned away, but at the sound of sandaled feet against the stone floor he drew up his head and then allowed his chin to settle on his folded hands.

"Ah, minister. They neglected to tell me you were coming today."

This, of course, was not true, but such polite fictions were required for a ruler who would not have altered his daily routine for anyone less than the Roman prefect.

"I apologize for the intrusion, sire," Eleazar replied, bowing from the waist. "If this is not a convenient time . . ."

"Nonsense! We're finished here." He pulled himself up into a sitting posture, his legs dangling over the edge of the block, and then, scowling at the slave, waved a hand in dismissal.

"Go on, go on, you fool. See if the stones are sufficiently heated."

He turned back to his minister and smiled. "Come and take a little steam with me," he said, as if to an intimate and trusted friend. "You look as if it would do you good."

Eleazar sighed and proffered his thanks to his benevolent master. He hated from his soul all these foreign innovations, and Antipas doubtless knew it, but it made no difference. He stepped into a changing closet, put off his priestly garments, and wrapped himself in a strip of linen that would hardly have done for a loincloth.

When he came out, Antipas was already in the steam chamber.

"One cannot entrust this to a slave," the Tetrarch said in Greek, the language he preferred in private, as he ladled water over black, twisted stones. The water hissed and bubbled, and the air was rapidly thickening. "The steam has to gather at a certain rate or one doesn't begin to sweat properly. I learned the trick in Rome, when I was a boy."

He looked about him, admiring the white marble that enclosed a space hardly bigger than a tomb, and suddenly he grinned with mischief.

"Sit down, Eleazar. Here you may relax. Here, with just the two of us, we can for the moment put court etiquette aside."

Eleazar sat down, but he could not relax. He had been acquainted with Antipas for thirty years, and had served him for twenty, and he knew that the man was never so dangerous as when he assumed this affable manner.

"Now. What did you wish to see me about?"

They talked of administrative matters first. It was perhaps an hour before the First Minister broached the subject which had tortured his mind ever since the preceding evening.

"Sire, there is the question of this preacher, John. . . ."

"Who?"

"John, Sire—called 'the Baptist'. He immerses people in the Jordan, claiming to take away their sins."

"Oh, him. What of him?" The Tetrarch seemed to go inside himself for a moment, as if to recall some detail of the matter. "He insulted my wife, didn't he?"

"He said your marriage was an unclean thing, Lord."

"That's right. I remember now." And then, suddenly, he laughed. "But you, in your time, have said no less."

This seemed a comment wisest ignored.

"Caleb, it appears, has arrested him," the First Minister continued quietly, as if breaking bad news.

"Yes. I remember he said something about it."

"Then you gave your permission?" The inquiry was made to sound as bland as possible.

"Yes, I suppose so. Why? The fellow is dangerous."

"Perhaps, sire," Eleazar said at last. "Perhaps not. But I suspect he is more dangerous in prison than out of it. Many people revere him as a prophet, and even more respect him. If we put him to death—and we will almost be obliged to if we hold him for any period of time—then those people will be outraged."

"What do I care if they are 'outraged'? I am the law in Galilee and Perea, not they."

"Yes, sire. But discontent can boil over at any time. If there is a riot, then you will be forced to use soldiers to quell it. The Romans are watching us, and they might overreact."

The Tetrarch seemed not to have heard. Sweat was collecting in the creases of his face and he looked exhausted. He took a corner of his linen wrap and wiped his forehead, then his eyes.

But he had been listening. Any mention of the Romans always caught his attention. He could, to a degree, ignore the opinions of his subjects, but the Romans were a different matter.

"So what are you suggesting?"

"That the wisest course would be to let him go. He preaches that men should purify themselves against the time of God's judgment of the world. He is a harmless madman."

"He has a large following. Caleb says he might incite them to anything."

"I have heard nothing to suggest he will incite them against Your Majesty, and if he does, then there will be time enough to act."

It was in every sense an uncomfortable moment. The steam was oppressive enough that it almost made one gag to breathe it. And the Tetrarch had a dangerous look in his eyes.

"If I let him go, these people whose opinion seems so important to you will imagine I am weak. They will believe I am afraid of the Baptist."

Aren't you? Eleazar asked, though only his own mind.

"Not if we act quickly. Then it will appear as an act of clemency—an act, almost, of piety. Mercy proceeds from strength, sire. A wise and benevolent ruler, who respects a man of God and seeks only justice, corrects the act of a hasty official . . ."

"Ah! That is it." Antipas held up the index finger of his right hand, as if commanding attention. "You intend for Caleb to assume the blame."

"He is to blame, Lord."

Suddenly the Tetrarch rose to his feet, which meant that Eleazar was obliged to stand. The two men faced each other, with hardly the length of one's arm between them. It felt like a confrontation, the beginning of a bitter quarrel.

Antipas glanced about him, wary as a hunted animal. His hands clenched into fists.

"Caleb protects me," he almost shouted. "I am surrounded by enemies. The Baptist would lead a mob to the palace gates. Caleb wishes to crush him. Caleb would crush all my enemies."

In his mind he seemed to see it all—the howling rabble, forcing him to flee when they overpowered his household guards. The Roman prefect in Caesarea, shaking his head in silent contempt. And then the summons from Rome.

Then, just as quickly as it had begun, it was over. Antipas, perhaps realizing that he had betrayed himself, sat back down. Eleazar remained on his feet, which the Tetrarch noticed after a moment. He motioned wearily for Eleazar to be seated again.

For a long interval neither spoke.

"I am tired," the Tetrarch said finally. "I am old and weary."

Yes, of course, Eleazar thought. *Now he wants sympathy.*

"Your Majesty carries a heavy burden," he replied.

"A heavy burden . . . Yet I have you to help me. Haven't I, Eleazar?"

"Yes, sire. All that I have, all that I am, even my life, is yours."

"Yes. I know."

Antipas dropped his gaze a little and then looked sideways at his minister. He smiled. It was a smile full of menace.

"You think Caleb is becoming a danger to you," he said, as if the possibility had just occurred to him. "You created him. You brought him into my service. And now you want to destroy him."

"I am not afraid of Caleb, sire. I think, however, he needs to be curbed."

"No. I will not permit it."

Eleazar took a breath, intending to offer some protest, but then thought better of it. The Tetrarch, he knew, would not be moved. It had become a point of honor.

So, best to defer the question to another day, when heads might be cooler.

"Then would it be possible merely to hold the Baptist for the time being? An honorable detention, while we make inquiries."

"Caleb is already in Machaerus." Antipas made a gesture with his right hand, as if presenting a gift. His smile, however, betrayed him. "He has orders to question the Baptist and to act accordingly. If this 'harmless madman' of yours has dared to call my marriage into question, he dies. The audience is over."

He made a dismissive gesture with his hand. There was nothing to do except to rise once more and bow. Eleazar was already pushing against the door when he heard the Tetrarch's voice again.

"You really do fear Caleb, don't you, minister. Perhaps you are right. It will be interesting to see which of you is my true servant."

When he returned to the changing closet, Eleazar closed the door and was for the moment completely alone. It was then that his usual icy calm deserted him. He leaned his forehead against the cool marble wall and fear flooded his heart.

So this is what it all means, he thought. *He sees Caleb's ambition, so he will set us against each other like dogs fighting over a scrap of meat.*

And Eleazar knew what would happen if he lost. Antipas was extravagant, always building new palaces and always in debt. Even with the vast wealth of Galilee at his disposal, he was constantly borrowing money. The First Minister's property, his farms and houses, his money invested with merchants, all he had inherited from his father and had acquired since by his own labor, could not help but tempt a ruler who never felt himself rich enough.

Caleb had been clever. He had played on the Tetrarch's fears, for a despot was always afraid of rebellion. He had insinuated his wife into Herodias's inner circle. He had arrested the Baptist and now, doubtless, would begin a great purge of his followers. There would be accusations and forced confessions, leading to a series of carefully staged executions, all of it serving to impress upon the Tetrarch the narrowness of his escape. Thus Caleb would rise in power and influence. He would become First Minister, and his word would become law. Good men would go to their deaths that Caleb might buy up their property at a tenth of its value. He would become a great man, wealthy and feared.

And Galilee would become a realm of nightmare.

And Zadok, what would become of him? He would lose his inheritance.

The future to which his talents entitled him would be obliterated in a stroke. The best he could hope for was that his mother's family might be able to keep him safe in Jerusalem.

Unless the Romans, as a goodwill gesture, decided to make a gift of him to the new First Minister of Galilee. Caleb was of a vengeful temperament. Even with the father dead, it might gratify him to take out what remained of his resentment on the son.

"Unless I can stop him," he whispered to himself, and then added, bitterly, "my disciple."

These terrors were unworthy of him, Eleazar decided. He pushed himself away from the cold, comforting stone.

He dressed quickly, putting on his priestly robes, making sure that everything was in order. He would leave now, in silence but not in haste—he did not wish to appear to be running away, not least to himself.

4

On his return journey from Machaerus to Sepphoris, Caleb stopped off in Tiberias. He had to explain to the Tetrarch that it had proved necessary to execute John. The Tetrarch received him in the palace gardens, where he was taking his after-dinner stroll. The news was not well received.

"So now, instead of a living prophet, we have a corpse. You may have trouble with the Lord Eleazar about this."

Which meant, of course, that Antipas was disappointed. And, as his servant understood only too well, disappointment was a dangerous emotion in rulers.

"John could not be broken," Caleb replied, his voice low and confiding. "The man was not human. He cared nothing about pain, and he saw death as deliverance. Thus he had no weakness to exploit."

"You sound as if you admire him."

The Tetrarch smiled contemptuously, and Caleb could almost see the dark wings of death fluttering over his head.

They had stopped for a moment. The lord of Galilee and Perea needed to catch his breath. The two men stood facing one other.

"Admired?" Caleb could only shrug. "No, sire. John was mad. He had buried himself in his madness, too deep to be reached by the usual means—probably by any means."

He paused, knowing that on the next throw of the dice he was wagering his life. He glanced about him, and his gaze fell on a little tree, no taller than a man, and he noticed how black its leaves appeared. It occurred to him how beautiful the world was, and how much he would regret leaving it.

"However, his disciples were sane enough to run away," Caleb continued. "I had given orders to arrest them along with the Baptist, but of course the fools allowed them to escape. I will hunt them all down, and we will soon know how widely this conspiracy has spread."

For perhaps a quarter of a minute the Tetrarch's face was expressionless, even vacant. He might not even have been listening.

Caleb had the uncomfortable feeling that Antipas was already measuring him for his coffin.

Then the Tetrarch smiled, raised his hand, and placed it on Caleb's shoulder.

"I always know I can count on you in such matters," he said.

Half an hour later, Caleb was sitting in his study in the house that was kept for him against his visits to Tiberias. He was drinking wine to settle his nerves and, as his fear subsided, entertaining himself with regrets about the lie he had told. He had never ordered the disciples' arrest. It had not occurred to him.

However, such lies were necessary. Now it would be someone else's head on the block. The officer at Machaerus, probably—what was his name? *In any case,* Caleb thought, *better him than me.*

Or probably, by morning, the Tetrarch would have forgotten about it.

Michal sent word that she was detained by the Lady Herodias. Caleb spent an uncomfortable night alone.

As soon as he was back in Sepphoris, Caleb directed his attention to the Baptist's followers. He had long lists of them.

One name immediately suggested itself—partly because the man might prove useful not as a victim but as a spy, and partly because his arrest would be such an exquisite jest.

Judah bar Isaac was a Judean living in Tiberias. Caleb had made inquiries and discovered that his instinct had been correct. Judah received his income through a Greek merchant, the money coming from Jerusalem. Judah apparently was in disgrace with his family, but he seemed to be living an agreeable enough life. He was indolent and pleasure loving and enjoyed considerable popularity with an aristocratic set that included both Greeks and Jews.

It was a familiar pattern, one Caleb himself had followed in his youth. It seemed to run in the family, because Judah was a cousin, the grandson of his mother's elder sister.

However, it appeared that not all scapegraces were dismissed on quite the same terms. Caleb's father had given him a small purse of silver coins and title to a farm in Galilee, where presumably he would scratch a living out of the earth and acquire the virtues of a good peasant. His cousin had means enough to enjoy a leisured existence in Tiberias. Had his sins been so much less?

Caleb tried to recall if they had ever met. Probably, although he had no memory of this favored youth. Judah, who was five years younger, certainly would have none of him.

This business would require some care. Judah was a member of one of the leading Levite families, close to the high priesthood in Jerusalem. A common laborer can be arrested, tortured, and killed without risk, but not a Levite. The Temple was sacred, and the Levites were its servants.

So one had to take care. The arrest had to be managed quietly, so that Judah's friends in Tiberias would think he had simply fallen off the face of the earth.

Caleb had just the man for this kind of work.

Matthias was a palace guard, young, very strong, reasonably intelligent, and utterly without pity. He also drank, so much that he would long since have been dismissed if Caleb had not learned to value his interesting set of skills. When he was given a task, however, he stayed out of the wineshops until it was finished.

Caleb explained the difficulties to Matthias and gave him his orders: "Bring Judah bar Isaac to Sepphoris and put him in the lower prison. I want him to have no idea where he has come to, or why."

To Uriah, his faithful servant and master of the lower prison, he also gave instructions.

"You will receive a new charge. You are not to molest him or injure him in any way. Yet it is necessary that he learns to fear you. Can you accomplish that?"

Uriah's answer was a grin of pleasure.

In less than a week Matthias could report that Judah bar Isaac was safely installed in his cell.

"How did you do it?" Caleb inquired—not because he cared but because he knew the value of giving subordinates a chance to describe their accomplishments.

But if Matthias took any pride in his work it did not show. His face was as impassive as if it were made of iron. Only his eyes betrayed him, for in them there was a hint of something like anguish.

"He had a favorite whore. I bribed her to drug his wine. He slept all the way here."

"And you are sure the whore won't speak of this?"

"The whore is dead."

"I compliment you on your thoroughness, Matthias." Caleb opened a box on his desk and took out a small pouch containing a small number of silver coins. "Here. Tavern money."

He tossed the pouch to Matthias, who snatched it out of the air—nothing moved except his hand, which might have been plucking a grape from an arbor.

"Thank you, Lord," Matthias said, without emphasis. His gaze was directed at nothing in particular and his face was an unreadable mask.

Caleb had heard everything that Uriah had to tell him about the new prisoner, who had been in his care for two weeks now. Judah was probably ready for their first conversation.

What had it been like for him? What had he thought that first day, waking up, naked and in chains on the stone floor of a foul-smelling cell, the only light a faint gray patch coming in under the bottom of the door? Probably that this was a jest arranged by his friends.

Then gradually he would have realized the truth: that he had no idea who held him, or where, or why. But, whatever the reason, it was not a jest.

Of course he had begun shouting—then screaming. Uriah had come in and, one way or another, made him understand that he was to remain silent. Probably only then had he begun to know real fear.

After the first day, there had been no more shouting. During the first four days, there were fits of sobbing, but even these had subsided. Once a day Uriah came into the cell to bring food and take away the slop bucket. He never spoke. Sometimes the prisoner asked him questions, which Uriah ignored. Lately the prisoner had begun making remarks.

He clearly did not expect any answer. He seemed merely to be amusing himself.

Good, Caleb thought. Fear was beginning to subside. The mind possessed a wonderful capacity to adjust itself to anything.

And the mind was what mattered. Any man could be broken by torture—well, perhaps not *any* man; the Baptist stood in Caleb's experience as the one exception—but no matter how complete the surrender, its effects were not lasting. The point was to attack not the body but the mind. There was no shortage of prisoners in the dungeons of Sepphoris. For years Caleb had been trying out on them the effects of prolonged anxiety, arbitrary punishments and rewards, and the fear of abandonment that lurks in the dark corners of every human soul, and he had come to believe that these provided the keys to true mastery.

If he could have had five months with John, perhaps the story might have had a different ending.

"I will instruct the guards in the upper prison to bring one of their charges down to you," he told Uriah. "Take him into the prisoner's cell and kill him. I want the execution to make an impression, so a quick death won't serve. Then leave the body there, until I tell you to remove it."

The next day Caleb went down to the lower prison. Uriah opened the cell door for him and handed him a torch. Then, once they were inside, Uriah took the corpse by the heel and dragged it out, closing the door behind him.

The dead prisoner left behind him on the floor a smear of blood, which in the torchlight seemed black.

For perhaps a minute, Caleb did not speak. Partly this was strategy and partly it was fascination with what even a few days in this worst of places could do.

The young man of fashion, the frequenter of Greek plays and pretty whores, was gone. In his place was just another prisoner, filthy and helpless. He kept turning his head away, no doubt because the light from the torch blinded him. He tried to shade his eyes with his hand, but the chain was not quite long enough to permit it. He looked too dazed even to be afraid.

His family, when they sent him away, could never have imagined that he would come to this.

"Who are you?" Judah asked. "Why am I here?"

Caleb realized that he had made a mistake. He had kept silent too long and thereby surrendered the initiative. He would have to take it back.

"You are not here to ask questions. You are here to give information."

The ceiling was low and Caleb kept thinking he was about to bump his head. He did not wish to appear to crouch. He looked around for a stool, but there was none. In any case, better to remain standing.

"You will describe to me your relationship with the criminal John, called the Baptist. If you lie to me, if you suppress information, if you do not tell me the whole truth, then no one will ever know what happened to you."

Judah lowered his head until it rested on his arms, and after a moment he began to make a whimpering sound.

In his mind, Caleb recited the letters of the Greek alphabet. That would be sufficient time.

"I will give you one more chance to answer. If you do not, I will forget you. The world will forget you. Tell me of the criminal John and your relationship to him."

He hardly had time to finish the sentence before Judah cried, "*I only saw him once!*" And then, more calmly, "I only saw him once. Some friends thought it would be amusing to hear him speak. We listened, and then we left. I don't even remember what he said. It was a joke, a way to spend the afternoon. That was all."

Caleb seemed to consider this. He stared into a dark corner, where there was nothing to see. He tapped his foot a few times against the floor. Then he turned and walked out of the cell. Even before Uriah slammed the door shut, he could hear the prisoner shouting, "No, *no!*"

"Tomorrow we won't give him anything to eat," he said quietly, although there was no chance Judah would hear him over his own screaming.

Caleb decided he would give his kinsman three days—no, four—four days to consider the situation. It varied with the individual, but three or four days was the usual length of the journey into absolute despair.

Caleb decided he would work no more today. He would go to the baths and sweat out the stink of this place.

In truth he simply wanted to be out in the light. He wanted to be outside and to feel the heat of the sun on his face. Perhaps by the time he reached the baths his fear would have subsided into something tolerable.

In the prison the thought kept coming unbidden into his mind, *How long until I am in one of these cells, waiting upon the executioner's convenience?*

Soldiers were already out in the countryside, arresting anyone suspected of being one of the Baptist's followers, but the Tetrarch was not a patient man.

And behind the Tetrarch, Caleb always saw the Lord Eleazar, whispering in his master's ear, biding his time until he could strike.

That moment was never far from his mind, that moment in the Tetrarch's garden when he had felt himself in the shadow of death's dark wings.

There was a room, just beyond the door to the upper prison, which Caleb used when interrogations had reached a certain stage. It was a quite ordinary room, with a desk and chair and a stool for the prisoner. There was even a small window, high up on the wall, which allowed, at certain times of the day, a shaft of light that seemed to rest on the floor like a physical object—one felt almost as if one could lean against it.

The ordinariness of the room was the point. It reminded the condemned that there still really was a world outside. Through the one window they could glimpse the sky.

For their next interview Caleb ordered that the prisoner be washed and given clean clothes. He was brought in and directed by gestures to the stool. No one had spoken to him in four days.

Caleb, who was sitting behind the desk, studied Judah's appearance. He looked exhausted, but there were no abrasions on his feet, so apparently he had been able to make it up the stairway without being dragged.

His expression was almost defiant, but Caleb knew from experience that this was a pretense that would shatter the instant it met any resistance.

"Tell me about the Baptist."

"I know nothing." The prisoner—it was somehow difficult to remember that he had a name—shook his head. "I saw him once. Hundreds of people went to see him."

"Yet there were not hundreds who were baptized." Allowing himself a tight smile, Caleb held up a scrap of papyrus. He could not, at the moment, remember what was written on it, and it did not matter. "You were baptized. That is our information."

The prisoner, Judah bar Isaac, the scion of a family that had served the Temple since David's time, covered his eyes with his right hand.

"It was an impulse. I yielded to it. I don't know why."

Caleb wanted to laugh. It had been an inspired guess, nothing more. The papyrus, now that he looked at it, contained this week's guard roster.

"So you admit that you were one of his followers. You admit that you lied in your first statement."

"I admit that I was baptized." Judah looked up over the edge of his hand, seeming to hide behind it. "John was very persuasive."

"And why would you, a young man of wealth, popular and pleasure loving, why would you find John persuasive? That he should appeal to peasants and beggars, this I can understand. But why you?"

"I was growing tired of the life I led. John said that the sinful would find only misery, and I knew he was right."

"Then you *were* a follower."

Judah stared at him for a moment. He looked exhausted, as if the effort of explaining the obvious had worn him out.

"The pull of habit was too strong," he said finally. Then he laughed. It was a short, despairing sound. "I found I could only be virtuous a little at a time. And, in the end, not even that."

For a moment neither man spoke, the one because he perhaps realized that he had already said too much and the other because he was struggling to conceal his sense of triumph.

Caleb could sense it. Judah bar Isaac was on the verge of becoming his willing accomplice.

Judah was perfectly suited to the role he had been chosen to play—an aristocrat, cast off by his family, in search of redemption. He was all of these things in real life, so it was not a part he would need to learn. John's disciples might even remember him, the rich man from the city who was moved to accept baptism and reclaim God's favor. In any case, it would never occur to them that he was a spy.

Because it would serve no purpose simply to arrest and execute these people. Antipas had to be convinced that they formed a conspiracy against him, and for this Caleb needed witnesses and confessions. He needed people from within the group who were willing to denounce it.

But that end would never be gained by coercion. Judah had to be converted.

Fear, of course, had its role, since the final question was always the same: How did one deal with fear? The interrogator stripped away a man's defenses until he himself was the last defense. The prisoner came to live through his jailer. That process was an art.

And the key was always to find the weakness, the grain of self-doubt that lives in every man. Attack him from within and eventually he must surrender.

Judah bar Isaac had just revealed his weakness.

"Am I still in Galilee?"

The question was a surprise, and Caleb had to consider what answer to make. Or if he should answer at all. He decided it was the moment to give back a little.

"You are in Galilee."

"I wondered. Yours is the only voice I have heard since . . . this started. You speak like a Judean." He smiled, shyly, like a child. "Are you a Judean?"

"You will be returned to your cell now. Guard!"

Caleb saw the expression of terror in his cousin's eyes and felt a sense of relief. How close had Judah come to discovering his identity?

ى

As he stood in the doorway of his house, looking down the street, which gradually descended into the lower city, Caleb was thinking about his breakfast. He fancied his stomach was troubling him.

In matters of food he was abstemious, but he wished to take pleasure in what little he did eat, and this morning the melon slice had been too ripe. His kitchen woman was, of course, Galilean and simply could not be made to understand that melon should be slightly crisp and not sweet to excess. It was the eternal problem of dealing with provincials.

The street was empty, but he knew he had only to walk a few minutes to be in the market district, where he would be surrounded by crowds, and he hated crowds. They made him uneasy.

It was possible, although unlikely, that he might be recognized, and a mob was capable of anything. Usually, when he went into the lower city, he took a few soldiers as an escort, but his business today was best achieved without calling attention to itself, so he was obliged to go alone.

And the Baptist had been dead two months. Probably few even remembered him.

Still, he felt vaguely giddy. He knew he was subject to fits of apprehension—it was, after all, endemic to his work—but he preferred to credit this morning's disturbance to his digestion.

Or to the fact that his wife had remained behind in Tiberias. It was the wise choice, since Michal's closeness to the Lady Herodias was useful, but a man cannot always be wise in matters touching on his wife. He missed her. He had been away from her too much of late. Even when she was in a filthy mood, when she screamed at the servants and threw things, he was glad to have her near him. It was torture to have her a day's journey away.

Or to homesickness. He did not hate Galilee, but it was not Judea. He missed Jerusalem.

Eight years ago he had not imagined he could ever miss the city of his birth. When his marriage had brought him into disgrace with his family, with little more in his purse than the title to a small farm in Galilee, his strongest emotion had been relief.

As it happened, Caleb never reached the farm. Tiberias was on his way, and Tiberias turned out to be an entertaining city. He sold the farm, without ever having set foot on it, for enough money, he estimated, to keep him in comfort for at least three years. In that time something would turn up. He had been born under a lucky star, so something always turned up.

But after a year, largely due to the extravagance of his new wife, he was near destitution.

Michal liked to watch the chariot races. She always insisted on the most expensive seats, the ones nearest the track—so near that, once, a clod of mud thrown up by the horses' hooves hit her in the breast, a mishap which left her strangely excited—and when the winners took their victory lap she would throw coins to them as they drove by. An afternoon at the races could turn into an expensive business, and in the winter months, when the weather was agreeable, she would want to go two or three times a week.

And she was always buying clothes and new sandals and little jeweled pins, which she claimed were presents for her family but which somehow collected in the drawers of a small cabinet she kept in their bedroom.

Once—just once—Caleb tried to persuade her to be less lavish in her expenditures, but the approach was met with scornful derision.

"I am the daughter of a Levite family and was never taught to acquire the habits of poverty. Do you expect me to live like a porter's wife?"

Then she turned her back to him and refused to speak to him or even look at him.

Caleb found he had no defense against this. Finally, he even tried to apologize, but she wouldn't hear him. This went on through most of the day.

At last, in the evening, when they were preparing for sleep, still turned halfway away from him, she opened her lips, speaking as if to some third person in the room.

"Perhaps I should return to Jerusalem," she said. "I could live with my mother, as a widow. A husband who cannot support his wife might as well be dead."

In bed, she wouldn't allow him to touch her.

This went on for several days and then, quite suddenly, she seemed to forget all about it. She was not affectionate, but at least she was civil.

Perhaps she thought he had learned his lesson, in which case she was right. As the contents of his purse dwindled, Caleb became increasingly desperate. He was less afraid of poverty, or even of death, than of losing Michal.

If he had not met the Lord Eleazar, there was no telling what he might have been driven to.

The First Minister had seen in him qualities he had not even realized he possessed. And now, perhaps inevitably, those very qualities, ambition and cunning, had brought Caleb into conflict with him.

And of late the Tetrarch had seemed to favor the servant over the master.

Did Eleazar feel the cool breath of the ax upon his neck? Who could say. His demeanor was unchanged, but that meant nothing. Eleazar was an unreadable man and as cold as a pond eel.

But Eleazar was also a wily man, as wily as he was inscrutable—a fact affirmed by his twenty years at the center of power.

Still, he could be brought down. Anyone could be brought down. It was the one immutable fact they all lived with, that haunted their dreams.

Caleb looked back at his house and decided, quite suddenly, that it no longer pleased him. It was too small and was in the wrong part of the palace district. The Lord Eleazar lived in a far larger house and owned perhaps another ten or twelve larger still. He even had houses in Tiberias and Jerusalem.

Perhaps in time, Caleb thought, all of these would be his. Perhaps they would all be part of his reward, after the Lord Eleazar had fallen, for having saved the Tetrarch from his subjects.

And he would stand in the reception hall on one of them and receive the submission of all the great men of Galilee.

It was a pleasant idea.

Caleb decided that he had lingered in the shade of his doorway longer than was consistent with dignity, and he stepped out into the street.

The sun was unusually hot for so early an hour, which contributed to his almost voluptuous sense of grievance. The heat, as it shimmered over the cobblestones, really was unbearable. Nothing but his sense of duty could have called him out into the glaring sunlight on such a day, and he looked forward to spending the rest of it at the baths.

But first he must wheedle an ironsmith into an insignificant act of treachery. Judah had let fall a name, which had led to another name, which had led . . .

The shop of Noah bar Barachel was at the end of a street that opened into a small square, in the center of which there was a fountain. The women who were filling their water jugs were better dressed, and a few wore thin gold bracelets on their wrists. There was a general air of prosperity around the square.

This was encouraging, because the more the ironsmith had to lose, the more pliable he was likely to be. Wealth, even comparative wealth, makes a man fearful.

The interior of the shop was surprisingly cool. The door and the one window stood open, but the room was still dark enough that an oil lamp hung from one of the rafters.

Around counters on the sides were displayed numerous iron objects that glittered in the lamplight almost like silver: knives, saws, chisels, the blades of reapers, awls and hammerheads. On the floor were pots full of nails, and on a small table in the center of the room was a collection of pliers, some of them distinctly odd looking. Caleb picked up one of these to examine it more closely.

"Those are for extracting teeth, Excellency."

Caleb was not conscious of anyone having entered. He glanced at the instrument in his hand and noticed how one edge of the vice curved in slightly to conform to the shape of a tooth and allow for a better purchase. It was, in its way, very clever.

But he had not come here to admire a set of pliers. He frowned, feeling somehow that he had been tricked, and set them back down on the table.

"You are Noah?" he asked coldly.

"Yes, Excellency. I am Noah."

The man who was Noah smiled. It was not an ingratiating smile but one which suggested . . . what? Something like compassion, which Caleb always equated with contempt.

Caleb had to remind himself not to take offense.

Noah the ironsmith was slightly under average height and wore a plain, dun-colored tunic, beneath which were outlined the muscles of his arms and chest, so that the total impression was one of compact strength.

He reached up to touch the mustache of his short black beard. He seemed thoughtful, giving the impression that he was trying to remember something, and then he smiled again.

"Yet I perceive that your visit is not one of business. At least, not the business of pliers. May I then presume to offer Your Excellency a cup of wine?"

Caleb considered the question for a moment and then managed to nod, as if granting permission. He gained nothing by insulting the man, but the distinctions of rank must be preserved. It would not do to appear too cordial.

The wine was actually quite good, delightfully cold, and the cup was of hammered bronze.

"You honor me with your visit, Excellency. And I am curious to know what business brings you here, without your customary escort."

Caleb was first surprised and then amused. So, he had been recognized.

"You know me, then."

"Yes, of course, Excellency. Sepphoris is not so vast a place that the great are suffered to remain faceless. Particularly not one such as you, upon whom the Tetrarch depends for protection against his subjects."

The two men sat facing each other across a small round table, and Caleb considered how to deal with so politely phrased an affront. An affront, as it were, wrapped in a compliment.

He decided, with effort, to ignore it.

"Do you often go home, Noah?"

"Home?" The ironsmith seemed perplexed. "I am home now, Excellency."

"I had understood that you were born in a village called Nazareth."

"I was born in Sepphoris, Excellency. In this very house."

"Yet you are familiar with Nazareth."

"Yes."

"You go there often?"

"I am there every Sabbath, to accompany my grandfather to the prayer house." Noah leaned slightly forward, and for the first time a hint of anxiety showed in his face.

"May I know, Excellency, what there is to interest you in so small a place as Nazareth?"

"Probably nothing." Caleb, feeling that he had reclaimed control, allowed himself a thin smile. "Tell me, apart from your grandfather, do you have other family connections there?"

"Excellency, Nazareth is a small village. Perhaps four hundred people have their homes there. In such a place, everyone is related to everyone else."

"And is one of your relatives there a certain Joshua bar Joseph? A carpenter?"

There was a pause, lasting perhaps as long as two breaths.

"Yes, Excellency, he is my cousin. Our grandfathers were brothers." For a moment the ironsmith looked almost stricken, and then he seemed to come back to himself, even managing a faint smile. "So, precisely what could my cousin, the carpenter from Nazareth, have done to make him of interest to a man with your responsibilities?"

"That is what I want you to find out—*precisely* what he has been doing."

At dinner Noah seemed preoccupied. He tore off small pieces of bread and ate them as if he didn't realize what he was doing. He was silent and stared at the walls. Sarah hardly knew what to make of him.

"Is something wrong?"

The question intruded on his reverie and he took a sip of wine.

"Yes, something is wrong. I had a visitor today."

Sarah was relieved. Noah was a good man and a loving brother, who never found fault with her, but still she was relieved.

"A visitor? What did he want? Money?"

"No, not money." Noah smiled. It was a smile she had seen countless times before, a mingling of affection and amusement. "My visitor was from the Tetrarch's palace. A man named Caleb."

Sarah, who took little interest in anyone she did not know, had never heard of such a person. She needed to have explained to her that this was the man almost certainly responsible for the arrest of John the Baptist.

"Then he must be evil." She shook her head, as if to deny the possibility of such wickedness. "John was a holy man, much loved by God. How could the Baptist have threatened him?"

"By criticizing Antipas for marrying his half brother's wife. He said it was an unclean thing. Besides, Antipas was probably worried that so popular a man might have raised a rebellion against him. Despots always live in fear of rebellion."

"Is the Tetrarch a despot?"

"Yes. He is greedy and vain and he does not love God. He taxes the villagers so heavily that many are driven off their land. The land is our heritage from God, and he takes it so that the rich can have their great estates, and the poor have only enough to keep the breath under their ribs—sometimes not even that. Besides, the Baptist was right. It *was* an unclean thing for him to marry that woman. When have the sons of Israel ever fared well under kings—no matter how they style themselves?"

Criticisms of the great made Sarah feel uncomfortable, so she changed the subject.

"What did he want, this man?"

"He was asking about Joshua."

Noah shrugged, as if to say, *Doesn't that explain everything?* "My visitor wants to know if Joshua is dangerous. He wants me to find out."

"What will you do?"

"That is the question, isn't it."

Noah sat looking at his sister for a moment. He was conscious of the sacrifice she seemed to insist on making for him, and it pained him to watch her fading into quiet despair in his service. Besides, Abijah was a close friend and a good and pious man who could see beyond her awkwardness and appreciate the gentle, sweet creature that she was.

If he was honest with himself, he had to admit that he would miss her dreadfully. But it was time she became Abijah's wife. She had a right to a husband and children and the happiness they could bring. Besides, if this business about Joshua led to his arrest, he wanted Sarah safely married.

And prison was a real possibility. Soldiers could arrest him one day, and no one would ever hear from him again. It happened more and more.

Because this man Caleb seemed already to have made all the important decisions.

"I have not seen Joshua since the Passover," Noah had told him, convinced that God would pardon him the lie.

*"Then see him again, wherever he is, and make your report. I simply need
certain points confirmed."*

The implication was clear: the report, to be considered accurate,
would have to incriminate Joshua. Otherwise, Noah would be considered an accomplice.

*"Your cousin was the disciple of a man guilty of sedition. Therefore it fol-
lows that he is guilty."*

"But if you know he is guilty, why do you require my report?"

"Because the Tetrarch must know that justice has been done."

Yes, of course. This man's profession was to protect Antipas from his
enemies. Thus, enemies must be demonstrated to exist. This all fit with
Noah's general impression of this beardless murderer with the face of a
naughty apprentice.

But Sarah, sitting across from her brother, in the house where they
had both been born, could never be brought to understand a man like
Caleb.

So what was he, Noah, ironsmith of Sepphoris, to do?

Then, seemingly from nowhere, a memory swam up before his eyes.

"Joshua stole a fig once." Noah smiled, shaking his head. "Right off
the Passover table. I saw him do it. I was just tall enough to peer over
the edge, so I suppose we were about four years old. And there he was
on the other side. We stared at each other for a moment, and then he
reached out, grabbed his prize, and ran up to the roof with it. I don't
suppose anyone missed a single fig, but at the time I thought he had
committed the greatest crime imaginable."

"Did you tell on him?"

"No. So presumably that made me as guilty as he." Noah smiled. "Do
you want to know something? I don't think he would have done it if I
hadn't been there. He wanted me to see that he was a big boy, and not
afraid."

6

After dinner Noah retired to his bedroom. There was nothing unusual in this, and Sarah, who had long since grown accustomed to her brother's habits, did not inquire why. Perhaps, if she thought about it at all, she would have assumed he wished to study or to read, or perhaps merely to rest. The one thing that never would have occurred to her was that he withdrew to pray.

And Noah would not have described what he did—or tried to do—as prayer. For him, as for most people, prayers were the strings of words he had learned as a child, to be recited on set occasions. Prayers were ceremony, elements in the ritual of life. Before meals, one blessed God for sustaining one's life. While the Sabbath candles were being lit, one acknowledged God's commandments. Sometimes one reflected upon the meaning of the words and sometimes not, but the words themselves were unchanging.

Noah thought of what he did as "coming to God" or "talking to God," and he always began with the formula that contained almost the first words he could remember hearing: "Blessed art Thou, O Lord our God, King of the Universe . . ."

And yet that was never quite the beginning, for God was not to be approached in pride. Why should God listen except if a man recognized he did not deserve to be heard? So before he addressed God, Noah always addressed his own heart, humbling himself, numbering to himself his failures and his small list of sins.

And then he would open his soul to God—or try.

Sometimes he had the sense of being heard, but more often not. He never asked for good health or fortune or anything for himself beyond enlightenment and the comfort of being understood. He merely wished to feel God's presence, and when God would not listen he blamed himself. God was angry with him and the anger of God was always just. Who was he to claim God's attention?

It was the thing he had always envied most about Joshua, the ease with which he reached out to God. God loved Joshua. But who was Noah that God should love him?

Tonight, what burdened his heart was this man Caleb. Noah wanted to understand God's will. What should he, Noah, do about this trouble with Joshua and the Tetrarch's watchdog? But there came no answer. God was silent.

And then it occurred to him that God's silence was itself an answer. God does not repeat Himself. He had given His answer long ago.

For in the end it came down to the Law. The Law was from God, a gift more precious than life itself because it consecrated life. To reject the Law was to reject God, and thus to wander in darkness.

The Law commanded justice and mercy, and Caleb had turned his back on both. In their place he had embraced expediency. He wanted something—the Tetrarch's favor, the protection of the state, or some other, more personal satisfaction about which Noah could not begin to guess—and to these ends the man was prepared to sacrifice innocent people.

And yet, what was he except a reflection of the power he served? The Tetrarch, like his father before him, like his masters the Romans, knew no law except his own will.

Did Caleb say his prayers? Probably. But at some point he must have stopped listening to the words. The living God had faded out of his life without his even realizing it.

Did the Tetrarch say his prayers? Possibly. Or perhaps he prayed only to Rome.

And if Noah did what they required he would become like them.

So what could he do? He could flee. He could sneak away to Damascus or someplace even further, beyond the Tetrarch's reach. But then he would be leaving his family to the mercy of men who had no mercy. Or he could refuse, and suffer arrest and death. And neither of these would save Joshua, because Caleb would only find another and more willing spy.

The one thing he could not do was what Caleb required of him. He could not provide a report in which "certain points" were "confirmed" so the Tetrarch might "know that justice has been done."

Thou shalt not bear false witness. Such was God's commandment, and Noah dreaded to separate himself from God.

Thus, he must find Joshua and make him understand that his life was in peril, and then he must write a report that portrayed his cousin as a harmless preacher of virtue. He did not think that God would be offended if he left a few things out.

Whether Caleb would be offended was another matter.

So the following morning, after breakfast, he struggled through the crowds entering Sepphoris by the southern gate. The road led on to Jerusalem, but after perhaps twenty minutes a trail branched to the left, passed between wheat fields, then skirted around the brow of a low, terraced hill before it descended into another valley. There lay Nazareth.

It was an hour's walk, yet every time his feet left the main road he had the sense of entering another existence, a place as far removed from Sepphoris as the wilderness of Europe. Sepphoris was young, undefined, and as changeable in its moods as a child. Nazareth seemed as old as the earth. In Nazareth one found only the ancient, immutable patterns of peasant life.

It was small, even for a village. The houses, which were principally of mud brick, were scattered apparently at random but in fact followed an intricate pattern, reflecting the structure of kinship ties, which governed the whole of its people's lives. Noah's father had been born and was buried here. His grandfather lived here still.

It was the ancestral place, at once familiar and strange. But where was it any different? In Sepphoris, his birthplace, he sometimes felt like a rude peasant, and in Nazareth he felt—and was made to feel—a stranger. His own kinsmen did not entirely trust him, for the simple reason that he had ceased to be part of their daily experience.

Not for the first time, it occurred to him that home was not a place but a system of relationships, and his consisted of his grandfather and Sarah. His grandfather was old. Death would soon claim him. And Sarah had a right to a life of her own, to a husband and children, to a family in the midst of which he would be but the most welcome of visitors. What then? Then he would become what his grandfather was now.

The cluster of buildings, of which his grandfather's house was the approximate center, in a sense represented the disappointment of the old man's hopes. He lived surrounded by his brother's progeny, to whom he was Uncle Benjamin. His one son had moved to the city, returning only to fill an ossuary, and Noah, his sole male descendant, and childless, was little more than a frequent visitor.

The house itself consisted of three rooms: a main room, which included the kitchen; a bedroom; and the workroom, which was now largely left to the mice. A few years ago Noah had replaced the floor of packed earth with stone, something his grandfather had lamented as a useless expense, and he paid a village girl to clean and do the cooking. By the standards of Nazareth, Noah had prospered and could afford to see that the man who had raised him lived out his last years in comfort.

Noah heard him before he saw him. Benjamin was sitting on a stool beside his doorway, busy with a small object that seemed to require a file. He looked stooped and wasted. Even into middle age he had been a strong man, but time had worn him down.

"What are you working at, Grandfather?"

The old man looked up and then shaded his eyes with his hand. He peered for a long moment, as if trying to recollect something.

"Noah? What are you doing here on a workday?"

Noah ignored the question, with its implied disapproval, and crouched down so that his grandfather would no longer have to stare into the sun.

"What is it?" Noah asked.

"A padlock." Grandfather held it out for inspection. It was open like an oyster. "The mechanism is clogged with rust—you'd think they'd been keeping it at the bottom of a well. It just needs cleaning up."

Noah recognized the design as his father's.

"People don't remember to keep them oiled," he went on, allowing the disemboweled padlock to absorb his attention. For perhaps a minute the only sound was the remorseless rasp of his file as the old man patiently repaired the creation of his dead son.

What did he feel? Possibly nothing. Possibly that sorrow had become too remote to trouble him. Or possibly time had merely refined it.

"Why are you here, Noah?" he asked, without lifting his eyes. "You should be attending to business."

"A distinguished person in Sepphoris has asked me to make inquiries about Joshua."

"Joseph's boy?"

"Yes."

For a few seconds the file was silent. Then the work resumed.

"And this 'distinguished person,' who is he?"

"Someone whose existence it is better not to know about."

"I see. It appears you have acquired strange friends in the city."

"He is not a friend." Noah reached out his hand and let the fingers close over the padlock. "Believe me, Grandfather. I do not wish to be the Tetrarch's spy, but I need to speak to Joshua, if only that he may know his danger."

Noah lifted his hand from the padlock.

"How is Sarah?"

"She is well."

The old man nodded, if only to indicate that they understood each other.

"That cloth merchant of Sarah's should make up his mind. If he waits much longer, she will be past bearing his children."

"She is only six and twenty, and besides, I do not think it is *his* mind that needs making up. She seems to think I will perish if she is not there to look after me."

"Time you remarried."

Noah could only shrug. He knew what was coming next.

"Your wife has been dead four years," his grandfather went on. "There must be an end to everything, even mourning. Find another who pleases you, and then you can go on with your life. And so can Sarah."

He folded a piece of cloth around the padlock and laid it aside.

"God has not blessed us," he said. "Not you, not me, not Joseph. Your father died younger than you are now. Joshua's wife too is dead, and I believe grief has turned his mind."

"Joseph has other sons."

"Sometimes I believe God has cursed this family."

"I do not believe that."

Perhaps the old man felt that the subject had exhausted itself. Perhaps, as sometimes happened, he merely lost the thread of the conversation. In any case, for perhaps a quarter of a minute he appeared to stare at nothing, then he shrugged and changed the subject.

Noah slept that night in his grandfather's house. He did not return to Sepphoris, but directed his steps north.

About three hours from Capernaum the road made a long detour around a line of hills, adding several miles to the journey. There was, however, a well-worn path, too steep for wagons but easy enough for a man on foot, which cut across. It was just at the summit of this path that Noah encountered a robber.

Obviously the robber was not experienced at his trade, since he remained sitting on a large stone, a pruning hook balanced on his knees, even when Noah stopped within five paces of him.

"Peace be yours," Noah said, regarding the man with no emotion more stirring than curiosity. He was young, probably no older than sixteen. The red rims of his eyes showed luridly through the dust that covered his face enough to give him a corpselike appearance. He was obviously a peasant and just as obviously had been on the road for several days. That could only mean one thing.

"Peace be yours," he answered, and then, apparently as an afterthought, added, "If you have any money, give it to me."

His hand closed around the staff on his pruning hook, which was perhaps intended to be interpreted as a threatening gesture, but he made no attempt to rise. In fact, he seemed exhausted.

It occurred to Noah that he had merely to step forward a few paces and kick the fellow in the chest to send him sprawling.

"You mean to rob me?" he asked.

"Yes."

"With a pruning hook?"

The youth looked away, as if embarrassed, and Noah almost laughed, but restrained himself out of respect for his feelings.

He did smile, however. He couldn't help himself. The situation was ludicrous.

"I have bread and cheese and even a little wine," he said. "Enough to share. You will need to fortify yourself if you plan to lead a life of crime."

Noah walked up to where the man was sitting and opened his pouch. He held it out, along with his wineskin, but at first the man made no move to take them. He merely stared at them, as if he doubted the witness of his own eyes.

"Come. Eat."

The words seemed to snap the youth out of his trance. He took the wineskin, upending it to let the contents pour into his mouth. He had nearly drained it before he stopped, after which he let out a long sigh, as if he had been holding his breath, which perhaps he had. Then he took a flat piece of bread from the pouch and began tearing off pieces, which he stuffed into his mouth.

Noah sat down beside him, for the rock was long and flat, almost like a bench. A lifetime of hammering red-hot iron had given him such strength in his hands and arms that at any time he could have broken this would-be brigand's neck like a stick of kindling wood, but he was not one who thought in such terms, and he felt only pity.

"How have you come to this?" he asked.

The youth paused for a moment, staring out at nothing as, apparently, he gathered his thoughts.

"My father lost his land," he said finally. "The last few years have been hard, and he had to borrow. A week ago the moneylender came with writing that said he owned the land now. He told my father he could stay and work for wages. He took my sister for a kitchen servant. He had no work for me, so I had to leave. It was either starve or steal, so I thought I would head north and join the bandits."

"If you join them, all you can expect is to be caught in a few years and crucified."

"Better a bad death a few years hence than a bad death now."

Noah seemed to consider this and then nodded. The logic was unassailable.

"But the bandits won't take you."

"Why not?"

"Because you have nothing to offer them." Noah shrugged, seeming to imply that the point was obvious. "Look at you. You don't have a horse, you don't have a weapon. Why should they trouble to supply you with either when every day ruined farmers make the trek into the mountains, hoping to join them. Probably, they will cut your throat."

"Then what am I to do?"

"That is the question, isn't it."

They sat together for a time without speaking. The wine was gone, which Noah chided himself for resenting. After all, in three hours he would be in Capernaum, where he could drink all the wine he wanted. This poor soul might never taste wine again.

Then a thought occurred to him.

"I have a friend in Ptolemais," he said. "He is a merchant, and I have done business with him for years. He owns warehouses and a couple of ships. His name is Kreon. He is a Greek but a good sort of man. Just ask for him along the wharves. If you tell him that Noah the metalsmith from Sepphoris sent you, he will give you work."

"Where is Ptolemais?"

"It is on the coast of the Great Sea. If you walk west, keeping Mount Carmel on your left, and then turn north when you reach the sea, you will find it. You will be there tomorrow."

"Tomorrow."

Perhaps the same thought was in both their minds: How was this wretched, spent man to walk to Ptolemais, in one day or even five?

Noah fetched his purse from under his belt and counted out five silver shekels and then, after a moment's reflection on God's hatred of avarice, another five. To these he added a scattering of copper coins.

The man glanced at the money resting in Noah's palm and raised his hand as if to fend it off.

"Keep it," he said in an offended tone.

"I see. It would have been more honorable to have killed me with your pruning hook and then stolen my purse. I commend your scruples."

This was received with a cold silence.

"Listen, my friend. By assisting you I find favor with God, so in refusing out of pride you do that which injures us both. Besides, the day may come when you will be able to render me an even greater service."

He took the man's hand and poured the coins into it.

"Take these," he said. "Rest in the first village you find. The copper will be enough for a bed and food for a few days. Do not show anyone the silver. In Ptolemais, bathe and buy clean clothes so that you do not come to Kreon as a beggar."

"My name is Samson," the man said. It seemed to be his way of offering thanks.

"Then be careful in the city, lest they cut your hair."

7

When Noah arrived in Capernaum, he found he was more tired from the journey than he had expected, and he was hungry. In the market he discovered a wineshop where he could also buy a dinner of fish and millet, so by sundown he was feeling better.

"Come a long way, have you?" asked the proprietor as he cleared away the dishes and poured Noah a second cup of the local beer. It was his business to be sociable, but there was an edge of suspicion in the question. He was a large man who carried the extra flesh that only comes with prosperity. The threadlike scars on his fingers indicated that he had begun life as a fisherman.

"I left Sepphoris this morning."

"I've never been there. I've been to Tiberias three times, but never Sepphoris. It's quite a city, from what people say."

"I live there."

The proprietor frowned. Noah suspected that he felt cheated. If he had known, the man would have charged more for the meal.

"Do you know of a place where I could find a bed for a few days?"

"I might be able to oblige you." His eyes narrowed as he seemed to be straining after a way to accommodate a man wealthy enough to live in Sepphoris. "I don't know where else you might go—people hereabouts don't generally care for strangers."

Noah smiled and nodded agreement. With that settled, it seemed a propitious moment to inquire after his real business.

"I have a cousin," he said. "The last I heard of him, he was living somewhere here. I wonder if you know of him."

"What's his name?"

"Joshua bar Joseph."

"This cousin, he's from Sepphoris?"

"No. From Nazareth. That's a village just south of Sepphoris."

"And his name is Joshua?" The proprietor appeared to consider all this, and then suddenly the expression on his face changed, as if something unpleasant had just occurred to him.

"You don't mean the preacher, do you?"

"It seems likely enough. He's a tall man. He used to be a carpenter."

"That's him. He's been making a nuisance of himself around here for a couple of months now. You say he's kin of yours?"

Noah had the distinct impression that the price of hospitality had just gone up, so he reached into his purse and took out three silver shekels, one after the other, and placed them in a row on the table.

"You will put me in your debt if you can tell me where to find him."

The sun was just at the horizon when Noah saw a man sitting in the sand by the water's edge, leaning back against an overturned fishing boat. Even at a distance of a hundred paces, he knew it was Joshua.

He sat down beside him. He could make out little except his profile, with its high forehead and eye sockets deep enough that the darkness seemed to gather in them. Joshua gave no sign that he noticed his presence until Noah used his thumb to break the clay seal on the wine jar he was carrying with him. In his other hand were two small cups. He filled them both and offered one to his cousin.

"Where did you buy this?" Joshua asked. "Or did you simply scoop it up from a puddle of donkey piss?"

Noah laughed quietly and threw his arm across Joshua's shoulders.

"And hello to you," he said.

For a time they drank in silence. It was a warm evening, and the sound of waves lapping against the shore was agreeable. Neither wished to break the spell with questions that could have only unpleasant answers.

"Where *did* you buy this?"

Joshua held his cup out to be refilled.

"I don't notice that you are reluctant to drink it."

Joshua tasted the wine again and made a face, which was just visible in the gathering darkness.

"That is because it is your wine. Should I ever again have a few copper coins of my own to spend, I want to know what places to avoid."

"This one is just off the main square. It has a green awning."

"By chance is the owner a big, stout man?"

"Yes."

"Noah, you have an unerring instinct for trouble. His name is Ezra and he used to be a fisherman, until he married the previous owner's widow. She is ten years older than he, so perhaps she wasn't inclined to be fastidious. For a brief time she listened to my message, and perhaps it made some impression. Needless to say, *he* is not one of the saved."

"So I gathered."

"Does he know you are my cousin?"

"Yes, but for a consideration he will overlook it. I have a bed there."

"You will probably find yourself sleeping on the roof. The weather this close to the sea can be freakish, so let us pray it does not rain."

The idea seemed to amuse him, and he laughed. Then, suddenly, the laughter stopped.

"What are you doing here, Noah?"

"I have come as a spy for Antipas. He wants to know if he should have you arrested."

"No—really. What are you doing here?"

"That is the reason."

So Noah told him about Caleb. Joshua listened and then said, "I do not know this man."

"Believe me, it is my hope that you never will. If the rumors are to be believed, he is the one who put the Baptist to death."

"Then why have *you* come?"

"Because I have no choice and because if I do not someone else will. I, however, being your cousin, will report that you are a harmless crank who preaches repentance and that nobody listens to you anyway. Besides, I felt you should be warned."

"I am safe enough here."

"You cannot imagine how reassured I am."

"You worry too much, Noah." Joshua reached back and rapped his knuckles against the hull of the boat. "How long would it take me to have this in the water? And on the other shore Antipas has no authority?"

"They might surprise you before you can get to a boat."

"No. This town is like a drum—the slightest tap is heard everywhere within. Should Antipas send men for me, someone would tell me of it before they had left the main road. The Tetrarch is not popular hereabouts."

"What are *you* doing here, Joshua?"

"Getting drunk with you."

Joshua laughed at his own joke, and then suddenly he stood up.

"Come along," he said, holding out his hand to help Noah to his feet. "Let's walk. You can tell me your news. Has Sarah found a husband yet?"

They followed the shore. It was dark by then, but there was a long streak of moonlight across the water, enough to light their way. They took off their sandals and let the waves wash over their feet. It was as if they were boys again.

"How do you live here?"

"Simply." Joshua smiled, as if it were the answer to a riddle. "I have made the great discovery that a man, no less than a sparrow, needs little to be content. A friend of mine, who is a fisherman, keeps a bed for me. I am invited everywhere to dinner. Enough people listen to me that one or another will supply anything I may happen to need. The Baptist lived on locusts and wild honey and drank nothing but water. I am not so pure a soul as he was, but I am learning. I have stopped worrying about my little wants because I know that I live under God's protection."

"And this is enough for you?"

"Yes." He shook his head. "Yes and no. Now and then, when I remember Rachel, I have a twinge of regret, but in time I hope to overcome even that. God took her from me for a reason. Besides, very soon I will have her back."

Noah risked a glance at him. There was only moonlight, but he knew that face well enough to sense its perfect composure.

"Do you believe that death is final?" Joshua asked, without turning his head. Noah thought there might be a faint smile on his lips.

"I don't know." Suddenly Noah remembered his own dead wife. "I hope not."

"The Pharisees teach that one day the graves will yield up their dead. The Baptist believed it. I believe it. And I know that day is not far off."

S

They talked until late into the night. Then Joshua said that he wished to be alone to pray and Noah went back into the town to find his bed at the wineshop.

To do him justice, Ezra provided a cot near the remains of the kitchen fire, and Noah would have slept soundly had he been able to still the whir of thoughts racing through his mind.

The most troubling thing was Joshua's utter sincerity. It was impossible to listen to him and not be convinced that he believed the will of God had been revealed to him, and such was the force of that conviction that it was very difficult to stand against it.

But when had it ever been any different?

Once, when they were children, Joshua had somehow conceived the idea that Moses was the father of King David, whom he identified with his grandfather's father, who had recently died and whose name had been David. From this he concluded that his own grandfather must be king of Israel, which he identified with Nazareth. Thus Joseph, and then he, would in turn become kings.

Noah expressed doubts, so eventually the question was referred to his grandfather, who, with becoming gravity, explained everything.

"Can you count to ten, Joshua?"

"Yes."

"And if you have ten tens, how many is that?"

"I don't know—a lot."

"Ten tens make a hundred. And ten hundreds make a thousand. That is how many years since the time of King David. In those days Nazareth did not even exist.

"None of our family will be kings, Joshua, and that is well. For the children of Israel should have no king but God."

Joshua accepted this, since it never occurred to him that Uncle Benjamin could be wrong about anything, but for three days he would not even speak to Noah.

This did not seem unjust to Noah, who, for his part, was never able to overcome the sense that he had somehow committed a breach of friendship, that Joshua, somehow, had been entitled to be right.

But now they were men. They no longer enjoyed the child's luxury of surrendering to imagination.

Very early the next morning a man appeared at Ezra's tavern. He was thickset, with a massive curly black beard that suggested a certain ferocity. The impression was offset, however, by his eyes, which were constantly glancing down at the ground, as if he were embarrassed. To Noah he introduced himself as Simon, and he was apparently the fisherman in whose house Joshua found a bed.

"He sent me to fetch you. Perhaps you will take breakfast with us?"

"It would be a pleasure."

Simon actually seemed relieved, and they set off together in the direction of the sea. As they walked, Noah, more out of compassion than interest, tried to draw this shy man out.

"Have you known Joshua long?"

"We were both followers of the Baptist." Simon risked a sidelong glance at him. "Do you think it's true that they killed him?"

"Yes."

"Some say he ascended bodily into heaven."

"Would it were so, but I have never heard of anyone escaping that way from the Tetrarch's dungeons."

They were silent for a long moment as Simon appeared to be adjusting to this new reality. At last he shook his head.

"Joshua loved the Baptist," he murmured, giving the impression that he regarded this as a great secret. "He was closer to John than any of us. He says that God will avenge His servant."

"Does he say so publicly?"

"No. Only among those who are closest to him."

"It is just as well he does not. Antipas has a long reach."

Except for the nets drying beside the door, the fisherman's house might have been in any village anywhere in Galilee. The walls were of mud brick, painted a dusty white and enclosing two rooms. The floors were of earth, but they were covered with cut reeds.

In good weather, like today, meals were taken out of doors. Simon's yard faced the water, and there were perhaps sixty people assembled there. Among the adults, there were more women than men, and there were several children. They all were quiet, even the children.

It was easy to find Joshua—one merely had to follow everyone else's gaze. He sat on a stool beside the door, the center of attention. From the way he gestured with his hands, he was obviously explaining something. This was clear even before Noah could distinguish the sound of his voice.

". . . and death will be held in abeyance forever. The mighty shall grieve then, and the poor shall be exalted. Is not God a just God, and shall not the first be made last and the last first? We live in a world ruled by darkness, and shall not the light come? That we find evil everywhere is but a sign that the kingdom of God is near."

He glanced up and saw Noah. Then he raised his hand and smiled.

"Friends," he announced, "this is my cousin Noah, whom, as he tells me himself, Antipas has sent here to spy on me. Well, Cousin, what say you? Should the Tetrarch have me put in chains?"

"Oh yes, for you have been talking sedition."

"Yet I have not mentioned his name."

"You say the world is full of evil."

"But is that not the truth?"

"That it is the truth is what makes it seditious."

For an instant Joshua seemed perplexed, and then he threw back his head and laughed. A moment later he was on his feet and the two men embraced.

"Eat your breakfast," he said in a low voice. "I have almost finished. Then we can talk."

Breakfast consisted of a piece of flatbread wrapped around some fennel.

Joshua resumed his seat near the door. He buried his face in his hands for a moment and then looked up and smiled.

"Happy are the destitute, for they shall be exalted. Happy are the children, for their faith is pure. Happy are the children of man, for their father is God. Go in peace."

When the crowd had departed, Joshua and Noah walked slowly back down to the shore, where men were pushing their boats into the water in preparation for the day's fishing. The sun was in their faces, and Joshua had to shade his eyes with his hand in order to watch.

"I like fishermen," he said. "I wish I had been born a fisherman and had lived my life in sight of the sea."

"If you had been born here, you would be longing to be a carpenter in Nazareth."

"That is perhaps so."

"I know it is so. You always had too much imagination." Noah made sweeping gesture with his arm. "One world is not big enough for you."

"As it is, *this* world is not big enough for anyone."

"It eases my conscience to hear you say so. Now at least I know I will not be lying when I tell Caleb you are not in your right mind."

For the second time that morning, Joshua laughed. It was a good sound, reassuring and human.

"I am not afraid of him."

"Then you *are* crazy."

Joshua started to say something, but Noah waved his hands, commanding silence. Anger was boiling in him, mingled with an odd feeling of shame.

For a long time they walked along the shore without speaking.

"Go away, Joshua," Noah said at last, kicking clumsily at a small stone, which rolled only a few feet and then abruptly stopped, like an old man settling into a chair. "Take a boat and cross over, tonight, into Gaulonitus, and lose yourself. I have enough money with me to keep you for three or four months, and I will send you more. I have reliable friends in the gentile cities. In a year or two, provided only that you keep silent—that you refrain from preaching—Caleb will forget your very name and you can come home."

"A year or two?" Joshua smiled, as if in on the joke. "Long before then, Caleb and Antipas will both be swept away."

"Do you truly believe that?"

Joshua turned his head to look at him, as if for a moment he doubted Noah's sanity.

"I believe it certain. They are as dead men."

"And so soon?"

"Yes. The time is very close when we shall awaken from this bitter dream." He smiled and shrugged his shoulders, in apparent helplessness. "And if I do as you suggest, I would go down to destruction with them. God has called me, as He did the Baptist before me, to give notice of His coming, and if I shrink from the task He will not forgive me. So, you see, I cannot run away.

"Besides, what can they do?"

"Do? Tell me you are not serious, Joshua. They can put you to death."

"They can make me sleep for a while—a very short while—as they have the Baptist. But I doubt they will have time even for that. God grows impatient."

"God, or you?"

Joshua stopped and turned to face Noah, then smiled and reached inside the neck of his tunic to pull out a small leather bag hanging from a string. He opened the bag and pulled out a silver ring with a small red stone.

"I told you I wouldn't lose it," he said, putting it in Noah's hand. "I gave the money away, and the blue cloak is now in the possession of a beggar in Tiberias. So I am poor again.

"But I can offer you a better dinner than breakfast. A wealthy woman, a follower of mine, has invited me. Come to Simon's house at sundown and we will go there together."

Noah spent the rest of the day with his landlord. Trade, apparently, was always slow until the fishermen came back, so Ezra was perfectly willing to bear his company, especially since the wine they were both drinking came from his own cellar and Noah paid in silver.

And, once he realized that Noah was not about to take offense at any criticisms of his cousin, he was very willing to talk about "the preacher," the more so the more he drank.

"He hates anyone with a little property," Ezra told him, very confidentially, as if it were a secret. "He says God will sweep us away like dust. Now, does that sound reasonable to you? A man builds something up with his own labor and this is a sin, like murder or eating eels? I don't see the sense in it. I'm a pious man—I pay the Temple tax and contribute to the priests. I don't see what entitles him to turn my wife against me."

"Did he?"

"Oh yes." The landlord nodded fiercely. "She came home and said we had to sell everything and give the money to the poor. Can you imagine such nonsense?"

"Why did he tell her to do that?"

"Because God is coming, and God hates rich people."

"Are you rich?"

"No." The idea of his poverty seemed to depress him. "I have this tavern, which I admit pays better than fishing. But according to the preacher a man is rich if he has a house to sleep in and can afford to eat lamb on holy days. If you own more than your loincloth, you're a sinner."

"So, did your wife at last see reason?"

"What she saw was my fist. I blackened her eye, and since then she's been quiet."

After a while Noah began to tire of the landlord's conversation and was very glad to hear him complaining that so much wine in the afternoon made him tired.

"Take a nap."

"An excellent idea." He ducked his head submissively. "You won't be offended?"

"Not in the least."

Ezra then went inside and Noah found himself agreeably alone. He preferred the company of his own thoughts, at last.

If there is sadness in recollection, then that sadness can itself be a kind of pleasure. So it was whenever Noah thought about his own wife. He could close his eyes and almost feel her sharp little shoulder blades pressed against his chest as she slept. His memories of her were wordless—the sight of her, the way her body felt beneath his hand, the scent of her hair. The dark beauty of her eyes, with a glance saying all that needed to be said.

He tried to remember only that, not the way she had died. Her face drenched in sweat, the screams, the bleeding that could not be stopped. That final agony lasted almost a whole day, and the child had been born lifeless.

The following spring, Joshua's wife had died the same way.

Grandfather had once said he feared Joshua's grief had been too much for him. It was a possibility Noah had no difficulty in understanding. He could easily recall his own state of mind in the long months after Ruth's death. The sullen resentment, the feeling that all meaning had gone out of existence.

The worst was his sense of estrangement from God.

In the end, he and God, like old friends who have endured a deadly quarrel, managed to patch things up. Yet it was never the same—the conviction of living under God's protection had disappeared.

One Sabbath evening, as the light died, he had described these feelings to his grandfather, who, to Noah's surprise, had not been shocked but had merely pointed out that God offered no guarantees in this life, that even God's love for His children could not save them from the operations of blind chance.

Thus, over time, Noah had worked out for himself a notion of how it all fit together. There was life in the world, where one had to accept injustice and cruelty and the arbitrary workings of fate, and there was God, who offered the consolations of His Law and His understanding. One could not choose to be safe, for there was no safety, but one could choose to be righteous, which meant living in acceptance of Torah.

And righteousness opened the possibility of prayer—not prayer as a collection of words, but prayer as an appeal to God for His love. God read the hearts of His children as it was given to man to read the Law. God would forgive weakness and error, but not a turning away from Him. Life was short and uncertain, but one could live in the presence of God, and God was eternal. To live in the presence of God was man's consolation for having to live in the world.

But it seemed as if Joshua felt that God's love implied something more.

Just before sundown, Noah returned to the house of Simon the fisherman, where a little knot of men, with Joshua at its center, was waiting.

"Good. You came," Joshua said, with perhaps more emphasis than necessary. "I was afraid you had become disgusted with us and would stay away."

"I have grown hardened to your eccentricities, Cousin. Where are we going?"

"Ah!" Joshua threw his arm over Noah's shoulders, pushing him gently forward as if he lacked the capacity for independent movement. "The house of a widow. A wealthy widow. She has become a follower and gives much to the poor. She also—and this is more to the point—gives excellent dinners."

"Yet I have it on the authority of my landlord that you despise the wealthy, that you consider them sinners."

"I despise no one, and my ministry is not to the righteous but to the fallen, who have need of me. Besides, a man would have to be made of stone to despise Deborah. Wait and see."

Capernaum was not so vast a place that the great lived more than a few minutes' walk from the dwellings of the poor. Or perhaps the widow was not really so very rich. After all, Joshua, who had but rarely ventured into cities, did not encompass much in his ideas of wealth. Deborah's husband, as it turned out, had been a fish salter and merchant, and dead some two years. His house was no larger than Noah's house in Sepphoris and betrayed few symptoms of grandeur.

And Deborah, who met them at the door, managed in an instant to confound all Noah's expectations of her.

For one thing, she was young, by the look of her only a few years into her twenties, more fitted to be a bride than a widow. More than this, she was beautiful, with large, black, captivating eyes, and there was in them, as she gazed up at her unknown guest, an expression of sympathetic tenderness, which did away with all the awkwardness of first meeting.

There were sixteen at dinner, some of whom Noah had met earlier in the day and some who were strangers. These, from their appearance, seemed men of means and, from their conversation, outsiders, interested in Joshua's teachings but as yet unconvinced.

"Let me introduce you all to my cousin Noah," he began, after a servant girl had filled everyone's wine cup. "He is an ironsmith, a man of great skill who has prospered in his craft. He is also learned and devout and, like many of you, skeptical."

This was greeted with polite laughter, and Joshua turned to Noah, who occupied the couch on his right, and smiled, as if encouraging him to see the joke.

"When it is God's will to overturn the wicked and redeem His children, I believe that Noah shall be among the saved—for all that he is my cousin and thinks me a great fool." Again there was laughter, but less hesitant. "It is even possible he may be right, for I am neither wiser nor

more virtuous than others, and Noah, who has known me since childhood, could doubtless entertain you with many instances of my folly.

"But fool or not, it has been God's pleasure to make me His instrument. So disregard the man, who is no different from yourselves, and
hearken unto the message, which is from God."

He spoke for nearly an hour, and no one, Noah observed, touched
either their wine or the bread before them. Even the servant girl listened, shyly standing half concealed behind a curtain.

It was interesting to watch their faces, to hear the voice that was
almost as familiar to Noah as his own, and witness its effect on people
who had not grown up with the sound of it in their ears.

The poor among them, the servant girl and the few friends Joshua
had brought with him, seemed in a state of rapture. For them it was a
congenial teaching, and Joshua's words plucked at their hearts like the
fingers of a skilled musician playing a harp. They had no doubts.

"In God's kingdom, which is near at hand, so that one can almost
hear the first murmurs of the storm which shall sweep away injustice,
there shall be no distinction between rich and poor. The man who owns
two coats shall give one away, simply that the naked might be clothed."

The others, the men of position and wealth, were troubled. Why
shouldn't they be? They were being asked to give up everything that
defined them, that set them apart from and above their fellow men. It
was so easy to believe that because you were rich you were better.

And yet they too were being pulled along by the almost irresistible
current of Joshua's voice. For that moment, at least, they believed. They
felt the full weight of his gentle reproach. For perhaps the first time in
their lives, they knew shame.

"And while we wait—and that wait will not be long—we should anticipate God's will and live our own lives as if the Kingdom were already here. Thus I say to the mighty of the earth, the men who own
vast estates accumulated from the farms of those whom they have
driven into debt, repent of your sins, give away all that you have, and
seek God's forgiveness."

"But, Master, is every man who acquires wealth a sinner? Have we
not been taught that prosperity is the sign of God's favor?"

The question came from a well-dressed man who, when Joshua's
gaze settled on him, glanced down and began nervously playing with
the rings on his fingers.

"Each man answers that question in his own heart," Joshua answered. "Each man knows how he came by his wealth and if he has been just in his dealings, if he has shown mercy to the poor, if he has obeyed God's commandment to love others as we love ourselves. What does God whisper to you in the night?"

Noah glanced over his shoulder at Joshua, who was smiling. It was a wonderful, understanding, forgiving smile.

And it was not without its effect, even on Noah. He turned his attention back from the speaker to his audience, and he could see that they felt it as he did.

In a day or two many would shake off the impression. They would return to their accustomed lives and find comfort in their possessions and the envy of the poor. But for some this would be the defining moment. They might renounce their wealth, or they might not. But they would never see things in the same way again.

"And now let us break bread, my friends, for if we wait any longer God may forgive me but Deborah's cook will not."

While they waited to be served, Noah and Joshua talked quietly. "It is like staring at one's reflection in a pond," Joshua said. "The least breath of wind and it becomes unrecognizable. No wonder they seemed confused."

"But you made an impression—even on me."

"Did I?" Joshua seemed genuinely pleased. "Then can I number you among the saved?"

"We'll see."

This made Joshua laugh.

When everyone had been attended to, Deborah came and sat down between the two men. She spoke briefly to Joshua and then turned to Noah. This, he told himself, was because he was the stranger.

They talked of inconsequential matters, of the inconveniences of travel, of village life and whether it was to be preferred to life in the great cities, of the best way to cook leeks. Yet it seemed to him, in that moment, the most interesting and important conversation of his life.

Was that because of Joshua's sermon? He didn't know. Still, Noah felt as if some closed place in his heart had suddenly been thrown open to the light.

9

Noah lingered in Capernaum for three more days, remaining for the Sabbath, during which Joshua preached in the house of prayer to a sullen audience. They took dinner that night at Deborah's house, where there were no other guests. The three of them sat at a small, round table, their heads almost touching, like conspirators.

"I have it in mind to visit the north," Joshua said suddenly, as if the idea had just come into his mind.

"That is an excellent idea," Noah answered—he discovered, to his surprise, that he was almost angry. "Disappear into the villages. Lose yourself in places no one in Sepphoris has ever heard of."

Deborah said nothing, but the exchange caught her attention. She seemed perplexed.

Joshua saw this and smiled.

"My cousin seems to imagine I am in some danger of arrest."

"Why?"

"Because the Tetrarch is afraid of him," Noah said.

Having spoken the words, Noah suddenly realized that they sounded like a jest. Perhaps the jest was that they were the truth.

"But why would the Tetrarch be afraid?"

"Why was he afraid of John the Baptist?"

Still, she did not seem to understand. It was perhaps to rescue her

from this confusion that Joshua once more picked up the thread of his
original idea.

"I will wipe the dust of Capernaum from my feet and search for a few
more ready to listen to God's message."

"If that message is anything like what I heard this morning, you will
find few enough," Noah said.

Deborah was sufficiently shocked that she actually put her hand to
her mouth, as if beseeching silence, but Joshua seemed amused.

"They weren't very responsive, were they."

"Fortunately for you."

Noah turned to their hostess and smiled. It was a perfectly unpremeditated gesture—for that instant he was unmindful of Joshua's existence.

Then he was recalled to himself.

"I think the Sabbath prohibition against work was the only reason
you weren't taken outside and soundly thrashed," he went on, seemingly concentrating his attention on the cup of wine he held in his left
hand. "Peasants and fishermen generally have few enough possessions
that they are not enthusiastic about being called upon to give them
away to anyone. They grow suspicious, and with reason. Isn't this what
our masters, Antipas and his jackals, say to us all: 'Divide your goods
with me'?"

"I do not think that God would accept the comparison."

"Doubtless not. But many of your listeners would."

"Yet . . ."

It was Deborah who had spoken, and they both turned to her. Their
attention seemed to embarrass her into silence.

"Go on," Joshua said quietly, as one would encourage a child's first
steps.

"Pardon me." Her eyes rested on Noah's face for an instant, and then
dropped. "Does not God command us to share with the poor? And is
this not what the Master bids us do?"

"The Master . . . ?"

Joshua threw back his head and laughed.

"You see, Noah? This is how one gains a reputation for wisdom—by
proclaiming the obvious. Apparently I have used it to great effect, since
they *will* call me that."

The next morning, as Deborah was finishing her breakfast, her servant girl announced that there was a man at the door.

"It is the man who was here last night—not the Master, but his friend."

"Thank you, Hannah."

It was indeed Noah, and it was immediately clear to her that he was not at his ease.

"Won't you come in?" she asked him, standing just inside her doorway, smiling as sweetly as she knew how. "Have you eaten?"

"No—yes." He actually grinned with embarrassment. "I have had breakfast, thank you. I am going home . . . to Sepphoris. I just thought I would stop and say farewell."

It was obvious he had no intention of crossing her threshold, and she had no difficulty divining the reason. Although her acquaintance with him was slight, she could easily believe him to be the sort of man who would be delicate about the reputation of a young widow living alone.

"Well, thank you."

They stood facing each other through a long moment of silence, and she began to suspect that he had intended something more than a mere visit of courtesy. But he would not speak. It puzzled her.

"I hope you have an agreeable journey," she said finally, simply because she could think of nothing else. "Sepphoris is a great distance, I hear."

"Not so far." He smiled, with something like gratitude. "A good day's walk. No more. I will dine with my sister this evening."

He glanced away, silent for a moment, and then said, quite suddenly, "I had thought of coming back in a few weeks' time."

"Oh? Won't the Master have left by then?"

"It is not Joshua . . ." He shrugged and turned his eyes aside, seemingly at a loss.

"Lady, I am like you—alone," he went on, speaking with a careful deliberation that was almost like a rebuke. Almost, but not quite. "I lost my wife four years ago, and since then I have hardly thought of another. Grief gives way to numbness, which becomes nothing more than a habit."

He paused, apparently waiting for some response, but of course there was none. Deborah would not have known what answer to make. She could only listen, with stunned fascination. She was conscious of nothing except the man before her, and the rapid beating of her own heart.

"And then I met you," he went on. He smiled again, but it seemed a smile from which all hope had fled. "I would know you better."

Again he waited, and again she could say nothing. It was not in her power.

"But I can see that I have offended you, for which I can only apologize. I will trouble you no longer."

Never, she thought, never in her life had she seen such sadness in a man's eyes.

He took a step backwards and then turned to go. He had almost reached the corner of the building, where he would turn and disappear, perhaps forever, when she found her voice.

"No, wait . . . please."

He stopped and turned his head. There was nothing in his face except resignation, not even curiosity. It was the face he would wear while waiting for death.

Suddenly she felt a flood of pity for him. She wanted to comfort him, to tell him she would do anything to make him happy, to see him smile again. But of course it was impossible to do any of these things, so she took a step down from her threshold stone, which brought her that one step closer to him.

He did not move. He did not seem to understand.

"When you come back . . ." she began, and then stopped. The difficulty was that words defined intention and, beyond the simple desire to keep him from departing out of her life, she had no idea what she intended.

But she must say *something*.

"Where would you stay?"

He smiled—he did smile. The hopelessness vanished. Or, perhaps more accurately, was translated into a certain wariness.

And he took a step back toward her.

"My good friend Ezra," he said, "who keeps a tavern, and has decided to forgive me for being Joshua's cousin, can doubtless be persuaded to furnish me with a bed."

The smile vanished, as if he felt it was out of place, or implied too much.

"I would do nothing to compromise you, Lady. I have business

dealings with men in the gentile cities to the east—Capernaum would make a convenient base from which to visit them."

His expression became faintly playful, the way it did sometimes when he argued with the Master.

"I would turn up with a pack animal laden with my wares, and for a few months I would play at being the itinerant peddler."

He had thought it all out, it appeared. But, then, he would. It surprised her a little to discover how distinct was her impression of him. They had met only twice, and yet she believed that she understood his character. He was the sort of man she believed she could trust.

Perhaps she had been paying more attention than she realized.

"You have taken me by surprise," she said, glancing away out of sheer embarrassment. "I can give you no encouragement. I need time to think. At this moment I have no idea . . ."

"I understand that." He took another step toward her, but only one. "I ask for nothing beyond the opportunity to know you better, and to have you know me better."

"I would know you better, Noah."

He smiled, and she realized it was the first time she had ever spoken his name.

"Then we will see each other again, in a few weeks' time."

"What did he want?" Hannah asked. She was sixteen and had worked in the household since she was twelve. Like her mistress, she was utterly alone in the world, and her loyalty to Deborah had the absolute quality of a blood tie. The question was therefore not an impertinence.

"Merely to say good-bye."

"I think he likes you."

"Really?" Deborah smiled, as if at an interesting but indifferent fact, and hoped she was not blushing. Her face felt hot, so probably she was. "The Master loves him, so he must be a good man. I would value his regard."

Hannah said nothing, but the expression on her face betrayed a suspicion that her mistress was not being entirely candid.

"I have some accounts to go over," Deborah announced, suddenly eager to get off the subject of Noah and his regard. "I will be in my bedroom."

Her bedroom was on the second floor and possessed of a balcony that faced onto a small kitchen garden surrounded by a wooden fence. The balcony was just large enough for a chair and a round table not much bigger than the lid of a cooking pot. Only one person could sit there comfortably, and during her husband's lifetime the door to the balcony had always been kept closed. It had become, since his death, a kind of sanctuary.

She disliked her bedroom, although she was rarely prepared to admit this to herself. Still, to this hour, after two years of widowhood, she found it disquieting, as if, at any moment, he might come in, with his heavy, *I am master here* manner that had always made her feel like an item of furniture.

The balcony was her own. She could close the door to the bedroom and be in a place that had no associations with her married life.

Because Deborah could not hide from herself that she had not loved her husband, and that awareness filled her with remorse. God commanded that a wife should obey her husband in all things, and should love him. She had obeyed him, but to love him was not in her power.

She was fifteen at the time of her marriage. Her father, who was clerk to a tax collector, had wept when he told her. She was his only child and he loved her, but he was in debt. Bukkiah the fish merchant admired her, would take her without a dowry, and would provide her father with the money to pay his creditors. He had no choice.

Her mother told her that to be poor and unmarried was the worst fate that could befall a woman. She said it was a daughter's duty to submit to her parents' will. Deborah submitted.

But, as God willed, her submission was to no purpose. The wedding feast was hardly cleared away when there was an outbreak of fever, which claimed both her parents in the same day.

Bukkiah was forty-two and a widower. His only son had died in childhood. He was not handsome and his conversation was without charm. Deborah found him coarse, but he was not brutal and treated her with decent respect. His respect increased when he discovered that her father had taught her to read and to do sums. He had an illiterate man's respect for anyone who could "do letters," as he called it, and such an accomplishment in a woman seemed to him almost magical. She kept his books and he listened to her advice in matters of business, although he did not like people to know. A man's wife should not have such authority with him. And a man's wife should not know how to read. Somehow it didn't seem quite proper.

Many women would have envied her. Her husband was tractable and rich. Yet this very consciousness of privilege only made Deborah more unhappy, since she reproached herself the more because she could not love him. He deserved his wife's love, although he did not seem to notice its absence.

She was his wife, and that was itself the problem. If she had been merely his servant she might have been reasonably content, but she was his wife.

Perhaps twice a month he had need of her and she would submit. At first it hurt, but after a time she felt nothing—or almost nothing. She hated the touch of his hands on her breasts. She hated the weight of his body over her. It felt like being trapped in a cave.

Yet, somehow, she had the sense that it might have been otherwise. The relations between husband and wife were supposed to be a pleasure for them both, and sometimes, even with Bukkiah, she had the sense that this might have been possible. But then he would be finished, and roll away, and fall asleep.

And such had been married life, until the day he cut his thumb on a broken piece of iron that had somehow found its way into the belly of a fish he was gutting. The wound grew putrid and his hand and then his arm swelled up so that he could no longer bend his elbow. By the third day he could not rise from his bed. She nursed him without rest and listened as, in his delirium, he called out the name of his first wife. In the week of his illness she was closer to loving him than in all the years before, and when his life flickered out she sincerely mourned him.

Almost nothing changed. The widow, who had come to understand the business at least as well as her husband, simply hired a few more men and things went on as before. Since Bukkiah's death she had received a few offers to buy the business, but she had declined them. The work gave her something to do.

And now, it appeared, she had a suitor.

Noah was not the first. Since being alone, she had received two offers from local men, both politely but instantly refused. Noah was the first to whom she felt herself inclined to listen.

She liked him. That was the difference.

She could list to herself various reasons for liking him: He was intelligent and pious. The Master loved and trusted him. He seemed a man whose emotions one could take seriously. He was not handsome, but she liked his face. His hands seemed to combine great strength with an almost feminine dexterity. Did these account for her liking him?

How long since he had declared himself? Not half an hour. In his walk from her door, he would hardly even have reached the main road. Yet the surprise was beginning to wear off.

She had only to close her eyes and in imagination she was sitting beside him. He was speaking, not to her but to someone else. His attention was directed elsewhere, but she could feel the warmth of his body. The sound of his voice, its rhythm, the way the words would trail off at the end of a sentence, was more beguiling than any music. She wanted to touch him but did not quite dare.

She was aware of a great tenderness in herself. It was like nothing she had ever experienced.

She forced her eyes open and looked around. She was sitting on her balcony. The morning sun was bright and came from over her left shoulder. Noah was gone, once more on the road back to Sepphoris.

Instantly, she missed him.

10

"What could it be?" the priest asked, examining the mysterious object he held with the tips of his fingers, turning it this way and that. It was made of iron, so highly polished that it could almost have been silver, and about the length of his hand.

"It is a pair of pliers. For pulling teeth." Caleb was mildly irritated that the Lord Eleazar should express such interest in a trifle. "It was brought this morning by messenger, a gift from my informant, along with his report."

"Look at the hinge mechanism," Eleazar said, with childlike delight. "Except that you cannot see it, can you. It almost appears as if there is no hinge. Your informant must be a very clever man."

"Yes, he is. Rather too clever, I suspect. His report is worthless."

With an air of reluctance, Eleazar set the pliers back down on his desk and accepted the single sheet of papyrus. The writing, he observed, was Greek.

"'Joshua bar Joseph has a negligible following, mostly women, to whom he preaches forgiveness of sins and the virtues of humility and charity. He believes that God will restore the world to its original perfection, for the enjoyment of which men must prepare themselves by purifying their hearts and practicing mercy and forbearance.'"

He looked up at Caleb, who was standing respectfully to one side, and raised his eyebrows.

"I can believe his following is negligible," he said. "Such lofty sentiments are unlikely to attract much interest.

"Then he goes on to write, 'It is difficult to imagine in what light Your Excellency could regard such a person as of any danger to the state.'"

"Joshua bar Joseph was a follower of the Baptist," Caleb insisted. "He is doubtless proclaiming the same message of sedition."

"Your informant suggests otherwise."

"My informant is his kinsman. He has a motive for softening the truth."

"His kinsman? Yet you selected him."

Caleb shifted his weight a little. He seemed uncomfortable.

"It is almost customary for members of the same family to denounce one another," he said finally.

"But not, apparently, in this case."

Eleazar examined the papyrus again, as if the object itself, apart from the meaning of its words, might offer some clue. "Why does he write in Greek? And why does he accompany his report with a tool for drawing teeth?"

Neither of these questions held much interest for Caleb. He had assumed the pliers were merely a gift—a bribe of sorts. A fruit peddler might have sent a basket of oranges, but Noah was an ironsmith.

"Why shouldn't he write in Greek? As for the pliers, he makes them. I saw a pair like this in his shop."

"Is he a learned man, this maker of pliers?"

"I believe he has that reputation, yes."

Eleazar smiled faintly, as if at some idea he felt no temptation to share.

"His report is worthless," Caleb repeated, without quite knowing why.

"It is only worthless if it is untrue. To know that a man is not your enemy is also valuable information."

At last he raised his hand in a gesture of dismissal. "You may go, Caleb. Continue to gather evidence, if it amuses you, but I am inclined to leave this cloud dweller in peace."

"As you wish, Lord."

When he was alone, Eleazar reread the report from this kinsman of Joshua bar Joseph, enjoying the ingenuity with which it managed to say everything and nothing. He almost envied Caleb the acquaintance of such a person, except that Caleb was too blunt to appreciate him.

Eleazar picked up the pliers again with his left hand, still holding the report in his right. Upon reflection, he decided they were much alike. The two halves of the pliers were joined, apparently, by a barrel piece, no further across than the width of the smallest finger on a man's hand, which projected from one half and fit into a circular hole of corresponding size in the other half. The riddle was, what held them together? Was there some fastening concealed within the joint? Did the barrel piece widen? In either case, how would a man construct such a thing? It was a mystery, concealed from view.

The letter was much the same. This Joshua preached a message which was identical to that proclaimed by the Baptist yet which, restated by Caleb's informant, sounded harmless enough. It was not sedition to teach that God would redeem his creation, less still that men should purify their hearts. Yet the Baptist had gone well beyond both. The Baptist had dared to rebuke the Tetrarch himself.

And then there was the argument from obscurity. The Baptist had been regarded by the common people as a prophet, and his arrest had been unpopular. His follower Joshua was heeded by almost no one, if his kinsman could be believed, so that to arrest him, and thus bring him to the attention of the mob, would be to create a danger where none currently existed.

The Tetrarch could not afford to elevate another religious zealot to martyrdom, at least not so soon. A ruler, if he is to continue to rule, can be hated only in moderation.

"It is difficult to imagine in what light Your Excellency could regard such a person as of any danger to the state." *But not impossible,* the informant seemed to be implying. *If you are sufficiently set upon shedding innocent blood, you will find a pretext.*

Why was the report in Greek? Why not in Hebrew or, at least, Aramaic? Why? There was no reason, except perhaps to suggest that Caleb had made himself a foreigner in the midst of his own people. Still, this was no more than the truth.

And then there were the pliers. What could the man possibly have meant by sending Caleb an instrument for drawing teeth?

None of the answers were flattering.

Caleb was angry because his spy did not tell him what he wished to hear. Caleb was becoming blinded by his own ambition. He should have been angry because the man rebuked him.

Eleazar felt himself included in that rebuke, although the author of the letter and the maker of the pliers probably had no idea that he was involved in the business. However, he took no offense. It seemed to him that the rebuke was deserved.

Eleazar had been born into the priesthood, but what did that mean? A few times a year he traveled up to Jerusalem to take his turn offering sacrifice in the Temple, and for the rest he wore a priest's vestments and lived like any other man. Perhaps the servants of God had no business serving any other master, yet what choice did he have?

Eleazar knew that Caleb had only brought him this report because he thought it valueless. He was playing at being the First Minister's humble servant so that their rivalry would not become too open. One could only imagine the things he was keeping secret.

His humble servant. The words themselves sounded like a particularly tasteless jest. *I do evil—or, at least, countenance it—and tell myself that I do it to serve some greater good,* he thought to himself. He wondered if the kinsman of Joshua bar Joseph would be impressed by his justification.

And then it occurred to him that this maker of pliers might have his uses, if not for Caleb, then for himself.

Eleazar decided he must learn the identity of Caleb's informant. Normally he did not wish to know such things, but now he needed allies, and this man seemed both clever and prepared to risk Caleb's hostility. Eleazar would make an exception.

Caleb knew he was in no fit state to speak to anyone. Rarely in his life had he been so irritated. He was beginning to find the Lord Eleazar intolerable.

So he went outside the palace walls and stood staring at the Galilean countryside for a full half an hour, and gradually, watching the green fields undulate in the wind, his mood became more tranquil.

He owned several farms in Galilee. There was one, with a large stone house, where he thought he might like to retire one day. He imagined himself sitting in the shade of a grape arbor, holding his wife's hand, enjoying her smiles.

It was a fantasy of course. Michal would never consent to such a life. Michal spending her days feeding the chickens and picking wildflowers— what a picture.

He had pleaded with her to return with him to Sepphoris, but even this she had refused.

"Sepphoris? What is there in Sepphoris?" She had actually laughed at the idea. "Sepphoris is a dog hole. Besides, the Lady Herodias requires my presence."

"*I* require your presence. I *love* you. Life without you is a torment."

But she had merely turned on her heel and left the room. When he departed from Tiberias, she would not even come to bid him farewell.

Michal living with him in a stone farmhouse, holding his hand beneath a grape arbor. Yet it was pleasant to think of, even if he knew it could never happen.

When he was convinced that he had returned to a state of perfect calm, tinged perhaps with a hint of melancholy, he returned to the palace.

He went down a stone stairway to the guardroom. The captain at first merely looked up inquisitively from his wine cup, and then rose to his feet.

"Where is Matthias?"

"Not on duty, my lord," the captain answered, his gaze apparently fixed on a point just a span to the left of Caleb's head.

The reply was, of course, precise and to the point. It meant that Matthias was in the city, unquestionably drunk, and probably in the arms of some slut.

"Well, find him. And when he is sober enough to keep his feet under him, send him to me. I shall be at home."

"Yes, my lord."

As always, Matthias awoke with a start. His sleep was dreamless, like death, and there was no interval between that and the terrible panic that always seized him in the first instant, sometimes before he even opened his eyes.

There were men in the room. One, his face very close, meant to kill him. No, it was only Lamech from the barracks, shaking him awake.

Relief, followed by shame, flooded his heart. He was such a coward.

"Come along, wake up," Lamech murmured, as if soothing a child. "Time to get on your feet. Little Ahab wants you."

Little Ahab—the guards' name for the Lord Caleb.

Matthias was lying on a pallet on the floor of a room he did not know and could not remember entering. Someone was lying beside him. He turned to see who, but that was a mistake, because a spasm of pain pierced his head like a nail.

Anyway, it was only some woman, asleep or maybe dead—no, she was breathing. She was on her belly with her face toward him, uncovered down to the rise of her buttocks, a little old for a whore but not bad. He couldn't remember her at all.

"I need a drink."

There was a wine jar beside the pallet. He could remember that. He reached out blindly and knocked it over, spilling some on the floor. He grabbed it by the neck and rolled himself in that direction until he was resting on his elbow. The whole process was agony. His head felt as heavy as an anvil, and just as battered.

There were about three fingers of wine left in the jar. He took a swallow, then another, and then he felt a little better.

"You need to wash your face and get on your feet," Lamech told him. "He wants you to go to his house."

The whore rubbed her nose with the back of her hand, opened her eyes, and sat up, without bothering to cover her breasts. She didn't seem at all surprised to see three armed soldiers in her room, all staring at her hungrily. She smiled.

Matthias reached for his tunic and extracted a small leather pouch from the pocket. Inside were two silver coins, the last of this quarter's pay.

Why should he care? The Lord Caleb needed him again, so there would be more silver to buy wine and pleasure. The Lord Caleb, whatever else, was not ungenerous.

He gave the pouch to the whore.

"Here. You were wonderful."

He always told them that.

Outside, Lamech dismissed the other two guards. "Have you had anything to eat?"

"No, and I don't want food. I want some wine."

"You know, the way you drink, you'll be dead in five years," Lamech said, after they had found a tavern and Matthias had quickly downed two cups of something that smelled worse than a corpse. "You don't even water it."

Matthias glanced up and briefly considered becoming angry. He decided against it. Lamech wasn't his friend—Matthias didn't have any friends—but they had trained together. That was close enough.

"Five years? Do you think it will take as long as that?"

"Why do you do it?"

"Because when I've drunk enough, something happens in my head. I don't care about anything then. My whole life, past and future, is like something that belongs to a stranger."

"It sounds horrible."

"It's bliss."

Matthias smiled, not very pleasantly. Lamech had a woman, and when he wasn't on duty he lived with her, in a room above a potter's shop. He was a decent sort who had never darkened his soul with deeds that cried out for vengeance. Probably even his dreams were innocent. Of course he wouldn't understand.

Matthias's dreams were terrible.

"That's enough wine," he said. "Two cups and I'm sober again. Now I'm hungry."

Lamech's orders were to find him, clean him up, and escort him to the door of the Lord Caleb's house, and it was there the two parted. Lamech disappeared around the corner of a building, while Matthias tried to summon the courage to knock.

The porter answered. All porters were either very young or very old, and this one was old. He knew Matthias by sight.

"The master is up on the roof," he said. "Do you remember your way?"

Without answering, Matthias went to the rear stairway the servants used. By the time he reached the roof his head had begun to ache again.

"You look dreadful," the Lord Caleb announced, glancing up from his chair for a short, scornful inspection. "Are you fit for work?"

"I will be, Lord, when the work requires me."

Matthias was always careful to fix his gaze a little to one side of the Lord Caleb's head, not simply because the mighty regard being looked at full in the face as a presumption, but because he hated and feared the man. The Lord Caleb had ordered done many terrible things, and yet he seemed untroubled by them.

To do evil and not to care—that required a devil.

The Lord Caleb had turned his attention back to the view. From his rooftop one could see for miles, and the sight seemed to please him.

"Of course you remember the Baptist," he said, without turning his head.

"I have heard of him, Lord."

Matthias closed his eyes, grateful that he had had no hand in that business. No one had rejoiced when John was arrested.

"He had followers—disciples, men who participated in his plans to overthrow the Tetrarch. Here is a list. A partial list."

Without looking at it, the Lord Caleb gestured to a table beside his chair. On the table was a bowl of fruit and, held down at one corner by the bottom of the bowl, a folded scrap of papyrus.

Matthias picked it up and opened it. He could read just enough to sound out the names. There were five, and against each name a place, usually a village no one had ever heard of.

"Find them," the Lord Caleb continued. "None is a person of consequence, so if they resist, you can kill a few and no one will object. Otherwise, bring them to me. Take as many men as you will need."

"And there is one other matter."

The Lord Caleb looked up at his obedient servant and smiled. "A certain Noah bar Barachel, who is an ironsmith here in Sepphoris, has offended me. I wish him punished."

"Shall I kill him, Lord?"

"No, do not kill him, since he may still be of use. Merely chastise him. Give him a good beating, but don't break anything. He goes to Nazareth every week to spend the Sabbath with his grandfather. I imagine he comes home after sundown, so you can catch him alone on the road. This is a warning best delivered in private."

"Should he know the warning comes from you, Lord?"

"I think he will know without being told."

11

Noah was almost the last through the city gates on the evening he returned home from Capernaum. It was already dark when he opened the door to his house, so he called out his sister's name, that she might know it was he and not be frightened.

"Have you eaten?" Sarah asked, as soon as she had kissed him.

"No, and I find that I am extremely hungry."

He smiled as he sat watching her prepare his dinner, because he knew he was going to make her happy.

He waited until he had drunk a cup of wine, and it had taken hold, before he spoke.

"I have met someone," he said. "A widow. She is young and beautiful. Her husband was a fish merchant and seems to have left her well provided for. Yet, in spite of all this, she is willing to receive me as a suitor."

At first, Sarah appeared stunned, and then, when her mind had adjusted to this new idea, she clapped her hands together in sheer joy.

"Beautiful? Oh, wonderful! And young? Young enough to bear children? And is she sweet tempered? Oh, Noah! I am so happy for you."

"She is sweet tempered. You will like her very much. She is also intelligent and pious. She is a follower of Joshua, which is the only flaw I can find in her."

He laughed, but Sarah seemed not to have heard.

"And she loves you?"

"As to love . . ." Noah cocked his head a little to one side and shrugged. "She wishes to know more of me—that is the most I can say. I will go back in a few weeks, and we shall see how it develops. At least she did not refuse me outright, which is what I expected."

"And do you love her?"

He seemed to consider the question for a moment, and then nodded.

"Yes, I think so. Or, more truthfully, I think if I see her again I will come to love her quickly enough. She strikes me as the kind of woman a man cannot stop himself from loving."

"What is her name?"

"Deborah."

"Well, she has conquered you."

As was his custom, Noah spent the Sabbath in Nazareth with his grandfather. They took the evening meal with Joseph and his family, who wished to hear news of Joshua.

"If he stays where he is, I think he is safe enough," Noah told them. "In Capernaum there are people who will protect him."

"Do you think my brother is mad?" Jacob asked. The tone of the question reflected his anxiety.

"No." Noah shook his head. "He believes he does God's work, but that does not make him mad. He may truly be a prophet—I don't know."

"How can he be a prophet?" Joseph asked, in a tone that suggested he already knew the answer. "The prophets of old performed miracles. They raised the dead and brought down plagues upon the enemies of Israel. He is not a prophet."

Noah shrugged, as if to say the mystery was too great for him. "Was the Baptist a prophet?"

No one seemed willing to answer.

When the meal was over and it was time to leave, Joseph embraced him. Noah could not remember another time he had done that.

"I thank you," Joseph said, and there were tears in his eyes. "You stand up for him. I know you love him."

"I think Joseph won't last the winter," Grandfather said as he and Noah returned to his house. "His lungs are failing. Joshua should come to him while he lives."

"I'll tell him. I'll be seeing him again soon." Noah found that he did not want to talk any more about Joshua. "I have something I wish to discuss with you."

Grandfather said nothing more, but once they were inside he took down a pair of cups and poured them both some wine. Then Noah told him about Deborah.

"It seems as if you have made a good choice."

"If she will have me. At least she is willing to listen."

"How did you meet her?"

"She is a follower of Joshua's."

The old man glanced at the ceiling, as if to say, *I knew there would be something.*

"She does not strike me as a silly woman, Grandfather. Many people, good, pious, sensible people, listened to the Baptist."

"You keep comparing Joshua with John."

"He was John's disciple. He preaches the same message." Noah shook his head. "All I am saying is that it is not unreasonable for her to be drawn to Joshua."

"Let us hope that she is not more drawn to him than to you."

"Let us hope."

The next morning Noah and his grandfather went to the prayer house. It was Jacob's turn to recite the Law, which this day happened to concern the treatment of criminals put to death. Since no one in Nazareth had ever been put to death, the topic did not excite much comment.

When prayer was over, they sat outside Grandfather's door.

"The Sabbath is not the least of God's gifts," the old man said, his head tilted back so that he could enjoy the sunshine on his face. "And that because it gives one time to think and to remember."

"To remember what?"

"First God, and then people." Grandfather smiled, without opening his eyes. "I remember you and Joshua, sitting with me just here, learning your letters."

"Joshua was quicker than I."

"Yes, but you were always wiser. You saw the truth of things when he did not."

"But he saw possibilities that never occurred to me. That also is wisdom. And he loves God."

"All men love God."

"Yes. But that love consumes Joshua."

Grandfather nodded. They did not speak of Joshua again. After a while, the old man got up and went into his house. A moment later he came back, carrying a scroll in his hand.

"Read to me, Noah," he said. "At my age it is a great pleasure for a man to listen to his grandson read the Law."

Thus the Sabbath passed away, much like every other Sabbath Noah could remember.

When the sun had set, it was time for Noah to return home. It was an hour's walk, and the light would not fail utterly before he reached the city gates.

After the inactivity of the day, it was a pleasure to move his legs, to let his arms swing free, and to know that tomorrow morning he would be back at the forge. As he walked he allowed himself to plan the journey that would bring him back to Capernaum and to Deborah. In his mind he selected the wares he would take and considered what he would say to the merchants in distant cities who would buy them.

He tried to avoid thinking about Deborah herself because the ideas that suggested themselves were not congenial. After all, by now she might repent of having encouraged him and dread his return. He could understand how that might be so—was probably so—because he had no illusions about his personal charms. He was neither tall nor handsome. Why should she love him?

He tried to keep his thoughts from her, but he was not particularly successful. So, by the time he reached the main road, he had worked himself into that state of melancholy which is perhaps love's most sincere form of tribute.

Otherwise he might have noticed that there was someone else on the road. He might have heard the footfalls behind him. He might have sensed that someone was gaining on him.

As it was, he had no inkling until he felt a hand on his shoulder.

The hand swung him around. In the darkness the man who held him was no more than a massive shape.

"You are Noah, the ironsmith?" a voice asked. It was a voice that went with the shape, as unmelodious as a rockslide.

"Yes. I am Noah."

The first blow caught him just below the ribs, and the breath went out of him so suddenly that for an instant he was not aware of any pain, only of a desperate need to fill his lungs. When he tried to take a breath, the pain was like the flesh being torn from his bones.

His legs began to buckle beneath him, but the man held him up, his left hand grasping the front of Noah's tunic. Then, with his right hand, he began delivering quick, precise blows that hurt like nothing Noah had ever experienced. The man's fist was like a stone, battering his face over and over so that each strike was an explosion of suffering. He could almost hear the pain as well as feel it.

At last he gathered enough breath to cry out, but he was instantly silenced by another blow under the ribs. Then his attacker spun him around and punched him in the back, low and to the right of his spine. That was the worst.

So, of course, he did it again.

Then the man let him drop. He released his grip and Noah went down, first to his knees and then down on his face.

Noah lay curled up on the ground, waiting for the next blow. But it never came. After a few moments, when he could bear to open his eyes, he realized that he was alone.

Twenty or so paces down the road, he saw a huge shape walking away, in the direction of Sepphoris. Unbidden, it came into Noah's mind that for someone so big the man had a surprisingly graceful stride.

For a long time—he had no idea how long—he just lay there by the side of the road. He might even have lost consciousness. He wasn't sure.

Finally he knew that he had to get up. It was an excruciating process, but at last he made it to his feet. Then his legs gave way and he was back on his knees. He rested for a moment, resisting the temptation to collapse, then he stood up again.

Would he stay up this time? Yes, he thought so. Could he walk? It seemed doubtful.

But he took a step, and then another. Movement was possible.

He did not consider what had happened to him, much less why. It never occurred to him to wonder. All he had in his mind was the next step, and then the next.

The city gates were no more than half a mile distant, yet Noah consumed the better part of an hour reaching them. They were shut, of course, but the guards recognized him.

"Noah?"

All at once his strength vanished. The next instant he was on the ground, with no notion of how he got there. The guards pulled him inside. After a moment he was able to sit up, and they offered him a cup of water.

"What *happened* to you?"

"I was set on."

"Robbers?"

"No." Suddenly it struck Noah as interesting and significant that the man had not taken his purse. "Has anyone else come through the gates in the last half hour? A big man?"

"No. No one."

He knew, of course, that they were lying—they had hesitated just an instant too long with their answer—and that too was significant.

"Can you make it home?"

"I think so."

The guard captain, whose name was Theudas, shook his head.

"Seth, you go with him."

Ten minutes later Noah was standing in front of his own door.

"You needn't stay," he told the guard. "I'll be all right."

He reached in his purse to give the man a few coins in recompense for his trouble, but Seth waved them away. The next instant he was gone, as if the night had swallowed him whole.

They were good fellows, Noah thought to himself. They meant no harm. But something had frightened them.

Sarah answered his knock. She looked at him and her eyes grew large. Her hand crept up to cover her mouth.

"I'm all right," Noah told her. "I had an accident."

She helped him into the kitchen, the first room after the shop. Then Sarah went back and bolted the door to the house.

She didn't ask questions. She took a cloth, dipped it into one of the water urns, and began cleaning his face. Her touch was light, but it hurt nonetheless.

"It probably looks worse than it is," he said.

"I think I should fetch you a physician."

"What would he do?" He smiled as her, and that also hurt. "I'll be fine."

"Then drink some wine to take away the pain."

"That is an excellent suggestion."

For the next hour Noah sat at the kitchen table, drinking wine cut with only two parts of water. It had the paradoxical effect of clarifying his mind.

His sister watched him.

"Now, tell me what happened," she said finally, in a tone that suggested she would not be receptive to any evasions.

"Someone attacked me. He knew me by name."

"He knew your name? Then why? Was he a robber? You have no enemies."

Apparently I have now, Noah thought. Then he shook his head—which turned out to be so painful an operation that for a moment he thought he might vomit.

"No. He wasn't a robber. He didn't take anything. And he didn't kill me, which means that it was a warning."

"A warning?"

"Yes—delivered by someone with considerable skill in such matters."

Noah drained his cup and poured himself another. The wine was helping. Provided he stayed still, he was beginning to feel almost numb.

Yes, he thought, it was a skillful piece of work. Here he was, almost two hours later, sitting, drinking wine, apparently in no danger of dying from his injuries. The damage was mainly confined to his face, with one eye almost closed shut but his nose unbroken. Whoever he was, his attacker had been careful. The object had been not to maim or kill but to inflict pain and thus inspire fear, and that he had certainly accomplished.

"I think I shall go to bed now," Noah said, when he had finished the second cup.

"Take the wine with you. You might need it during the night."

"Another excellent suggestion."

12

The next morning, at about the hour Noah usually opened his shop, there was a knock at the door—a loud knock, the knock of someone who did not mean to be ignored.

Sarah was in the kitchen. At first she hesitated, fearful after what had happened. Noah, as far as she knew, was still asleep. Then she decided it was cowardly to hide. She went out to the shop and opened the door.

"Is this the house of Noah?"

"Yes."

The young man smiled, not to make himself agreeable but because his wish had been gratified. He was tall and about twenty years old. His tunic was of embroidered linen and his hair and beard glistened with oil. He raised his eyebrows slightly, the way a certain kind of man might when addressing a servant.

"Then I must see him."

"He is ill. He is still asleep."

"What is wrong with him?" Without actually retreating, the young man seemed to pull himself back slightly.

"He had an accident."

"Oh," he said, the way he might have said, *"Then it is nothing contagious."* He reached into a pocket concealed by his thick leather belt and removed a sheet of papyrus, carefully folded into quarters. "Then show him this. I am sure he will want to see me."

He gave the papyrus to Sarah and, without being asked, stepped across the threshold.

"If you will please wait. I will take it to him."

Noah had spent a troubled, painful night and had only begun to sleep a little toward dawn. His ribs ached and his face was covered with tender, throbbing bruises, but this purely physical misery could not distract him from the fear that gnawed at his belly like a hungry animal.

Last night had been merely a warning. What would be next?

Yet sleep did come—and lasted until he became conscious of Sarah's hand on his foot.

"Someone is here," she said. "He brought this."

He sat up in bed, and she gave him the sheet of papyrus. He opened it, glanced at its contents, and then refolded it.

"What does it say?"

"I hardly remember." Very delicately, he wiped his face with his hands, wishing he had not drunk so much wine. Now he had a headache that had nothing to do with his injuries. "It is the letter I wrote about Joshua. What a coincidence."

Of course. He smiled at his sister, and it occurred to him, as a real possibility, that after today he might never see her again.

Because the man who attacked him could only have been sent by Caleb. And now he had sent the letter. What did he want? Another draft? Something properly incriminating?

"Thou shalt not bear false witness," he said, quoting the Hebrew. When Sarah looked puzzled, he asked her, "Where is this someone who has come?"

"In the shop."

"Then I mustn't keep him waiting."

Noah was relieved to find that their visitor was not Caleb but a haughty young priest who carried himself as if his first wish was to avoid the impurity of his surroundings.

Noah discovered that he was not in a mood to be polite.

"Yes? You wished to see me?"

For a moment the priest said nothing, merely stared at Noah's face.

"I had an accident, as perhaps you knew."

"Yes—your wife—"

"She is my sister." Noah paused, letting the priest's embarrassment take hold of him, and then repeated, "You wished to see me?"

"Yes." With visible effort, the priest reassumed his disdain. "Do you know the house of Kenan bar Dathan? It is on the Street of the Doves, just outside the gates of the palace district."

"No, but I imagine I could find it. Why?"

"A certain person, an eminent man, would be pleased if you would visit him there, at noon."

"But I take it this eminent person is not Kenan?"

"No, he is not."

Had he not been sure it would make his headache worse, Noah would have laughed.

"And I assume it would be quite pointless to inquire his name of you."

"Yes, it would. May I tell him that you will come?"

"Of course. How could I possibly refuse such an elegant messenger? Good day to you."

After another hour of sleep and a light breakfast, Noah discovered that he felt better. His face was still very tender, but his headache was nearly gone and the pain in his ribs, provided he did not breathe too deeply, was no more than a dull ache. He had just started to wash himself when he decided to take the basin of water over to a window and examine how he looked.

He waited for the water to be still and then studied his reflection. The face he saw was dreadful. He was covered with bruises, which by now had grown quite black, and his left eye was no more than a slit.

But he supposed he would recover—if allowed to live that long.

He selected a coat with a hood, so that when he went outside his face would be partly concealed in its shadow. The morning was cool, so perhaps no one would think it strange.

"I want you to leave here," he told Sarah, when he was at the door. "As soon as I am gone, I want you to set out for Nazareth and stay with Grandfather. Do not come back here until I tell you it is safe."

"Oh, Brother! What has happened to us?"

"I don't know, but I want you somewhere safe. Will you go?"

"Yes, of course. If you wish it."

"As soon as I am gone. Do you promise?"

"Yes."

———

The way was all uphill, but he had given himself plenty of time. There was no reason to hurry. He was not eager to reach his destination.

Nevertheless, the walk seemed to do him good. Warmed by a little exercise, Noah felt less stiff. The sunshine was a pleasure.

Life was God's gift to us. Whether long or short, it was a gift. Every minute of one's time was precious. Suddenly, and for the first time that day, he thought of Deborah. Memory showed him her face, and in his imagination she moved and lived and beckoned to him.

"Thou shalt not bear false witness." Such was God's commandment. It was better for a man to die, to surrender the breath under his ribs, than to break any one of the commandments.

If that was to be the choice, if that was what they demanded of him, that he lie and accuse Joshua—and thus provide the pretext for destroying him—then Noah hoped he had the courage to accept death.

The house of Kenan bar Dathan was vast. The floors were of polished marble. Some of the walls were painted with landscapes, so that the effect was to open the room out into a distance endlessly receding. It was the sort of thing that showed a fashionable Greek influence.

The owner, Noah reflected, might be a Jew, but he seemed to wish he had been born a pagan.

The boy who had answered the door ran to fetch the chamberlain, an awesome figure of about fifty, exquisitely dressed, who regarded Noah as he might a dog with mange.

"Your business?" he asked, implying that he suspected Noah had none.

"My name is Noah. I believe I am expected."

"Yes of course, my lord," the chamberlain answered, instantly adjusting his tone of voice. "If you would be good enough to follow me."

There was a room, large and empty, probably intended for the reception of many guests, then there was a corridor, then a smaller room, more comfortably furnished. Against one wall there was a couch, and on the couch reclined a man, leaning on his right elbow, his attention apparently focused on an object he held in his hand.

The man was of middle years, and thin. His hair was cut short, his beard a little longer. His eyes were intelligent, and there was that in his face which suggested life had disappointed him many times.

His dress revealed him to be a priest. Noah of course knew who he was.

At last he glanced up at Noah, smiled thinly, and gestured to a chair near the head of his couch. Noah sat down, his knees nearly touching a small table on which rested a silver tray holding two stone cups and a jug.

"My nephew told me your face was much bruised, and for once he did not exaggerate," the priest said, his tone dispassionate. "What happened to you?"

"That was your nephew this morning?"

"Yes." He tilted his head slightly, as if disclaiming responsibility. "My sister's son. He is rather spoiled."

"Perhaps he will grow out of it."

"Perhaps."

The Lord Eleazar held up the object in his hand. It was a pair of pliers, one Noah had made himself.

"This is an ingenious device," he said, laughing silently. "I am at a loss to discover how the hinge works. You must explain the trick to me."

He held the pliers out to Noah, who took them.

"At least they made it easy to discover your identity. I had them shown to one of your competitors, and he instantly recognized them as yours. 'I know of only one man who could have made these,' he said. 'His name is Noah and his shop is near the eastern gate.'"

"Why didn't you simply ask Caleb?"

"About certain matters it is not wise to appear curious."

The Lord Eleazar leaned forward, picked up the jug, and filled the two stone cups with water. He held one out to Noah.

"But you have not told me about your injuries. I am curious about that as well."

"I was set upon." Noah took a tentative sip of the water and found it astonishingly cold. "On my way home from spending the Sabbath with my grandfather, I was attacked by a man who, it seems, had also gone to some trouble to discover my name."

"Then perhaps you are lucky to be alive."

"I don't think luck had anything to do with it. My assailant was very skillful and had no intention of killing me. It was a warning. He meant to cause me pain and to frighten me. He succeeded."

"Did he?"

"Yes. But there are worse things than pain and fear, just as there are worse things than death."

"And what is worse than death, Noah?"

"Breaking the commandments."

For a long moment the two men remained silent as each seemed to assess the other. Then the priest set down his cup of water.

"Do you know who I am, Noah?" he asked.

"You are a man to whom Caleb would give the letter I wrote about my cousin Joshua. Is there anything else I need to know about you?"

Eleazar shrugged slightly, refusing to be insulted.

"I know who you are," Noah added flatly, as if contradicting an obvious falsehood.

"Then know that I did not order the attack on you. I knew nothing of it. Caleb did what he did for his own reasons."

"That is, of course, very reassuring."

The First Minister laughed. One had the sense that he did not laugh often.

"You have fulfilled the promise of your letter, Noah. I must grant you that. You are not impressed by the grandeur of my office, any more than you are frightened of Caleb."

"I am very frightened of Caleb."

"Yes, but not enough to suit him. Why did you write your letter in Greek?"

"I thought I would make it easier for him."

The Lord Eleazar smiled. Then, in the next instant, he became very serious.

"I think there are a few things you need to understand, Noah. I believe it possible that we could be of use to one another."

Their conversation lasted for more than an hour. For most of it the Lord Eleazar spoke, with Noah interjecting the occasional question or expression of surprise—and nothing surprised him more than the priest's candor. If any third person had been listening at the door, it might have meant both their lives.

But the Lord Eleazar, who seemed to have a refined understanding of all such matters, had taken his precautions.

"You are perhaps wondering why we have met here," he said, gesturing with his hand to take in all the space around them, "rather than at the palace or my own home. But Caleb has his spies, some of whom, no doubt, are among my servants. At least, that is my assumption. A few of his servants also provide me with information. Such are the conditions of life, no less than the sun and the rain, and we both accept them. I own this house. The man who lives here is my tenant and indebted to me. We are safe here."

"But why do you submit to being spied on by your own servant?"

"Because that is what he does." The Lord Eleazar leaned forward and refilled Noah's cup. "Caleb has an inborn talent for treachery, which is why I raised him to his present position. Further, the Tetrarch, who is deeply afraid of his subjects, likes him. He believes Caleb's persecutions protect him from his enemies. He is encouraged in this by his wife, the Lady Herodias, and she numbers Caleb's wife among her intimate friends. You see, the situation is complicated."

"You make me deeply grateful to God that I am only a humble ironsmith."

Although Noah had been sincere, the Lord Eleazar chose to interpret it as a jest and laughed accordingly.

"But you see that your relative obscurity has, at last, offered you no protection," he replied, still smiling. "Caleb reached down and found you. Now you are in as much danger as I am myself. If Caleb's ambitions are realized, and there is no longer any restraining hand on him, he will surely destroy you. You, and probably your whole family, since Caleb is a man who believes in thoroughness."

His words made Noah afraid, but not so afraid that he stopped listening. He had heard the words he had been meant to hear: *In as much danger as I am myself.*

"How does he threaten you, my lord? You stand at the Tetrarch's right hand. How can this man possibly threaten you?"

"He threatens me because he wants to replace me. *He* wishes to stand at the Tetrarch's right hand, and this he may achieve. He needs only to convince Antipas that he is necessary to the Tetrarch's survival.

"Actually, Caleb himself has become the greatest threat to the Tetrarchy. The execution of the Baptist caused much resentment. If there is enough resentment, there will be a revolt, and if there is a revolt the Romans will suppress it. Then they will probably decide that Antipas, like his brother Archelaus before him, is a bad ruler—which, from their point of view, means that he cannot keep the peace and thus guarantee the flow of tribute to Rome—and they will remove him.

"Do you wish to see Roman troops garrisoned in Sepphoris, Noah? But of course you won't see it because you will already be dead. So will I."

"But surely the Tetrarch wouldn't . . ."

"Wouldn't he?" The Lord Eleazar could only shake his head at such innocence. "Of course he would. My father was warden of the city, before me. Our family has acquired extensive properties, which by now, no doubt, the Tetrarch has come to regard with covetous eyes. If he decides that I am no longer useful to him, he will also decide that I am a traitor. All that I own will be forfeit to him.

"Do you see, Noah? I am fighting for my life. And if I perish, so will you. And so, eventually, will countless others. And the Romans will seize yet another piece of our homeland. They are bad masters, my friend. Eventually it will all end in war and slaughter."

Noah believed him. Indeed, it was impossible not to believe him. Yes, it was all true.

"Why are you telling me all this?" he asked. It was the one thing he did not understand.

"Because I think you can be of use to me. You can help me, and by helping me you can save yourself."

"How? I am as good as a dead man."

Noah looked down at the water in his cup. Suddenly it seemed important to drink it, as he might never have another chance.

"Last night I was beaten," he continued. "It was a warning, but Caleb might just as easily have decided to have me killed. When I received your message this morning I thought it was from him, and that I would be arrested. What he wants from me I cannot give him, and when he discovers that, he will send his man back to me, but with different orders."

Suddenly he reached down and took the cup, drinking it off at once. The Lord Eleazar watched him with undisguised interest.

"You are probably right," he said, nodding his head in agreement. "I think it may be necessary for you to go into hiding."

13

Noah returned to his house and confirmed that it was empty. Good. That meant Sarah was safely on her way to Nazareth. It would be better if he himself stayed away from there. Sarah would explain everything to Grandfather.

The Lord Eleazar was right. The wisest thing would be to disappear.

And he had a pretext. He went to the workshop and told his apprentice that he had decided to go on his trading expedition sooner than planned. He would leave at once. He did not know how long he would be gone. Hiram looked shocked when he saw the condition of Noah's face, but he asked no questions. He helped load the donkey with two boxes that contained the smaller, more precise tools that would fetch a better price, and promised he would look after things. Hiram was a good fellow.

The trip was not simply an excuse to get away, since Noah had planned something of the sort for over a year. He did business with the gentile cities in Philip's realm, and even up as far as Damascus, but it was on a small scale. He was sure, however, that he could find a larger market there and, if he started receiving regular orders, he could expand, take on a few more apprentices, perhaps even purchase another workshop, and grow wealthy.

But now that aim was secondary to preserving his own life and perhaps helping, in some small way, to rid the world of Caleb.

"I wish you to make inquiries," the Lord Eleazar had told him. "I am informed that you have extensive trading contacts outside of Galilee. I want you to find out for me how events here are perceived in the larger world—the world of practical men, men like yourself."

"What can I discover that you do not already know?" Noah had asked him. "The Tetrarch is widely hated. This is not a secret."

The Lord Eleazar had smiled thinly, acknowledging the uncomfortable truth. They were two men who could speak bluntly to one another, he seemed to suggest.

"No, this is not a secret. It is also beside the point. You will recall that his father was also hated, and yet he held sway over a far greater territory than Galilee. Even on his deathbed his power went unchallenged. The criterion of success for such men is not popularity but stability."

"So what sort of information do you seek?"

"How shall I put it?"

The Lord Eleazar seemed to look at nothing as he considered his own question. Then he raised his hands slightly, as if the obvious answer had only just occurred to him.

"Think of the Tetrarch not as a ruler but as a man of business—the manager of an estate, if you will. Or, perhaps more accurately, the landlord of the estate, for at bottom he is no more than that. Other men do business with him. They may not love him, but nonetheless they do business with him. And their approach to that business is based on an assessment of how well or ill they think the estate is being managed."

He paused for a moment, apparently depressed by the image he had conjured up.

"I want that assessment, Noah," he went on, when the moment passed. "I do not ask for any names because I know you wouldn't provide them. I don't expect you to betray anyone's confidence. But I want to know what men think. They would not tell me, or anyone they knew I had sent, but they will tell you. Over a cup of wine perhaps, at the end of the day."

So that was one more object of his journey. First Deborah had given the plan urgency, and now he was running for his life while gathering up the gossip of the marketplace.

Deborah. There was another question that needed an answer. What was he to do about Deborah? Everything had changed.

But perhaps she would save him the trouble of deciding. By now she may have come to regret her moment of acquiescence.

Since the last time he had seen her, there had been intervals when it seemed that the obstacles in his way were insurmountable. She was young, beautiful, and independent, and he was, after all, what he was: a thirty-year-old widower whom no woman, probably not even his dead wife, had ever considered handsome. By the standards of the village in which he had been raised, he was a prosperous man, but it never crossed his mind that Deborah would be tempted to marry him for his riches.

She was free—that was the point. Her late husband probably had been chosen for her, but the choice would lie with her now.

Noah's own marriage had been arranged. He had found no fault with his wife. Love had followed marriage. The union had been happy, and he had sincerely mourned her when she died.

Yet would she have chosen him if she had been in Deborah's position? Until now it had never occurred to him to wonder. What if she had been required to heed no voice but that in her own heart?

Such thoughts had tormented him ever since his departure from Capernaum, and now he was returning. To what?

And now he was a fugitive. What business did he have dragging her into this trouble? Best, perhaps, to leave her alone.

He slept that night in a village even smaller than Nazareth. A single silver coin bought him dinner, forage for his animal, and a mat by the kitchen fire in some farmer's hut. He hardly slept.

It was not until he came within sight of Capernaum that he decided he would see Deborah after all, if only to explain. He could not bring himself to part from her without a word.

It was about noon when Noah found himself knocking on the door of Ezra's wineshop.

"Oh, it is you! By the devil, what happened to your face?"

"I had an accident a few days ago. It looks worse than it is."

"Well, you are always welcome. Come back to visit your kinsman again? You will be disappointed. He has gone away, praise God."

"I know. I am here on business. Can you accommodate my donkey as well as me?"

Ezra ran his fingers through his beard as if considering a difficult passage of Scripture, but at last he smiled.

"I know someone in the next street who has an empty stall. Leave it to me." He gestured toward the donkey. "What have you got in the boxes?"

"Tools."

Ezra immediately lost interest.

Provided with a basin of water, Noah washed with more than usual care, changed out of his travel-stained clothes, and combed his beard. Then he went to Simon's house. He would inquire after Joshua. It was just a way of putting off the moment of decision, but he told himself that if his movements were noted it would call less attention to his visit to Deborah.

Simon was out fishing, his wife said. He would return at sunset.

So be it.

"Mistress, that man is here again. You remember him? He was a friend of the Master's. He looks like he's been in a fight."

Deborah experienced the news as a shock. Of course, "that man" could not be anyone but Noah. She hardly heard anything beyond the first sentence.

She was sitting on her balcony, and for an instant she was sure her heart had stopped beating. These sensations lasted only a moment, and then she forced herself to smile, with an expression of perfect uncon- cern, and directed Hannah to show their guest into the garden. It did not strike her as quite respectable to receive him in her house, and, in any case, at this hour of the morning, the garden was cooler, and more private.

The water jar she kept in her bedroom was almost empty, but there was enough to allow her to wash her hands and face. Should she change her dress? No—her dress was clean and it was the morning, so to appear in fine clothes would make an odd impression. She settled for combing her hair again, since she must do something.

There was a bench in the garden—only one, so they would of necessity be sitting beside one another. It was in the shade of a grape arbor, which screened it from the house. She had never considered its advantages for this kind of meeting, and as she descended the stairs from her bedroom she smiled to herself. This was the first time it had ever occurred to her that she might possess that kind of feminine cunning.

Noah rose to his feet the instant he saw her, a courtesy that would never have occurred to her husband. The first thing she noticed were his bruises.

"What happened to you?" she asked, experiencing a kind of tender panic.

"It's not important. I'll tell you about it."

Which of course meant *not now*.

He smiled, and there was an uncertainty in his eyes that touched her. She reached out her hands to him, a completely unpremeditated gesture that surprised even herself, and as he took them his expression changed to something that was less like confidence than gratitude.

"I hope you are well," he said, in a voice that could have said many other things. It was then that, with a visible reluctance, he released her hands.

"Yes, thank you. And you? How was your journey?"

"It was dusty and uneventful, which is the best that one can expect. I am very glad to see you again."

For a moment there seemed nothing more to say. They were both embarrassed, but it was the sort of embarrassment that had its own peculiar pleasure. He seemed on the verge of saying something which, she somehow sensed, she did not want to hear, so she took refuge in the mundane.

"Are you hungry? Shall I call Hannah . . . ?"

"I have not yet broken my fast, but at this moment I could eat nothing. Later, perhaps, it will occur to me to be hungry."

It seemed to her the most beautiful declaration of love she could have imagined. She wanted to embrace him, but of course that was impossible.

"I have thought much of . . . of what passed between us," she said. As soon as the words were spoken she considered that they were too bold, but in the same instant she knew she did not care.

"Is it possible you have reached any conclusions?"

"Yes."

She smiled. She was on the verge of laughing. When in her life had she ever been so happy?

Noah did not smile. Strangely, he appeared stricken.

"Something has happened," he said finally.

And then he told her a story, one she could hardly comprehend. It involved a man named Caleb, an evil man who had killed the prophet John, and a priest, and a letter Noah had written that had angered the man named Caleb, enough that he had had Noah beaten, and now Noah had been forced to flee.

"And this is all because of the Master?"

"Joshua? Yes, I suppose."

"Because you would not write lies about him."

"Yes." Noah shrugged, as if there were no more help for this trouble than for a summer of drought. "If I did as he expected I would not only betray Joshua and consign him to death, I would separate myself from God. I would be breaking the commandment against false witness, and I cannot bring myself to enter that darkness."

"Then you have acted as a good man and an obedient servant of God. If this is a crime, then the times are as bad as the Master says."

"The times are bad enough, but they are the times in which we are compelled to live."

"But you are right not to bend to them."

"But I would not be right to involve you in this."

Noah looked about him, as if trying to memorize every detail of this moment, and then his eyes settled on Deborah's face.

"I think it wisest that we do not see each other again. The dangers are too great."

"Women are braver than men," she said, smiling almost defiantly. "If you can face this trouble, so can I."

"Deborah, you don't understand. This man—"

"Be quiet, Noah. You will not move me."

She offered her hands to him again and he took them eagerly. They stood there like that, saying nothing, wishing only to behold each other and to be possessed of this moment.

"Won't you sit down?" she asked, as if they had just then encountered each other and no word of this trouble had been spoken. He released her hands and they took their places on the bench, not touching, their bodies at least a span apart.

Good, she thought. They were back at the start. They still had a courtship to go through, and many things to learn about each other, but a beginning had been made.

They talked through a good share of the afternoon, although neither of them was conscious of the passage of time. In an offhand way, as if he were merely making idle conversation, Noah told her about Sepphoris, which, to a village girl who had never journeyed ten miles from her birthplace, seemed a city of wonders. He told her about his grandfather in Nazareth and his sister, Sarah. She listened, and watched the gestures he made with his hands, which were at once strong, thick with muscle, and wonderfully clever. She noticed for the first time the tiny, star-shaped scars that must have been made by sparks from the forge. She remembered how gently those hands had held her own.

Eventually, when the sun was halfway through its descent, it seemed to occur to both of them that it was time to part.

"I had best take my leave," Noah said, seemingly unsure, all at once, whether he had overstayed his welcome.

"Come again this evening." She could see the question in his eyes: *What will your neighbors think?* She wanted him to know that she did not *care* what they thought. "By then, I assume, you will be hungry again."

They both laughed. It seemed strange and wonderful to her that she could share a joke with this man.

She led him through the house to the front door and, under the eyes of Hannah, they said their good-byes, just as if no understanding existed between them. But Hannah was not deceived.

Deborah turned to her as soon as the door was closed.

"He is coming again for dinner," she said, not even trying to conceal her excitement. "We must have something special."

"I told you he liked you," Hannah said.

What could Deborah do except laugh?

"Well, it seems you were right."

Dinner went well, unconstrained by the presence of Hannah, who, like a good servant, seemed to hear and see nothing. Rather than reclining on couches, they sat at a table, which allowed them to face one another.

"On my way here, I called upon Simon," Noah announced casually, as if it were of no particular concern. "He says he expects Joshua's return within the next few months, so I suppose I shall see him. I hope to persuade him to return to Nazareth, at least for a visit. His father is ill."

"What is wrong with him?"

"His lungs—my grandfather thinks he won't last the winter. This turn of Joshua's is a great grief to him."

"Why? Joshua is a man of God."

"Joseph doesn't want him to be a man of God. He wants him to be a carpenter. He wants him to remarry and father little carpenters. He

thinks Joshua has lost his wits. What his son is doing makes no sense to him."

"Does it make sense to you?"

"I can see why it would make sense to Joshua, and that is much the same thing. But I am enough like his father that it causes me to worry. For one thing, the fate of John shows what the world does to 'men of God.'"

"Will Joshua go to see his father, do you think?"

Noah appeared to consider the question.

"Yes," he said finally, "and I may accompany him, for I think we are both safe enough in the villages."

"Will you stay here long?"

"Only a day or two—lest my presence become irksome to you."

It was spoken jestingly, but Deborah sensed that behind the jest was a real anxiety.

"If I were to consult only my own wishes, you would stay even longer." Her own boldness made her blush. "Oh, what must you think of me."

Noah reached out to cover her hand with his own.

"I think you are everything I could wish you to be," he said.

"I feel so awkward."

"It is an awkward situation." He lifted his hand away from hers at what struck her as precisely the right moment. "Neither of us is a child, and you have no family to make everything run smooth. We must fend for ourselves, and find our way to each other as best we can."

"Will you really leave so soon?"

"Yes. Caleb knows about Capernaum. I doubt if I am important enough to him to mount a search, but he might inquire here. No one knows of my presence except you, Simon, and the innkeeper, but it is dangerous."

"Where will you go?"

"To the gentile cities—probably Canatha and Hippos. Caleb's reach does not extend that far."

"When will you come back?"

"Soon." He touched the back of her hand with his middle finger. "It is not in my power to stay away."

14

Noah lingered in Capernaum through the next day, although hardly anyone there would have been aware of his presence. The walls of Deborah's garden concealed him, and only she and Hannah knew he was there and not off trading, as he had told his landlord.

"My head apprentice believes I am on my way to Ptolemais," he told her. "I seem to be developing a talent for duplicity."

"Do you really believe they might attempt to hunt you down?"

"It seems possible." Noah shrugged, implying that the mind of a man like Caleb was unknowable. "It strikes me as a reasonable precaution to sow as much confusion as I can."

He took Deborah's hand. It did not seem too dreadful a liberty.

"In any case, I would rather not have anyone know that I spent this day courting you."

It would be several months before the first buds began to appear, but the arbor, as if it retained the memory of every past season, was fragrant. The air was deliciously cool.

All the time they sat together on the bench, he held her hand. A few times, when he began to imagine that she might find it irksome to be thus imprisoned in his grasp, he would relinquish it, but after a minute or two she would slip her hand back inside his.

Intimacy can grow in the spaces between words, in the silences. It can be discovered in the things that are not said, in what is not revealed or even implied. Thus Noah came to understand that for a long time Deborah had not known happiness. From their first meeting, he had been struck by her stillness, her apparent tranquility, but that was not the same as happiness. She might never bring herself to tell him of her sorrows, but he felt their presence in her life.

When the sun was down but there was still enough light to see, he slipped his box from underneath the bench.

"I had best be getting back to my friend Ezra," he said. "I will have dinner at the inn and bore him with stories of my adventures. I'll leave for the north at first light tomorrow, and I think it best we not see each other again until I return."

And then he was gone.

As usual, when there were no guests, Deborah and Hannah ate their dinner together at a small table in the kitchen. For half the meal neither of them spoke. The same subject was in both their minds, but perhaps each hoped that the other would break the silence.

Finally Hannah, who was younger, could restrain herself no longer.

"I had thought you would have a guest for dinner," she said at last. "You haven't quarreled, have you?"

"Is that what you thought?" Deborah asked, as if the idea amused her. "No, we haven't quarreled. In fact, I think that today has been the happiest day of my life."

So it had progressed as far as that. Hannah was surprised but not amazed. That her mistress might wish to remarry had of course occurred to her, and that she might be prepared to settle for this man Noah from faraway Sepphoris had not seemed unlikely. After all, Hannah, who was all of sixteen, could understand the desperation that must inevitably seize upon a childless woman of twenty-four. But in her heart of hearts, she found her mistress's enthusiasm remarkable. Noah from Sepphoris was not her ideal. For one thing, he wasn't tall.

"So you like him, then?" she said, merely to keep the conversation from lapsing into silence. "Is he agreeable?"

"Yes. He is agreeable." Deborah actually laughed. "He is the most agreeable man in the world."

Hannah must have look unconvinced.

"What? You don't like him?" Deborah reached out and patted her hand, as if reassuring a child. "Tell me."

"I like him . . ."

"But . . ."

"Well, he is not as handsome as some. The Master, for instance."

"The Master?" Deborah could but shake her head. "We all love the Master. He is a great and good man, a prophet. But the Master loves only God. It is not in him, I think, to love a woman the way a wife wishes to be loved by her husband.

"Besides, I think Noah is handsome—handsome enough. I will never tire of his face. And he knows how to talk to a woman. He makes me feel that he *sees* me. Not just as flesh but as a person. When I am with him I feel human. Do you understand?"

"I understand that you are in love with him," Hannah answered, letting her eyes grow wide in mock astonishment. "Obviously I have missed something."

Then they both laughed.

The next day Deborah was in a trance of happiness. Noah was gone, on the road to places she had never been, and all she wanted was to be alone with her thoughts of him. In the morning, when, as was her custom, she went to the warehouse, she gave no orders, only smiled and was agreeable to everyone. She spent the rest of the day on the bench beneath her grape arbor, where she had sat with Noah, thinking over every word that he had said, remembering every gesture of his beautiful, expressive hands.

How could anyone think he was not handsome? He was the most perfect man in the world.

This dreamlike state was brutally interrupted just after noon of the next day, when Hannah returned from the market.

"Lady, there is a stranger in the village. He is asking questions about Noah."

"Do you really believe they might attempt to hunt you down?"

"It seems possible."

She had not so much forgotten as put aside what he had said of his danger. In memory, the bruises on his face had faded, only to be recalled with conscious effort.

She had been a little fool, besotted with blind happiness, and now his enemies had come for him.

Hannah, to whom the arrival of an unknown man asking about Noah was merely an item of news, was startled by her mistress's reaction.

After a moment Deborah remembered herself and smiled.

"Did you see him?" she asked, as if the matter were of no importance.

"No. I only heard about him. Simon's wife told me."

"Did *she* see him?"

"Yes. He came to her house. Lady, is something wrong?"

"No, I don't think so." By sheer force of will, Deborah assumed a calm she did not feel. "It is probably some friend of his from Sepphoris."

"He came by boat, Lady. From Tiberias."

"Did he?"

She had no right to involve Hannah in this. Hannah must know nothing. Deborah waited through the longest quarter hour of her life and then put on her shawl.

"I am going to the warehouse," she announced.

"He came by boat. From Tiberias."

The Tetrarch ruled in Tiberias. He had built the city on the Sea of Kinneret, purely for his own pleasure. Whoever this stranger might be, he was no friend.

At that hour the streets were nearly empty. The men were fishing and the women were in their homes—or at one of the village's three wells, where they could fill their jugs and gossip.

Deborah had grown up poor in Capernaum, so she knew everyone. When she married Bukkiah and became wealthy, she had not forgotten her birth, had made no attempt to transform herself into a great lady, and so she had remained, to most people, Deborah the clerk's daughter and still one of them.

As a result, she was not an unusual sight on the village squares and no one would feel any reluctance about sharing the news with her.

Of course, everyone knew about the stranger.

"Very much the aristocrat, though he tried to hide it," said Orpah the net maker's wife, who had been a friend of Deborah's mother. "He dressed like a farmer, but his clothes were so new I doubt he'd ever worn them before. And his *sandals* . . . Very grand, very grand indeed. Those sandals would have cost my Remiel two months' earnings."

Orpah had put on weight since her sixth child, so there was something truly imposing about her indignation over the sandals.

"What do you suppose he wants?" Deborah asked, with an almost childlike innocence of manner.

"Some other foreigner," Orpah answered, with contempt. "No one *I* ever heard of. They should stay away—all of them. They have no business here."

Since many people drew their water from the lake, there were only three wells in Capernaum, and village life revolved around the wells. If you wanted the news—who had died in the night or had a new baby or had come into a little money—you visited the wells. Thus, it was not very long before Deborah had learned everything the village knew about the stranger from Tiberias, even to where he was at that precise moment.

"He is in there," said Jahleel, an old man, good for no work, who lived with his grandson. He spent his days hanging about the western well, watching the women and drinking weak beer. He was pointing across the square to a door beneath a green awning, a few tables scattered about in front of it. The entrance to Ezra's tavern.

"He has been in there . . ." Jahleel glanced up at the sun and then down at the shadow cast by the well's stone rim, "oh, half an hour. Though what he finds to talk about with Ezra is beyond me. Ezra's conversation is as bland as his beer."

This observation was followed by a series of high-pitched squeaks, only just identifiable as laughter.

Deborah had but to linger, to mingle with the village women as they waited to fill their water jugs, until the door to Ezra's tavern opened and the stranger came outside.

Orpah had been right—the man was in disguise. His tunic was simple homespun, but it was too new. His beard was longer than the village average, and carefully cut. As he walked away, Deborah noted the glint of a ring on his left hand. Orpah had even been right about the sandals. He was a rich man from the city, trying to seem like someone else.

Deborah followed him, keeping in the shadows of buildings and out of sight. He went straight down to the water, climbed into a boat that was too sleek to have been built for fishing, and was rowed away. The boat was heading south, toward Tiberias.

And the last person this stranger from Herod's city had spoken to was Ezra.

Was that significant? Deborah wasn't sure. She decided it was time to go home.

"Hannah, did you mention to anyone that Noah was here? You wouldn't have been doing anything wrong, so I won't be angry. However, I need to know."

Hannah shook her head, suddenly on the verge of tears. "No, Mistress. I would never . . ."

Deborah embraced her, the way one would a frightened child.

"I didn't think you would, but I had to be sure. Do you understand?"

"Yes, Mistress—no."

There was no escaping it. An explanation had to be made.

"Noah has been protecting the Master, and now evil men want to hurt him. The stranger today was one of those."

"What do you want me to do?"

"I don't want you to do anything," Deborah told her, kissing her on the forehead. "If someone asks you a question about Noah, or the Master, tell them the truth. I don't think anyone will ask, but you know nothing that can hurt either of them. For the rest, put this thing from your mind."

"Yes, Mistress."

Deborah retired to her balcony. The afternoon was more than half over. In a few hours the fishermen would be returning and Capernaum would come back to life. At sundown the Sabbath would begin, during which nothing could be done.

Her mind kept returning to Ezra.

Why? If a stranger comes to a village, seeking information, where would he go if not to the tavern keepers? It was an obvious choice.

How long had the man been among them? Perhaps three hours. He had gone to Simon's house first and talked to his wife. Why? Because he knew that Simon was a follower of the Master and that Noah was the Master's cousin.

No, no. She was starting at the wrong end. The real question was, what had brought this man to Capernaum? Why did he appear just two days after Noah had left?

Answer: because someone had sent a message to Tiberias that Noah was here.

There could have been nothing easier. Boats went between Capernaum and Tiberias every day. By water, the trip was only a few hours.

So who had sent the message? Who knew that Noah was in Capernaum?

Herself and Hannah. Simon. Ezra. Anyone else, even if they saw him in the street, would probably not know his name.

Would Simon betray the Master's cousin and friend? No. Simon had his faults, but treachery was not among them.

That left Ezra. And his tavern had been the last place the stranger visited.

And what more convenient occupation for a spy than tavern keeper? Travelers are drawn to a tavern. All manner of people went in and out all day long. Ezra was particularly well placed to pass on information without drawing attention to himself. The conclusion was inescapable. Ezra was the Tetrarch's spy in Capernaum.

But what to do about it? When Noah came back, Ezra would send another message to Tiberias. She would have to warn Noah, and then he would have to leave and would be without a safe place in the world to hide his head.

Better, far better, to silence Ezra. The Tetrarch was hated in Capernaum—all she would have to do was to mention her suspicions to any one of perhaps fifty people, and Ezra would disappear forever.

Then Deborah would have his life on her conscience.

But perhaps she could leave the decision to Ezra. Yes, that would even be safer. Better by far to have the Tetrarch's spy in her power than to have him dead, in which case the men in Tiberias would only recruit another spy.

Deborah went downstairs and found Hannah.

"Go to Ezra's tavern," she told her. "Buy a dozen jugs of beer and tell him they are too heavy for you to carry. Tell him I will expect him to deliver them personally within the hour."

A quarter of an hour later, Hannah was back. "He will bring the beer as soon as he can get away, Mistress."

So there was nothing left to do except to wait.

When he came, Ezra brought the beer to the kitchen door in a hand-cart. It was put away in a small cellar, and then he was told that the mistress was in the garden.

When he presented himself to be paid, Deborah was standing beside her grape arbor. She took some coins out of her purse and scattered them at his feet.

"You must pick them out of the dirt, Ezra. I am sure you have stooped even lower to collect your money."

A tradesman becomes inured to the insults of the wealthy, so, hardly even allowing himself a reproachful glance, Ezra went down on his knees and began gathering up the coins. He had almost the last one before Deborah spoke again.

"Tell me, Ezra. How did the man from Tiberias know to come to Capernaum?"

"Lady, I know nothing about any—"

"Don't lie to me, please," she interrupted sweetly. Under other circumstances her smile would have warmed a heart colder than Ezra's, but he understood at once that he was in mortal danger. "I know that you passed a message. For the moment I only wish to know how."

"Lady, how can you—"

"I will tell you again, and for the last time, do not lie to me. You are aware of what will happen to you if it becomes known that you have been spying on us for your friends in the Tetrarch's palace. You will disappear into the sea, your corpse wrapped in a fishing net, weighted with stones. Now, if you wish to live, answer my question."

One could see the struggle in Ezra's face. How could she possibly know? She knew. It didn't matter how. Which was more dangerous, to deny everything or to tell the truth? She was only a woman. Could he somehow bluff or frighten her? No. But would anyone believe her? Yes.

Watching his indecision, Deborah saw that she had guessed right. She felt a cold fury rising within her. This man had wanted to sell Noah to his enemies. For money. He had bartered with Noah's life as if the man she loved were no more than a basket of fish.

Yes. She had it within her to kill Ezra. If he did not confess, this would be his last Sabbath.

And perhaps Ezra saw this in her face.

"There is a boatman," he said at last. "His name is Ruben. He makes the journey from Tiberias every day and always takes a meal at my place. Sometimes he brings me orders—I don't know from whom—and I tell him whatever I see. In Tiberias they had wanted to know about the preacher. And now they want to know about this fellow Noah."

He was still on his knees, and now he really looked like a beggar. The fear in his eyes made them shine like wet stones.

"Lady, I am only Ezra, the fisherman turned tavern keeper. These people could crush us all with a word. What was I to do?"

"I can't answer that question, but I can tell you what you will do now."

Deborah leaned forward and put her hand on Ezra's shoulder. It was a gesture not of love or forgiveness or even pity, but of authority. She was like a queen accepting the submission of a subject.

"You will make no more reports about Noah. You will never again whisper his name in this boatman's ear. He can come and go, and you will be blind to it. More than that, you will tell me everything these men in Tiberias tell you. Everything. Do you understand me?"

"But, Lady, what if they learn that I have betrayed them? They will surely put me to death."

"They may never learn, Ezra, but that is in the future. If you do not do as I bid, you will have no reason to fear them because you will already be dead.

"Now—will you obey me?"

"Yes, Lady."

"Then we understand each other. If any harm comes to Noah, the very next day the fishes will be feeding on your eyes."

She dismissed him without a word, with the merest wave of her hand. And when he was gone she went over to the bench beneath the grape arbor and sat down. Suddenly she bent over, put her face in her hands, and wept. It was like a spasm of pain and disappeared almost as quickly as it had come. The grief she felt after was dry eyed and sullen. It was for the loss of something within herself, and she knew not what.

25

The village of Gischala in northern Galilee was famous for its olives. Matthias knew it well, since his native village of Meroth was only a few miles to the south. His mother had been born in Gischala, so he had family there.

He used to think that everything good in him had come from Gischala, for he had loved his mother. He was not a man to cultivate sentiment, but even now, ten years after her death, tears came to his eyes whenever he thought of her.

Hers was the fate of the gentle and the meek. She had been given in marriage to a distant cousin, a man named Abiud, ten years her senior who had already worn out a wife. Matthias could still remember the way, when his father had had too much beer, he would lament the death of his first wife, praising her beauty and virtue. In fact, he had led her a wretched life, so that, if family lore was to be believed, she had been glad to die.

As he grew older, the brutality of his father's nature had intensified, possibly because it met no resistance. Abiud's children—Matthias had two elder half brothers and a sister—were terrified of him, as was his wife.

Matthias could not remember a time when his mother's face had not carried bruises. Twice Abiud beat her into unconsciousness.

Then, quite unexpectedly one Sabbath, she died. No one was surprised except Matthias, who was fourteen at the time.

She couldn't get out of bed that morning. His father became angry and began shouting threats and, finally, she got up. She went into the kitchen and sat down. A few minutes later blood began to pour out of her mouth. She collapsed to the floor and died.

Matthias knew, of course, that his father had killed her. He had beaten her once too often, or too savagely, and had given her a mortal injury.

He knew, but there was little a boy of fourteen could do. He could not match his father, so he waited.

After that Matthias never thought of him as "my father," only as "Abiud." He was a stranger and an enemy.

He waited for two years. Then one day he caught Abiud alone, sowing wheat in a field about a mile from the village. Matthias had provided himself with the wooden handle of a scythe, and he took his time beating this man to death. He broke a knee and both arms, then he went to work on the face. Finally he broke Abiud's neck, so that the head collapsed to one side. He never forgot the way his father first laughed and then, after the first blow struck, howled like a cur—and then, toward the end, how he begged for his life.

When Abiud was dead, his son ran away. It was a terrible sin to murder one's father, and the villagers would have stoned him to death. He did not stop running until he reached Sepphoris, where he joined the Tetrarch's army.

The army taught him that brutality was the price of order. The Tetrarch's rule depended on his soldiers. If there was a riot and the soldiers came out of their barracks and killed two hundred people, the next day people stayed in their houses and there was peace. Soldiers were men set apart. Necessary, but hated by everyone. The only loyalty was to your comrades and to the Tetrarch, and to the Tetrarch only so long as the soldiers were paid.

These were the conditions of life, Matthias decided. Where else could he go? What other kennel would hold him?

The first year was the worst. Recruits were drilled until they lost the power to think. One became a soldier by acquiring a soldier's reflexes. Thinking had no part in it. A soldier was better off without memories or feelings or thoughts. This was the hardest lesson to learn, and Matthias never really mastered it. What he learned instead was that you cannot escape the things you have done. They haunt your dreams.

Even wine, which he had hardly tasted before he joined the army, could not banish his dreams forever. You could drink until it was almost as if you were dead, until even your dreams were stilled, but you would always wake again. And it was not possible to be drunk every night.

A Greek once told him that some professions do not allow a man to be virtuous. He said some wise man among his people had written this long ago. It was true.

A potter makes jars, a farmer harvests wheat, a soldier kills. That is his work. He is given a sword when he finishes his training, and the sword defines him.

Some men could not bear the burden. They ran away. They tried to go back to their villages, or to melt into the city crowds, but armies everywhere made a point of hunting down deserters, so they were al-most always caught. And deserters were crucified.

But sometimes they were granted a quicker death.

About a month after Matthias won his sword, a batch of six deserters was scheduled for death. Each one, with his hands bound behind his back, had a noose put round his neck, and the other end of the rope was tied to the back of a wagon. When the wagon started its journey to the execution grounds they had to trot to keep up. One prisoner fell down—perhaps deliberately, hoping that the rope would strangle him as he was dragged along—but they merely stopped the wagon, flogged him to his feet, and set off again. It was a good three miles to the abandoned stone quarry called "the place of crosses."

The guard had to quick march to keep up with the wagon, but at least their hands were free. The guard consisted of twenty men. A few were still green. Matthias was one of these.

When they reached the execution ground—a barren place—the squad commander chose four of the prisoners, apparently at random, cut the leather straps that bound their hands, and told them to go sit down. The remaining two were stripped of their tunics.

"Now these boys, who wanted to run home to their mothers, will be allowed to provide a few of our new men with a chance to wet their swords," the squad commander announced. "And don't feel sorry for them, because you'll be doing them a favor. They get to die quick, in-stead of after four or five days on the cross."

He grabbed one of the condemned men by the arm and pushed him forward.

"You there," he shouted, pointing with his free hand at the man standing beside Matthias, "Ebed, isn't it? Just step up here and kill him. You know how it's done."

Ebed was only fifteen, and he looked more frightened than his victim as he drew his sword.

"Go on now. Finish him." The squad commander pointed to a spot just under the prisoner's breastbone. "Right there."

After a tentative stab, which did little more than break the skin, Ebed seemed to lose heart entirely.

"Come on, don't be such a coward! Kill him, or I'll have *you* up on a cross before you're an hour older. Kill him!"

After a second attempt the prisoner was on his knees and bleeding heavily, but still alive. Finally the squad commander jerked him back up on his feet. Then he took Ebed's hand in his and guided his sword point to the first wound.

"Now push! That's all you have to do, just push."

It seemed to take forever, with the prisoner screaming in pain and fear, but at last he went down on one knee and then simply toppled over. He lay there, panting for breath, and then he was still.

"Ebed, I'll make sure you get twenty strokes for this. What a dog's dinner! Matthias, see if you can do better."

Matthias had already decided that he wouldn't hesitate. To hesitate is to let fear seize you, so he didn't even wait for the next prisoner to be brought forward. He covered the distance in a few long strides, drawing his sword as he went. The prisoner simply watched him, as if he hardly knew what was happening.

In the last instant the prisoner snapped awake and tried to pull himself back, but Matthias's downward slash caught him in the throat. There was a great spray of blood. The man stared at Matthias in what seemed like disbelief, and then collapsed.

The squad commander had been standing a foot or so too close. He wiped some of the blood from his face and then looked at it on his hand. Then he nodded.

"A little messy," he said calmly, "but I'm not complaining. At least someone here knows how to kill."

They spent what was left of the morning watching the progress of the executions. As part of his punishment, Ebed was forced to help with the nailing. When all four men were up on their crosses, a guard was left to keep watch, and the rest of the soldiers were marched back to barracks. Ebed wept the whole way.

A week later, in the middle of the night, Ebed went into the toilet and slashed his wrists.

Brutality was the price of order. And of life. Those were the alternatives—kill or die.

And now Matthias found himself back at Gischala.

"Why couldn't the cursed man live in some other place?" he asked under his breath. He was thinking not of his mother but of topography.

Gischala was on a hill. There were only four trails to the summit, but from any direction it was not a steep climb, so the trails were more a convenience than a necessity. This meant that a man in fear of his life could flee in any direction.

So they would have to enter the village at night. They would have to surprise Reuel bar Omri in his bed—him and his two brothers—and either kill them or take them away before the villagers had time to organize any resistance.

Matthias sat on a rock at the edge of a grove of trees, contemplating the problem. The village was no more than two miles distant. He had ten men with him, and twelve horses, but the horses would never manage the trails up to Gischala at night. He would have to leave the horses, and two men to guard them. The rest of the men would enter the village from the south and east, since those trails offered the easiest ascent, and they would converge on the southern edge of the village. The climb would probably take about half an hour. They would carry oil lamps to light their ascent, an unavoidable risk. With any luck they would be on their way back down before more than a dozen people even knew they had been there.

It was late afternoon, so they would have a few more hours to rest before it was dark.

There were perhaps four hundred people in the village. Matthias knew many of their names and where they lived. He did not know Reuel bar Omri, but when he was a boy, visiting his cousins, there had been a man named Omri living four houses away from his uncle Jethro. It was a place to start.

He spoke to his men, drawing a map of the village in the dirt. All were dressed in peasant clothing, so if they were caught or killed people would assume they were merely bandits. They watched him with hungry, attentive faces. They were looking forward to the raid.

Keeping them focused on the task was always the most difficult part. They cared nothing about Reuel bar Omri and, indeed, for that he did not need them. They thought only of plunder and rape, and wetting their swords with blood. They were with him in case the alarm was raised and they had to fight their way out.

They were the accursed of God.

So also was he. He led these men and he was one of them. Matthias bar Abiud, son of a brute and a brute himself—murderer, kidnapper, torturer, drunk. The foul servant of a foul master. Matthias bar Abiud, who had killed his own father in the coldest of blood, had no illusions about himself.

He knew he would kill in Gischala tonight, and if he brought Reuel out alive it would only be to deliver him up to torture and death. He would do these things because it was the Lord Caleb's will, and the Lord Caleb was a devil.

Matthias, he now recognized, had begun his journey into darkness the moment he took that scythe handle out of the toolshed, and it had brought him here, to his mother's village, where he was about to do things that would have made her heart wither.

And there was no escape. God had cursed him for his sins.

It was always worst in the hours of waiting, before the thing was done, while it loomed in his imagination like a ghost. Matthias knew he would be all right again once they started up the trail. Doing evil was always easier than imagining it—or remembering it.

Reuel bar Omri was the last. Matthias and his men had raided five other villages within Galilee and had taken away eight prisoners. He had saved Gischala to the end because it was his mother's village and would for that reason be the worst.

And when it was over he would deliver Reuel to the Tetrarch's dungeon and then go out and find himself a whore and jar of wine and forget all this. He would drink until he could sleep with no dreams, until even waking would seem a dream. He would stay that way until the Lord Caleb had more work for him to do.

His consolations in life were whores and wine and the hope that death was extinction.

Matthias sat watching the sun set. There was a line of hills to the west, so the darkness came earlier in the valley. That darkness would cover their movements as they approached the trails up to Gischala, but they would need their lamps on the trails, and the light from them would alert anyone in the village who happened to look down.

So, before they made their ascent they would have to wait until everyone went to sleep.

When did that happen? First dinner, then prayers, then sleep. How long had it been, Matthias found himself wondering, since he had prayed? How long before that had God stopped listening?

There was nothing to do but wait, and no company except his own dark thoughts.

After a while, as the night began to take hold, he noticed a faint glow that seemed to cover the top of the hill like a fog. It was the light from the hearth fires, escaping through open windows and lighting the sky.

They would wait until the light had been gone for an hour. By the time they reached the village, everyone would be asleep.

For village people, sleep was a pleasure. They did not fear sleep the way Matthias did. They did not fear their dreams. You went to bed with a full belly, you went into your wife, if you had one, and you slept. A few hours before dawn the women woke up to start the fires, but until then no one stirred.

The glow from the hilltop did not so much flicker out as slowly collapse. People were shutting their windows against the night's cold. They were going to bed.

One more hour. The men watched their leader as they checked their weapons and filled their lamps with oil. They were impatient to begin. Matthias ignored them.

Finally it was time. Matthias stood up, drew his knife, and tested the point with his thumb. The blade was half a cubit long and carried an edge on both sides. For close work it was better than a sword.

"Let's go," he said quietly. "You know what to do."

The trails seemed steeper than Matthias remembered. He kept thinking that some old man might get out of bed to piss and see them. He kept waiting for that shout of alarm.

But it never came. They reached the summit and regrouped. The village was theirs.

Three men would stay and guard the escape route. Five would come with Matthias to Omri's house. He might need them.

They walked soundlessly through the village.

Suddenly, as they rounded a corner, a man came out of his doorway. He turned and faced Matthias, and then stopped. He was surprised but not afraid.

Matthias, who was almost close enough to touch him, did not hesitate. The knife was in his hand, carried low. He took a step forward and brought the knife up so that the point entered the man's left side, just below his rib cage. All that registered in the man's face was disbelief. He seemed to try to say something, but no sound escaped him, only a short, panting gasp. Matthias gave the knife a sharp twist and pulled it out. The man fell dead at his feet.

Matthias listened for a moment. If he had to he would enter the house and kill everyone he found, but nothing stirred within.

He stepped around the corpse and went on his way. It was several seconds before he realized that, in his youth, that house had belonged to his mother's brother.

Whom had he just killed? He struggled to put it out of his mind. He had no time now.

The house in which Omri had lived when Matthias was a boy was like all the others in the village, like all the peasant houses in Galilee— mud brick and just large enough to encompass two rooms, a kitchen and a sleeping room for the owner and his wife, and often their children. The door was made of wooden slats and probably had a crossbar on the inside, but in a village like this, who took the trouble to secure his door at night?

Matthias signaled to his men to wait outside, and then he pushed against the door with his hand. It moved soundlessly on its leather hinges.

Inside, embers were still glowing in the fire pit. Someone was sleeping on the floor, covered with a rough wool blanket. It was impossible to tell if this was a man or a woman.

Matthias knelt down beside the shape under the blanket. There was just light enough from the fire to see that it was a young man with a short black beard. He was lying on his side, deep asleep.

So be it. Matthias covered the man's mouth with his hand and pressed the point of his knife against his throat, just under the chin. The man's eyes popped open.

"If you struggle, I will kill you this instant." Matthias whispered. "Do you understand?"

The man nodded, as vigorously as the knife point at his throat allowed.

"I am going to ask you some questions. You will answer them. If you cry out, you die. Do you understand?"

The man nodded.

"I will take my hand away now."

He lifted his hand a little from the man's mouth. He made no outcry.

"Where is Reuel bar Omri?"

"In there."

With his eyes the man indicated the door to the sleeping room. Matthias blessed his luck. Old Omri must have died and Reuel, as the eldest son, had inherited.

"Who are you?"

"His brother—Nereus."

"There is another brother. Where is he?"

"Dead."

This presented a problem. The Lord Caleb had spoken of three brothers. Reuel was the prize, but he had wanted all three. Now one was dead. Could he bring this one? How? Reuel was in the next room, and there was too much risk of waking someone. No. Nereus would have to stay.

"How? How did he die?"

"The fever. Two months ago."

"Lucky for him."

With a quick thrust, the knife point went into Nereus's throat, through his tongue, and into his brain. His eyes widened, but he gave no other sign that he knew he was dead.

Matthias wiped the knife blade on the woolen blanket and went into the sleeping room.

There was a bed under the window, sideways against the wall. A man and a women slept in it, the man next to the wall. In another, smaller bed slept a child, a little girl, perhaps two years old.

The woman must have been a light sleeper, because she turned her head. She started to get out of bed—probably she thought to check on the child. She was naked and, as far as one could judge in the darkness, quite beautiful.

It had to be done. Matthias strode across the room. He was almost on her before she realized he was there. He took her by the throat and drove the knife up under her ribs. She lived just long enough to reach up and close her hand over his arm.

The knife through her heart was all that held her up. Matthias pulled it loose and she slipped quietly to the floor.

Reuel did not wake until he felt Matthias' hand over his mouth.

"I have already killed your brother and your wife. If you make a sound I will have to kill your daughter as well."

He waited, his hand tight on Reuel's mouth. The reality of the thing had to find its way into the man's mind.

"Do you understand me? If you cry out, you will die and the child will die."

Reuel nodded.

"Then get up."

The woman's tunic was hanging from a hook on the wall, along with her belt. Matthias took her belt and used it to bind Reuel's hands behind his back. All the while, Reuel stared at the body of his dead wife.

Matthias couldn't trust the man not to panic. He grabbed the woman's tunic and tore off a long strip to make a gag.

"Now, let's go."

Outside, a man took the prisoner by each arm and forced him along almost at a trot. They rejoined their comrades at the beginning of the south trail.

"When you are ready to come down," Matthias told them, "find something to use for a torch."

"We will use the village for a torch," one of them answered. The others laughed. At this point they did not care how much noise they made.

Matthias looked around at their eager faces. This was a moment they had all been waiting for. He nodded. He understood perfectly.

"You know where the horses are tethered." He raised his arm and pointed into the darkness. "I will wait there an hour—or until I see the villagers swarming down the trails. Then I and any who are with me will leave. I will take the horses, so if you get there alive you will still be on foot. You all know what kind of death you can expect if you fall into these people's hands."

He made a gesture of dismissal.

"Go then. Amuse yourselves."

Matthias started down the trail, holding the oil lamp in one hand, the other hand clamped on the back of Reuel's neck. He knew he was leaving behind him an orgy of rape and murder, but it was necessary. His men would keep the villagers distracted enough that no one would think of coming after him. He was the servant of evil, but to serve well was the only shred of integrity left to him.

By the time they reached the foot of the hill, Matthias could already see the fire above. It was a short walk to the horses.

When they reached the grove, Matthias cut away Reuel's gag and unbound his hands.

"You killed my wife," Reuel said. "You are a murderer."

"Yes."

The admission seemed to stun Reuel into silence. Then he shook his head, as if trying to wake himself from a bad dream.

"Who are you? Why have you done this?"

"You do not need to know who I am. Reasons can wait."

"Where are you taking me?"

"Somewhere you do not wish to go."

They waited, both of them watching the fires as Gischala burned.

Slowly the men began to filter back. At the end of the hour, Matthias counted only nine.

"Where is Abraham?"

"Dead. He was careless. He got what he deserved."

He got what we all deserve, Matthias thought. And then, out loud, said, "Let's go."

16

Of late Caleb had had many interviews with Judah, of varying duration but always tending to become longer. As the prisoner abandoned himself to confession, and thus rendered himself increasingly defenseless, he was rewarded by being allowed to confess even more. He became dependent upon this man who controlled his fate. His nameless persecutor became his protector, as the hope of forgiveness became his only hope.

"Why am I here?"

"You are here because you have offended God."

"My whole existence has been an offense against God."

"It is more specific than that. You followed the Baptist, who was an enemy of the Tetrarch and therefore an enemy of God. Guard!"

Sometimes Judah was taken away to be beaten and starved. Sometimes he was rewarded. It seemed to follow no logic and was intended so to seem. One did not earn forgiveness through merit. There was no merit. Forgiveness was both arbitrary and tentative.

And gradually, as it became necessary, Caleb began to reveal himself.

"Who are you?"

"I am a servant of the Tetrarch, which is to say a servant of God. My name is Caleb."

"I had a cousin named Caleb. Like me, he went into exile—in Galilee."

"Did he. I wonder what became of him."

"No one seems to know."

"Perhaps that is best. Guard!"

After this conversation there were no more punishments. Judah was taken to a cell in the upper prison. The cell contained a real bed. He was given better food and was allowed exercise, for one hour every day, in a small walled courtyard. For that hour he felt almost free.

The interrogations, of course, continued. Judah seemed to regard them as almost a pleasure—certainly a release. It must have seemed to him that his interrogator was the one person in his life who actually understood him. It followed, therefore, since every man believes that it is impossible for him to be understood without being loved, that he had come to regard his interrogator as his only true friend.

Therefore his punishment, whatever it would come to be, was God's justice.

"Come. Get up. We are leaving here for a while."

Caleb stood at the cell door. He seemed impatient.

"Leaving?"

"Yes, for a while. We will be back by nightfall. Get up."

The stairway was familiar because at the top, immediately on the right, was the doorway to what Judah had come to think of as *his* courtyard. But today they followed a corridor that branched to the left. It was a long, airless space that seemed to go on endlessly. Judah had not even suspected its existence.

Then there was a door, which opened into a broad cobbled courtyard. The walls cast long shadows, and from the feel of the air on his face Judah guessed it was early morning. There was a cart, like a farm cart, hitched to a pair of horses. Caleb climbed up and took the reins.

"Come." He made a beckoning gesture with his hand. "Don't be afraid."

But Judah was afraid. He had no clear idea how long he had been in prison, and now he was afraid to leave it. He was filled with dread as he climbed into the cart and took his place beside Caleb, who handed him a jug that turned out to contain wine mixed with water, one part out of eleven, the sort of thing they gave to babies.

"Drink," he said. "I know you haven't had your breakfast, but today's work is best done on an empty stomach. It isn't far."

A pair of gates opened and they drove down a wide road that seemed to pass through a city of some size. Judah glanced back and noticed two guards behind them, on horseback.

"What place is this?"

"Sepphoris." Caleb looked around him, as if seeing it himself for the first time. "Not a bad place. It is not Jerusalem, or even Tiberias, but it isn't bad."

"Where are we going?"

"To bear witness to God's triumph."

There was something almost threatening in the way he said it, so that Judah was not tempted to inquire further.

They passed under what must have been the eastern gates, since the rising sun was directly in their faces, and took a road that followed the city walls for a time and then descended into a valley before rising again to go up a barren, rocky hill.

"It's just ahead," Caleb said finally. "Twenty years ago it was a stone quarry. Now we find other uses for it."

Judah glanced over his shoulder and saw that the two mounted guards were still following them. Were they there to prevent him from escaping? Oddly, he had felt no temptation to try.

As soon as they arrived at the quarry, Judah realized that he had been brought to a place of execution. He experienced a convulsion of fear that was like having the breath sucked from his lungs.

Around about were wooden beams, one end buried in the ground so that they looked like the dead stalks of trees, shorn of all life. There was a small crowd assembled. The focus of their attention was a man nailed to a cross.

"Do not be afraid," Caleb said quietly. "You have not had such trouble lavished on you merely as a preparation for death. Someone will die today, but it will not be you."

The condemned man was in his middle twenties, gaunt and hard like a peasant. He seemed already half dead, as if the world beyond his own suffering no longer existed for him.

"Do you recognize him?"

"No."

"Truly not?" Caleb seemed genuinely surprised. "He is here because of you. You gave me his name."

"I . . . ?"

"Yes. His name is Reuel. Do you remember him now?"

"No. I . . ."

The truth was he couldn't recall. He studied the man's face and half convinced himself he might have seen it somewhere before.

He had given Caleb many names in connection with the Baptist—so many that he could not be sure if they had belonged to real people or he had simply imagined them. Could one of those names have been Reuel?

"Who is he?"

"He was one of John's disciples." Caleb smiled, apparently amused at the idea. "We captured him three weeks ago. He has been interrogated and has, in his turn, given us yet more names. Yours was not among them, however.

"He had two brothers, by the way. Also followers of John. They, however, did not survive."

"There was someone among the disciples whose brothers accompanied him. Perhaps he is this one," Judah muttered

"Presently you will remember."

One of the soldiers, clearly the officer in charge, glanced expectantly in their direction, but Caleb responded with an almost imperceptible shake of his head.

The officer immediately looked away.

The exchange made Judah uncomfortably aware of the crowd.

"Why are all these people here?" he asked. "Are they friends of his?"

"No. I doubt if there is one among them who even knows his name."

"Then why . . . ?"

"Because one does not go to the trouble of crucifying a man except as an example to others. Thus there must be witnesses. We simply rounded these people up and marched them out here, although doubtless they will find the spectacle entertaining enough. They will tell their friends, and in a day or two people will be coming of their own volition to look at Reuel's corpse as the flesh rots off the bones. The point is to make an impression."

Judah listened, hardly understanding the words. He wanted to turn his eyes away but could not. The sight held him.

"How long has he been like this?"

"Since yesterday morning."

Caleb smiled pleasantly.

"How long will he live?" Judah asked. He could hardly speak. His heart was pounding wildly and, try as he might, he could not take his eyes from the man writhing in agony on the cross.

"If he is strong, he might last three or four more days. I have heard that some suffer as long as a week. But that will not be Reuel's fate. Very soon, when I give the order, they will break his legs. Then he won't be able to push himself up to fill his lungs, and death will follow quickly. So, you see, there is mercy even for such as he."

Caleb produced a small box from beneath the wagon's seat. Inside were grapes, bread, and two stone cups. He popped a grape into his mouth and offered the cluster to Judah.

"Eat something. We will be here for a time."

Judah waved the food away, which made Caleb laugh.

"The first time I saw a man nailed up, it was the same with me," he said, pouring himself a cup of the watered wine. "I did not break my fast until the next day. But one grows used to it. Punishment is necessary in this wicked world and, like all necessary things, it is to the greater glory of God."

They waited. The crowd waited, to the sound of thirty or forty simultaneous conversations. Some of them drifted away. Here and there one even heard the odd burst of laughter.

The soldiers, who had done their work and would have nothing more to do so long as Reuel was required to suffer, played at dice or slept with an arm thrown across their eyes. None of them paid any attention to the man on the cross, who sometimes, when he tried to take a breath, made a faint squeaking sound, like a rusty hinge.

The sun grew hot as midday approached. Reuel, whose face was drenched in sweat, so that even his blood was washed away, kept moving his mouth soundlessly.

"What is he saying?"

"I expect he's asking for water," Caleb answered.

"Won't they give him any?"

"No." Caleb glanced up at the sun and then flinched away. "I wish I had thought to bring a sunshade," he said.

By the middle of the afternoon the crowd was almost gone. At last Caleb raised his hand and beckoned to the officer in charge, who came running.

"Do it," he told him. "Finish this."

The officer trotted back to his men and said something to one of them, who pulled a mallet with an iron head out of a sack upon which he had been resting his feet.

The thing was done almost before one realized what was happening. The soldier broke Reuel's shinbones just below the knee, three blows to each leg. The pain registered in Reuel's face, but he made no sound.

"He'll be dead soon," Caleb said quietly, as if offering consolation. "Have you seen enough?"

"More than enough."

"Good. Then let's be on our way."

Judah never spoke the whole way back to Sepphoris. He seemed dazed, or as if he were somewhere else. Perhaps he was. Perhaps, in his imagination, he had never left the execution ground, where he watched Reuel die one breath at a time.

That night he did not even try to sleep. All night, in the perfect darkness of his cell, he sat on the edge of his bed and tried to remember.

Did he remember Reuel? Perhaps he remembered that John had had a disciple whose two brothers accompanied him. He wasn't sure. Perhaps he remembered that the disciple's name had been Reuel. Perhaps. Probably. He wasn't sure.

If he remembered, then certainly he had betrayed Reuel. Under interrogation he had named every name that came into his head. It had had nothing to do with his will. The words came out of their own volition.

And yet the guilt was his. Before his very eyes, Reuel had suffered and died on the cross. Caleb said that he had betrayed the man. How could it not be so?

Sometime in the early hours after midnight, when time seemed to have stopped altogether, Judah's doubts withered, to be replaced with a sense of shame that was identical with certainty. He had handed a man over to death.

Yet Caleb had said, not once but many times, that all of this was in the service of God. Judah had heard the words without understanding them. Only now were they revealed as the truth.

The service of God. Perhaps that idea alone was enough to render life supportable. There was nothing else.

Judah put his hand up to his face and discovered that he had been weeping.

The service of God. He would never know, of course, that Caleb had lied to him.

17

Judah bar Isaac had hardly known what to think or feel when told that he was about to be released.

"You will be given clean clothes and money," Caleb announced. "You will be allowed to bathe and to trim your beard. You will be allowed to purify yourself, for you will be acting as a useful servant of God. You will be under my protection on every step of your journey."

Which of course meant that he would be watched. It was an understandable precaution, but unnecessary. Judah had not the slightest intention of betraying his cousin—for that was what he now knew him to be. If he did that, where could he hide, where could he go for safety? Caleb had already demonstrated that he had a long reach.

Besides, Judah did not want to. He had discovered himself in prison. He had had revealed to him his own utter unworthiness. And now God was putting his feet on the path to self-respect.

But even this was temporarily obscured by those first few giddy moments of freedom.

His cell had a window, which allowed him to know when the dawn broke. At first light he was given breakfast. Then, when he was washed and combed and dressed, Caleb came.

"You will leave by the main entrance, as befits an honest man. Then you will take the road north, until you reach a town called Capernaum. You will be looking for one Joshua bar Joseph, a preacher, a self-styled holy man who profanes the name of God among the poor and ignorant. If he is not in Capernaum, you will find him. You will attach yourself to this man—he is known to have followers, so it should not be difficult—and you will store in your memory everything he says and does. For the time being, you need concern yourself with nothing beyond."

Judah would remember forever his walk down the palace steps, his first moments in the swirling crowds, the intoxication he felt at the chaotic mingling of a hundred human voices. After a quarter of an hour he had to go into a wineshop to steady himself. He recalled holding the coins in his hand, the pattern they made across his palm, the deep pleasure of counting them out in payment for a cup of something that was worse even than the wine in prison but seemed to flow through him like quicksilver.

Then he glanced about and found himself wondering which of those whose faces were half turned away would soon be reporting to Caleb that he had entered this shop, that he had drunk a cup of wine, that he had left hurriedly.

For he must be about his business. The leash was short.

He found he had to stop for rest many times that first day. Prison had taken away his strength. His legs ached and his breath came quickly. He was like a man recovering from an illness.

There were few travelers on the road. Judah walked on alone, letting his eyes run along the line of the horizon, and the vast emptiness filled him with fear. At times he found himself longing for the walls of his cell.

He stopped the first night at a nameless village and bought lodging and food for a single silver coin. His host shared a jar of beer with him. He was a man of about fifty, with heavy streaks of gray in his beard and a hard, peasant face.

"Come from the city?" he inquired, with a diffidence suggesting he was merely making conversation and had no desire to pry.

"Yes, this morning."

"I hear it's a big place."

"Have you never been there?"

"No." The man shook his head. There was an absence of curiosity in the gesture that implied he could imagine no reason for going. Its wonders meant nothing to him.

"The countryside is better," Judah said, without conviction.

His host nodded in agreement. The matter was settled—or, more ac-curately, had never really been in dispute.

"I came from Jerusalem," Judah said.

"Ah, Jerusalem!" The man smiled, his face seeming to crack under the strain. "I was there once, for the Passover. Took the whole family. A week getting there, ten days in Jerusalem, a week coming back. What a time we had! I bought a lamb there and had it sacrificed in the Temple. What a place! I never guessed it was possible for men to make anything that big."

"It was the work of many thousands. Herod had only just finished it when he died."

"Who is Herod? A friend of yours?"

Judah arrived in Capernaum late the next day. He found an accommo-dating wineshop, where he ate dinner and was promised a bed for the night. The landlord was even able to give him information about the preacher Joshua bar Joseph.

"Oh him, yes." He was a broad, tough-looking man, beginning to run to fat, as if from soft living. "He made a nuisance of himself around here for some time, but he's gone now. Good riddance!"

"Any idea where?" Judah offered a confiding smile. "I have business with him."

"Well, if he owes you money, you'll never see it again. He's a ragged beggar. The women like him, though. My own wife . . ."

"Do you know which road he took when he left?"

A silver coin somehow found its way onto the table, and the landlord picked it up with his broad, clumsy fingers.

"North."

"Thank you, Ezra."

Judah spent the next day seeking more specific information and grad-ually began to form an impression of his quarry. Joshua bar Joseph did, in fact, have followers in Capernaum, and they were not simply a gaggle of hysterical women. They all believed him to be the instrument of God, and many were convinced he was the successor to John the Bap-tist. Even among those who did not subscribe to his teachings, no one spoke of him in terms that would suggest he was some half-crazed boor who believed that God spoke to him through his stomach. He was not mad, he was not ignorant, he was reported as being very far from stupid. Judah looked forward to meeting him.

But that was not to be in Capernaum.

The following morning Judah started north. At every town and little village, he inquired if there was any news of a prophet named Joshua who taught that the world was to be redeemed from sin. Sometimes people told him that "the Master" had stayed among them for a few days or a week and then moved on. Sometimes his questions were answered with incomprehension and mute suspicion.

Gradually he came to understand the pattern of Joshua's wanderings, which kept him away from the cities and was proceeding in a great arc that had already crossed over the tributaries of the Jordan River and would sweep back to Capernaum. It was a journey through places unknown to all except those who lived there. It was an embracing of obscurity, as if obscurity itself had become the only real virtue.

Judah was three weeks on the road before he found Joshua, just outside the village of Bethsaida, sitting under a tree with three other men, who appeared to be his followers, repairing the strap of one of his sandals. He seemed wholly absorbed in the task.

Joshua was a tall man, with long legs and arms, and his bearing, even as he concentrated on trimming a strip of leather, was impressive. There was that about him which commanded one's attention. Judah had no difficulty imagining him addressing a multitude of eager listeners.

But he was also, and obviously, a peasant. That was the great surprise. This fomenter of rebellion, this dangerous revolutionary, really was a village carpenter. To be suddenly confronted with this inescapable fact was in itself a kind of revelation.

"I have been a long time searching for you, Master."

Joshua raised his eyes from his work and spent a moment studying the face of the man who stood before him. Then he smiled.

"I remember you," he said. "You came to hear the Baptist, with a group of your city friends. It was like a street festival to them, to hear the madman from the desert preach."

Judah felt the reproach and apparently looked it, because Joshua continued, "I remember you because you were the one who did not mock."

"I was baptized."

"Yes, I remember."

"And yet I slid back into my old life. I repented of my sins and then sinned again."

The men who were with Joshua exchanged glances suggestive of a certain mistrust.

"Then you had not truly repented," Joshua answered. "Repentance is not the impulse of a moment but a rebirth that changes everything. However, I will not reproach you, for it is an old story. The pull of worldly things is strong."

He stood up and, when Judah approached him, threw an arm over his shoulder to embrace him.

"Well, if you have been searching for me, you have found me. Now, what do you want of me?"

Judah told him a story. It was not so much a lie as a recasting of the way he actually felt. The details were an invention, but the mood reflected his experiences over the last few months.

"The merchant who invested for me had losses and used my capital to cover them. Then he lost that and ran away. I found myself with little more than the money in my purse and the clothes I stood up in. My family could not help me. I was alone. I took this as a sign from God, a punishment for the empty life I had been leading."

"It was not a punishment. It was a mercy. You have, by your own account, led a wicked life, and now you have been separated from the root cause of that wickedness: wealth, which, one way or another, was stolen from the poor."

"You make me sound like a bandit."

"A bandit robs because he must. If he steals from the rich he is merely taking back some part of what they have robbed from the poor. You were worse than any bandit.

"But God, in His wonderful compassion, has taken your money and left you your life, which you now have an opportunity to redeem. You are better off than your laughing friends who came down with you to the river to hear John. Very soon God will sweep the world clean of sin, and your friends will lose everything, including their lives. You are like a man released from prison."

They were walking now back toward the village, which was like every other village Judah had been to on his search. The streets were dusty and the houses were made of mud brick. It was yet two hours before sunset, so most of the men were still in the fields. Children played their incomprehensible games, and women, when you saw them, were usually carrying water jugs to and from the village well.

Judah had lived all his previous life in cities, first Jerusalem and then Tiberias. In the cities, property was spoken of in the abstract—a man owned farms in Galilee, which produced a reliable income of so much per year. The farm was like a hen that lays an egg. The owner of the hen-house takes the egg from the nest. He commits no sin because, among other things, he prevents the world from being overrun with chickens.

The countryside was nothing like what Judah had imagined. People were poor in the midst of abundance. These were the peasants, whom he had been raised to regard with contempt and suspicion. Here, in their midst, a farm was not a mechanism as impersonal as a millstone, grinding out income; it was the very life of these people.

"You are like a man released from prison."

The lie becomes a parable, and the parable points to a truth that transcends the facts the lie denies. It was perfectly possible to understand why Caleb saw this man as a danger.

"I would follow you, Master. I would attain salvation."

And the peculiar thing, the truly puzzling thing, as Judah suddenly became aware, was that he did not know if he meant it or not.

Joshua was silent for a moment or two, and then he said, "We will be leaving here soon. You are welcome to come with us if you like. Along the way we may discover if your repentance is sincere."

The next morning they were on the road, and in the middle of the afternoon they came into a village that seemed abandoned. There were not even any animals in sight, not even a dog. It was as wretched a place as Judah had ever beheld, with houses left unrepaired after the spring rains, amid a general atmosphere of dilapidation and neglect.

"What has happened here?" he asked. "Where are the people?"

"In the fields," was Joshua's answer.

"What, everyone?"

"Yes, everyone." Joshua glanced about, as if hoping to observe some sign of life. "The man who has come to own all the land hereabout allows his tenants food only if they work, and then only enough to keep them alive. Instead of each householder working his own land, they are sent out to labor in crews. It is a more efficient method of farming, I am told. Those whose labor is not needed, or who can't work, are forced to leave—or, if they are old and can't leave, they die here.

"So everyone in this village—men, women, even those women quick with child, even the children themselves—works from dawn to dusk in the landlord's fields. They are not slaves, but they might as well be. And the landlord sits in Tiberias or Sepphoris or perhaps even Jerusalem and collects the money. His conscience is clear, for he does not live among these people to witness their misery. He probably congratulates himself on his good management.

"And this is happening more and more. God gave the land to His people, to be their inheritance, and it is being taken away from them."

"Will we be stopping here?" one of the disciples asked. Judah thought his name was Jacob, but he wasn't sure.

"Oh yes." Joshua nodded vigorously, as if to suggest that stopping in this desolate place was incontestably necessary. "These people need to hear that God, at least, has not forgotten them."

And then he laughed.

"Yet I fear no one will invite us to dinner. How can they? They have no food to spare. So we will leave as soon as I have finished speaking, lest we embarrass them."

They visited several more towns and villages in the following weeks. The pattern was always the same. Joshua would wait until sundown, when the men began returning from the fields, and then he would find a spot where groups of people began to converge, usually near a well, and he would begin to preach. The villagers, some of them, would listen for a time, and then the crowd would begin to drift away. Unless conditions were really bad, usually someone—perhaps because they were impressed with the teachings, or perhaps only because God enjoins hospitality to strangers—would invite them to dinner. There Joshua would tell stories, which in the end would point back to his central message.

That message was always the same: Very soon, God would send a heavenly judge to separate the righteous from the wicked. Not even the dead would escape this judgment, for they would rise from their graves to answer for the sins they had committed in life. Then, when the wicked had been condemned, those few remaining would inherit a world cleansed of evil. There would be no illness, no poverty, no sin, no death. All would live in harmony under the Law of God. It would be the rebirth of Eden.

And, in the time while the people waited for this redeemer, whom Joshua always described as "one like the son of man," they must live their lives as if they had already entered into the kingdom of God.

It was at this point that the message ran into difficulty. Joshua's peasant audience found it easy enough to identify the wicked—tax collectors, Herod, their landlords, soldiers, anyone who lived in a city—and they could look forward to a time when these would be overthrown and they themselves would be left in peace. In the kingdom of God they would live lives of plenty. The problem was that in the present they were poor.

"If you have two cloaks and you see a man who has none, give him one of yours. Do not turn away the destitute, but feed and shelter them. The Law of God commands us to love our neighbor as ourselves. Love the stranger as you love your own life."

The village householders, hearing such words, would turn away. They did not dispute with Joshua because it was obvious that he was a clever man, a learned man, and argument would be in vain. They simply stopped listening.

Most of them.

"Master, what must I do to inherit eternal life?"

The man was perhaps twenty. His robe was of fine linen, embroidered at the sleeves and borders, and his hands had the look of never having done work. His eyes were anxious, but one gathered that this was not their habitual expression.

When Judah looked at him, he had the sense of peering into his own face.

"Keep the commandments," Joshua answered him. "Honor your parents. Do not steal. Do not bear false witness. Do not kill. Love God. Show charity to the poor."

"I have never broken the commandments, Master."

Joshua studied him for a moment, as if trying to make up his mind about something.

"Then give away all that you have."

It was as if the man had been slapped in the face.

"But how can I do that?"

"Your possessions are a burden to you. You cannot enter the kingdom of God until you are free of them."

The man seemed to struggle for words, but none came. At last, when
he realized there was nothing else he could do, he turned and walked
away.

They watched him until he disappeared from sight.

"He seemed very upset," Judah said. "Perhaps he will think better of
it and come back."

Joshua smiled and shook his head.

"Riches, as you would know better than I, are very consoling. In a
month he will have forgotten us. Or, if he remembers us at all, it will be
with relief at his escape."

They never did see him again.

But the incident must have remained on Joshua's mind. A week or so
later they were in a fishing village on the eastern shore of the Sea of
Kinneret. Joshua had been there before and was known to the villagers,
so at least in a few houses they were received as friends.

Capernaum was just on the other side of the water, and someone had
promised to row them across, the next morning. It was the last evening
of their journey together.

"How much money do you have left in your purse?" Joshua asked.
He and Judah were walking along the shore, watching the birds dive
into the water for fish. Joshua found the sight amusing.

"I'm not sure. A few silver coins, no more."

"Then count them up."

There turned out to be eighteen drachmas and twelve shekels. Judah
was a little surprised there was even so much.

"Go into the village and give it away," Joshua told him. "There are
many poor here."

"All of it?"

"All. It is time for you to strike off the last of your fetters."

So that was what he did. He left Joshua on the shore and returned to
the house where they were to spend the night. The woman who was
their hostess, whose name was Martha, accepted two shekels and sent
her son with him that he might be directed to the houses of the poor.

Judah experienced an odd sense of exhilaration. He knew the scattering of these coins meant nothing, for there was money enough awaiting
him in Tiberias, along with the threads of his old life.

Yet sometimes he felt he might never go back there. He imagined himself living as Joshua's disciple forever. He knew this was impossible. He knew that one day Caleb would swoop down on this, his enemy, and everything would be over. Yet sometimes it was possible for days together to forget that Caleb existed.

So, while he distributed his meager wealth among those who perhaps had never before even seen a silver coin, Judah was happy.

Until an old man, sitting beside his doorway, shook his head as he regarded the three drachmas in the palm of his hand. The hand closed into a fist and he looked up at Judah with obvious resentment.

"It is only the rich who make a game of charity," he said.

18

Saul, Noah's friend and host in Damascus, tended to regard him as a hopeless provincial. Saul was a trader in every imaginable commodity, whose business contacts extended as far west as Greece, and it was rumored—though he would have winked and denied it—that in the east he numbered among his customers the royal house of Parthia. He was also a Pharisee and learned in the Law and the Prophets, even if he preferred to read them in Greek translation.

Greek was his first language. He collected the Greek poets and playwrights and was as likely to quote Sophocles as Isaiah. Around his table one saw as many Greeks and Romans as Jews. He was a man of broad sympathies, and his letters, which Noah always looked forward to receiving, were full of jokes and gossip and interesting interpretations of Torah.

And Damascus was overwhelming. Noah had visited it twice before, but he simply could not adjust to the scale and diversity of the place. It made even Jerusalem seem like a village.

"You should move here," Saul told him during one of their walks to his warehouse. "A man of your skill would grow rich beyond counting."

"Thank you. I prefer to live among my own people."

"'My own people.' Listen to the man. Considered rightly, the Jews are your own people, along with the Greeks and the Anatolians and even the Romans. God is the father of us all. I keep the Law, as you know, but all men are my brothers. I believe that God gave us Torah that we might lead all the nations to Him."

"Yes, but thus far we have not been terribly successful."

"That is because men like you keep themselves shut up in Palestine. Do you realize that there are Greeks and even a few Romans who attend our synagogue? They are *interested*. The money for our new floor came from a Roman tribune. Wait until the Sabbath and you will see for yourself."

Noah made no reply. He always felt slightly dwarfed by Saul—by his vitality and his enthusiasms, and by the sheer physical presence of the man. Saul was tall and broad, with a thick, impressively cut beard, heavy, dramatic eyebrows, and the face of a bird of prey. He seemed all nose and eyes. One had the impression he could burn a hole through granite with those black eyes.

Saul's warehouse was across the street from one of the small Roman garrisons scattered throughout the city. This was probably not a coincidence, and he seemed on friendly terms with the soldiers, greeting some by name as they lounged around the entrances to the wineshops that lived by their trade. These exchanges were in Latin, in which Noah was halting at best but which Saul spoke with fluency.

"Behold the legionnaires of Rome—poor children," he said, switching back to Greek. "Farm boys, for the most part. Their commanders tell them they are masters of the world, but from the look of them they miss their mothers."

"Then they should go home."

Saul glanced down at Noah. His expression was at first fierce, as if offended, but quickly dissolved into a wide grin.

"Then where would *we* be?" he asked. "Everyone complains about it, but, believe me, Roman rule is a good thing, particularly for us. The Romans guarantee Jewish rights in every city in their empire and, for the rest, as long as the taxes are paid and there is no trouble, they leave everyone alone. You prefer the Seleucids? Or the Herodians? May God deliver us from the sons of Herod!"

"At least Antipas is a Jew," Noah answered, with perhaps more emphasis than he intended. "One of our own."

"Is he? Are you sure?"

"No."

They both laughed.

It was the impression of an instant, the sense of being watched. Something at the edges of his consciousness had alerted him, and Noah turned his head slightly to the right, just enough to allow him a glance at the arrangement of human figures along that side of the street.

Two men in Greek dress were arguing—a friendly dispute apparently, at least that was what their gestures indicated. Three young men were laughing, sharing a skin of wine and flirting with a woman not quite so young. Their voices were loud enough to allow one to hear that they were speaking Latin. They were obviously soldiers from the garrison. A woman, about forty, was sweeping her doorstep.

A man in his thirties was eating out of a small bowl, using his fingers. His tunic was belted with a rope, knotted at the left side. He seemed intent on his meal. Too intent.

Was this man known to him? His face was half hidden, perhaps intentionally, as he bent over his bowl. No, there was nothing about him that struck a chord in Noah's memory.

It was with a flood of relief that he decided this could not be the man who had attacked him on his way home from Nazareth. This one was simply not big enough.

In that brief moment, no longer than a few beats of one's heart, Noah felt the world change around him. He was far from Galilee, and yet Galilee had caught up with him.

"What would you say if I told you that I am being followed?"

Saul appeared to consider this for perhaps the time it took to cover ten paces—they had turned the corner now and were almost at the door of his warehouse. Then he stopped and turned to look at his friend. His expression was detached and speculative.

"I would not be surprised," he said. "I am *not* surprised. You appear here in Damascus with no warning, and I have to wonder why. Were you suddenly seized by an impulse to see me? Charming as I am, I don't think so. You are not the spontaneous type. And then there are those yellow patches on your face that look like fading bruises. Noah, what have you been up to?"

"It's a long and complicated story."

"All the better. I have plenty of time."

They went into the warehouse, which was huge and cluttered and strangely quiet, and Saul locked the door behind them. On the floor in his office was a square made of wooden planks, which he pushed aside with his foot to reveal a shallow well. He bent down, rolled up his sleeve, and reached inside to extract a jug, dripping wet, the contents of which turned out to be a wine dark as blood, delicious and strong. Saul poured some into two stone cups.

"Taste it," he ordered. He waited until Noah had taken two sips and then nodded. "Now. Tell me."

So Noah went through the events of the last few months, beginning with Joshua's appearance at his workshop door and ending with the man eating on the street. When he was finished, Saul nodded, as if every word had conformed to his expectations.

"And this priest," he asked, "this Eleazar—do you trust him?"

"No. He is the Tetrarch's man."

"Good. Then you are finally learning cynicism. And this cousin of yours. What of him?"

"Joshua may be a prophet. Or he may be just another poor fool. I don't know. But I do know that his life is worth saving."

"And he cannot be persuaded to leave Galilee?"

"No. I've tried."

"Then it seems an insoluble problem. You know, of course, that there has been a great harvesting of the Baptist's followers lately. Antipas has been busy."

Noah felt something clench his heart.

"No. I didn't know that."

"They may already have your cousin—in which case it doesn't matter what you do. You won't be able to save him."

"Yet I must try."

Saul pursed his lips, apparently considering this answer.

"I think you would be wiser to stay in Damascus. I can arrange to have your sister brought here."

"No. I must go. Soon."

"Then I can at least arrange for the Romans to detain our hungry friend outside."

"I can imagine how they would 'detain' him. No. I prefer not to have anyone's blood on my hands. He might be perfectly innocent."

"No one is perfectly innocent. Except, perhaps, you, my friend."

———

That night, the men who had accepted Saul's invitation to dinner might, had they found it expedient, have settled among themselves any question touching on Rome's province of Syria. The imperial legate himself was there, along with two of his military commanders and leading figures from the Greek and Jewish communities. Saul, who lived by his friendships and the influence they afforded him, was in turn courted by them all, and tonight Saul had steered the conversation around to Herod Antipas, Tetrarch of Galilee and Perea.

Noah, the least in so distinguished a company, occupied a couch farthest from his host. He did not enter into the discussion, nor was he expected to. The other guests seemed not even to have noticed his presence. He merely ate and listened. This suited his purposes nicely.

"I would not, of course, dream of criticizing the emperor for supporting him," said Phineas bar Kidron, nodding to the legate, Lucius Flaccus, his intimate friend, whom he had helped to make rich, "but he is an odious creature. Like his father before him, he is an insult to the people he governs."

The legate, who did not seem to have taken offense, busied himself with the breast meat of a sparrow as he considered his answer.

"The emperor," he said at last, "must manage his affairs with the tools he has at hand, and Galilee has been quiet for decades." He shrugged, suggesting that the point was unanswerable. "You, Phineas, my friend, do not like him. Your reasons are religious, but what is that to us? In any case, aside from direct Roman rule, which everyone would find inconvenient—you should hear my man Pilatus on the subject of governing the Jews—what alternative is there?"

"Still, I notice you keep that nephew of his safely tucked away in Rome, well out of his uncle's reach. What's his name again?"

"Agrippa. Herod Agrippa."

"Yes, that's him. His grandmother, at least, was a Hasmonean, and *they,* at least, were actually Jews. Saving him for something, are we? A little insurance in case the current Herod disappoints you?"

This was greeted with general laughter, in which the legate did not scruple to join in.

"Well, one thing at least," said Panaetius, a white-haired Greek of vast age and absolutely incalculable wealth, "that fellow Antipas certainly knows how to make the money fly. In debt I hear."

"Perhaps that is your solution, my dear Phineas," the legate suggested.

"Perhaps, if his creditors grow too insistent, you can persuade him to sell you Galilee."

This was widely appreciated as the best jest of the evening. It was several minutes before the laughter died away.

"Unfortunately, Herod has an easier source of money." The speaker was one Amos bar Benjamin, an elegant man and reputed to be a great scholar. "He simply increases the taxes. Galilee is a land of plenty, and yet one hears that in the villages they are starving. He risks a peasant revolt if he is not careful."

"And now he has killed one of their heroes."

It was not clear who spoke, but the silence that followed this reference to the Baptist was itself painful testimony.

"Yes," Amos replied at last. "He has murdered one of God's prophets. He will be made to pay for that."

Noah glanced at the imperial legate, a man who could not be suspected of sympathy with someone like John, and noticed that he, in his turn, was carefully observing the reactions of the other guests. Perhaps he was silently readjusting his appraisal of Antipas. The Romans did not like trouble in their subject lands.

"About a year ago I had an interesting exchange of letters about John," the legate said at last. "Pilatus was afraid of him. He argued that the man had many followers and was preaching the overthrow of the existing order. I wrote back, 'Where is he? What does he do?' Pilatus replied that he immersed people in the Jordan, in the wilderness of Perea, and I asked, 'So then, they go to him?' and he answered, 'Yes. Large crowds collect to hear him preach and to have their sins washed away.' I gave instructions that he was to be left in peace, that we have nothing to fear from a holy man in Perea, that it is never wise to tamper with religion, that we would gain nothing by creating a martyr. It would appear that I was right."

"So, my friend," Saul asked as he and Noah enjoyed a final cup of wine together, after the last of the guests had departed, "what did you learn?"

"Nothing I have not heard elsewhere in my travels. That the moneylenders do not have confidence in Antipas. That the execution of John is resented and, what is worse, regarded as a sign of weakness."

"And you will put all this in your letter to your priest friend?"

"He is not my friend, but yes, I will report what I have heard."

"And what will you say of the legate?"

"Only a general statement that the Roman authorities do not seem unwilling to hear criticism of the Tetrarch."

"Ah, then of course you would have no interest in reading the reports that Flaccus sends to the emperor."

Noah could do no more than put down his cup and stare. It seemed impossible.

"Oh yes, my friend," Saul went on, smiling with pleasure at the reaction he had elicited. "The legate dictates his correspondence to a scribe, who prepares a copy for the emperor and a copy for the legate's archives—and another copy, which by a mysterious process finds its way into my hands. When he writes to the emperor, by the way, he writes in Greek. Tiberias is a great scholar who surrounds himself with philosophers and poets. His Greek, they say, is better than his Latin. Did you know that?"

"No, I did not. But then, I am not personally acquainted with the emperor."

"Neither am I, but I read everything that he reads touching on this little corner of his empire. Would you like a peek?"

"Yes, I—"

"Then tomorrow. You will have complete access. I only ask that you make no copies and that, in your letter to this priest, you leave out names. Agreed?"

"Yes. Yes, of course. This is a very great favor."

"Nonsense. I would simply have them know that you are well connected. That you are a man with powerful friends who would resent your death at their hands."

He touched Noah on the shoulder and smiled.

"I am a selfish brute, you see. Besides, you make such amusing toys."

Noah had the name of a man in Paneas who could be trusted to convey to the Lord Eleazar any communication put into his hands, but first it was necessary to reach Paneas alive.

The city was on the main trade routes, about seventy miles south and west of Damascus. It was in Philip's realm, which might or might not be a problem, depending on Philip's current degree of cooperation with his brother, a matter more unpredictable than the weather.

Yet Paneas had certain advantages for a fugitive. It was almost on the Syrian border, which facilitated escape to the north, and if one preferred to flee south, it was directly on a tributary of the Jordan River. Noah also had friends there who, if the need arose, would probably be able to smuggle him to Tyre. In Paneas, Noah would feel reasonably safe.

But first he had to get there. He had not seen the hungry man again, but wherever he went in Damascus he could not shake the sense of being watched. Seventy miles of road meant at least two days of traveling, more likely three. Two days—or three—gave an assassin many chances.

Saul arranged for Noah to leave his house in disguise and then to travel with a caravan on its way to Ptolemais.

In Paneas, Noah immediately found the man who would convey his letter to the Lord Eleazar. He was a shopkeeper named Dothan. He took the letter, sealed it, and put it in a drawer. That was the end of the transaction. Dothan, one suspected, did not want to know any details.

The question then was, what to do? The hungry man was nowhere in sight, but that meant nothing.

Noah spent four days in Paneas, which was a pagan city, named after one of their countless gods. He visited the famous grotto and stood with a crowd of people watching the water gush from the mouth of a cave. At the end of his visit he set out for the city of Seleucia, a good day's journey to the south. Except for his donkey, he was alone.

He arrived in Seleucia before sundown, having encountered no one on the road except strangers traveling north.

In Seleucia he stayed away from people he knew. He was gripped by a strange passivity. He ate, he slept, and to comfort himself he said his prayers and read Torah, trying to pretend that there was no world beyond these things. For ten days he never left the city. He began to think he would never leave it.

Then, late one afternoon, while he was sitting on a bench in front of the inn where he stayed, reading about the deliverance of Isaac, he saw the hungry man again. The hungry man was across the street, watching him. When he caught Noah's eye, he smiled. Then he crossed the street and sat down on the bench beside him.

"I am sorry if I have frightened you," he said. He glanced at the scroll in Noah's trembling hands. "What are you reading?"

Noah forced himself to look down at the writing—in that moment he could not have recalled what it was.

"The story of Abraham and Isaac," he said, after a pause in which he struggled to find his voice.

"Where the angel stays Abraham's hand?"

"Yes."

"I always liked that story," the hungry man announced, with evident satisfaction. "The stories are the best part of Torah."

Noah did not reply. He was too busy adjusting to the idea that he was not about to be killed.

"The Lord Eleazar sends you his greetings. He wants you to know that he found your report beyond anything that he expected. When you reach Hippos there will be a letter from him awaiting you."

"How do I know that you are from the Lord Eleazar?" Noah asked. It did not seem an inappropriate question.

"He wished me to tell you that he has not forgotten what you said about it being better to die than to break the commandments."

Noah allowed himself a deep breath and the hope that he might live to be a few months older. Was it also possible that he might also live to see his home again, or Deborah's face?

"Am I going to Hippos?" he asked.

"Yes. Perhaps I could accompany you. It would be safer. But you must promise not to slip away from me again."

"I promise. By the way, have you eaten?"

"No."

"Then you must join me for dinner." Noah observed that the sun was low in the sky and allowed himself to smile. "I thought you might be hungry."

19

Upon reading the letter, which covered several pages, the Lord Eleazar at first suspected that Noah had simply made it all up, that it was all a self-serving fabrication, the sort of thing one expected from paid spies who knew the market value of dramatic information. However, he was not far along before he abandoned this idea. It was all too specific, too full of direct quotations that had the ring of authenticity.

Thus it was with a mingling of excitement and fear that Eleazar made his way from line to line of Noah's Hebrew, so magisterially perfect that it was almost like reading an intelligence report written by the Prophet Isaiah. Indeed, the rebuke of Antipas was all the more stunning for coming from a chorus of voices, their identities concealed, but in one case, at least, perfectly obvious.

Eleazar knew that Noah had dined with Lucius Flaccus in Damascus, and many of the expressions attributed to a "high Roman official" sounded exactly like the man who over the years had honored Eleazar with several private conversations.

Although, judging from the candor of some of his remarks, the imperial legate must have been deep in his wine that night.

But it was all perfectly believable. Besides, Eleazar tended to trust the ironsmith, who did not seem to possess the temperament of one who simply made things up.

So, having digested the letter and being satisfied of its veracity, Eleazar was faced with the problem of how best to present it to the Tetrarch.

First of all, as Antipas hardly even knew the Hebrew alphabet, it would have to be translated into Greek. Then the source would have to be disguised. He owed Noah that, and besides, the man was revealing himself to be too valuable an asset to risk. The best plan, he decided, would be to present it as a summary based on several different reports. And last, of course, many of the actual words would have to be softened, since Antipas was so quick to take offense.

All of these were tasks that Eleazar felt he could entrust to no one else. He himself would prepare the document he would carry with him to Tiberias.

He suspected that this interview with the Tetrarch would turn out to be both difficult and dangerous, so he gave himself three days to prepare. He made a Greek transcription and then burned the original. Then he undertook the difficult task of editing it into something at once sufficiently convincing and yet not too offensive to the self-conceit of the Tetrarch.

As he read over the final draft, he tried to anticipate how Antipas would react, what questions he would ask, whom he would blame and for what. The man was as unpredictable as a bull in the breeding season.

In the last few hours before he undertook the journey to Tiberias, Eleazar made over certain properties to his son—not enough to excite the Tetrarch's avarice, but enough to keep the boy in comfort for his lifetime. It seemed a reasonable precaution.

As his wagon rolled under the eastern gate on his way out of Sepphoris, Eleazar kept trying to imagine some way of avoiding this confrontation. What did he hope to achieve? An end to the purge of John's followers. The destruction of Caleb. Did he need both? Yes. The purge was pointless and destructive, and if he did not somehow manage Caleb's fall, sometime or other there would be another crisis, and then another. It would end badly. Almost certainly, Eleazar knew, Caleb would destroy him if he did not strike first. Was this report of Noah's the best means? Yes. He could not believe that God would provide him with a better means. It even had the advantage of being true.

There had been rain all that week, but today the skies had cleared.

There was hardly enough wind to stir the curtains, which he had drawn back so that he could see the countryside. Somehow the aftermath of rain always clarified things. Colors were brighter, and the lines of the hills sharper. The world was a paradise, another Eden.

But once again the serpent was coiled and waiting.

When he arrived in Tiberias, Eleazar went to his house and bathed and changed his clothes. Then he had a meal and talked to his steward about domestic matters. He inquired after each of the servants and affected to take an interest in a plan for enlarging the drains. He knew he was simply putting off the moment.

At last he wrote a note to the Tetrarch's scribe, informing him of his presence in the city and requesting an audience. The sun had already disappeared over the western walls. Eleazar assumed a reply would not come until the following day.

He was mistaken. Within an hour he received word that the Tetrarch was prepared to receive him as soon as Eleazar might find it convenient—which meant, of course, immediately.

There was a garden beside the main banqueting hall. A stone balustrade around two sides of it faced the water, which created a quite illusory sense of openness and accessibility, for below the balustrade was a ditch, perhaps ten cubits deep, its walls deliberately sheer and lined with smooth stone. Such was Antipas's fear of his subjects that the outer lip of the ditch was patrolled night and day.

The garden itself was lovely during the day, but at night it took on an atmosphere of secrecy and menace. It was illuminated by oil lamps, each on top of a thin bronze shaft, so that there were pools of vague, shimmering light amid the darkness.

Eleazar was shown out into the garden and told to wait. He did not sit down on any of the benches that could be found along the gravel paths. He waited, standing, staring down at the walkway.

Why gravel? It seemed an odd choice. The walkways in all of his own homes were paved with stone. And then it occurred to him that, on stone, one had merely to remove one's sandals to move about quite soundlessly. Gravel was noisy and therefore perfect for a monarch who lived in dread of assassins.

He was alone for perhaps a quarter of an hour before one of the doors

to the banqueting hall opened. The Tetrarch stepped out and began glid-
ing between the little circles of soft light. He was resplendent in a robe
shot through with silver, and his hands twinkled with gems. As he came
near, Eleazar made a deep bow and Antipas nodded curtly.

"You arrived three hours ago," he said. "Why did you not send me
word at once?"

"I knew Your Highness would be with his guests and I did not wish
to intrude."

Antipas seemed to consider this answer, cocking his head a little to
one side. Probably he knew it was only an excuse, but the timing fit, so
he seemed willing to ascribe the delay to Eleazar's famous sense of tact.

"What did you want to see me about?"

Eleazar did not immediately answer. Suddenly he could feel Noah's
report, which he carried in a pocket inside his robe, pressing against his
heart like a slab of stone.

"Reports have reached me, sire," he said at last. "Matters I would
bring to your notice."

"Reports?" Antipas's face seemed to contract. When did anyone ever
bring him a report that did not contain bad news? "Reports from whom?
What about?"

"Reports from abroad, sire. From various places. Reports of opinion,
of how we here in Galilee are perceived by the larger world."

The Tetrarch moved his foot impatiently, so that the toes became
visible beyond the hem of his robe. One of them—the middle one—
glittered with a jeweled ring.

"What do I care about *opinion*, Minister? I am indifferent to what
they say in the bazaar."

"Roman opinion, Majesty. Along with others, almost as important.
Men of commerce. Merchants. Men whose feelings we would be wise
not to ignore."

"Why? What are they saying? What is this *about*, Minister?"

"It is about the Baptist, sire. It was a mistake to kill him."

"*That* again?"

Eleazar found it prudent not to reply. He merely waited until the
Tetrarch's exasperation had found release for itself in an impatient kick
that sent the gravel flying like startled birds.

"What are they saying?"

Antipas sank onto a bench, apparently exhausted by the effort of restoring himself to calm.

"They are saying, Majesty, that it was a sign of weakness."

Eleazar, who had of course remained standing, found he could almost pity the man who stared up at him with something like disbelief.

"Weakness?"

"Yes." The First Minister of Galilee placed his right hand over his heart, as if pledging his own fealty. "The Baptist was respected, sire, and no one can understand why we thought it necessary to execute him—unless, perhaps, because our grasp on power has become so weak that we fear even the crowds who gathered by the Jordan to have John wash their sins away."

"Who says this?"

"Many, sire. Including the imperial legate in Damascus. He made reference to the affair in his correspondence with Rome."

Even in the flickering, heavy light of the oil lamps, it was possible to see the Tetrarch's eyes grow wide.

"His letters to the emperor? You have seen these?"

"Copies, sire. I have seen transcripts, which I have reason to know are genuine."

Antipas shook his head.

"Is *nothing* secret from you, Minister? It would appear not." He held out his hand. "Let me see."

With vast misgivings, Eleazar took the folded sheets of papyrus from his pocket and allowed the Tetrarch to snatch them away from him.

"This is your own writing," the Tetrarch announced, almost triumphantly, as he flipped through the pages. "I know your hand—I have seen it often enough."

"I prepared a summary, that Your Majesty might be inconvenienced as little as possible."

The only immediate reply was a grudging nod while Antipas tried to make sense of what he held in his hand.

After a few moments of absorbed silence, he looked up.

"I must read all this and consider it," he said. "I will not keep you, Minister. I will send word when I have need of you."

With a wave of his hand he indicated that the audience was over. Eleazar bowed deeply and retreated, slowly.

———

Fear is the most private of emotions. It thrives in darkness and solitude. It hides in the shadowed corners. It gnaws at the hearts of lonely men.

The Tetrarch was a ruler of uncertain temper. His actions would be guided by his moods, which were as fluid as quicksilver. And Eleazar had put into his hands information that could only frighten him and, worse, threaten his self-esteem. The Tetrarch could make himself believe anything, and therefore it was impossible to know how he would react to so telling a blow.

It was perfectly conceivable that he would order Eleazar's arrest. The First Minister of Galilee knew that he might be dead before the next dawn, that he might be led straight from his bed chamber to the executioner's block.

Eleazar had no confidants. His wife, whom he had been unable to love, was long dead. His nephew was a shallow young man who could never be made to understand the complexities of life. And his son was still a boy.

As he sat in his room, drinking wine and gathering the courage required to take off his clothes and go to bed, he kept thinking of Noah. Noah, who had found himself helpless before Caleb just as Eleazar was helpless before the Tetrarch.

What had he said? Oh yes, something about how there were worse things than death. What was worse than death, Eleazar had asked. And Noah had answered, breaking the commandments. Thou shalt not bear false witness.

Eleazar, a priest of ancient lineage, was scrupulous in his observances. He kept the Law, honored God and prayed to Him, and believed himself a pious man. Yet he had never found much of comfort in the religion of his ancestors. Did he love God? He didn't know.

It was possible to envy Noah.

The night passed slowly. At last Eleazar went to his bed, but sleep failed him. He simply waited, for the sound of sandaled feet upon the floor, for the excited voices of his servants, for the loud knocking at his door that would tell him his life was over.

At last dawn came. Rose-colored light found its way in through the windows, and it occurred to Eleazar that the Tetrarch must have been asleep for some three or four hours and that, therefore, the order for his arrest had not yet been given. The Tetrarch would not awaken for another five hours at least, and until then, Eleazar concluded, he was safe.

Thus he was at last able to sleep. He slept for three hours and then awakened in a cold terror. Death seemed very close.

But it was only a servant, knocking at the door, inquiring if he would care for some breakfast.

Eleazar was able to laugh at himself. Yes, he would have breakfast. He would eat, and then bathe and dress himself and face like a man whatever awaited him.

It was the middle of the afternoon before he received word that the Tetrarch would receive him. The bearer of this message was not a squad of soldiers, but a boy, probably no more than ten years old—too young to be afraid of the great—who smiled and said that His Majesty would be pleased if the First Minister would attend on him in his private chambers.

His private chambers. That by itself was interesting.

The Tetrarch thought it consistent with his dignity to live on a lavish scale, but the room into which Eleazar found himself being conducted was elegant in its simplicity. He understood why at once. This room belonged to the Lady Herodias. She was sitting beside her husband.

Eleazar made a deep bow to the Tetrarch and, if possible, an even deeper bow to his wife.

"Very well, Minister, what are we to do about this?" Antipas almost shouted, holding up the report Eleazar had given him the night before. "Oh do sit down, man. Her ladyship will forgive you, and you give me a crick in the neck standing there like that."

The First Minister bowed yet again to Herodias, in recognition of this courtesy, and, when the lady smiled, subsided into a chair. He was rather pleased with himself, for he was reasonably sure that nothing of the immense relief he felt showed in his face.

They were alone in the room, and Eleazar discovered an interesting contrast between husband and wife. Except for the jeweled rings that never left his hands, Antipas was quite plainly dressed, in an embroidered tunic without even a cloak over it. And he had neglected to comb his hair. He looked as if he might have come directly from his bed.

Herodias, however, had obviously taken some pains with her appearance. Her black hair shone from the brush, and her dress, of blue silk with white sleeves, was both modest and elegant, with only a loose white cord for a belt. Eleazar guessed that this was for him, that she wished to make the right impression, to avoid antagonizing him.

She was better prepared for this interview than was Antipas, probably in the contents of her mind as well as the adornment of her person.

"Come now, Minister—what am I to do?"

Antipas was afraid. He was hiding it behind a screen of bluster, but he was afraid. Herodias was afraid as well. That was useful.

"I would suggest to Your Majesty that this would be an appropriate time to end the purge."

"Purge? What purge?"

The Tetrarch of Galilee and Perea seemed genuinely perplexed.

"The purge of the Baptist's supporters, sire. They are being rounded up and imprisoned. Some of them have already been crucified."

Antipas started to say something, but his wife touched his arm with her hand and he fell silent.

"Will that be enough?" she asked. "Simply to stop the purge?"

"No, Lady, but it will be a beginning."

Herodias made no reply. She would have liked to, but she restrained herself. Eleazar allowed the silence to endure while he counted silently to five.

"I would urge Your Majesty to declare an amnesty," he said finally. "'The Tetrarch is moved by compassion for his subjects and forgives their errors,' and so forth, and so on. I have no doubt that those chastened by a few months in prison will give no further trouble, and we need an interval of calm."

"The Blessed One alone knows what the Romans will think," Antipas blurted out, holding a hand over his eyes as if afflicted by the light.

Yes. Noah's quotations of the imperial legate's correspondence had had their effect. Nothing else could have frightened the Tetrarch into such cowering submission. Eleazar reminded himself that he must think of a suitable reward for the ironsmith.

"The Romans will think you are wise, sire," the First Minister announced soothingly. "The Romans care only for domestic order and their taxes. The one insures the other. Any steps taken to pacify Galilee will be approved by Damascus—and by Rome."

"It shall be as you think best, Minister," Antipas answered wearily, his hand still covering his eyes. "I leave all of this to your management. And now . . ."

Eleazar made a small sound, as if clearing his throat, and Herodias, like a hunting dog that has found the scent, lifted her head. Again she touched her husband's arm, and again he fell silent.

"There is more, of course," she said, not so much to the Tetrarch or his minister as to herself.

"Yes, Lady. There is one other matter."

"And that is . . . ?"

"Caleb," the First Minister answered, addressing himself rather pointedly to the Tetrarch. "He has demonstrated his unworthiness. I must assume my share of the blame, sire. I brought him to your attention. It was a mistake. When this crisis is past, I hope you will allow me to accept the consequences of my failure and retire from your service, but Caleb also must render his account."

At last the Tetrarch, like a man coming out of hiding, lifted his hand from his eyes. He glanced first at his minister and then at his wife, who, almost imperceptibly, shook her head.

Yes, of course. She had already considered the probability that Eleazar would assume such an attitude and had coached her husband accordingly.

"I cannot part with you, Minister," Antipas said, like an actor reading a part. "You must continue in my service, for I have grown to depend upon your wisdom. We will speak no more of blame. As for Caleb, rein him in if you will, but he too must remain with me. Have no fear—I will make it plain to him that he is *your* servant as well as mine."

Eleazar placed his hand over his heart and, as well as one can while seated in a chair, bowed to the will of his master.

"Then I have a favor to ask of you, sire."

"Name it." The Tetrarch smiled benevolently, the interview having veered in a more comfortable direction. "You have but to name it, Eleazar."

"My favor is this: that you will allow me to draw up a list of names, and that it shall be Your Majesty's pleasure that no one whose name appears on that list shall be subject to arrest or shall be interfered with in any way without Your Majesty's express warrant."

The Tetrarch waved his hand, as if consenting to a trifle, and a faint trace of irritation registered in the Lady Herodias's face.

"And of course, Minister," she said sweetly, "you would expect to be consulted before any such warrant is issued?"

She had created the trap for herself. Eleazar smiled at her, almost pityingly.

"Lady, I advise the Tetrarch when and if he condescends to seek my opinion. I serve his will—nothing else remains to me. He consults me at his pleasure."

He risked a glance at the humbled ruler of Galilee and Perea and then turned his attention back to Herodias. Antipas feared the Romans, and Eleazar could read their thoughts. It would be the Tetrarch's pleasure to consult his First Minister on all matters touching his realm, and his wife understood that. For the moment, at least, Caleb was checked.

20

Among the small number of his followers, Joshua's return to Capernaum was a cause for rejoicing. That first evening they all assembled at Deborah's house for dinner and to hear the Master recount his journey.

Throughout the evening, as Deborah listened to Joshua describe his reception among the villages of the north, she found herself wondering, over and over again, what Noah would make of it all. Even Joshua related his adventures as comedy.

"In the countryside, it seems, nothing changes but the tax rates. Men have grown so deaf they can hardly hear the wind blow. They ask me, 'Why now? Why do you say that God will come now?' and all I can answer is 'Why *not* now? We have Herod pretending to be a king, building cities of marble for the rich, and farmers being driven from their land like goats herded to pasture. The whole world has been given over to wickedness. How much longer can God be expected to stay His hand?' They merely shrug and pick the lice out of their beards. It is like trying to wear away a stone by kissing it.

"Still, here and there I change a few hearts. You see, Deborah? I bring back to you three new disciples to feed."

These three glanced away, not quite in unison, but as if they were suddenly ashamed of the bread they put into their mouths.

"They are welcome," she said, smiling.

Hannah, in compassion, refilled their wine cups.

"And now I have eight," Joshua went on, gesturing with his arm as if to a multitude. "When it pleases God to make them twelve, one for each of the twelve tribes, then we will be fortified, ready for the day of His coming. I am not discouraged. Galilee hears the truth, Jerusalem shall hear it, and then the world shall be brought to repentance. The harvest is sown and shall be brought in. All things proceed according to the will of God. All things."

The three who had accompanied Joshua back to Capernaum were named Judah, Jacob, and John. Jacob and John were brothers, day laborers from near Chorazin, big, strong men who could agree on nothing except their devotion to Joshua, given to shouting at each other so that he called them the Thunder Brothers. Nevertheless, they fitted in easily to the rhythms of village life. They were poor and Galilean. Simon and his brother Andrew took them out fishing, so that they earned their keep.

Only Judah was a problem. His hands were soft from a lifetime of leisure, and his accent betrayed that he came from the south. To the others, for whom their little corner of Galilee was the world, he seemed almost a foreigner. He was a city dweller, and he had been rich. They did not know what to make of him, so they were suspicious.

At first his only friend was Levi, the reformed tax collector, who understood what it was to be an outcast. When Levi repented of his old life and became one of Joshua's followers, Deborah had given him a job salting fish, that he might not starve. She did the same for Judah, and Levi taught him the work.

But Deborah too was suspicious. She could not justify her suspicions, even to herself, but they persisted. Judah said he was from Jerusalem, which would account for his accent. Deborah had never been to Jerusalem; however, she could credit that people who lived so far away would not talk like the fishermen of Galilee. She herself was thought rich in Capernaum but, like villagers everywhere, she imagined people from the cities to be rich beyond reckoning. She knew that rich people sometimes lost their money. But did not the rich and mighty have families, no less than the poor? Would not his family have helped him? Perhaps not.

She knew also that Judah had been baptized by John, because Joshua had witnessed it. And he had lapsed back into sin. Well, he would not be

the first. There were those in Capernaum who had listened eagerly
enough to Joshua, only to turn away at the last.

Yet there was something about Judah that seemed not quite real. The
story and the man somehow failed to match. There was some flaw in
Judah, which Deborah could not identify but only sense.

But perhaps her suspicions were no more than the sum of her village
prejudices. A rich Judean from the city seemed out of place salting fish.
Perhaps it was no more than that.

When Noah was away, as she had come to realize, she was given to
brooding.

How many more days before he would come back? What was keeping him in Damascus, or wherever he was? Where *was* Damascus?
Somewhere north, in the gentile lands—that was all she knew. She did
not care anything about Damascus. The name was hateful to her. How
many more days?

Then, late one afternoon, Hannah came back from the market.

"I saw him," she said, smiling slyly. "He and his donkey were covered
with dust, but it was him."

There was, of course, no need to specify who *he* was.

"Perhaps I should have bought meat."

Deborah could only shake her head. There was less than an hour
until sunset—he would not come today. First he would go to Ezra's,
where he would see to his animal and clean up. Then, probably, he
would go see Joshua. The one certainty was that he would do nothing
to compromise her. He would wait until tomorrow, probably until the
early afternoon, before he called.

But she wanted to see him. Now. Tonight. She didn't care what the
neighbors thought. She didn't care if the whole of Capernaum believed
that Noah the ironsmith was her lover.

"Go first to the Master. Invite him to supper. Insist. Tell him there
will be honeyed lamb. He will not say no. And tell him to bring whom-
ever he likes. Then go back to the market."

And if Noah didn't come with Joshua, she would send to fetch him at
Ezra's. It simply was not possible to wait through another night without
seeing him.

As soon as Hannah was gone, Deborah went upstairs to her bedroom
and washed her face and hands. Then she changed her clothes. Then

she sat down and began combing her hair. Noah admired her hair, and tonight she wanted it to glisten.

Her preparations were not in vain. Two hours later, when Joshua arrived, he had Noah with him. Noah took her hand and smiled to show that he understood her cunning.

"You remember my cousin, who is back safely from a sojourn among the pagans," Joshua announced. "Those people eat the most abominable things, so doubtless he is starving."

"Then we must see to it that his hunger is satisfied. It was good of you both to come."

"Goodness played no part in the decision, and you cannot pretend to be ignorant of the fact. You, better than anyone, know of my particular weakness for honeyed lamb."

The evening answered all of Deborah's reasonable expectations for it. Noah, as the more recent traveler, was allowed his fair share of the conversation and described the wonders of Damascus, which he said was a city greater than Sepphoris—in extent, greater even than Jerusalem, which Joshua disputed, perhaps only from motives of piety, since he admitted he had never set foot in Damascus. It was a point of little interest to Deborah, but she had the pleasure of listening to Noah's voice, the music of which she was now quite sure she would never tire.

"Was the trip a success?" she asked, simply to fill a lull in the conversation.

Noah seemed to consider the point for a moment and then nodded.

"Yes, I think so. Damascus is a trade center that reaches into the whole of Asia, and I made many useful contacts. When I return home, I think I shall have to hire a new work space and begin training a new set of apprentices."

"And you will prosper," interrupted Joshua.

"That is possible. If I do I will provide the world with objects of use, and ten or fifteen young boys will earn money for their families and learn a trade, which will one day allow *them* to prosper."

"I was not implying a criticism."

"Yes, you were," Noah answered, with a smile. "You see the misery that afflicts the countryside, and the vast wealth of princes and land-lords, and you draw the conclusion that all wealth is a form of pillage."

"I have offended you."

Noah laughed and placed his hand on Joshua's shoulder.

"You have not offended me. The world is burning down around us and you are throwing water on the flames. Sometimes, in your haste, your aim is a trifle defective, but if you wet the hem of my cloak I can overlook it."

"Then you may become rich with God's blessing."

"And grow fat and complacent and learn to hold the poor in contempt. About that, at least, you are right. Indifference to the suffering of others is one sin God will not forgive."

"Then there is no disagreement between us." Joshua glanced at Deborah, holding her gaze for a moment as if to let her in on the jest. "For certainly when you are rich you will give all your money away."

"Perhaps not all of it."

Late the following morning, for he too was impatient, Noah called at the house of the fish merchant's widow. He was received, as usual, in the garden, where Deborah looked as beautiful as he had ever seen her.

"Have you decided?" he asked, almost as soon as he had sat down beside her—it was simply impossible for him to begin with any other subject.

She lifted her hand a little away from her lap, and he required no other invitation to take it in both of his own.

"Yes." She smiled, although she seemed almost on the verge of tears. "Have you?"

"I don't think there was ever any decision for me to take. I think I knew the first moment I saw you."

"Then it is settled?"

"We will be married?"

"Yes. Of course."

They both laughed. It seemed so absurdly easy. A common impulse drew them together and, for the first time, he kissed her on the lips.

Then, to his surprise, she returned his kiss, allowing it to linger until his heart began to race.

After a while propriety reasserted itself and she drew away—not far, not more than a span, but enough to reclaim herself.

Still, she kept reaching out to him, as if to confirm his presence.

"How was your journey?" Deborah asked finally, simply because it was necessary to say something.

"Adventurous." Noah smiled, showing his teeth. "Four days ago I thought I might never see you again. I even thought I might be murdered. But the man I thought would slay me turned out to be a friend, and it seems both Joshua and I are out of danger. The Lord Eleazar has convinced the Tetrarch to end his purge of the Baptist's followers. I have it all in a letter he sent me. Would you like to see it?"

As soon as he took it from his pocket, she grabbed it eagerly. It was a simple sheet of papyrus, covered with writing in a small, precise hand. She read it through in silence, only her lips moving, until she reached the end.

" 'Caleb is in disgrace and his wife has been sent home to Sepphoris, so even the Lady Herodias has noted a change in the wind.' Who is the Lady Herodias?"

"Herod's wife. Before he married her, she was his brother's wife."

"No! Is such a thing possible?"

Noah smiled. "It is if you are Herod."

" 'I do not think Caleb is such a fool as to bother you again.' Now that *is* good news."

"Yes. It means we won't have to go into hiding in Syria. We can live in Sepphoris." He frowned suddenly. "*Can* you live in Sepphoris?" he asked her. "It is very different from Capernaum."

"I suppose I can. Other people do, so why shouldn't I? I will sell the house and business, and the money shall be my dowry. May I bring Hannah with me?"

"By all means bring Hannah. You would miss her."

"Yes. For a long time she has been almost my only friend."

"You will find another in my sister."

"She will not resent me?"

Noah smiled and shook his head.

"She loves you already, and she has reason. Now she can marry her cloth merchant."

This amused Deborah, and she wanted to hear the complete story of Sarah and the cloth merchant, which was of course impossible because Noah's knowledge of the matter was confined to the public facts.

"But do not despair over my ignorance," he told her. "She herself will tell you all that you might wish to hear. Sarah, who I think has been lonely, will confide many things to a sister that she would not tell her brother."

They spoke of other matters. He described, as best he could, his house in Sepphoris. He tried not to conceal its deficiencies, which suddenly, although he had never been aware of them before, appeared to be many.

However, she seemed to think it would do quite well.

"And it is made of stone?"

"Yes."

"Good. Stone is cooler. And Hannah will appreciate the fountain in the square. Here it is such a distance to the well. It sounds like a very convenient house."

"There is no garden," he answered, feeling suddenly that he had been overpraising it. "There is only an alleyway behind, across from which is my workshop and forge. And there is no balcony. The houses are jammed up against each other."

"I can live without a balcony. I can even live without a garden. I have never liked this house. The balcony and garden are merely places to which I can escape from it."

"Still, it is pleasant to feel the sun on one's face. We can take walks outside the city walls. The main gate is only a few minutes from my door, and the countryside is quite beautiful."

He smiled at her, wondering why she suddenly seemed pensive.

"Joshua must be told," she said quietly, almost gravely.

"I will speak to him this afternoon. I will bring him to dinner, with your permission. By the way, am *I* invited to dinner?"

Deborah seemed not to have heard.

"Do you think he will approve?" she asked. There was real anxiety in her voice.

"Why shouldn't he approve?"

21

It was perhaps two hours past noon when Noah left Deborah's house. He had promised her that his first task would be to find Joshua and tell him.

At that hour Capernaum was almost deserted of men. At sunset, when the fishing boats returned, it would fill up again, but for the moment the only person who might know about Joshua's whereabouts was Levi, the former tax collector, who now did penance in Deborah's warehouse, a building near the water.

Except for Simon, Noah had never exchanged more than a few words with any of Joshua's disciples, but he had always suspected that Levi was a bit mad, an impression he did not now find it necessary to revise.

"Have you repented?" Levi asked him, forgoing the customary introductions. "Have you truly repented? I have repented and Joshua has said that God forgives me. Yet the weight of my sins is heavy upon me. Do you think it is always thus?"

"I think the hardest thing is to forgive oneself. Do you know where I might find Joshua at this hour?"

"Yes, the hardest thing is to forgive oneself. Perhaps that is what it means to repent—not to forgive oneself but to understand truly how much one has offended God. Even after forgiveness, there is the punishment of remorse."

Levi was a small, frightened man whose beard looked as if some animal had clawed out strips of it. His hands fluttered about, giving the impression that he wanted to touch you but did not quite dare.

"Remorse is like poison," Noah agreed, "but if you are forgiven you are allowed to take comfort in that. Where can I find Joshua?"

"Do you wish to confess your sins to him?"

"No. I merely wish to speak to him, on family business. I am his cousin."

"Oh yes. I remember you now. He would be at his prayers at this hour. He talks to God. What a gift, to be able to talk to God!"

"Yes, I agree. It is remarkable. Where does he go to pray?"

There was a grove of trees about two miles north of Capernaum. It was too far to go for wood and, from the perspective of the villagers, it had no other attractions. Thus it was the perfect place for one who wished to be alone with his thoughts—or with God.

It was here that Levi directed him, and it was here that Noah found Joshua, sitting on the trunk of a tree that had somehow become uprooted in the sandy soil. His hands were clasped in his lap. He looked stricken.

He raised his eyes and beheld his cousin, without apparent surprise.

"Is something troubling you?" Noah asked, sitting down beside him.

"What you said yesterday, about my father. I don't know what to do."

"Have you prayed? I was told you come here to pray."

"I have prayed. God is silent."

"So, which afflicts you, that God is silent or that your father is dying?"

"Both." Joshua shook his head. "I do not understand why God will not direct me."

"Perhaps because He already has."

"Do not mock me."

It was now Noah's turn to shake his head.

"God has commanded us, 'Honor thy father and mother.' This we were taught in childhood. Have you forgotten?"

"No."

"Then you know what is God's will, and it is no wonder that He is silent. Return with me to Nazareth and see your father. If Grandfather is right, you may not have another chance."

"Father and I never got along. If I go back, we will only quarrel."

"Nevertheless, he loves you. His eyes hunger for the sight of you. And he is your father."

For a long moment Joshua was silent. Finally he rubbed his face with his hands, as if driving away sleep.

"All right. When you leave I will go with you. How long will that be?"

"After the Sabbath."

"The Sabbath is four days from now. Why so long? You have business in Capernaum?"

"Yes."

"I can guess what it is. So tell me—have you seen Deborah yet today?"

Noah turned to look at his cousin and smiled. "Has it been as obvious as that?"

"It was obvious last night. The way you avoided each other's eyes, I thought at first you had had some sort of quarrel. You were better at the deception than she. When she finally did look at you, from the expression on her face she seemed likely to crawl into your lap right then. Are you going to marry her?"

"Yes. We agreed this morning. She sent me to tell you."

"That was considerate of her."

"You don't seem pleased."

"I am merely a little disappointed."

Joshua stood up and helped Noah up from the tree trunk. They walked in silence out to the edge of the grove, from which one could see the water stretching far enough that the shore opposite was hidden.

"It is so near. It is so very near, and she can only think of being married."

"What is so near?" Noah asked, struggling to keep the irritation out of his voice.

"God's kingdom." Joshua turned to him and smiled, as if embarrassed. But he was not embarrassed. "He is sending His messenger to be judge of the world, of the living and the dead. Then there will be no evil, no sin, no death, no unhappiness. God's law will rule to the ends of the earth. The time is so short. The hour is nearly upon us."

"Why do you believe this?"

"What?"

"It is a simple question. God has visited worse times upon us."

Noah stood, not quite facing his cousin, his gaze focused on the line where sky and sea met, the prey of emotions he did not wish to speak of.

"Only consider," Noah continued, his voice almost toneless. "The Jews have been through captivity and exile. We have endured worse rulers than Antipas—his father, for instance. The Romans are less dreadful than were the Babylonians. This is not so terrible an age, so why does God choose this moment?"

"Because it must end sometime."

"You have not answered my question. Why *now*?"

"I don't know." Joshua shook his head. He seemed genuinely perplexed. "I only know that it is so."

"How do you know?"

"Because He tells me."

Noah realized that they had come to a dead end and, as he thought of Deborah and what she might feel listening to this, he felt her slipping away from him. Perhaps desperation made him cruel.

"Two months ago, when I saw you last, you spoke then of God's kingdom as if it might arrive before dinner. Since then the days have rolled by without the heavens parting to show the face of your son of man. Will it happen today? This month? Before the Passover? Within your lifetime? Do you know?"

For the first time, something like doubt showed itself in Joshua's face.

"I know only that it *will* come," he answered at last. "The time and the place are known only to the Father."

"And therefore it is vanity and presumption to believe that mere men can understand the mind of God."

"I have never claimed to understand His mind. I know only what He tells me."

"But He has not told you when."

"No."

"Then *I* will tell you something, Joshua." Noah touched him on the arm and they began to walk down toward the beach. "If God's kingdom should come and He should allow me to live in it, and if, as you say, life there would be everlasting, then I would choose to live in your renewed Eden with Deborah and with no other. For without her there could be no happiness, even in a perfect world."

"Then you should marry her. Does she feel the same?"

"How could she help it? Am I not handsome, charming, and clever—not to mention tall?"

This allowed Joshua to laugh, and he swung his arm playfully over Noah's head, the top of which barely reached his shoulder.

It was agreed between them that Joshua would come to dinner and that he would give his blessing to the proposed marriage. Joshua displayed no reluctance. He seemed amused by the whole business. Yet, when the appointed hour arrived, Joshua did not.

They waited dinner. The time passed.

"He is angry with us," Deborah said at last. "I knew it would be so. He thinks we should put away all thoughts of happiness in this sinful world."

"He does think that, but he is not angry."

"Then why has he stayed away?"

The instant she phrased question, Noah was sure he knew the answer. It was not something he felt he could explain to Deborah—not because she would not understand, but because she would.

"I will go find him," he said.

"Will you bring him back?"

"No."

"How will you find him? He could be anywhere."

"It will not be hard. I think he wants to be found."

There was a large jar of wine resting on a side table. The seal had not yet been broken. Noah picked it up.

"Have no fear," he said, with a joyless smile. "He will drink to our happiness."

A full moon filled the streets with light, and Noah had not far to go. Only to the shore.

In his experience there was nowhere on earth as deserted as a seacoast at night. It was the same at Capernaum as at Sidon and Caesarea, where the docks grew ghostly quiet after sunset. Those who make their livings by the water withdraw from it as from a thing accursed.

On the beach the fishing craft were overturned and, in the harsh moonlight, looked as if they had been abandoned forever. There was no one about—except, of course, God's messenger to Galilee, the prophet Joshua, who was sitting disconsolately on the sand, with his back resting against the hull of a boat.

"You didn't come," Noah announced, taking his place beside him, "so I thought I would bring the celebration to you."

"Go away. Leave me alone."

Noah ignored him and broke the seal on the wine jar. He took a sip himself, decided it was not entirely contemptible, and offered the jar to Joshua, who took it without apparent reluctance. He drank in silence for several minutes.

"Is Deborah angry with me?" Joshua asked finally.

It was, in some ways, an interesting question.

"You have known her longer than I have. Have you ever seen her angry?"

"No. Somehow I cannot imagine her angry."

"Neither can I." Noah shrugged and took back the wine jar. "No, she is not angry. She thinks you must be angry with her. I assured her that was not the case, but she remained unconvinced."

"I am sorry for that."

"You should be."

"Are *you* angry?"

"A little. But not enough to make a difference."

As if to demonstrate this, he gave Joshua back the wine jar.

For a long moment Joshua sat with the jar resting on his knee. He seemed lost in contemplation.

"Drink," Noah told him, almost harshly. "Either drink or give it back."

"Do you want to make me drunk?"

"Yes."

"Why?"

"Because sometimes that is the best use one can make of wine. That is one reason why God in His mercy taught us how to make it."

"When the time arrived, I simply could not bring myself to enter Deborah's house and smile on her happiness." He took a swallow and then another. "Do you understand?"

"Yes, I do. It brings back the past—for me as well."

Joshua nodded and handed him the jar.

"Do you remember, the night after we buried Rachel, how you and I went up on the roof of Uncle Benjamin's house and drank ourselves into oblivion?"

"Yes. We woke up the next morning with the sun in our faces."

"I think you saved my life that night." He put a hand on Noah's arm. "I don't know what my despair would have brought me to if you hadn't been there."

"I understood how you felt. My own wife had been dead less than a month."

"Did you love her?"

Noah took a swallow of wine, as if to help him clarify his response.

"Yes. I loved her. But not, I think, as you loved Rachel. I don't think I am capable of such intensity of feeling, and I am thankful for it."

"Do you still think of her?"

"Yes. Sometimes, against my will. I have learned that is a pot best left unstirred."

"I think of Rachel all the time."

Noah shrugged, although in the gathering darkness the gesture was more likely felt than seen.

"You should let her go," he said. "It is not possible or even desirable to forget, but one should recognize the will of God. The dead have left us."

"And yet she has never left me." Joshua tilted his head back in a way that suggested he was close to weeping. "I feel her presence. There are moments when she seems so near that I imagine I have but to glance around to see her smiling at me."

Noah handed him back the jar, since it was clear he had need of it, but Joshua did not drink. The jar rested on the sand beside him.

You poor fool, Noah thought, but did not say. It would have been a thousand times better if they could both have gotten fuddled with wine, but it was not going to happen.

And perhaps there was no escape, not even in drunkenness. Joshua, it seemed, was one of those who could not accept the permanence of misfortune. He had no gift for resignation.

"Even in God's kingdom she will not be my wife again," Joshua announced suddenly. "Those who have passed through the grave will be purified of desire. Yet I do not regret this. She will still be herself. She will still be Rachel. I will see her again, and that will be enough."

"God's kingdom," Noah murmured, hardly even intending to be heard. Yes, of course. In a world full of death and injustice, where a Herod ruled and Rachel lay rotting in the earth, how could someone like Joshua help but believe that God would come to set everything right?

Noah picked up the wine jar and took a long swallow. The wind from the sea was growing cold.

22

Caleb sensed his danger the moment he received the Lord Eleazar's note. The First Minister was still in Tiberias—he had been there five days, which for him was an unusually long visit—and now Caleb's presence was requested: "The Tetrarch wishes you to attend him," was all the note said. It had been brought by mounted courier and was not even signed, but Caleb recognized the long, precise, faintly slanting hand.

There was nothing to do except to go. Within half an hour Caleb was on his horse, with an escort of only two soldiers, and he reached the gates of Tiberias a full hour before sundown.

However, sundown brought the Sabbath, during which nothing could be done.

Caleb was accorded the use of a small house near the palace, and he went there now to wash and change. He was surprised to find his wife waiting there for him.

"Were you told I was coming?" he asked, experiencing a small thrill of anticipation. Michal was a beautiful woman, a fact which always impressed him anew whenever he saw her.

"No. I have been turned away."

"What?"

"I have been banished from the Lady Herodias's presence," she announced, with suitable emphasis, as if she had been accused of jesting.

"Why?"

She turned her gaze aside for a moment, seemingly gathering the strength to cope with such stupidity.

"No reason was given," she said finally. "*I* was not at fault." And then, as an afterthought, "Why are you here?"

"I was summoned."

Michal covered her mouth with her hand and then slowly shook her head. But the conclusion was too obvious to deny.

"Then you have fallen from favor."

Immediately, and without another word, she left him. There was a room in the house that she sometimes used when she wished to be alone. Caleb knew better than to follow her there.

So he was alone, with the Sabbath, that empty day, looming before him.

Caleb did not consider himself an impious man, so he felt uncomfortable when his wife did not appear for the lighting of the Sabbath candles. A servant woman performed that office, and Caleb recited the prayer, which he knew so well that the words almost spoke themselves.

"Blessed art Thou, O Lord our God, King of the Universe . . ."

The words were just collections of syllables, somehow pleasing to God. He had long since ceased to reflect on their meaning.

As he recited, his mind was clear. He knew Michal was right. He had fallen from favor. How Eleazar had achieved it, he had no inkling.

"Who has sanctified us with His commandments . . ."

He counted his alternatives. They did not make an impressive list.

"And commanded us to light the Sabbath candles."

It was over, at last. A little ceremony he had performed hundreds of times, which lasted less than a minute, yet which, this Sabbath evening, had seemed to stretch on forever.

He was glad when he could be alone. He went to his bedroom, where the servants had already set out wine and bread for him. He was not hungry, but he drank the wine, searching for a means to dull the edge of his fear.

He lay down on the bed, thinking that somehow, sometime, sleep would come. He needed to sleep, but even this was denied him.

In the small hours of the morning, his wife came to him. She carried a candle, which softened her face, and she was wearing her nightdress. Probably she hadn't been able to sleep either.

"What will you do?" she asked, sitting on the edge of the bed.

"What can I do?" He even laughed—he was beginning to regard his situation as, in certain lights, amusing. "I will see what the Tetrarch wants of me."

"You could run."

"Where? And if I did, what would they do to *you*? I can't run."

She let her hand rest on his arm, and it occurred to him that perhaps that was what she had come to find out, whether he would simply disappear and leave her to the mercy of his enemies.

Apparently he had made the right answer, because she crawled into bed beside him.

Suddenly he was stiff with desire. Was this to be the seal on his pledge? He would make love to her and thus commit himself to face the Tetrarch's wrath? It seemed likely.

She had no doubt been kept awake, wondering how best to extricate herself from her husband's downfall, and this was what she had settled on.

Did it matter? He considered the question for an instant and then decided that no, it didn't.

It was a hope which years of experience could never quite extinguish, that somehow, someday, Michal would realize how much he loved her and feel some small regret at what she had wasted. Perhaps it could only happen after he was dead, but even that was something to hope for. He would stay now, and it was likely the Tetrarch would have him put to death, and then . . .

But no. Love was folly. Love was a trap from which there was no escape. Fool that he was, he didn't even want to escape.

He turned on his side and she began to shift herself, to crawl beneath him. When he went into her she let out a long, ragged breath. As he moved to his climax she began to moan and to claw at him. Probably it was all pretense. Probably she felt nothing. It didn't matter.

When it was over they lay together. She turned to him and let her small, fragile hand rest on his thigh. It was a delicious sensation.

And then he slept through until dawn.

He would never be able to remember how he got through that long Sabbath. After he had dressed and washed, and leaving Michal still asleep, he went down to the room he used as an office. All through the day he did not eat and only drank water.

When would the Tetrarch summon him, and what would he say? The first was difficult to answer and the second impossible. The one certainty was that the Tetrarch would try, was already trying, to break down his courage, and this was the one victory it was crucial to deny him. Antipas despised fear—probably because he was so consumed with it himself. Thus the one necessity was to hold himself together.

He felt fortunate, then, that the summons came about an hour after the Ceremony of the Four Blessings, which ended the Sabbath.

The Tetrarch, he was told, was in his garden, enjoying the night air, and wondered if the Lord Caleb would care to join him.

It turned out to be a short interview, and anticlimactic.

"Well, Caleb, my boy, I know you only meant to protect me, and I love you for your zeal, but this business with the Baptist and his followers has become dangerous. Eleazar says we need an interval of calm, and of course he's right. He's usually right. So I want you to stop the raids and let everyone go. I'm going to issue a general amnesty to celebrate the Lady Herodias's birthday—which won't be for a few months yet, but I'll issue the amnesty tomorrow—and all those fellows you have locked up can crawl back to their homes.

"Beyond this, I want you to remember that you take your orders from the First Minister. You are his servant as well as mine. You are to take no major steps without his approval. He'll have specific instructions for you when you get back to Sepphoris.

"Now, you keep your head down for a while and this wind will blow itself out. You've just been a little too full of yourself is all, but you're a good boy.

"Now go home and kiss your wife for me. You are dismissed."

As he walked away, as he made his way through the corridors and reception halls, Caleb could hardly keep his legs under him. He kept expecting soldiers to appear out of nowhere and seize him.

He had found Antipas's manner toward him unnerving. The loving father reproves his son for making too much noise.

Except that Caleb knew how these games were played. He had heard of men who had left the Tetrarch's presence glowing from his praise and then had found themselves under arrest before they reached the main gate.

So it was with a sense of only conditional relief that he at last stood in front of his own front door, waiting for a servant to open it.

Instead, it was Michal.

"What happened?" she asked, clinging to the door frame as if she might otherwise collapse.

"I am here," he answered with a shrug. "If by tomorrow morning I haven't been arrested, then we will go back to Sepphoris. If I am not arrested on the way, I will go back to work. How is it that you answered the door?"

"The servants have fled. As soon as the Sabbath was over, they vanished. I wonder how they could have known."

"The servants always know."

"Yes. I suppose so."

Suddenly Caleb felt immensely weary. He no longer cared what happened to him, provided he could have a few hours of sleep.

"What did the Tetrarch say?"

Caleb made a vague, dismissive gesture with his left hand. "I have been chastised for being too zealous. I have been a naughty boy, but he loves me."

"Then you are safe?"

"No."

He found his bed and slept soundly for about four hours. Then, suddenly, he was stark awake. Had some noise alerted him? He listened. There was nothing. Gradually he began to relax. Only when his fear had lost its edge did he notice that he was alone.

Yes, of course. She had nothing more to gain from him, and she wouldn't care to be in the room if the guards came. It was safer to sleep somewhere else.

He sat up in his bed, thinking about Michal's shortcomings as a wife. It made a pleasant diversion from thinking about how close he had come to the abyss.

Michal was a beautiful woman, and her manner, when it suited her, was playfully seductive. When it did not suit her, she had the disposition of a shrew. Yet even when she plagued him, Caleb always felt a strong desire for her.

He had not known her long before he was prepared to sacrifice everything to possess her, and that was very nearly the way it had worked out.

In a sense, it was well they had had to leave Jerusalem. If one is to grow disillusioned with one's wife, it is perhaps better that this process take place among strangers. Caleb found it painful enough to imagine his friends' amusement at his plight—probably most of them had known he was making a catastrophic mistake—but it would have been unbearable to discover Michal's true nature and to see each step in that gradual revelation mirrored in the knowing smiles of every casual acquaintance. In Sepphoris, a week's journey from Jerusalem, he could comfort himself with the thought that, if his wife was empty, childish, selfish, and unbearably ill natured, at least he was aware of the fact before it became common knowledge.

Still, she was not always dreadful. When they were back in Sepphoris, and she had settled down a little, she would begin to feel the need to reaffirm her power over him, and for a week or so their bed would be a very warm and comfortable place.

Then, her confidence returned, she would find it less and less necessary to make herself agreeable and, as he witnessed the change, Caleb would experience first disappointment, then contempt for his own self-delusion, then a peculiar mingling of lust and shame that he could only believe was God's special curse on him.

Michal disliked Sepphoris, which she considered a hopeless village, and probably she would begin sending pleading little notes to the Lady Herodias, hoping to be allowed to return to Tiberias. Otherwise, she might travel to Jerusalem to visit her family.

Or, at least, that would be the pretext. Her father was dead and her mother was a tiresome woman whose principal interest in life was surviving as many of her acquaintances as possible. She had a sister, who disapproved of her and whom therefore she regarded as a bore, and her brother . . . Well, her brother was one of those invisible young men whose name no one could ever seem to remember.

It had, of course, occurred to Caleb to wonder if his wife might not have a lover in Tiberias—someone to lavish money on her and satisfy her flesh and give her someone to torment. A lover might be prepared to meet her in Jerusalem. Caleb could arrange to have her watched, even in Jerusalem, and the penalty for adultery was stoning. It was an agreeable thought.

But then, of course, the whole world would know and he would look a fool. A man whose business is creating fear cannot afford to look a fool.

And, worse, he would lose her.

An hour before dawn he fell asleep again.

In the morning, after breakfast, Caleb went to the garrison and arranged for an escort and a wagon for his wife. It was reassuring to see that he still had the power to do such things.

The journey back to Sepphoris was uneventful. Caleb rode with the soldiers, keeping away from his wife, who would only complain to him about the dust.

When they arrived, his servants—who, unlike those in Tiberias, had not run away—prepared them dinner, after which Caleb went up to the roof to sit in the twilight and enjoy the view.

But this evening the view did not work its customary magic. He hardly noticed it. His mind, like the gaze of a circling hawk, was fixed on a single object.

It appeared that he had survived this particular crisis. Antipas did not mean to bring him down—not yet—but this reprieve was only temporary because, whatever the Tetrarch might intend, the Lord Eleazar meant, in the end, to destroy him.

Tomorrow, when he called upon Eleazar, Caleb would play the repentant servant. And Eleazar, who certainly understood his own part in this little drama, would sternly admonish him and then put him to work on a series of trivial assignments. Caleb's implied task would then be to earn his way back into the First Minister's confidence.

All of which was, of course, perfectly meaningless. Both men knew there would be neither mercy nor forgiveness. Each would be bent on ruining the other as the only possible means of insuring his own survival.

Bad news traveled faster than any horseman, and by now every petty official in Sepphoris would have heard that the Lord Caleb was out of favor. How many of those who worked under him had already made their way to Eleazar, eager to pledge their loyalty? Thus, when Caleb returned to his desk, he would find himself surrounded by spies.

He had to find a way out.

23

When the sun had at last set, and he came down from the roof, Caleb discovered that a messenger had left a note. It was from the Lord Eleazar, inviting him to breakfast the next morning. The note was kindly phrased. It was the sort of note one might send to an intimate friend who had recently suffered a bereavement and needed cheering.

So, when the sun rose, Caleb went to the Lord Eleazar's house and was shown into the garden, where he found the First Minister. They made a meal of figs and wine served in little cups of solid gold.

Eleazar was never brutal in his speech, but he was also not a man to waste time on pleasantries. The interesting thing was his subtlety. He made no reference to Caleb's interview with the Tetrarch but instead talked to him as to a trusted, confidential servant.

"We need an interval of calm," he said, his attention apparently absorbed in the task of cutting open a fig with an exquisite little silver knife. "The Tetrarch has issued a general pardon, which should help to quiet things. He needs continuing access to loans and, even more, he needs the support of Rome, which is contingent upon the tribute being paid on time and the absence of any trouble that might require them to intervene—we all prefer that their legions remain in Syria. This business with the Baptist and his followers, whatever its original merits, upsets the merchants, which worries the moneylenders, which in turn encourages the Romans to think dark thoughts. It is time for all the dogs to curl up and go back to sleep."

He looked up and smiled. He was not finding fault, but explaining policy.

"You will release our prisoners—all of them, no matter what their offenses—and you will arrange for them to be returned to their homes. It might even be a good idea to distribute a little silver. The emphasis must be on the Tetrarch's mercy."

"It shall be as you direct, Lord."

"I knew you would understand."

Eleazar's gaze and his smile never wavered. The only trace of irony was in the words themselves.

"It is of course in the nature of things that there will be other criminal prosecutions," the First Minister continued. "Such is the depravity of men. I have, however, prepared a list of names, which I will send to your office later in the day. Without the written consent of the Tetrarch, no one whose name appears on that list is to be touched."

He made a small, despairing gesture with his left hand, as if to suggest that we must all learn to submit ourselves to the caprice of princes.

"I have prepared a list." Even before it reached his desk—and he did not have to wait long—Caleb had arrived at certain conclusions about its contents. First, since the list was Eleazar's, he was protecting his friends. Second, he now had sufficient authority with the Tetrarch to persuade him to endorse the list.

The question was, how had he suddenly acquired such power? The answer, of course, somehow involved the Romans. *"The Romans think dark thoughts."* How did Eleazar know what the Romans were thinking?

The list was brought to him a little before noon. The first name was Joshua bar Joseph, carpenter, formerly of the village of Nazareth, which was, perhaps, expected. But the second was Noah bar Barachel, ironsmith, resident of Sepphoris.

The Lord Eleazar threw a wide net. Caleb would have assumed that the First Minister had never even heard of Noah bar Barachel, and now he was to be regarded as untouchable. Which meant that Eleazar regarded him as an asset. *His* asset.

Noah had disappeared. He had left Sepphoris after his encounter with Matthias, had briefly surfaced in a village named Capernaum, and then had vanished.

And now Eleazar was protecting him. Why? What made Noah bar Barachel, ironsmith, resident of Sepphoris, so valuable?

"The Romans think dark thoughts."

Had Noah somehow been the source of Eleazar's information about the Romans' dark thoughts? It seemed preposterous.

And yet . . .

"This business upsets the merchants, which worries the moneylenders. . . ." Noah moved comfortably in that world. He was a craftsman whose goods were sold far beyond Galilee.

Those damned pliers—*that* was how Eleazar had found him!

Suddenly Caleb felt very stupid and very afraid.

He decided he would do no work today—in any case, there seemed no work to do. He would go to the baths and see if the steam couldn't clear his head.

The public baths were comfortable and luxurious without being spectacular. The Tetrarch had built them in emulation of the Great Herod's in Caesarea, but on a far smaller scale because, although just as despotic as his father, Antipas was not as rich. One could walk around the outside of the building in about the time it took to recite one of the shorter Psalms, and many of the walls were plaster painted to look like marble. The pools, however, were marble, as were the walls of the steam rooms and—most blessed of all—the benches. It was wonderfully soothing to lie there on that cool, smooth Parian, wrapped in linen, sweating like a chariot horse.

The baths were also less crowded than those in Caesarea. The Greeks and Romans, of whom there were very few in Sepphoris, regarded baths as indispensable to civilized life, but they were a custom the Jews had been slow to adopt. Every house of any size in the city had a stone immersion pool, but these were for ritual purification rather than pleasure, and the Jews as a whole resisted foreign ways. Antipas had a taste for all things Greek, and those of and around his court emulated him, but the general population, even those who could easily afford the twenty *prutot* admission price, tended to stay away.

From his youth, Caleb had had many Greek friends. He had even, sometimes, dined in their homes, which of course was forbidden. Well, he had not died of it. He had always admired the Greeks, who had spread their culture and language over half the known world—and that, the better half. Even Jews, when they came on pilgrimage from outside Palestine, tended to speak Greek. They read Greek philosophy and literature and bought Greek art for their homes. They worshipped the God of the Jews, but they lived in a wider world, and he envied them.

Caleb liked to begin his time at the baths by washing himself in warm water, then taking a sudden plunge into the cold pool, then, and finally, teeth chattering, hunched up in his towels like Methuselah staggering toward death, making his way into one of the steam rooms. Those first few moments, as he breathed in the warm, thick air and felt himself begin to sweat, were a deliverance, a return to Eden. The sense of well-being was so profound that his mind simply emptied.

Not to think, that was the great blessing.

Except today the blessing was withheld. Lying there, the sweat welling in his eyes, he could not escape the memory of this morning's interview.

"We need an interval of calm."

Noah, the artisan, the petty tradesman with his saw blades displayed upon the walls and his pots of nails, had had the last word. His cousin, Joshua bar Joseph, disciple of an executed criminal, was now to be regarded as a dreamer and a harmless crank, preaching love and forgiveness to peasant women.

So the preacher of sedition becomes the messenger of God's forgiveness. Noah becomes a spy for the First Minister, and all is peace and light. The last word.

"Caleb—why do I always find you here?" he heard someone say, in Greek.

Caleb wiped his eyes and saw, sitting on the bench opposite him, a corpulent, middle-aged man with his thinning hair wet from the plunge pool and plastered to his forehead like fangs, as if his face were peering out from the jaws of some huge serpent. He was actually smiling, seemingly glad to have discovered an acquaintance.

But, then, why shouldn't he be? He was the sort who need fear no one.

"Kephalos. I thought you were in Alexandria."

A slave brought in a tray with a stone bottle of ice water and two cups. Kephalos filled them both and handed one to Caleb, who sat up to accept it.

"I was, but the Tetrarch is short of money again. I am on my way to Tiberias to see his chief steward."

He raised his cup in salute and smiled once more, as if sharing a jest with a friend. *Yes, of course,* he seemed to be implying, *when is the Tetrarch not short of money?*

This, naturally, was the reason he was not afraid. Not of Caleb, not of the Lord Eleazar, not even of the Tetrarch. Kephalos was indispensable. Nor was he subject to arrest or confiscation, being protected by a network of highly placed friends, all of whom owed him money. And, in any case, no one would gain by his removal. Although immensely rich himself, he never loaned out from his own treasury but preferred to broker loans for certain interests in Egypt, who were themselves protected, it was rumored, by members of the imperial family.

"Have you come from Caesarea?" Caleb inquired, to deflect the conversation from the Tetrarch's finances, which was never a safe subject.

"Yes. One must put in an appearance from time to time." He made a rueful face, for, as everyone knew, his wife was a harridan whom, because her family was influential, it would have been inconvenient to divorce. She lived in Caesarea. "Whenever I am there it occurs to me that the city has grown more brutish. In my youth, when Archelaus still ruled, I thought it charming, but with the prefect there it is full of Romans—a coarse lot."

"You Greeks are such snobs," Caleb said, laughing in spite of himself.

"Mark my words, you don't know how well you have it. Antipas may not be a perfect ruler, but at least he is one of your own. The Judeans were fools to petition Caesar to remove Archelaus."

"I was a child then, but I have always heard that Archelaus was worse than his father."

Kephalos threw up his hands in a despairing gesture. "No one could be worse than Great Herod. There were disturbances in the Temple—when are there not disturbances in the Temple?—and perhaps Archelaus went a little far in putting them down. But is it better now? This new prefect, this Pilatus, just look at the trouble he has caused already. Wait until there is some new crisis in Jerusalem and he will crucify so many that they will run out of wood."

He sighed, perhaps a trifle theatrically, and poured himself another cup of ice water, which seemed to restore him to a more philosophical temper.

"Believe me," he said finally, "it is a curse to live under the Romans."

An idea was beginning to form in Caleb's mind, so, characteristically, he tried to deflect the conversation in some other direction.

"The whole world lives under the Romans," he said casually, wishing suddenly he were alone.

"This is true, but at least here in Sepphoris one does not have them constantly breathing in one's face. Why else do you imagine I spend so much time here?"

"I thought it was to escape the Greeks."

This made Kephalos laugh.

After another cold plunge to wake him up, Caleb dressed and went home. It was late afternoon, so he told a servant to bring him some wine and fruit up on the roof, where he could be alone with his thoughts.

His wife, praise be to God, was out of the house.

This time the view from his roof was a refreshment to the spirit. He could ignore the city and see the valley below, green, stirring with every breath of wind. And through the valley, no more than a silver thread, slowly curving east until it disappeared behind a range of hills, the road to Judea. The road he had followed, coming into Galilee and his long exile.

In the extreme distance, near the summit of one of the hills, he could see a man working. He knew, rather than saw, that the man was tending vines. The slopes were steep, and little else but grapes would grow there, so they were covered with terraces. The man was moving sideways, making his way along a ledge, and from time to time he would reach up with both arms, the left hand a little above the right, which meant that he was probably trimming away dead shoots.

The man tending the vines was doubtless a peasant living in some village beyond the crest of the hills. The chances were he had not been in Sepphoris above three times in his life, and he probably mistrusted city people. The cities belonged to the wealthy and were full of corruption—that would be his opinion. He had probably thought well of the Baptist and regarded Antipas with sullen hostility. This man, Caleb understood, was his natural enemy.

The peasants were capable of anything. They might come into the city for some holiday and begin to riot, simply because some one or another of their heroes had been arrested. Sometimes the Tetrarch's officials went into their villages and were never heard from again.

Caleb did not worry about the city dwellers. There was no danger from the wealthy, or even from the small traders. Men were easily controlled, provided they had something to lose, but the peasants were another matter.

It had become Caleb's destiny to protect the Tetrarch from those who wished him harm. Most of his subjects wished him harm.

But now it had been decided that all was to be love and forgiveness. The Tetrarch had no enemies.

So what need had he of a protector?

To be unnecessary was to be in a dangerous position. Servants who were unnecessary had a way of disappearing.

Caleb's problem was how to demonstrate to the Tetrarch that the danger was real, that men like Joshua bar Joseph constituted the natural opposition to his reign.

The Lord Eleazar, he decided, might be right. It would not do to allow the Tetrarch's unpopularity to reach intolerable levels. Arresting Joshua bar Joseph might prove dangerous, even if he had no following.

Nevertheless, it was necessary that he be arrested.

However, if it could be arranged that he was arrested outside of Galilee and executed by the Romans . . .

The Romans were hated, but they were feared even more. The Romans could execute a hundred religious fanatics and it would hardly be noticed.

And they would destroy anyone they saw as a threat to their power, so certainly they would execute Joshua bar Joseph. It was merely a question of putting him within reach of the lion's paw.

Caleb thought he might have the means close at hand.

24

Jerusalem.

Eleazar could not remember the first time his parents had brought him here, but it always inspired in him the same sense of awe. God filled the universe. He was everywhere. But He was more here, in this city, than anywhere on earth.

Eleazar returned to Jerusalem five or six times a year, for the festivals and to take his turn performing the duties of the priesthood. He maintained a house here, and he had purchased a tomb just outside the city walls. He did not believe in any life after death, but still it gave him a certain comfort to know that when his time came he would lay down his bones here.

He sometimes felt that he was permitted to be a different person in Jerusalem, that the politician was an identity he left behind in Galilee, that here he was allowed to be merely God's servant. He understood that this was an illusion, but a part of him believed it nonetheless.

So it was with a lightness of heart that he passed under the great arch of the western gate. He had come up to fulfill his twice-yearly obligation as a priest by serving his turn in the Temple. For two weeks he would work in twelve-hour shifts, offering sacrifice at the altar of God. But he had arrived a week ahead and planned to remain a week after. At least for the time being, Galilee was calm, and he had needed to get away.

He arrived at his house just half an hour before the beginning of the Sabbath and was present to recite the prayer while the Sabbath candles were lit. Afterwards, and until it was time for bed, he read from a collection of the Psalms of David.

The next morning he walked to the Temple and was purified. He spent the rest of the day, until sundown, in a close study of Isaiah.

The Sabbath over, Eleazar went to see his son. While pursuing his studies, Zadok lived with his aunt—his late mother's sister—and her husband, Micah, with whom Eleazar had been friends since childhood. Micah promptly invited Eleazar to dinner.

Micah was a plump, convivial soul and deserved to be happy, and his choice of a wife indicated that he had the better judgment in such matters. Elisheba was a pleasant woman, very different from her younger sister, and Eleazar had often thought that his own life might have been happier had he married her instead. He had been misled by a certain teasing quality in Rebekah, imagining it to indicate a sweet nature. Perhaps he had more than imagined it. Perhaps it had even been there, disguised as flirtatiousness. But he had not been the husband to draw it out.

Perhaps, then, the blame was his, and it wouldn't have mattered which sister he had married. In either case, the marriage had been a misery for them both.

Micah and Elisheba had two daughters, ages ten and twelve and both fancying themselves in love with Zadok. After dinner Elisheba and the girls disappeared and the men went up to the roof to enjoy the cool darkness of a Jerusalem night and to drink wine.

The wine was excellent and was served in heavy silver cups, for Micah was a man of substance who owned several valuable farms in Judea and Samaria.

"At least they can't take this away from us," Micah said, setting his oil lamp down on a small, circular table. "Except during the festivals, you could almost imagine you were living in the City of David."

It was a commonplace enough remark, hardly more than a sort of verbal clearing of one's throat, and requiring no response, but Zadok, who was full of student idealism—or perhaps needed to assert his claim to be taken seriously—nevertheless offered one.

"You mean you don't have to see the Roman soldiers strolling along the tops of the Temple walls?" He smiled and took a sip of his wine.

"I don't know why they bother to come. Their presence undoubtedly provokes more trouble than it discourages."

His uncle laughed, probably because he was the host.

"I believe you," he said, looking off into the darkness. "A mob is always fearless—until the Romans come down from the walls."

Zadok did not seem entirely satisfied with this.

"Without the Romans, the people would be guided by the priests, who are, after all, their natural leaders." He took another sip of his wine, which in the darkness appeared almost black. "Under the Persians the high priest ruled, and there was peace."

"But today he is no more than a functionary," Eleazar said without emphasis, only putting his hand on his son's arm. "The Roman prefect can dismiss him with a word—as Old Herod could and did when he was ruler here. The prefect even keeps the high priest's regalia under lock and key, only allowing him to wear it during the festivals. The people see this, and draw the inevitable conclusions."

"And what conclusions would those be?" Micah asked, making it sound like a challenge.

"That the priesthood serves the Romans and not them. That we have forfeited our right to be regarded as their 'natural leaders,' as my son put it."

Eleazar smiled faintly and shook his head.

"It was a necessary compromise," he went on. "But it was still a compromise. And now they look to those who refuse to compromise."

"Like this John, whom they called the Baptist." Micah uttered a grunt of contempt. "A fanatic who dressed in animal skins and ate locusts. Let us thank the One True God there are not many like him."

"There are more than you would imagine."

Eleazar leaned forward, resting his elbows on his knees. Suddenly he felt old and worn out. He began to reach for his wine cup but then thought better of it. Wine was not the remedy he needed.

What he needed was to tell the story.

"I met one recently," he said at last. "A tradesman—an ironsmith to be precise. He failed to provide properly incriminating evidence against a kinsman and was beaten for it—not by my order, I am relieved to say. He understood the warning, but do you know what he told me? That breaking the commandment against bearing false witness would be worse than death. I thought it was an interesting remark from a man who only a few hours before had been so starkly reminded that he was mortal."

"The ignorant always see life in terms of such absolute choices."

"But this man is not ignorant. Why would you assume, Micah, that he is ignorant? Merely because he is not a priest? He is reputed to be a man learned in Torah, and from my knowledge of him, I have no trouble believing it.

"My point is that such men are a moral force to be reckoned with. The Romans, granted, are themselves little better than common ruffians, incapable of appreciating any virtue in their subjects except submission. But we, God's priests, are not Romans, and we need the support of men like my ironsmith because such men are rapidly taking our place as the 'natural leaders' of the common people. What is a priest these days, when he is beyond the Temple walls? A landowner whom his tenants never see, and who is therefore hated as an oppressor, or the servant of a ruler like Herod Antipas, and thus hated even more."

As was their custom when Eleazar was in Jerusalem, Zadok stayed with his father. That evening, as together they walked back to the First Minister's house, they had little to say to one another.

They went to Eleazar's study, and a servant brought them a pitcher of cold water and a pair of cups. When the servant was gone, Eleazar filled the two cups and they drank in silence.

"I have never heard you speak that way," Zadok said at last. "I have never heard you say such things."

"It was an unguarded moment. Perhaps I had a little too much wine." His father shrugged and smiled faintly.

"You hardly touched your wine."

"Didn't I? Then perhaps that is the reason. Some things it is a mistake to see too clearly."

25

As soon as it became known that Deborah was to marry the ironsmith from Sepphoris, which was almost as soon as she knew it herself, both of the other fish merchants in Capernaum offered to buy her business. Within two days the matter was settled. Even her house was sold.

She explained it all to Noah as they sat beneath her grape arbor.

"Perhaps you could even accompany Joshua and me to Nazareth." He made a small, self-deprecating gesture, as if shooing away a fly. "You could stay with Joshua's mother until we are married. Of course, I can imagine many reasons why that might not be practical. There is your packing . . ."

"All of which Hannah can manage without me. There is nothing to hold me here."

When he could summon courage to look her full in the face, Noah discovered that she was smiling.

"Please take me with you," she said. "I have been unhappy here so long, and I do not wish to be separated from you again."

"Then you will not be."

He leaned forward and, very softly, kissed her on the lips.

After the first star had proclaimed the end of the Sabbath, Noah and Joshua walked to Deborah's house to celebrate the journey, which would begin at first light the following morning. The house was in disorder because Hannah had begun packing and sorting as soon as she heard her mistress's news. Although she had never known any place but Capernaum, staying behind in it formed no part of her plans.

Deborah, sensing Hannah's distraction, prepared dinner with her own hands.

To be out of Hannah's way, the three sat outside, resting their plates on their knees. There was a faint breeze from the sea, just enough to stir the air, and the moon shone like bronze.

"One would think she is the one getting married, instead of you."

Joshua had clearly intended a jest, but something in Deborah's expression suggested that he had come close to the truth.

"What have you promised the poor girl?" he asked.

"I have said that whatever I do not take to Sepphoris she may regard as her own to sell towards her dowry. There." She shrugged her shoulders—quite prettily, Noah thought to himself. "Is that so evil? She too wants a husband."

"Is that all women think about anymore?" Joshua asked.

"We have been through this before," Noah interjected. Neither of the others betrayed any symptom of having heard him.

"She is poor—as I was once poor," Deborah said. "And she is alone."

"She is not alone as long as she has you." Noah covered her hand with his own. "In you she has a better friend than most people can lay claim to."

But Deborah was not mollified.

"A friend is not a husband. I cannot give her a family. She wants children, and a man's arms around her. A man can lead many different lives. He can wander the earth if it suits him, and there is always time to settle. A woman has only one chance at happiness, and that is marriage."

"The only happiness is in God," Joshua announced, as if that settled the matter. He tried not to show it, but Noah could see that he was nettled. "In God's kingdom we are all His children."

"This is true. God is our refuge," Noah said.

He felt Deborah's hand turn under his own, and the fingers close around his thumb. She understood.

"But we are not vessels of light," he went on, a strange sadness filling him as he contemplated his cousin's face. "We are not the angels who surround His throne. We are only men and women, and to each of us

God in His mercy gave the other, to support us in our imperfection. Even in God's kingdom we are still only men and women."

Joshua made no reply, and the conversation drifted in other directions, but the mood of their little celebration remained somehow darkened. Soon, on the pretext that tomorrow's journey would be long, it broke up.

"Shall I walk you back to Simon's house?" Noah asked, with a cheerfulness he did not feel.

"No." Joshua shook his head, as if he had just reached a decision. "I won't go there—at least not for a while. I need to pray."

"Good night then."

They parted, and after a few steps Noah stopped and turned to watch his cousin's departing figure as it faded into the darkness.

"He has become a stranger," he thought, *"someone I do not know. When, I wonder, did that happen?"*

The next morning, at first light, Noah found Deborah's door already open. He heard the sound of women's voices within, so, as he was leading a donkey, he called out. Deborah appeared almost at once, carrying a small bundle, presumably of clothes, and a wineskin.

"I am ready," she said, smiling in a way that made his heart clench. Then she looked at the donkey and noticed that there were no packs on its back.

"I thought perhaps you would find the journey less tiring if you could ride."

"Would the donkey find it less tiring?"

"The donkey is accustomed to far heavier burdens than you."

"I think I would sooner walk."

For reasons he could not define, Noah found himself elated by her answer.

"Then at least the donkey can carry your luggage."

"In that case, I'll go pack another bundle."

She disappeared inside, and when she came back a few minutes later she found that Joshua had turned up with five of his disciples—the Thunder Brothers, Simon, Levi the former tax collector, and Judah.

"We shall need another wineskin."

"Probably two," Noah answered her. He did not seem pleased by this increase in the number of their traveling companions.

"And food—we shall need more food."

"Oh yes."

When she returned with the extra provisions, Hannah was with her. Hannah was in tears as the two women embraced.

"We shall see each other again in Sepphoris very soon," Deborah told her. "Noah will make arrangements for your journey."

"I shall miss your wedding."

"Perhaps. But I shall not miss yours."

This brought on another flood of lamentation, and Deborah herself was close to weeping by the time they set off. She said not a word until they were outside of Capernaum and on the road south.

"Tell me again about this apprentice of yours."

Noah found he was almost startled by the sound of her voice.

"His name is Hiram and he is a good fellow. He is past twenty and has learned as much as he ever will, but he wishes to stay with me until after the Passover. The plan is that he will then set up on his own. I will help him with tools and a little money, which was my understanding with his father when he was apprenticed to me. When he finds a work-space, I will also help him to build his forge."

"In Sepphoris?"

"Yes. Like me, he was born there."

"He will be your competitor?"

This made Noah laugh. "There is work enough in Sepphoris for two ironsmiths."

"Do you think they will like each other?"

"That is up to them." He brought Deborah's hand up to his mouth and kissed it. "In a week or so I will send him up to fetch Hannah. They will have plenty of time to become acquainted."

"She is very young. He will not . . ."

"No, nothing like that. As I said, he is a good fellow, and he wants a wife. It is a thing one can sense."

"Was it a thing you sensed about yourself?"

There was a playfulness in her words, which Noah was glad to hear.

"Not until I saw you," he answered, kissing her hand again.

They were left to themselves as they walked along. Joshua seemed to prefer the company of his disciples, who made an appreciative audience for his many jests—their talk was constantly punctuated by laughter. During the first hour he never so much as glanced back at them.

Their party was following a footpath that crossed over a hill. The hill was low and wide, like a loaf of bread, and the main road made a long detour around it. On the other side, Capernaum would disappear from sight.

"Can one see Sepphoris from here?" Deborah asked, when they had reached the summit.

"No." Noah shook his head, struggling to conceal his amusement. "The day will be half gone before we see Sepphoris, and then only as a smudge on the horizon."

"Can one see it from Nazareth?"

"No. There are hills in the way. Are you so eager?"

"Of course. I have never seen any great city. Sepphoris will be my home. I cannot help but be curious."

"It is not so vast a place. As soon as it pleases you, I will take you for a stroll around the walls. Believe me, you will not find the exercise tiring."

"You cannot judge what a girl brought up in Capernaum will think vast."

"That is true."

The road south curved around the base of the hill and then ran straight south for almost as far as the eye could see. It was empty except for an indistinct cluster of movement some five or six miles away.

"Joshua. I think we should stop here for a few moments. It would be just as well if everyone sat down."

Joshua was in the midst of telling a story. He stopped and turned to face Noah, seemed about to say something, and then apparently changed his mind. The expression on his face was somewhere between impatience and bewilderment.

Noah merely pointed, and Joshua followed the gesture with his eyes.

"Yes?" Joshua said at last.

"Sit down," Noah commanded, and everyone obeyed—even, at last, Joshua.

"They're riding horses."

Joshua, whose eyesight was better suited to distance, nodded agreement.

"How many, do you think?" Noah asked.

"Four . . . no, five." Joshua brought his right hand up to about shoulder level and made a gesture as if counting. "Yes, five. And they are keeping their horses to a walk. See how little dust they raise?"

"Five men on horseback. That means the likelihood is they are either soldiers or brigands." Noah allowed himself a syllable of bitter laughter. "Not that the distinction is much worth drawing."

"What should we do?" Deborah asked. It was clear from her tone that she was not yet greatly alarmed. She put her hand on Noah's arm.

"Wait here. Perhaps they haven't seen us yet, and even if they have, the trail is too steep for horses. I think it unlikely that they will clamber all the way up here on foot on the off chance we might have something to compensate them for their trouble."

Simon nodded vigorously. "We have the advantage of height," he said, almost triumphantly. "Even if they are armed, there are plenty of stones lying about. We could make a mess of them before they came anywhere near us."

"We will not resist evil with evil."

Joshua looked his disciple full in the face, that he might know the full weight of the rebuke. Simon clearly felt it, for he lowered his eyes.

For a moment the only sound was the faint stirring of the wind.

"It is not evil to defend oneself," Noah said. "And, in any case, this does not seem the moment to be discussing ethics."

"What better time?" Joshua smiled, as if he had made a jest. "God's commandments exist for occasions precisely like this. And God commands that we resist evil with good."

"Then let us hope they do not come up here, so the matter will not have to be put to the test."

Noah touched Deborah's arm and pointed to a large boulder only five or six feet away.

"I want you to crawl over there and conceal yourself. They are still far enough away that they won't notice one person's movements."

Deborah nodded and started toward the boulder on her hands and knees. She must have been frightened, but she did not betray any sign of it.

The thought flitted through Noah's mind that if he died this day he would miss a lifetime of happiness with her.

"There is nothing gained from sitting here," Joshua announced. "We have little enough worth stealing."

"There are men in this world who will kill you to steal your sandals."

"We all live at God's sufferance, Noah."

"And a man should not try God's patience."

"Nevertheless . . ."

Joshua stood up. Almost at once the riders halted.

"They have seen you. Congratulations."

"In any case, they would have seen us soon enough. I think we might as well go down to meet them."

Noah started to say something and then thought better of it, for he realized that Joshua was right. The great thing was to keep these men away from Deborah.

He glanced at her and smiled.

"No matter what happens, do not move," he said. "They will not come up here for nothing, so they must not see you. Promise me that you will stay just where you are. Promise me that you will not even turn your head to look, no matter what."

"I promise."

By then all the men were on their feet. The disciples looked nervous. Judah occupied himself with brushing the dust from the skirt of his tunic. Levi seemed ready to flee in panic.

"There is nothing to fear." The expression on Joshua's face reflected a perfect serenity of mind. "God holds us cradled in His hand."

The walk down the hill occupied about a quarter of an hour. Joshua took the lead. No one spoke. Noah observed that Simon clutched in his right hand a stone about the size of an apple.

"Drop it, Simon," said Joshua. "Let it go, along with your fear." He had not so much as turned his head. Suddenly he laughed.

"Let that be your new name," he said. "From this day on, you shall be called 'the Rock.' "

When they reached the road they had to wait until the horsemen, who seemed in no hurry, overtook them.

As they approached, it became obvious that these were not soldiers. They were dressed like peasants, which meant, it being a reasonable assumption that a poor man in possession of a horse had probably stolen it, that they were brigands.

"Good morning," Joshua said, as soon as they were close enough to save him the trouble of shouting. "God be with you."

None of them answered. The lead rider cocked his head a little to one side and smiled in apparent amusement. It was not a reassuring smile.

When they were about ten paces away, they allowed their horses to drift to a halt. Their faces and clothes were caked with dust, as if they had been on the move for several days. In their gray-brown anonymity, they hardly seemed human. But for their eyes, which were still alive, they seemed as menacing and insubstantial as ghosts.

A few of them carried swords slung across their backs, so that the hilts were visible over their shoulders, and no doubt the others all had some sort of weapon.

"These roads aren't safe for unarmed men," said the horseman who had found Joshua's greeting such a jest. He was tall, and so thin that his legs, which were bare up to the middle of his thighs, looked spindly and useless, as if they would collapse the instant they had to bear the weight of his body. "It could be all your lives are worth to be out here unprotected."

He seemed to enjoy a reputation as a wit among his comrades, for an appreciative ripple of laughter could be heard behind him.

"We are not unprotected," Joshua answered him.

"No?"

"No. God, Who sees all, is our protection."

The horseman appeared to consider how to respond, and then he shrugged and once more cocked his head to one side.

"Well, if that is all . . ."

"That *is* all, and it is enough."

Joshua took a step forward. His whole posture was like a challenge.

"Have you so far abandoned yourself that you imagine God has abandoned you?" he asked. "You do not know that He Who made you hears every beat of your heart? This moment His gaze is upon you, and He remembers, if you do not, that He is your father and you are His son. So beware of what you do in the presence of the Father, lest you forfeit His mercy."

The horseman leaned forward, if not intimidated, then at least perplexed.

"Who are you then? Are you a prophet? Are you Isaiah?"

"No, I am not Isaiah. I am Joshua bar Joseph, born in Nazareth, yet I ask you, in Isaiah's words, 'against whom have you raised your voice and lifted your eyes in Pride?' It is not my life you hazard but your own."

"We'll see."

The horseman was already reaching back to draw his sword when Noah stepped forward. He drew a small leather pouch from inside his cloak and threw it on the ground. It landed close enough to the horse's feet to make the animal start.

"This is what you seek," he said. His voice was level, as if he had just made the last decision of his life. "Take it. It is all I have, and these men are poor. Take it. It holds silver. Take the donkey as well, and be satisfied."

"How do I know that is all you have?"

Noah was framing an answer when one of the other riders urged his horse forward a few steps, put a hand on his companion's arm, and whispered something to him. There was a brief conversation, and then the horseman turned his attention back to Noah.

"My friend says that you are known to him. He says that you once saved his life. He says that we should let you and the prophet go in peace."

All the while the second man smiled at Noah with obvious pleasure, apparently expecting to be recognized.

It was a moment before he was.

"Samson?" Noah experienced an instant of disappointment. "Then I gather you did not go on to Ptolemais."

"No." Samson shook his head, still smiling broadly. "I bought food and rested. Then I bought a sword. Then I stole a horse."

"And became a brigand?"

"Yes."

"I am sorry to hear it."

Samson's friend seemed to take offense at this.

"There is nothing wrong with being a brigand."

26

Samson and his companions, as it developed, had not eaten since the morning before. They returned Noah's pouch to him with just enough formality to indicate that he and his friends were no longer considered as among those upon whom it was permissible to prey, but at the same time they regarded with covetous eyes the food sacks and wineskins which burdened the donkey. They would not steal, and they were too proud to beg, but an invitation to share, it was implied, would not be declined.

The donkey was quickly unloaded.

Then Noah remembered Deborah and, reproaching himself, called out to her. Instantly he saw her face appear above the boulder behind which she had been hiding, and he gestured to her to come down.

They met halfway up the trail and embraced.

"We are safe then?" she asked as they walked down together. "They are not brigands?"

"We are perfectly safe, but yes, they are brigands. One of them, however, is a friend of mine."

"You have friends who are brigands?"

"He wasn't a brigand when I knew him before."

By the time they returned, most of the wine had been drunk and everyone was on convivial terms. There was much laughter, and Joshua was attempting to explain to Samson about God's kingdom and how its imminent arrival should make him reconsider his choice of career. Samson listened politely but did not seem convinced.

The brigand leader, holding the last wineskin by its neck, stood up to greet the new arrival.

"Aha! I knew you were holding something back."

He slapped his thigh and laughed. He was a good fellow and meant no harm. He invited Noah to share the wine.

"This is my betrothed, Deborah. We are on our way to Nazareth to be married."

"Then we should drink to your happiness."

On the pretext of seeing to the donkey, Deborah left them. The two men sat down in a patch of shade reluctantly provided by an acacia tree. When the wineskin was offered to him, Noah observed that the brigand leader's hands were narrow, with long, slender fingers.

There were at least two hours wanting until noon, but somehow it did not seem wise, under the circumstances, to decline any friendly gestures.

"Peace be with you." Noah took a long swallow.

"Peace be with you," the brigand answered. "My name is Lemuel, by the way."

They sat together in silence for a time, passing the wineskin back and forth.

"That friend of yours, is he a preacher?"

"Yes. He was a follower of the Baptist. He is my cousin."

"You should tell your cousin to curb his tongue."

His voice betrayed no hostility. He was merely offering useful advice.

"I have told him that many times. He does not listen."

"Well, it brought him within a heartbeat of being killed today. Does the man have no fear?"

"It would seem not. He believes he lives under God's protection."

"God's what?" This struck Lemuel as funny, and he laughed again. "God protected David, and maybe a prophet or two, but He does not care about ordinary men like you and me and your cousin—what was his name again?"

"Joshua."

"Joshua? I think I have heard of him." He took back the wineskin and seemed about to drink, but then apparently lost interest. "Well, maybe God does protect him, if he's lived this long. Yes, maybe He does."

Then he remembered the wine, took a swallow, and handed the skin back to Noah.

"She's a pretty woman, your Deborah. You are fortunate."

"I know I am."

"I was married once."

Lemuel sighed and shook his head. It was obvious that he wanted to talk.

"What happened?"

With his long hand, the brigand made a surprisingly graceful gesture, suggestive of the perversity of fortune.

"I was a weaver," he said. "I owned my own loom. Then I fell into debt to the wool merchants—I had no choice. I bought the wool from them and sold the finished cloth to them, and the prices were not in my favor. Then one day a man came and said that the loom and the house we lived in belonged to him now. We went to stay with my wife's family, but my wife caught a fever and died. She did not struggle against it and died quickly. I think she wished to die. Then I was by myself."

"And you became a brigand?"

"Yes. It came down to a choice among being a thief or a beggar or starving to death. I wanted to live, and a man must have a little pride. I don't rob the villagers, so they will hide me when the soldiers come looking. Only the rich think ill of a robber, and they are the worst robbers of all. To the poor I am a champion because I oppress those who oppress them."

"You almost oppressed me today."

"Anyone can make a mistake."

Lemuel and his companions had decided that the pickings were too thin in Galilee and so were on their way to Judea. Thus, because the southern road was on their way, they volunteered to accompany the little group to within sight of Sepphoris—any closer would run the risk of encountering the Tetrarch's soldiers—and for this they agreed to accept fifteen silver pieces, which was close to the amount in Noah's purse. Thus was their honor as brigands satisfied.

They all parted as friends, about an hour and a half's walk from Nazareth.

The encounter left Joshua exuberant and, as it was obvious he had exhausted the subject with his disciples, for the first time in the journey he sought out Noah.

"I was never afraid," he said, his voice confidentially low as he threw an arm across Noah's shoulders. "I felt as if God had me cradled in His hand."

"When were you ever afraid? You weren't even afraid when we were seven and you jumped from the top of the vine terrace, but you broke your arm anyway."

Joshua threw back his head and laughed.

"You are an inconvenient friend for a prophet. You have a perfect memory of every time I have made a fool of myself."

"*Are* you a prophet then?"

"If I am not, then I am mad, for God speaks to me. I hear His voice in my heart. Do you think I am mad, Noah?"

It was not a jest but a real question, and Noah weighed his answer accordingly.

"No," he said at last. "I do not think you are mad."

"But you are not prepared to repent and join me in awaiting the Kingdom."

Then it was Noah's turn to laugh, and it was not a pleasant sound.

"Do you imagine, Cousin, that you have a monopoly on repentance?" He turned and looked up into Joshua's face. "Anyone who tries to live under God's law tastes repentance every day of his life. Since I was received as a man in the prayer house, I am not conscious of having broken any of the commandments, but I know that God requires more. I am honest in my dealings and I give to the poor, but I have been guilty of a thousand compromises with life, so that sometimes I wonder if it is even possible in this world to be a good man."

"In *this* world, probably not." Joshua smiled, as if he had just guessed the answer to a riddle. "And why is it you only call me 'cousin' when you are annoyed with me?"

Noah could laugh again, and this time with pleasure, for thus easily was the estrangement between them bridged. They could talk again with the effortless understanding of old friends.

One time Noah looked over his shoulder at Deborah, who was leading the donkey, wondering if she felt neglected, but she merely smiled at him, as if guessing his question, and shook her head. The renewed intimacy between the two men seemed to please her.

"I suspect it is a great folly for me to return to Nazareth," Joshua announced suddenly, for they had been speaking of other matters. "Father and I will only quarrel."

"Try to avoid it. The excitement will only wear him out."

"It will be almost impossible to avoid."

"Nevertheless, try." Noah made a gesture with his right hand, as if to silence objections. "I know that it will not be easy, but try not to be provoked by anything he says. He does not understand the turn your life has taken, and he will never be made to understand, so let it pass."

"Why is it so difficult for him to see? *You* see, don't you?"

"I suppose, in some sense. Yet this path you follow can only lead you away from what most of us call happiness. What did the Baptist's father think, I wonder."

"I never heard him mention his family." Joshua shook his head. "Until this moment, it never occurred to me to think he might have one."

"Yet he must have. Perhaps in some village his parents grieve and wonder why their son chose to live, and to die, as he did."

"Except that perhaps he did not choose, but was chosen."

"Perhaps. But that is not a possibility that would occur to your father."

"That is the truth."

By then they were within a few minutes' walk of the village, along a road dividing fields whose owners they could have named. The familiar world of their childhood was closing in around them.

Joshua picked up a small stone and threw it, just as Noah had seen him do hundreds of times before. When they were boys, it might have been a gesture of pure exuberance. Now it suggested that his thoughts were not pleasing to him.

"What plagues me, more than anything else," he said, his eyes still following the trajectory of the stone, "what I cannot bring myself to be reconciled to, is that the truth of my message is as transparent as water. I am like one who points his finger and says 'Look! The enemy comes,' and anyone who troubles to turn his head can see the dust raised by the approach of a hostile army. And I know that my father will not think to turn his head, and only because I am his son."

As they walked through the outskirts of the village, people looked up from their daily occupations, and a few smiled and waved their hands in friendly recognition. Most ignored them. Noah and Joshua they of course knew, but the others were strangers and thus objects of suspicion.

The first member of the family to see them was Noah's grandfather, who was sitting on a stool beside the door of his house. His face, only the instant before vacant of expression, registered first surprise and then pleasure. He stood up and embraced them, first Noah and then Joshua, and then his attention fell on the only woman with them.

"Is this then she?" he asked, his smile almost flirtatious. He took her hands in his. "Are you Deborah?"

Deborah was so overcome with embarrassed pleasure that she could only nod.

"I think you will make Noah very happy."

"She has done that already, Grandfather," Noah said, at which they could all laugh, as much in relief as anything else.

Suddenly the old man frowned. He glanced at Noah, as if in reproach.

"Your sister should be here."

"Why isn't she?" Noah felt a sudden surge of anxiety. "I told her to stay with you."

Grandfather smiled, as if at a story he had heard many times before.

"She doesn't go near your house," he said. "She stays with a friend in the next street. I think she doesn't want her cloth merchant to forget her."

"Yes, of course," Noah answered, feeling a trifle foolish. After all, the danger was past, wasn't it? "She will be with Abigail. I shall have to get a message to her."

"I'll go." It was Judah who spoke. He pushed himself forward. "I'll be happy to. Just give me directions."

At first, Noah's only reaction was astonishment, and then he remembered himself.

"It will add another two hours to your journey," he said. "I could not ask it. . . ."

"Two hours is nothing. I have been so long in the country, it will be good once more to have cobblestones beneath my feet. Simply tell me where she lives."

It was obvious he meant to do it, so Noah told him where to find the house.

"Do you know Sepphoris at all?"

"No."

"It is not so vast a place. There are a number of streets that branch just to the left of the eastern gate. Follow the Street of the Carpenters south until you see a house with a green door. It will be on your right and, believe me, there is only one. My sister's name is Sarah. Tell her I hope to see her in the morning."

There was an awkward moment as Judah departed. He turned and suddenly found himself facing Joshua, and for an instant he seemed ashamed. But Joshua merely smiled.

"Go," he said. "It is a good thing that you do."

When Judah was gone, Joshua put his hand on Noah's shoulder and bent his head, as if to whisper a confidence.

"Now, will you do something for me? Come with me to my father's house."

It was not a thing that required explanation.

"Of course."

Noah glanced at Deborah, offering an unspoken apology.

"She will be safe enough with me," his grandfather announced. "I will entertain her with prodigious lies about your childhood."

Since there were still a few hours of daylight left, Noah and Joshua went to the workshop, where they could expect to find the men of the family. They were not disappointed. Both brothers were there. Joseph, who could no longer work, occupied a stool in the middle of the room, where he could sip water from a jug resting on the floor and watch his sons with envious eyes.

He was the first to see Joshua, and was so taken by surprise that he actually stood up. Joshua immediately strode over and embraced his father.

"So. You are here. Well. Good."

These were all the words Joseph could bring himself to utter, but they were enough. The two men stood with their hands on each other's shoulders, and all they could not say was reflected in their faces.

"Noah." Joseph's voice, when at last he did speak, was choked with emotion. "I have you to thank for this."

At last, when his father had released him, Joshua went to his brothers, each in turn, and embraced them. Jacob seemed glad to see him. To Little Joseph he might have been a stranger.

"Are you home to stay?" Little Joseph asked him. His tone suggested that he already knew the answer. But Joshua was wise enough to act as if he hadn't heard.

He stayed for perhaps a quarter of an hour, sitting beside his father and speaking to him in a low voice. Noah could not hear the words, but it was clear from the expression of something like gratitude on Joseph's face that Joshua was keeping the peace.

At last Joshua stood up.

"I should see my mother now," he said, and went through a door into the house.

Joseph looked up at Noah and shook his head.

"He is much more his mother's son than mine," he said, as if resigned. "We will not see him again before supper."

Noah, his duty done, went back to his grandfather's house, where he found Deborah and the old man sitting together beside the doorway, deep in conversation. His grandfather, he noticed, was holding his future wife's hand.

He was so pleased with the picture they made that he was almost disappointed when they noticed his presence.

"Ah, you are back," his grandfather announced. "How was it?"

Noah shrugged. "A good beginning. For the rest, we'll see."

"You don't sound hopeful."

"Grandfather, some collisions are inevitable."

Benjamin nodded sadly. Then he released his hold on Deborah's hand, but not without giving it a final pat.

A few minutes later Gemariah, Jacob's wife, turned up with an invitation to dinner.

"Miriam sent me," she said, addressing herself mainly to Deborah. "She wants the whole family to be together. And we all want to meet Noah's intended."

"Can I help?" Deborah asked. "Another pair of hands . . ."

Gemariah, who was a plain, good-natured country woman, seemed both pleased and embarrassed by this and didn't know how to reply.

"Please?" Deborah smiled prettily and the matter was settled. They bade the men farewell and went off together.

When they were out of earshot, Grandfather shook his head and laughed.

"As you see, she conquers us all," he said.

———

As the sun began to descend below the hills, they all sat down to eat. As was customary on such occasions, tables were set up outside. Miriam, marshaling her daughters and daughters-in-law with a precision a Roman general might have envied, managed to arrange things so that nothing disturbed the felicity of her son's homecoming. Joshua sat with his father, his brother Jacob, Uncle Benjamin, and several children. Little Joseph sat with Noah and Joshua's disciples. When the meal was served and the women could take their places, it was apparent that Deborah had already established herself as a great favorite.

About an hour later, Sarah appeared out of the darkness. Noah rose and embraced his sister.

"You shouldn't have come all this way in the dark," he said sternly, trying to conceal his pleasure.

"It was perfectly light until a few minutes ago." She laughed. "Besides, I wanted to meet my new sister."

"Did you come alone? Where is Judah?"

"He told me you were here, and then he left. Didn't he come back?"

"No."

"Then I expect he is still in Sepphoris."

"So it would seem."

27

The next morning, nothing would do except for Noah, Sarah, and Deborah to walk to Sepphoris. The danger was past, so Noah assured them, and Sarah announced to her brother that his betrothed would certainly be eager to see her new home. Sarah was insistent.

A single evening had been enough to make the two women friends. Noah had watched their developing intimacy with pleasure, but without surprise. They were almost the same age, both sweet tempered, and neither had a sister. Certain affinities were inevitable.

During the hour from Nazareth to the eastern gate, Sarah carried most of the burden of conversation. She described all the rooms of the house: which had the best light at what times of day, the strengths and deficiencies of the kitchen, the problems of storage. Deborah added a word or two about the furniture she was bringing from Capernaum and was content to listen to everything Sarah had to say concerning the probable best placement of each piece. Noah, for the most part, kept silent, occasionally shaking his head in amazement. He would never have imagined that domestic order was so complicated.

It also occurred to him that Sarah was uncharacteristically excited, almost hectic, and he was pleased to observe the placid kindness of Deborah's responses. She seemed to understand whatever was afflicting his sister.

Probably, Noah thought to himself, it all had something to do with the cloth merchant.

Abijah and Noah had known each other for a little over two years. There was a circle of men in that quarter of the city who met at irregular intervals in one another's homes to discuss Torah with perhaps more freedom and greater intensity than was quite appropriate to the prayer house. Abijah lived only two streets from Noah, and they had formed the habit of walking to and from these meetings together. Their conversations along the way were frequently more interesting than the meetings themselves. Eventually, and without the hint of an ulterior motive, Noah had invited Abijah to dinner, and that was when he met Sarah.

Abijah was a few years lacking of thirty. At nineteen, while still living with his parents in Caesarea and apprenticed to his father in the cloth trade, he had been engaged to marry a young girl, the daughter of his mother's cousin. For some reason—which, apparently, he felt bound in honor not to explain—the engagement had been broken off, and Abijah had moved to Sepphoris and set up in business on his own. He worked hard and achieved success, and apparently had given no thought to women until he set eyes on Sarah.

That was a year ago, and ever since, he had been her ardent suitor. He was handsome, prosperous, learned, and agreeable. He could have secured the favor of any girl in their stratum of local society, but only Sarah would do. It was Sarah, plain, awkward Sarah, who had presented the obstacles. She loved Abijah—that was apparent. She valued his many good qualities and was grateful, as only an unmarried woman of twenty-six can be grateful, for his love, his ardor, and his persistence. But she would not leave her brother.

Then, providentially, her brother had fallen in love with a widow in Capernaum. Was it any wonder that Sarah was eager to discuss housekeeping arrangements with her new sister-in-law to be?

When they entered the city gates, Deborah was as one struck dumb. Sepphoris seemed a place beyond belief. All she could do was look about her and stare.

At the house, after Noah had unlocked the door, Sarah and Deborah passed quickly through the shop and into the living quarters. They simply vanished, and Noah was left behind to count the stock.

Half an hour later, Abijah turned up. They embraced, as if they were brothers already, and Noah offered him a cup of wine.

"I hear you are soon to be married," Abijah said abruptly.

"Yes." Noah could only laugh. "Sarah and my betrothed are inside now, deciding on all the details of my future life."

"And on the strength of your engagement, Sarah has finally consented."

Abijah did not laugh, but he smiled broadly. They were sitting at a small, circular table in the shop, and Abijah was stroking his beard with the back of his left hand, the way he did when he felt he had offered an unarguable interpretation of Torah.

"Are you, too, prepared to consent?" Abijah asked.

"When has my consent ever been in doubt?" Not without difficulty, Noah preserved a becoming gravity of manner. "I was never the obstacle. I would sooner have Sarah married to you, my friend, than to any man living. Does that put your mind at ease?"

"She is a wonderfully loyal sister," Abijah declared with admiration.

"And she will make you a wonderfully loyal wife." Noah took a sip of wine and set the cup down with a certain emphasis. "Now. Shall we discuss terms?"

"I do not care anything about terms."

"Yes, but I do. I will not shame my sister by sending her to her husband like a beggar. She shall have a suitable dowry—furniture, clothes, kitchen utensils, and money."

"Then, because I know you to be a just and pious man, I leave the details to you."

"You honor me, brother."

Noah refilled their wineglasses, and the conversation drifted first into predictions of their future happiness and then, gradually, into a discussion of the fine points of the Mosaic law concerning marriage.

After perhaps an hour, they were interrupted by a knock at the shop door.

Noah rose to answer it and was surprised to discover that his caller was the same man who had visited him once before, the First Minister's nephew.

The elegant young priest stepped inside—tentatively, a step at a time, holding his robes close around him as if fearful of contagion—and Noah closed the door. When the priest saw Abijah he frowned.

"You may speak freely," Noah said, perhaps more harshly than he was aware. "This man is a member of my family."

The First Minister's nephew turned around to face him. He did not seem impressed by Noah's assurance.

"A certain distinguished person—"

"Your uncle."

"Wishes to speak to you, in a place you know—"

"The house of Kenan bar Dathan, on the Street of the Doves, near the palace gate."

For a moment the young priest seemed to consider if he should become angry, but apparently decided against it.

"And wonders if tomorrow morning would be convenient. The first hour after prayers."

"Tell the Lord Eleazar that I am at his disposal. Now, was there anything else? Perhaps you will join us in a cup of wine? We are celebrating an engagement."

"I think you upset him," Abijah observed, once the priest had made his somewhat hasty departure.

"How? Was I rude?"

"Yes."

"Let us hope so." Noah sat down again and poured them both another cup of wine. "I would hate to think he has taken a liking to me."

"Is he really the Lord Eleazar's nephew?"

"Yes."

"Then perhaps you should be more careful not to offend him."

"His uncle knows he is a puppy. Besides, the Lord Eleazar is a great admirer of my dental pliers."

Eventually, Deborah and Sarah finished their tour of the house. Noah performed the little ceremony of introducing Deborah to Abijah, which Sarah watched, holding one hand tightly clenched in the other as if afraid it might escape. Then Sarah announced that they were going to the marketplace, which was three streets away.

"Would you like an escort?" Abijah asked, addressing the question to Sarah. "I can carry your purchases for you."

"We are only going to look, not to buy," Sarah answered, seeming somehow relieved. "However, if you would enjoy a tour of the stalls, you are welcome."

Noah smiled, a little sadly.

"I might as well come with you. You will need to buy enough for dinner, since we will be spending the night here. It seems that I have an appointment in the morning."

"Then we shall have a feast!" In pure exuberance, Sarah actually clapped her hands. "The four of us have so much to celebrate."

On the way there, the lovers paired off, but as they reached the marketplace, which completely filled one of the large public squares, the feminine alliance reasserted itself and Sarah led Deborah off through the rows of stalls, so close together that their awnings almost touched above the walkways. Noah and Abijah could follow, if they liked, but their presence was rarely acknowledged, and then only with a backward glance and a smile.

"I had no idea you moved in such distinguished circles," Abijah said at last. He phrased it as a jest, as something which could be easily turned aside, but his curiosity about the Lord Eleazar was obvious.

"He sends his nephew because he cannot trust his own servants, which is also why we will meet tomorrow in someone else's house. We are not bound together by friendship but by the fact that we have a common enemy, whom we both fear."

"Who in all of Galilee does the Lord Eleazar need to fear?"

Noah put his hand on Abijah's arm, only to capture his attention. He wanted his new brother-in-law to see his face, to read its expression.

"It is better for you that you do not know. I say this not because I do not trust you, but because you will be Sarah's husband."

"I understand."

Noah could only laugh.

"No, by the mercy of God, you do not. But let it rest. And say nothing of this to Sarah."

Eventually they went home, the men silent, laden with bags of food, the women cheerfully conspiring about how it should be cooked.

Would that it could be just so, Noah thought, *just as it is now, every day for the rest of our lives.* Which of course was not possible. Life was not a trip to the marketplace.

Once they were inside the door, the women disappeared into the kitchen and, to while away the time until dinner, Noah and Abijah walked back to Abijah's house, which was larger than Noah's, and the first floor of which he used as a shop and warehouse.

When they arrived, Abijah led Noah up to the living quarters and begin soliciting his opinion about the household arrangements.

"It's a musty old place," he said, looking around him as if seeing it for the first time. "I haven't kept it up, I'm afraid—I'm hardly here except to sleep. The kitchen is a shambles."

"It doesn't look so terrible," Noah lied, noting the cobwebs. "I gather you've been taking most of your meals out."

"A man living alone falls into bad habits."

"I remember," Noah replied, thinking of the time before his marriage, when he had first moved back into his father's house and was just setting up in business. His bride, when she arrived, had been appalled by the condition of the place.

Then it occurred to him that this was the first time he had thought about his dead wife in days. It seemed to him wrong that she should have been so easily forgotten, as if he had somehow betrayed her.

He found that he envied his new brother-in-law, who would soon be a husband for the first time. No baggage, no divided heart, no sense of one loyalty sacrificed to another.

"I wonder if there is time to have it rebuilt."

The sound of Abijah's voice came as a surprise. As Noah readjusted himself to the present moment, he smiled.

The kitchen. Yes.

"I'll tell you what I think you should do," Noah said. "After you are married, ask Sarah her opinion—one thing you will discover is that women love to be asked their opinion—and tell her she shall have a free hand in making whatever alterations she thinks best. Sarah is careful about money, so you will end by paying less than if you had done it yourself. And Sarah will have everything as she wishes it."

"That is excellent advice."

"Yes, it is."

When they returned, dinner was almost ready, so there was only time to mix the wine—six parts to five, in honor of the occasion—and then to be herded into the little room next to the kitchen where they always ate.

It was, indeed, a feast. The lamb was braised and served on a bed of Egyptian rice, and there were dates, sliced cucumbers, grapes, and bread still hot from the oven.

The conversation consisted mainly of Abijah's lavish praise of the cooking, all directed at Sarah, who blushed and smiled and said nothing as she squirmed with pleasure. Noah and Deborah were left in peace to look at each other, exchanging a word or a smile now and then.

When the meal was over, the two men were shooed out like geese, so they went up to the roof to finish the wine. Abijah, with every cup, expressed greater enthusiasm for Sarah's many perfections. Finally he wanted to know how soon he could expect to be blessed with her as a wife.

"The sooner the better," Noah replied, thinking of the Lord Eleazar and his servant Caleb, from whom he wanted his sister safely distant. "Tomorrow afternoon you will return with us to Nazareth, to receive our grandfather's consent, and then, as soon as the festivities can be arranged . . ."

Finally, after it had grown dark, Abijah returned home.

"I am finished with this day," Sarah announced, almost as soon as Abijah was out the door. "I am going to bed."

As she said it, Noah observed that she and Deborah exchanged a glance. Then Sarah kissed her brother and was gone.

"You have arranged this between you," Noah said, taking Deborah's hand in his own. He never ceased to marvel at the delicacy of her fingers. "You have plotted with my sister to give us this time alone."

"Yes."

"Whose idea was it?"

"Hers. I think it was a way of making amends."

"Why 'amends'?"

"Your sister is not very sure of herself," she answered, smiling at him in an unusual way, with none of her customary shyness. "I think she was uneasy about Abijah. But she needn't have worried, as she saw for herself. He hardly even looked at me."

"You mean she . . . ?"

This made her laugh. "Yes—of course. Women are human."

She glanced about, as if embarrassed. But she was not embarrassed, as Noah could see clearly when her gaze returned to his face.

"The kitchen is hot," she said, letting her free hand run down his arm. "Let's go up on the roof, where it will be cooler."

The roof was dark and solitary. Here and there one could see lights from the nearby houses. In another hour, however, these would all be gone, snuffed out as people prepared to go to bed. It was no longer the season during which one slept outside in hopes of catching some cool breeze, but there was still a sleeping mat rolled up and leaning against the parapet. Deborah had merely to touch it and it uncoiled itself and flattened out on the roof. They sat down on it.

"This is really the first time we have been alone together," she said.

"There was the bench in your garden," he offered, knowing perfectly well what she meant.

"Yes, but there Hannah was always somewhere about. Then there were the neighbors."

"There are neighbors here."

"But they can't hear what we say, and they can't see us." She crawled up on the sleeping mat and stretched out. "Come lie down beside me. There is no one in the world but you and me."

He lay down so that they were on their sides, facing each other. He found that he desperately wanted to kiss her, and had nearly made up his mind to do it, when she kissed him first. It was a long, slow kiss, as if she wanted him to learn everything there was to know about her mouth. Her tongue came out and delicately touched his upper lip.

Suddenly she pulled a little away.

"I never loved my husband," she said. It sounded like the confession of some dreadful sin. "I shouldn't tell you, but it's true. He wasn't a bad man, but I never felt anything for him. He owned me, and did what he wished with me, but I never gave myself to him—not freely, not with joy, as I will give myself to you."

"I loved my wife," he said, without knowing quite why. Somehow, not to say it would have been to violate this woman's trust.

"I'm glad. You are a man who would make any woman happy, so I'm glad she made you happy. I mean it. I do."

"I love you."

He reached up and touched her face, and she took his hand and brought it to her breast. He could feel her breath on his face. She kissed him again, only this time as if she meant to devour him. When she was finished, she laughed.

"I don't think this was quite what Sarah had in mind, but your sister is a virgin and there are some things she doesn't understand yet."

Suddenly Noah became aware that his member was stiff enough to have been cast in his own workshop. Deborah reached down to touch it beneath his tunic.

"If you want me . . . ," she began.

"There is no doubt that I want you."

There was an awkward moment as she struggled out of her clothes. It seemed to take forever. When she was naked, he wished that he could see her, but it was too dark. As he slid his hands over her body she drew closer to him.

"Is this against God's law, Noah? I feel I am your wife, from this moment and for as long as either of us lives. Is it wrong if we do not wait?"

"In another week we will be married. I hope—I believe—God will allow us this."

28

The next morning, when Noah awakened alone in his own bed, his first sensation was disappointment. He had been dreaming of Deborah, of the feel of her body against him and the little sounds she made as she reached her passion, and now she was somewhere else, asleep in Sarah's room, and he was full of longing.

Or perhaps she was awake and tormented by regret. Last night, in the dark, it was one thing. This morning, in the pitiless light of dawn, it might appear as something very different.

He sat down on the stool beside his window and began reciting his prayers. The words, which he had spoken every morning for as long as he could remember, almost said themselves, but their automatic quality freed his mind and allowed him to turn to God. *Was it a sin?* he asked. *Have I forfeited Your grace? I love her. That is my only excuse. And I promise I will love her until I die.*

He felt comforted, as if God understood. What did God not understand? God was tolerant of weakness, but not of selfishness or cruelty or of turning away from Him. He, Noah, son of Barachel, ironsmith in the city of Sepphoris, had merely loved a woman, and God winked.

He went downstairs for his breakfast and found Sarah in the kitchen. She kissed him, as was her custom in the morning, and turned back to her cooking pot.

"Where is Deborah?" he asked.

"Still asleep."

A few minutes later Deborah came down. "Good morning," she said, almost singing the words as she threw her arms around Noah's neck and then kissed him on the mouth. When he seemed startled, she laughed.

Sarah, apparently, had noticed nothing.

As they ate, the women talked. Noah was silent, for he had remembered, for the first time since last night, that he was to see the Lord Eleazar this morning.

The first hour after prayers.

"I must go," he said.

He rose from the table and was already in the shop before he realized that Deborah was behind him. He turned around and she held out her hand to him.

"Are you angry?" she asked.

Noah took her hand. "No."

"Then . . . disappointed?"

"No." He shook his head and smiled. "If I had nothing to think about except you and last night, I would be perfectly happy. I can't imagine being disappointed in you."

"Then what troubles you?" she asked, not even allowing herself to be flattered.

"My appointment this morning is with the priest."

Deborah nodded. She did not need to have explained to her which priest. For them, there was only one priest.

"What does he want?"

"I don't know."

Suddenly she was in his arms.

"When will they ever leave us alone, these people?"

"I don't know."

For a long moment they stood there, silently holding each other.

"This is our marriage ceremony," Noah said finally, as their embrace began to subside. "This, even more than last night, has made us one. We know what we are to one another, and God blesses us."

"Last night I loved you *so* much. This morning I love you still more."

That was the sight of her that Noah carried away with him as he headed up the steep streets that would take him to the great houses clustered around the palace. All his life he would remember her face as it appeared in that moment. And he thought of Joshua's dead wife,

Rachel, and understood, for the first time, the depth of his cousin's grief, which went beyond the longings of the body, beyond even love. It seemed to him really possible that a woman might weave herself so into the fabric of one's soul that to lose her went beyond pain, into something like disbelief.

"And yet she has never left me," Joshua had said, that night only a few days before, when they had sat together on the beach at Capernaum, sharing a jar of wine while he tried to explain why he couldn't bring himself to come to Deborah's betrothal dinner. *"I feel her presence. There are moments when she seems so near that I imagine I have but to glance around to see her smiling at me."*

Now, at last, Noah understood. As he waited in front of the door of the house of Kenan bar Dathan, on the Street of the Doves, he understood perfectly what Joshua had meant.

The same boy answered the door and ran away to fetch the same distinguished chamberlain, who conducted him to the same room, where Noah found the Lord Eleazar reclining on the same couch, in front of the same silver tray holding two stone cups and a jug, doubtless filled with cold water.

"Welcome back," the First Minister said, smiling and raising an arm in salutation. "Please be seated. I am very glad you were able to return."

Return to what? Noah could only wonder. This room? His own house? The life he had lived before he had ever met a man named Caleb? Nevertheless, the priest seemed actually glad to see him.

He filled the two cups from the pitcher and offered one to Noah. And, yes, it held water. And, yes, the water was cold.

"Did you encounter any dangers on your journey?" he asked. It seemed a bland enough question, but of course it was a trap.

"You would know, my lord. You had me followed."

"For your own protection, yes." The Lord Eleazar seemed faintly amused, as if at a jest he did not choose to share. "But my man did not pick up your trail until Sidon. And by Damascus you had noticed him. I suspect you have a talent for this sort of thing."

"Am I to go on yet another journey, Lord?"

It was a question which, apparently, the First Minister did not yet choose to answer, so he merely glanced away, the way a man will when he is considering a choice of possibilities, and then his eyes returned to Noah's face and he smiled again, but this time without warmth.

"I hear you are to be married," he said. "God enjoins us to take a wife, but you are a widower, are you not?"

"Yes, I am."

"Then you must be an enthusiast. I hope you will not be disappointed."

"Not in my choice, certainly."

"But in other things?"

"That is for you to tell me, Lord."

The Lord Eleazar picked up his cup, studied it for a moment, and then set it back down on the silver tray. One had the sense that there were things he knew had to be discussed but that he was reluctant to begin.

"Your report was very useful," he said finally. "I showed parts of it to the Tetrarch—he did not inquire as to the sources of my information— and he agreed that the purge of the Baptist's followers must end. The Tetrarch has issued an amnesty. Those of John's followers who were imprisoned, and still alive, have been released and allowed to return to their homes."

He paused for an instant and his eyes fell on Noah's face, as if he sought some reaction. But the ironsmith was impenetrable, so he continued.

"I prepared a list of those who are not subject to arrest without the Tetrarch's express warrant, and the Tetrarch agreed that such a warrant would require my approval. This protection extends to their families as well. Your name and that of your cousin are both on the list."

"Thank you, Lord. That was generous of you."

The First Minister nodded slightly in acknowledgment. He had grown accustomed to Noah's way of enclosing an impertinence in an apparent submission. He had even developed a taste for it.

"Your gratitude is perhaps premature," he answered, with a faint shrug. "Caleb is bright enough to know that your name on that list means that I took the trouble to find you out, and that I consider you some sort of asset. Before, you were his, and now you are mine. He will regard this as a betrayal. That is the way his mind works.

"I had hoped to use your report as evidence that he had blundered, creating a danger to the Tetrarchy where none existed before. In short, that he should be removed. But the Tetrarch would not allow it. The Tetrarch likes Caleb. He finds him amusing."

"Why are you telling me this, Lord?"

The First Minister regarded the ironsmith with unsympathetic eyes. He seemed almost annoyed, as if he thought Noah should have spared him the task of explaining something so distasteful.

"Because you must understand that as long as Caleb lives you have an enemy. He has been curbed, and for the time being he will be careful. But eventually he will find a way to come back at us both. He will bring me down because he needs to, because I stand in his way and because he knows that if he does not I will eventually find a way to destroy him. He will kill you simply because you have affronted his vanity."

The Lord Eleazar held out his hands, palm upwards, as if to ask, *"Is it not apparent? Do I not make myself clear?"*

"And yet, my lord, you still have not told me what purpose of yours is served by my knowing this."

At first it was as if Noah had reached out and struck him in the face. Then he smiled and allowed himself an instant of laughter.

"You are right, of course. I want you to do something for me."

Noah did not respond. He merely waited.

"A prisoner was released here in Sepphoris—a secret prisoner, given special treatment." The Lord Eleazar smiled thinly. "You see, I also have my informants. I want you to make inquiries."

"A prisoner? What is his name?"

"I do not know his name. No one seems to know his name."

"As you yourself have said, my lord, there has been an amnesty. Many prisoners have been released."

"This one was released before the amnesty. I want to know why. Caleb scoops a man up and holds him anonymously for some months, and then the man is released. I think it would be worthwhile to know what is happening."

"There is nothing else you can tell me about him?"

"No."

"It seems a hopeless task."

"As I have already said, Noah, I think you have a talent for this sort of thing."

As soon as her brother had left, Sarah excused herself and went up to her room. When she came back down, she had changed her clothes and her hair was combed. She sat at the kitchen table, talking with Deborah, but she seemed distracted.

The reason became clear half an hour later, when Abijah came calling. He too was very carefully dressed, his beard freshly trimmed.

"Since Noah has other business, I thought your new sister-in-law might enjoy a morning's tour of the city," he said, addressing Sarah.

The two women exchanged a glance, and Sarah's eyes were almost pleading.

"That is very kind of you," Deborah answered. "I have a great curiosity about this place which is to be my home."

A few minutes later they all were out the door.

"What would you like to see?" Sarah asked, peeking around her lover like a child hiding behind a curtain.

"The place is so vast, I hardly know. Things I would not see in Capernaum."

"What is Capernaum like?"

"Like Nazareth, except a trifle bigger."

"Then you must see the palace district," Abijah announced. "Besides, from there the views of the countryside are quite spectacular."

"Certainly there are no palaces in Capernaum," Deborah answered, and they all laughed. They hardly needed an excuse to laugh, for it was a fine day, not too hot, and they were off on an expedition of pleasure.

The streets of the lower city were crowded, noisy, and narrow, but as they proceeded up the hill, away from the districts inhabited by workers and tradesmen, the streets widened and the crowds thinned. It became possible for two people to walk abreast, and naturally those two were Sarah and Abijah, holding hands, Sarah frequently glancing back at her sister to be and smiling with happy embarrassment.

Deborah was not sorry to be taking up the rear, for it was pleasant to watch the lovers together and it gave her a chance to be alone with her thoughts.

She wished Noah were along, but if he could not be with her, at least she could think of him. There was pleasure in that as well.

There was, among others, the pleasure of a great gamble made and won. The idea of offering herself to Noah had occurred to her early yesterday, when Sarah was showing her through the house. She had seen the sleeping mat on the roof, rolled up and apparently forgotten. That had been enough. She did not know that he might not reject her, perhaps angrily. Perhaps angrily enough to refuse her altogether. He was a pious man who feared God and honored His commandments.

But he was still a man, and he had not rejected her. He had loved her and had treated her body with a kind of reverence. She could still feel the touch of his hands on her, still feel the warmth of his mouth.

And she had learned, in the covering darkness of night, that her life with him was not to be a desert. She had learned that the coming together of man and woman could be love and passion and joy.

Twice he had entered her. The first time had been urgent, quick, and very pleasant. It had been enough to convince her that she could be happy. The second time was beyond describing.

By the time the three reached the palace district, there were about two hours lacking until noon. The sun slanted down on the marble buildings, making the roofs and columns gleam. They were huge. Deborah had never seen anything like them.

"Those are the baths," Abijah said, pointing to a structure so white it hurt one's eyes to look at it. "Behind it, there, is the theater. The Greeks like to sweat without effort, so they lie about in little rooms and pour water on hot stones. They spend hours every day, naked as babies, the sweat pouring—they think it's good for them.

"So we have public baths because the Greeks have them. And we have a theater where all the performances are in Greek. All this because, when the Romans put down the rebellion after Great Herod's death, they burned the old city, and the worst destruction was up here, at the crest of the hill. So when Antipas took power he leveled the whole area and rebuilt it. And that is why it looks like a Greek city."

Sarah and Deborah exchanged a glance. Sarah looked apprehensive, as if she wished her lover would talk about something else, but Deborah ignored her. The fact was, she was curious.

"You don't sound as if you approve," she said.

"I don't." Abijah turned to face her, his expression almost challenging. "Jews are not Greeks. Foreigners have been trying to turn us into Greeks for three hundred years—first the Seleucids and now the Romans—but we remain what God made us. Sometimes we have had to fight to keep the old ways. Perhaps someday we will have to fight again. But in the meantime our Tetrarch, who is hardly a Jew at all, builds theaters where the plays are about foreign gods."

"Joshua says that God is coming to redeem His people."

"Who is Joshua?"

"My cousin," Sarah answered, in little more than a whisper. "He is a preacher, and Deborah was one of his followers. That is how she met Noah."

"Oh, *that* Joshua." Abijah smiled. "I have heard of him. He was a follower of the Baptist?"

"Yes," Deborah answered almost defiantly. "He carries on John's work."

"Well, the Baptist was a servant of God."

That seemed to conclude the discussion to everyone's satisfaction, and Abijah went back to describing the architecture.

As they walked about, Deborah almost stopped listening. The scale of everything filled her eyes. She could hardly believe that men had built such things.

Eventually they wandered away from the great public buildings and into the surrounding district, where the homes of the wealthy and powerful huddled around the palace complex like blind puppies searching for the teat. These too were mainly Greek in style, with columned entrances and generous use of marble.

"You ought to see Caesarea," Abijah said pleasantly as they walked along. "It's much worse. By comparison, Sepphoris is the only Jewish city left in Galilee."

He had hardly finished speaking when Deborah stopped in her tracks.

"Could we pause here a moment?" she said. "I'm tired."

The other two huddled around her, which was what she wanted. She wasn't at all tired, but she had seen something. In a doorway, on the other side of the street and perhaps fifty paces away, two men were standing. One was speaking to the other, but the distance was too great and the street too crowded for even the sound of his voice to reach them. The man who was speaking was emphatic in his gestures, like one issuing commands, and the other was like a beggar, his posture a little stooped as, now and then, he nodded his head in submission. Everything about him suggested that he was completely humbled. They could have been master and slave, but they were not. A slave would not have been so afraid.

Deborah had never seen the speaking man before, but the other man was Judah.

The conversation in the doorway lasted hardly a minute. Then the door opened and the speaking man disappeared inside. Judah walked hastily away down the street. He looked like a thief escaping into the darkness.

"I'm fine now," Deborah said, trying to smile. "I just needed a moment to catch my breath."

"Perhaps we should go home," Sarah suggested.

She really did look concerned, and Deborah felt guilty for deceiving her. But it was better that she and Abijah not become involved in this.

"Yes, perhaps. Perhaps Noah will be back by now."

29

Noah had indeed returned, and Sarah explained that Deborah had become tired and needed to lie down for a while.

"Don't worry about me," Deborah whispered to him, just before she went upstairs. "I'll explain later."

Sarah accompanied her, and the two men were left together. Abijah almost immediately took a small papyrus scroll from his pocket and handed it to Noah, who knew at once what it was. He opened it and read it carefully.

"Five hundred silver shekels is a considerable sum," he said finally. "My grandfather won't know what to make of it—no bride from Nazareth has ever commanded a tenth of such a figure."

"I want Sarah to know that I value her."

Noah could only shake his head and laugh. "She knows that already, and she is a practical girl who will think you have taken leave of your senses to part with such a sum. But never fear. Grandfather will doubtless request me to invest it, and it will come to Sarah at his death."

Abijah, for whom it was not a question of money but of respect, merely shrugged. In any case, Noah would make it up to him in Sarah's dowry. It would all come out right.

"How was your walk?" he asked, to change the subject. "Was Deborah taken ill?"

"She complained of fatigue, but I didn't believe her." Abijah smiled, as if sharing a secret. "I think she just wanted to come back, probably to be with you."

Certainly she seemed well enough half an hour later, when she and Sarah came back downstairs. She smiled at Noah and touched his hand.

"Do you feel well enough to walk back to Nazareth?" he asked.

"Oh yes. There was nothing wrong with me. I'll tell you about it later."

And so the two couples started out together, but it was not long before Abijah and Sarah, who paid no attention to anyone except each other, were a good twenty paces ahead.

This was agreeable to Noah and Deborah, since it gave them a chance for private conversation.

"You see how well suited they are to one another," Noah observed, gesturing toward his sister and her lover. The sight of them seemed to amuse him. "Abijah is such a great, tall fellow and Sarah always had long legs. You and I will never be able to keep up with them."

"Sarah is a sweet girl. I think they will be happy."

"Let us hope so. They both deserve to be happy."

"So do we."

She smiled and he took her hand.

"I am already happy," he said, and then instantly wished it unsaid. Deborah would imagine he was alluding to last night and he did not wish to distress her.

But she was not distressed.

"There are a few details we need to settle," Noah said. "We need to settle who will act in place of your father in discussions of the bride price, and we need to settle on an amount. Abijah is going to offer five hundred silver shekels for Sarah."

"Five *hundred*? Such a sum?"

"That was my reaction. However, I can hardly allow myself to be outdone by my future brother. I was thinking of six hundred. Of course, if I were obliged to pay according to your true value, I couldn't afford you."

"You are very sweet," she said, and squeezed his hand. "But can you afford six?"

"Oh yes. You see, I am about to marry a wealthy widow."

They both laughed, loud enough that Sarah and Abijah glanced back.

The expression on Sarah's face was a reminder.

"You were going to tell me about this morning," Noah said.

"I saw someone. I didn't want him to see me, so I pretended to feel ill."

"Who was it?"

"Judah."

It took a moment before Noah remembered who she was talking about.

"Then he must have stayed in the city. But why did you not want him to see you?"

As they walked along the dusty road, Deborah seemed to stare out at nothing. Noah put his hand on her shoulder, and she turned her face to him and smiled.

"You don't like him, do you," he said.

"No. I don't." She shook her head, as if admitting some failure in herself. "I never have. But that is not it. He was with another man."

"Someone you know?"

Noah was immediately struck by the absurdity of his question. Who could Deborah know in Sepphoris?

"No. I had never seen him before. But Judah was afraid of him. I could see that, even at a distance. They were like master and slave."

"Perhaps Judah was trying to beg money from some stranger, and the application was not well received."

"No. This was someone he knew. Whatever was between them had nothing to do with money. The other man was . . . I don't know how to put it. He has some power over Judah."

She shook her head again, this time with emphasis.

"Besides, Judah has no reason to beg for money. When Joshua first brought him to Capernaum, I gave him work. When I sold the business, I paid everyone off."

"And so you felt—what?"

"That whatever was happening between Judah and this other man was best left between them."

Noah nodded in agreement.

"Well, perhaps it will all be explained when Judah comes back."

"Perhaps. But I have the feeling this was something we are better not knowing anything about."

———

By the time they arrived in Nazareth, Judah had almost been forgotten.

Sarah entered her grandfather's house and Deborah went in search of Joshua, whom she wished to stand in place of her father for the betrothal ceremony. Noah and Abijah were left standing outside Benjamin's door.

"I think we can go in now," Noah said at last.

They found Sarah and Benjamin sitting at the table in the kitchen. Benjamin seemed not to notice their entrance, but Sarah could not restrain a smile of something like relief. There was a jug of wine on the center of the table and one cup in front of Sarah.

Noah and Abijah sat down.

"Grandfather," Noah began, "my friend Abijah wishes to be introduced to you. He has a matter dear to his heart, which he wishes to discuss."

The old man, who knew his part in this little drama, raised his eyes to Abijah's face and nodded.

"What business can he have with me?" he asked.

Abijah then took the marriage contract from his pocket and read it aloud. He promised to love Sarah all the days of her life. He promised to take no other wives. He promised to pay five hundred silver shekels to her family as a compensation for their expense in raising her.

During this recitation Benjamin seemed not to be listening. When it was over he glanced at Noah, who nodded his approval.

"It seems in order," he said at last, his face remaining expressionless. "But my granddaughter must signify her consent."

Abijah took up the jug of wine and poured some into the cup that rested in front of Sarah. After a few seconds she raised the cup to her lips and drank.

"She has accepted your offer," Benjamin announced, and for the first time he smiled.

He rose from his seat and went into his bedroom. When he returned he was carrying a piece of cloth. He stood behind Sarah's chair and held up the cloth by the corners, revealing it to be about two cubits square and of a linen so fine as to be almost transparent.

"This was your mother's veil," he said, as he let it flutter down to cover Sarah's head. "You will wear it whenever you go outside, that all may know that you are spoken for."

There followed, of course, the gift giving. A silk shawl, dyed the purple of kings along the borders. Bracelets of silver. Little leather bags filled with spices. Noah and his grandfather made appropriately admiring remarks and Sarah smiled and blushed. It was a moment of unblemished happiness.

At last Abijah rose from the table. "I go now to build a house to receive my bride," he said, and made a slight bow. When he was out the door, the old man shook his head.

"If he can afford to pay five hundred silver shekels for his wife, doubtless he already has a house." Benjamin picked up one of the bracelets that was lying on the table, considered it for a moment, and then set it back down. "Such a sum. I think you young people must all be mad."

"One must honor the forms, Grandfather. And he loves her."

"Yes, Noah. I have eyes to see that."

Then the old man reached up and lifted the veil from Sarah's face.

"I think he will make you a good husband, Sarah. Provided he doesn't beggar himself."

Then everyone could laugh.

In the evening, after the first stars had appeared, Noah and his grandfather sat outside and drank water, dipping their cups into a jar filled from the village well. The well was deep and the water was cold, and the emerging darkness was still pleasantly warm.

"Where is Sarah?" the old man asked.

"Gone to see Deborah. As you can imagine, they have a lot to talk about."

"Then they get along?"

"Like sisters, as if they've known each other all their lives."

"That is a blessing."

Benjamin sat with his head resting against the wall of his house, his eyes closed. Anyone might have thought he had drifted off to sleep, but he had not.

"Two grandchildren betrothed in the same day," he said finally. "That too is a blessing. Perhaps God has forgiven us."

"Forgiven us what?"

"Only He knows that."

He closed his eyes again, and a faint smile played across his face.

"Who will be married first?"

"Deborah and I, after the next Sabbath."

"Here in Nazareth?"

"Yes."

"Good. The family will appreciate that." And then suddenly, as if the question had just come into his mind, he asked, "How much did you give for her?"

"Six hundred silver shekels."

"Joshua drives a hard bargain."

"Yes."

They both laughed, for it was an exquisite jest.

"I was a little surprised you didn't return here yesterday," Benjamin said—quite casually, as if the matter were of little interest.

"I discovered I had an appointment this morning."

"I see."

The old man seemed to regard the subject as closed, but suddenly Noah, like a little boy with an overburdened conscience, found that he wanted to tell him everything.

Except, how could he do that? He settled for telling him about his meeting with Eleazar.

"I see."

Benjamin nodded. He had never heard of the priest Eleazar, who sat at the Tetrarch's right hand, but he knew that his grandson, who had suddenly disappeared for almost two months, had left many things out.

"Are you in danger?" he asked.

"Not now."

Benjamin looked away for a moment, as if he did not care to meet his grandson's eye, and then with elaborate care he dipped his cup into the jar of water.

They sat for a while in the gathering darkness, saying nothing. Benjamin seemed to savor the water like wine.

"Is Joshua in danger?"

Noah shook his head. "For the present we are all safe."

"And how long will the present last?"

"I don't know."

The old man, accustomed to accepting the uncertainties of life, merely nodded.

Then, apparently, he decided to change the subject.

"Joshua spent the morning with me," he said. "I suspect he merely wished to escape his family for a time. We had a long talk."

"What about, Grandfather?"

"About God, and the mystery of His intentions." Benjamin made a gesture with his hands, lifting the palms upward as if balancing some object. "And it became clear to me that he has thought more deeply about this question than I have. Would you like to hear what he said?"

"I already know what he said. He does not make a secret of his beliefs."

"And what, then, do you think?"

"I don't know what to think. I have no answers, only questions."

The invisible object in Benjamin's hands became two objects. He seemed to be trying to decide which was heavier.

"What questions are those?" he asked. It was not a challenge. He seemed genuinely curious.

"I wonder how someone I grew up with can see into the mind of God."

"The same question his own family asks."

"Yes."

"Perhaps he does not see at all. Perhaps God whispers these things to him, as a father whispers to his son while he falls asleep. He trusts in God as a child trusts in his father."

"Do you believe Joshua is a prophet, Grandfather?"

The old man shook his head.

"I do not know. Perhaps he is not a prophet. But perhaps our family has produced one whom God loves as a son."

"We all call God our father. Yet He is the greatest of mysteries. Joshua presumes to speak for Him, to know His heart, and for that reason I dread what may become of him."

The old man dropped his hands.

"Yes, I understand what you mean," he said. "To be loved by God is to assume a fearful burden."

30

The next morning, after breakfast, Joshua came and invited Noah to take a walk with him. They set out together for the hills, where they had played together as boys, and for a long time Joshua was silent.

"You paid six hundred silver shekels for Deborah's bride price," he said at last, making it sound like an accusation. "That is a great deal of money. Who were you trying to impress?"

Noah laughed. It seemed such an odd way to begin a conversation.

"It is about the sum she received for her house and business. All of that comes to me as her dowry. The bride price is hers alone, since she has no family. Do you begin to understand my reasoning?"

"Yes. You wanted her to have her own property. But if you ever divorce her, you forfeit the dowry and thus you lose both halves of the transaction."

"Who would ever be fool enough to divorce Deborah?"

"That is a point."

The ground under their feet was beginning to rise. Noah pointed to a grape terrace above a steep face of rock.

"Remember when you jumped from there and broke your arm?" he asked.

"You keep bringing that up." Joshua smiled and rubbed his elbow. "We were just seven. I didn't realize that the farther you fall the harder you hit the ground."

"After that, it was the rest of the summer before your mother let you come out and play again."

"But you kept me company." Joshua put his hand on his cousin's shoulder. "We read Torah together—it was the only thing I was fit for."

"So why now are you asking me about Deborah's bride price."

"Why? Did I offend you?" He looked at Noah as if that possibility had never occurred to him.

"Yes. A little."

"Then I am sorry. These days you and I don't think alike, at least not about things like money. Your motives were honorable, but such a sum, given to the poor, would abate much suffering."

"Deborah and I have set aside two hundred as a wedding offering to the poor."

"But two hundred is not six hundred."

"Joshua, you grow tiresome in your righteousness."

This observation was greeted with an explosion of laughter.

"Then truly it must be that I am God's prophet," Joshua announced triumphantly. "For we have it on the authority of their own writings that many considered them tiresome. Perhaps no one becomes a prophet until after he is dead."

They had reached the summit of a low hill, so they sat down to enjoy the view. With the sun at their backs, they could see Sepphoris in the distance, shining like a jewel on the other side of the plain.

"Noah, will you go to Jerusalem this year?"

"Yes. Deborah has never seen it."

"And will we meet there as always?"

Noah smiled to himself, for he knew this was Joshua's way of apologizing. They always spent the Passover together, at the house of a distant relative.

"Yes. We will meet there, as always."

"I wish Uncle Benjamin could go with us."

"He is too old. Even the thought of the journey wearies him."

"I know, but he will not be any the more wearied for my wishing it."

Joshua sat with his elbows resting on his knees, the expression on his face as keen as a hunting dog's. *What is he thinking of?* Noah wondered. *Merely Grandfather in Jerusalem?*

"When we come back, we can tell him all about it," Noah said.

"Perhaps he will know without our telling him."

Noah was about to ask him what he meant, but he seemed so concentrated on his own thoughts that it would have been an intrusion.

But then Joshua saved him the trouble.

"This Passover will see great changes," he said, almost as if speaking to himself. "And Jerusalem will be where they will begin." Then he turned his head and smiled. "You don't believe me, do you."

"I am like Grandfather. I don't know what to believe."

"Did he talk to you about me?"

"Yes. He thinks you may be one of the pious, whom God loves."

"Did he really say that?"

Noah could not help but be amused that Joshua was so pleased.

"Yes, he did."

"Well then, in Jerusalem we will see if he was right."

Suddenly Joshua climbed to his feet and then reached down to offer a hand to Noah. The two of them stood for a moment, looking at Sepphoris in the distance.

"Remember the summer Father and I spent working there?" Joshua shook his head, as if trying to clear his thoughts. "What was it we were building there?"

"The scaffolding for the baths. I remember I came along with you one day, just to see this great wonder."

"How old were we? Seventeen?"

"I think so."

"Father is so very sick now. And so afraid of death."

"Has he spoken of it?"

"No. But for the first time he listens to me. I tell him of God's kingdom, and how want and death and unrighteousness will be banished, and he listens. I tell him to embrace repentance, and it is a measure of his fear that he listens. He wants to believe."

"What is stopping him?"

"My brother, Little Joseph. Father favors him because he is the most like him. Jacob stands aside."

As if from a single impulse, they both turned and started back toward Nazareth.

"If I could bring my father to God . . ." Joshua began, and then smiled and shook his head. It seemed beyond his power to finish the thought.

"Then it would heal the breach?"

"Then I might save them all."

The path they took swung around a piece of rising ground and they came within sight of the road that ran south from Sepphoris. They saw a man coming toward them from the road, and almost immediately he raised his arm and waved.

"Look there," Joshua said. "It's Judah, returned from the fleshpots of the city."

The man started running toward them, and it was perhaps half a minute before Noah, who was not as farsighted as his cousin, could make out that in fact it was Judah.

He remembered Deborah's odd story about him, and his own answer: *"Perhaps it will all be explained when Judah comes back."*

Suddenly he knew that it would not be.

By the time Judah was with them he was out of breath. He embraced Joshua and then quickly greeted Noah.

"I couldn't resist it," he said at last. "I have been so long in the villages that I longed to feel cobblestones beneath my feet again. I drank wine and took a bath. It was glorious!"

Joshua laughed.

"Well, you came back. That is the main thing. I pray you will be brought to repentance."

"Not yet! I enjoyed myself too much."

As they walked, Judah regaled them with his adventures, none of which seemed to have involved breaking the commandments. It was a sketchy narrative, Noah observed to himself—not enough to fill three days. There were things he was leaving out.

"I hope, at least, you didn't have to sleep in the street," Noah said.

"Oh no."

Noah caught Judah's sideways glance, as if the disciple realized he had made a mistake.

"But perhaps you had some acquaintance you could stay with," Noah continued.

"No. I know no one in Sepphoris."

"Well, you do now." Noah smiled benignly, for all that he felt as if a sliver of ice had pierced his heart. "Next time, you must make my house your own."

Judah's thanks were just a shade exaggerated. He was relieved, and could not quite disguise it.

Joshua, of course, noticed nothing. Why should he? He had not heard Deborah's story, and he was not a man given to suspicion.

They walked back toward the village together. For the most part Noah kept silent, merely interjecting a word here and there. He was more interested in listening, and more in the way the conversation proceeded than in its content.

"I should have come back sooner," Judah said, dropping his head in a show of repentance.

"Then why didn't you?"

"Perhaps because, until recently, I have lived all my life in cities. I feel comfortable with the crowds and the noise. I like buying a cup of wine at a stall, where the man who pours it looks not at me but at the coins I drop on his counter. With all its crush of people, one is somehow more alone in the city. I missed that."

"Cities encourage one to be selfish. In cities humanity becomes a blur, just part of the background. We forget the love we owe to one another."

"Yes. You are right. I have been selfish."

"Perhaps it is man's nature to be selfish, just as it is God's nature to be loving and forgiving. The path to salvation is the path of learning how to be like God."

"Yes. I am weak and sinful. I despair of salvation."

"God will uplift you. You have merely to open your heart to Him and He will bring you to Himself."

"I will try to be better. I won't drink wine again."

This made Joshua laugh, and he put his arm on Judah's shoulders.

"No one asks such a sacrifice of you. Wine is God's gift to us and we should accept it with gratitude, knowing it belongs to Him and not to us. But drink it with your friends."

So it went—the disciple accusing himself and the teacher opening the way to forgiveness. And it was impossible not to believe in the sincerity of Judah's repentance. He really seemed to believe that he had fallen into sin. He wished to be forgiven.

But there could be many sins besides drinking wine at a stall.

Noah, Abijah, and Sarah had agreed among themselves that they would leave for Sepphoris early enough to be back in the city by noon.

Deborah would remain in Nazareth, with Joshua's family, until Noah came for her, the day following the next Sabbath.

The wedding would be celebrated in Grandfather's house.

But that meant that three days would intervene until Noah would see his betrothed again, and four before he could claim her. It seemed an eternity.

He wanted to see Deborah one last time before he left.

In theory, the betrothed couple were not supposed to keep company together between the betrothal ceremony and the wedding, but, given the conditions of everyday life, the prohibition was largely ignored. After all, Sarah and Abijah would be walking back to Sepphoris together. All that was required was that some pretext be found so that the meeting did not seem arranged.

So, when Noah returned to his grandfather's house and learned that Sarah was visiting Deborah, presumably at Joseph's house, Noah had merely to go and fetch Sarah.

He found the two women sitting together outside, on a wooden bench in the shade of an ancient fig tree. They looked so odd in their veils that he was relieved when they saw him and uncovered their faces.

"Good morning," he said, and then, turning to his sister, added, "we will be leaving in less than an hour."

It was all the hint Sarah needed. Doubtless she was looking forward to the walk home, when she could be with Abijah.

"I suppose I should go put my things together," she said, and was gone.

Noah sat down beside Deborah and smiled.

"I hope this is the last time I shall have to construct an excuse for being alone with you," he said. He glanced about, to make sure no one was near, and then kissed her.

When the kiss was finished she studied his face for a moment and asked, "What is wrong?"

"Does something have to be wrong?"

"I can see it in your face. You smile at me, but not with your eyes."

It was a peculiar feeling to be understood so easily. He supposed he would get used to it. Perhaps getting used to it would be one of the pleasures of marriage.

"As it turns out, you were right about Judah."

31

It had become a habit. Almost every afternoon, about an hour before sunset, Caleb went up to the roof of his house and looked out over the Galilean countryside. His servants, and even his wife, knew not to disturb him. He wanted to be alone with his thoughts.

These days his thoughts were not pleasant.

He drank wine—perhaps more than he should—and watched the wind play across the wheat fields. Galilee was an abundant land. To own even a small share of it was to be rich, and Caleb's share was not small. He owned several large farms and all the land surrounding some ten or twelve villages—he had lost count—and twice a year the rents poured in like spring rain.

Still, the view from his roof no longer comforted him. It simply reminded him of all he had to lose.

There was not a day, not an hour, when he was free from fear. Fear haunted him. Fear had become his second self.

But on his roof at least he could be alone with it.

Eleazar had the Tetrarch's ear. Eleazar had seen to it that Caleb would not be received in Tiberias—neither he nor his wife.

Since the beginning of her exile from court, Michal had spent her days writing long, pleading letters to the Lady Herodias, which went unanswered. Caleb knew, because he had had the letters intercepted. Most he burned, but a few of the more temperate and supplicating he allowed to reach their destination—the mighty of this world like to be fawned over, and it would not do to have the tetrarch's wife feel herself neglected.

Still, no answers came. Forgiveness and reinstatement were not to be expected. Eleazar had seen to that.

And Michal, after a series of indescribable tantrums, had at last decided that life in Sepphoris was not to be borne and announced that she intended a visit to her family in Jerusalem. And Caleb found he lacked the strength of character even to refuse his permission. She would go— he couldn't stop her. And if he tried, she might punish him by never coming back.

Marriage was an ordeal, a thousand tiny steps toward despair.

He could divorce her, simply end it. But then he would lose her entirely, and that would be infinitely worse.

This was one more injury the Lord Eleazar had done him.

And Eleazar, Caleb knew, would not be content with merely this. Eleazar meant, in the end, to destroy him. He would be arrested one day and made to vanish. No one would even know where he was buried.

But there was still a chance of survival. Still a chance that he would live to enjoy the income from his various estates. He merely had to demonstrate that Eleazar was wrong, that the Tetrarch really was hedged in by enemies, that the danger was real. Then Eleazar would fall, and Caleb would be safe.

To do that he needed to destroy Joshua bar Joseph.

But he had to be careful. Joshua had to be exposed as a threat to the state. Joshua had to suffer and die as an insurrectionist. But it could not happen in Galilee, and it could not happen at Caleb's hands.

The Romans had to do it, in Judea. Antipas would be suitably impressed if the Romans crucified Joshua.

"Are you sure he plans to be in Jerusalem for the Passover?" Caleb had asked Judah.

"Yes. He always goes. He stays with his cousin."

The cousin being, of course, Noah bar Barachel, now attached to Eleazar. Well, provided the ironsmith didn't interfere, he could await his time.

Judah had quite a story to tell of his adventures with the peasant preacher. He had come out of the countryside more than half convinced that Joshua really was God's messenger.

"He is not a threat to anyone," Judah told him. "He is a wise and good man. He teaches love, charity, and forgiveness. He says we should not resist evil, but overcome evil with good."

"It is a question of what one defines as evil." Caleb smiled indulgently and poured Judah another cup of wine. It was a particularly good vintage, but Judah, in his old life, had been accustomed to the best. "If one defines as evil the social order, that is sedition. And since the social order is ordained by God, and since we must all submit ourselves to the will of God, it is also a sin. Your peasant holy man is nothing more than a rebel disguised as a prophet.

"What does he tell you, this peasant prophet? What words does he use?"

"He says God will send one like the son of man to judge the world. He says this one will come in power and glory and establish God's kingdom."

"'God's kingdom.' Is that the phrase he used?"

"Yes."

"This judge, he will be *like* the son of man, but not himself a son of man?"

"Yes."

"So he does not mean himself? He does not mean a human being?"
"No."

"An angel perhaps?"

"Perhaps. He does not say."

"And who will rule, once the angel has rendered his judgment?"

"He does not say, except that the first shall be last and the last first."
"I see."

He really did see. It was all painfully clear.

A palace guard had found Judah huddled by a doorway—the same doorway through which he had been released from prison. It was evening, and the guard, who thought Judah was a beggar seeking a little shelter for the night, was about to drive him away with a kick when he said, "Inform the Lord Caleb that I am Judah bar Isaac." So the guard told him to wait.

When Caleb, who happened still to be in his office, came down for a look, Judah was sitting with his arms wrapped around his legs, staring out like an owl. He looked up at Caleb as if trying to remember his face and then said, "Put me back in my cell."

"Nothing awaits you there but death," Caleb had answered him. "Do you remember the lower prison? Do you remember Uriah? Or perhaps you never knew his name. Uriah will make your death into an amusement lasting the whole afternoon. Do you want to suffer for hours and hours?"

"No."

"Then what do you want?"

"I don't know."

"Do you want to go back to Tiberias? To your old life?"

"I don't know."

He was a wretched creature. After two months with Joshua bar Joseph, he looked and smelled like a peasant.

"Come along," Caleb told him. "That's it. Stand up. I'll take you to the baths, where they'll wash your clothes and the steam will revive you."

They spent four hours in the baths. Caleb never let him out of his sight. He didn't dare.

After he was clean and had drunk some wine and had eaten a slice of cold melon, Judah began to return to himself. He began to complain that he could not remember the last time he had tasted meat, so Caleb ordered him a plate of grilled lamb. Judah ate it all and then curled up naked on one of the marble benches and fell asleep.

It was almost midnight when he awoke. The baths would have closed hours ago if Caleb hadn't bribed the attendants. The two men dressed and walked to Caleb's house, where they spent another two hours drinking wine. Finally the servants made up a bed for Judah in one of the rooms reserved for guests, and Caleb locked him in for the night.

Fortunately, Michal was in Jerusalem visiting her family.

The next morning Judah, who had lost the knack of drinking, was in a sullen mood and suffered from a headache. He cheered up after breakfast and another jug of the Cyprian wine Caleb had been saving against the day he was named warden of the city.

That was when Caleb began to interrogate him about Joshua.

"I see."

Joshua really was a dangerous revolutionary. The trick was putting that conclusion into terms that a political simpleton like Judah could understand.

"'God's kingdom,'" he repeated. "But God already rules the universe. Do we not pray to Him, every day, calling Him 'King of the Universe'? God rules history—one only has to read the Prophets to know that.

And He rules in Galilee and Judea and in all the lands where Jews worship Him. He lives in Jerusalem, in the Temple, in the Holy of Holies. Why does this fool Joshua preach the coming of a thing which is already here?"

"I don't know." Judah looked uncomfortable, but then, he was a little drunk. "Perhaps he means God will rule *directly*."

"Directly?"

"Yes."

Caleb could only laugh.

"What are men but His instruments? Does a mason chip stone *indirectly* when he uses a chisel? God rules *directly* now."

"I hadn't thought of it that way."

"I suppose not."

They were on the roof of the house, where Caleb could be sure no servant was listening. He knew that Eleazar had spies in his household, but none of them could have known the identity of his guest.

The sun had just broken free from the eastern mountains, so the morning was still cool. There was even a slight breeze. The world seemed both serene and beautiful.

But it was all an illusion. Caleb had long since concluded that life was no more than a cruel jest. There was neither mercy nor justice. There was only struggle.

Joshua bar Joseph might believe in angels, but Caleb bar Jacob knew better.

"If your prophet has his way," he said, pronouncing each word with elaborate care, "if this glorious, divine revolution ever happens, all it will mean is that mankind exchanges one set of masters for another. In place of the Tetrarch, we will have some peasant dictator. And the ground will be covered with corpses. Trust me. There will be death everywhere.

"But he will not have his way, because no one is listening."

"Then why did you send me to him?"

Caleb regarded his cousin with faint amusement. This child of a Levite family as old as his own, this pleasure-loving dabbler in religious fantasy, wanted to know *why*.

"That you might achieve your salvation," he said. It was perhaps as true an answer as anyone deserved.

"I don't understand."

"No, I am aware that you don't."

Caleb decided he had sufficiently baffled the man and it was time to change the subject.

"What is Joshua doing in Nazareth?"

"Visiting his family. His father is ill and not expected to live long."

Judah was eyeing the wine jar in a way that suggested he might like to hide inside it, so Caleb poured him another cup.

"His family, I gather, is not sympathetic."

Judah shook his head, even as the cup was at his lips.

"No."

"I gather few people are."

"Some are. He gains followers everywhere he goes."

Caleb considered this. A man goes about preaching that God's kingdom is at hand. He has small groups of followers scattered over the countryside, but he seems to stay away from the cities. Is such a man dangerous? Probably not. Probably Eleazar was right about that.

For one thing, revolutions usually began in cities, where there was power to be overthrown and the numbers at hand to accomplish it. You needed a mob to start a revolution. Peasants in the countryside did not pose a threat unless they were pushed to the edge of starvation, and sometimes not even then.

Joshua bar Joseph was not a threat to the established order, but he could be made to look like one. Jerusalem, after all, was a city.

"You are sure he is going to Jerusalem for the Passover?"

"Yes. He has spoken of it. He goes every year."

Caleb did not wish to know any more, primarily because he did not want to draw attention to his interest.

"What is your opinion of him, Judah? I am curious."

The disciple's face registered first surprise and then wariness, as if the question might be some sort of trap. His eyes fell to his empty wine cup, which rested on the table in front of him. He seemed to be trying to decide how it had come to be there.

"Just tell me. Don't be afraid," Caleb said, refilling the cup.

Judah took a swallow and then set the cup down. The gesture was like a decision made.

"I think he is a good man," he said. The look in his eyes was wary and at the same time almost defiant. "I think he is a man of God, and I believe he wants to redeem the world. He would save us all if he could.

He is without hatred or envy or malice. He truly loves his enemies. He would rejoice to lead the worst man on earth to the love of God."

It was a challenge of sorts, and Caleb felt a strong inclination to smile. But he did not. He met Judah's eyes with a steady gaze.

"Was it hard for you to say that?" he asked finally.

"Yes." Judah blinked and looked away, like a child expecting punishment.

"Why? Because you are afraid of me?"

"Yes. I know what you are capable of."

It was like a slap in the face—the rebuke all the more telling for being administered by a coward. Caleb waited until he was quite calm before he spoke again.

"Your holy man has nothing to fear from me," he said, filling his own wine cup for the first time. "I will not disturb him while he waits for his angel. What you say has eased my mind."

No one could have been more surprised than Judah. Whatever he had expected, it was not this. For a long moment he hardly moved, as he seemed to struggle to comprehend what he had just heard.

"You are free, Judah bar Isaac."

"Free?" He hardly seemed to know what the word meant.

"Yes, free. Go back to Tiberias and rejoin your friends, if that is what pleases you. Your old life awaits you there."

Caleb waited a few seconds and then smiled.

"Or perhaps that is not what you want. Do you want to remain with God's messenger?"

"I don't know." Judah shook his head. "I only know that I don't want to be who I was."

"Then think about it."

With an almost ostentatious casualness Caleb patted the pocket of his tunic, as if trying to remember where he had put something. Then he pulled out a small leather pouch and dropped it on the table.

"Here," he said. "You deserve a vacation from rectitude. Go out into the city and amuse yourself. Get drunk, stuff yourself with meat. Find a woman. Come back tomorrow morning and tell me what you have decided. But come back. Don't make me send the guards after you."

Caleb had issued orders to have Judah followed—at a discreet distance—and the reports were illuminating. The whores of Sepphoris went disappointed. The peasant prophet's disciple wandered aimlessly for several hours, speaking to no one, and then bought one simple meal and a small jar of wine, which he carried away with him. When night fell, he curled up in a doorway and, apparently having lost the habit of comfort, fell asleep with his head against the cold stone.

The next morning he found his way back to Caleb's house.

"I want to return to Joshua," he announced.

This was not a surprise. In fact, Caleb had counted on it.

"Well, at least stay for breakfast," he said. "And return the purse. It will seem strange if you go back to your friends with so much money. They might wonder where you got it."

They talked for a long time. Caleb made no effort to guide the conversation and was careful not to mention Jerusalem.

Judah simply needed to confess, first his own unworthiness and then his devotion to Joshua. Had it not been so foolish, it would have been touching.

"I truly believe God loves him," he said.

"Does he perform miracles?"

"Not that I have seen, but Simon speaks of a woman who was cured of a menstrual discharge merely by touching him. He turned to her and said, 'Daughter, your sins are forgiven,' and she was cured. Also, he once restored a blind man's sight."

"But you did not see it?"

"No."

"Curious." Caleb smiled faintly. "I have heard hundreds of reports of miracles, but I have never met anyone who actually saw one. If you ever do see one—if Joshua raises the dead, for instance—you must be sure to tell me."

"I will."

"Thank you."

At last, when they said their farewells, standing in the bright sunshine in front of Caleb's door, it was necessary to remind Judah that he had not quite slipped the leash.

"Remember who gave you back your life," Caleb told him. "Remember that I can reclaim it anytime I wish. If you betray me, I will make you wish for death long before you die."

It was interesting to watch the way fear seized him. Judah seemed to grow smaller even before his eyes. He was like a whipped dog that can think only to lick its master's hand.

"I would never . . ."

"I know." Caleb raised his arm in dismissal. "Now go back to your peasant friends." Then, seemingly as an afterthought, he said, "Be sure to come to me in Jerusalem when you are there for the Passover. I will not be difficult to find."

It was all quite simple, he thought as he sat on his rooftop. The peasant revolutionary, whom they would not allow him to arrest, would go to Jerusalem to be arrested, tried, and crucified by the Romans. No blame would attach to the Tetrarch, who would nonetheless be brought to see that the danger had been real all along. Then, as the Tetrarch's eyes were opened, he would remember to be afraid and would turn from Eleazar to his servant Caleb.

Power was the one goal in life and, behind it, fear lurked as the only reality.

32

Never in his life had Noah been so impatient for a Sabbath. In the early afternoon of the preceding day, Abijah arrived to accompany him and Sarah to Nazareth. Noah closed the shop and they started out.

As usual, his sister and her betrothed had no attention for anyone except each other, and Noah was content to be alone with his thoughts.

Tomorrow, or possibly even today, he would see Deborah again. At the Sabbath dinner they would probably have a chance to speak to one another. Then, in another two days, the wedding would take place. He would not see his house again until he was able to lead her into it as his bride.

He had not thought it possible to miss anyone the way he had missed her during these few days.

Be patient, he told himself. *Only three days.*

They found Grandfather sitting beside his doorway. He looked up and smiled. Then he put aside the latch lock he had been repairing, wiped his hands on a torn piece of cloth, and stood up to greet them. He kissed Sarah, who then went into the house. He put his hand on his grandson's shoulder and then nodded to Abijah, who took the hint.

"I have it in mind to call on my friend Abner," Abijah said.

When he was gone, Benjamin shook his head in mock dismay.

"Given a chance, he'd hang about all day, waiting for Sarah to come back out. I'm surprised you let him accompany you and Sarah here. City ways, I imagine."

"He loves her, Grandfather. And he's an upright man. There's no harm in it."

"I suppose you think I'm old-fashioned."

"Yes."

The old man saw the amusement in his grandson's eyes and smiled.

"Still, Deborah comports herself with more modesty."

Noah, who felt no temptation to inform his grandfather of certain events which had taken place earlier in the week, offered only a vague agreement.

"She's a proper village girl," Benjamin continued, patting Noah's shoulder as if this were all his doing.

"She's also a widow," Noah added helpfully.

"That is true. So she knows what to expect."

"I imagine she does."

The next morning Benjamin and his grandchildren went to the house of prayer. They were almost the first to arrive, so Noah excused himself from entering with his grandfather and sister by announcing that he would wait for Abijah. In fact, he was hoping for a glimpse of Deborah.

But Abijah also came early, perhaps hoping to see Sarah, and thus the whole stratagem was on the verge of collapse when Noah had the happy thought that they should both wait outside a little longer so that Abijah could be introduced to Joshua.

"Yes, I would like that," Abijah replied. "My friend Abner, who will be along in a moment, has become one of his admirers. He says he is an interesting man."

"Oh, he is certainly that."

Their patience was soon rewarded by the sight of Joseph approaching, with his family clustered behind him. The father walked slowly, leaning on the arm of his second son, Jacob. His face was damp with sweat.

"Peace be yours," he said to Noah, and then his eyes turned with faintly hostile curiosity to Noah's friend.

"This is Sarah's betrothed, my friend Abijah."

"From the city, then?" From Joseph, it sounded almost like an accusation.

"Yes, I live in Sepphoris."

Joseph nodded and then, as if he had decided to overlook the matter, he put his hand on Abijah's arm.

"Welcome to the family," he said, and turned to gesture toward his family behind him. "These are my sons—Jacob and Little Joseph, and my eldest, Joshua."

Each of these embraced Abijah in his turn, after which the introductions were over. The women, apparently, would have to wait until another time.

Everyone began a slow movement toward the door of the prayer house and, while Abijah and Joshua fell into conversation, Noah was at last free to direct his attention elsewhere. He took a step forward and grasped the hand of Miriam, Joseph's wife, stooping slightly that she might kiss him. Miriam had been a close friend of his mother.

"I have been looking after her," she murmured to him as their faces touched.

He had merely to turn his eyes to see Deborah, surrounded by Miriam's daughters and her son's wives, smiling at him through her veil.

He returned her smile, and that would have to do. There was now no time for anything else, and in the prayer house the women sat in the back.

The prayer house, which was in almost the exact center of Nazareth, was the largest building there. The structure was probably two hundred years old, although no one knew for certain, and it was of a piece with its rural origins. It was made of mud brick and the floor was earth packed hard by generations of pious feet. The benches and stools seemed haphazardly scattered but in fact reflected the kinship patterns that were part of the unchanging design of village life. Everyone knew their places and what to expect.

The moment came when the hum of voices and the shuffling of feet simply died away. Everyone was quiet, for they knew they were about to witness once more the eternal promise of God to His people, the reading of the Law.

Abner, Abijah's friend, who by rotation was this Sabbath's reader, rose and took one of the scrolls from the high, heavily built chair that represented the throne of God. He unrolled the scroll until he found his place, and began to pronounce the words of the Law, which Moses had received from God on Mount Sinai. The reading might have been about clean and unclean foods, or the rights of the poor, or the proper sacrifices to be offered in the Temple, or the remission of debt on the seventh year, or any number of other subjects, for the Law covered the whole of life and thus made all of life holy.

Today's reading happened to deal with the Law governing divorce.

"'When a man takes a wife and marries her, if then she finds no favor in his eyes because he has found some indecency in her, and he writes her a bill of divorce and puts it in her hand and sends her out of his house, and if she goes and becomes another man's wife, and the latter husband dislikes her and writes her a bill of divorce and puts it in her hand and sends her out of his house, if the latter husband dies, who took her to be his wife, then her former husband, who sent her away, may not take her again to be his wife, after she has been defiled; for that is an abomination before the Lord, and you shall not bring guilt upon the land, which the Lord your God gives you for an inheritance.'"

Abner, who was a heavily built, benign-looking man—a man of both wealth and scholarship, the owner of several vineyards in the area, known for his generosity to the poor—looked up from the scroll, raised his eyebrows, and allowed his gaze to wander over the congregation, seeming to invite comment. When no one immediately offered to speak, his eyes fell on Abijah.

"Perhaps we can prevail upon our learned guest from the city to open his thoughts to us."

Joshua, who was sitting next to Abijah, glanced slyly at Noah and smiled, as if to say, *"This should be interesting."*

Abijah hesitated just long enough to give the impression that he did not wish to intrude himself, and then slowly rose to his feet.

"I would only point out," he began, "that the passage is concerned not with divorce itself but with certain restrictions on remarriage. That divorce is permissible is implied, and the grounds are at best implied. In the case of the first marriage, the stated grounds are 'some indecency,' and in the second merely a 'dislike.' Thus Shammai, arguing from the first instance, states that divorce is permitted only if the wife is guilty of adultery, and Hillel, arguing from the second, claims for the husband an absolute right of divorce, even if he is merely annoyed because his wife has burnt his dinner."

As Abijah sat down, a ripple of suppressed amusement made its way through the front row of benches. Noah found it irksome, and so he stood up.

He waited for silence, his hands at his breast as if he were holding his prayer shawl in place.

"My friend the learned Abijah is correct in pointing out that the passage can and has been interpreted variously, but common sense and custom would seem to support the opinion of Shammai."

As Noah let his eyes wander over the faces of the congregation, he noticed that some were a trifle reluctant to meet his gaze.

"It is understood among us," he continued, "that if a man enters into a betrothal, he may not set aside his betrothed except if he finds that she is not a virgin or has been guilty of some other gross offense. Is it then reasonable to believe that, while the contract to marry is so binding, the marriage itself can be set aside on a mere whim?

"Beyond this, as a practical matter, marriage is the ground of family life, and the family is the ground of our life as the nation of Israel. If marriage is a tie no more binding than a cobweb, how are we to prosper and people the land? How can children be expected to thrive if at any time their mother can be dismissed like a servant?"

When Noah sat down, he was gratified to hear a murmur of approval, but it was cut short when Lot, an elderly farmer, sitting in the midst of his eight surviving sons, stood up. He was a small, frail-looking man, but he had the look of one accustomed to authority.

"My father chose my wife," he began. "He chose well and I have lived in happiness these fifty years. Still, Torah is clear. God said, 'I shall make a helper fit for man.' Woman was made to serve man. If a wife displeases her husband, he has the right to set her aside. He may be a fool to do it, but God has not forbidden us to be fools."

Lot resumed his seat, assisted by one of his sons, and to an approving undercurrent of voices. Here and there one could make out phrases like "the Law is the Law" and "master in his own house." It was clear that Lot spoke for the majority.

It was against this tide of concurrence that Joshua rose to speak.

At once a hush fell over the assembly. Everyone there knew Joshua, and knew that he had followed the Baptist and now preached on his own. Some approved and many did not, but everyone knew that Joshua was a learned man who loved God, and as such was entitled to a respectful hearing.

"Moses commanded that a man may put away his wife, that he may give her a certificate of divorce and put her out of his house."

He looked about him, and his eyes were full of contempt.

"But Moses gave you this commandment for your hardness of heart. God made both man and woman, and Torah says that a man leaves his father and his mother and cleaves to his wife, that they become one flesh. They become one instead of two."

"Listen how he speaks on his own authority," someone said, loud enough to be heard by everyone. "Is this not the carpenter's son?"

"And I say to you," Joshua went on, brushing aside the interruption with a contemptuous gesture of his hand, "that when God has established His kingdom here on earth, no man shall put away his wife, for what God has joined, man shall not divide."

Even before Joshua had sat down, his father was struggling to his feet. Joseph's face was almost black with anger.

"You must excuse my son, for I think his wits are turned. He wanders here and there like a beggar, telling fantastic stories of things to come. He lives in his own world—"

But he was cut short when Lot once more rose.

"Joseph, when else have we heard your voice within these walls? I cannot remember another time. A man has the right to speak his mind in the prayer house, even if he is your son."

In the ensuing tumult of voices, Benjamin put his hand on his grandson's shoulder and leaned toward him to whisper something in his ear.

"There is an old saying: when a man puts aside his wife, God weeps."

Joshua refused to leave the prayer house with his family. Instead, he went with Noah and Benjamin, and they sat outside Benjamin's doorway eating dates and drinking wine watered eight parts to three.

"At my age, I can't tolerate anything stronger," Benjamin said, shrugging his shoulders at the injustices of life.

Then he reached out and patted his grandnephew on the knee.

"You spoke well, Joshua. Both of you spoke well. I take pride in my two best students."

"My father took no pride in me," Joshua answered, cutting into a date as if he hated it. He was so restless that his hands seemed to shake. "It was a mistake for me to come back."

"It was not a mistake. It was the performance of a duty."

"And you see how it has ended. The scenes at home have been bad enough, and now he tells the whole of Nazareth he thinks me demented."

"Your steps are guided by the voice of God. This is a hard destiny for a father to accept."

"*Is* it the voice of God, Uncle Benjamin?" It seemed a real question. "Or perhaps he is right and my mind is possessed by demons."

"Was the Baptist possessed by demons?"

"No. The Baptist was a good man—a better servant of God than I ever hope to be."

"Ah, you doubt your own worthiness. The mad have no doubts."

Benjamin leaned back against the wall, and his eyes closed. He might have been asleep. They almost believed he was asleep, until he began to speak again.

"When I was nine years old we all went to Jerusalem for the Passover, and I remained behind to be apprenticed to a cousin of my mother's. He was an ironsmith. He taught me that, and he taught me to read and to love the Law and the Prophets. When I was sixteen I returned to Nazareth with nothing to show for my years in Jerusalem except a hammer and the scrolls of Torah. The hammer broke before either of you was born. The scrolls I still have, on a shelf in my bedroom.

"My father thought I had wasted my time, that I would probably starve, that my head was stuffed with useless learning. He was a carpenter, and the son of a carpenter, and that was all he understood. He was offended that I rose an hour before prayers to read Scripture. I tried to tell him that to study the Law is a form of prayer, but that seemed strange to him, even arrogant. The prayer house was enough, he said. I should not put myself above my elders.

"Yet he helped me gather the stone to build my first forge, and we collected old scraps of iron, which I cast into an anvil. In the end he lived to see me prosper.

"Unfortunately—or fortunately, for I do not pretend to know which—Joseph will not live to see how it ends with you. And a prophet's success or failure is harder to measure than an ironsmith's or a carpenter's. Yet ironsmiths and carpenters die and are forgotten. Prophets are remembered."

"And I may fail as a prophet," Joshua announced gloomily. "I seem to have failed in my own family."

The old man smiled. "Some failures are more precious to God than any success."

That evening, when the Sabbath was over, a party of friends collected at Abner's house for dinner. The guest of honor was Joshua, but Abijah and Noah were both invited. Although everyone was careful to avoid any allusion to Joseph's remarks about his son, the discussion over wine quite naturally gravitated back to the divorce question and what had been said in the prayer house.

"My only point," Abijah said, almost as if he were apologizing, "was that the text is ambiguous on the grounds for divorce. Grounds are implied, and they seem to be in conflict. I have always found it a puzzling text because it covers such a narrow point—how many men would put away a wife and then wish to remarry her after yet another man has divorced her?"

Noah was hungry, and he disliked sitting about, drinking wine on an empty stomach. It made him feel light-headed. He wanted to ask when they were likely to be served dinner. Instead, he asked a related question.

"Abner, would you divorce your wife if dinner was late?"

"She'd never allow it."

The exchange was greeted with appreciative laughter, even by Joshua, who seemed in an otherwise sulky mood.

"Hillel was a great man, I believe—humble, kind, and wise," Noah went on, once the laughter had died away. "But his decision on this question makes little sense to me. Nor does it, except as an assertion that a man is master in his own family, make sense to most people. Can anyone here remember the last time there was a divorce in Nazareth?"

"Only the great divorce their wives," someone said.

"Precisely. Look at Antipas. *And* his father."

"Tobias, I am ashamed of the way you abuse our late king," Noah replied, shaking his head at the speaker, who happened to be a cousin on his mother's side. "Old Herod did not divorce his first wife. To do him justice, he had her murdered."

Everyone could laugh, knowing they were safe from spies, for, with the exception of Abijah, who was vouched for by their host, the men assembled for Abner's banquet had all known each other since childhood.

It was just then that Abner's wife slipped quietly into the room and whispered something in her husband's ear. He listened and then spoke to her, pointing to the opposite side of the circle of banqueting couches.

The movement was sufficiently vague that at first Noah thought Abner was directing her attention to him, but she came around and, instead, spoke a few quiet words to Joshua, who was seated beside him.

When she was gone, Joshua sat up and threw an arm across Noah's shoulders, drawing him near.

"My mother and brother are outside," he said quietly. "I suspect I know what they want. Tell them to go home."

Noah went outside and found Miriam, attended by Little Joseph.

"I am to tell you to go home," he said, speaking to Miriam.

"His father insists that he return with us," Miriam answered, her gentle face filled with anguish. "He wants him to stay with us and work at his trade. He is sure that work will clear his mind."

Noah took her hand in his own. "Are you sure his mind needs clearing?"

What could she say? Noah had always known that Joshua, her firstborn, was her favorite child, and this collision between him and his father was exquisitely painful to her. Probably the only reason she had come was to render it less painful to Joshua.

"Noah, tell him to come out," Little Joseph almost shouted—Little Joseph, the baby of the family, his beard still only half grown in. "You heard him in the prayer house. His wits are turned."

"Are they?" Then something occurred to him. "Where is Jacob?"

"He wouldn't come," Miriam answered.

"And why was that?" Noah asked. He still held her hand in his own, and he could feel her fingers tightening around his thumb. "But I think I can guess. He refused to involve himself. Tell me, Miriam, do you believe your son is troubled in his mind?"

She could only look down and shake her head. What she was denying was not clear.

"He talks of the end of all things," Little Joseph said gloomily. "He says that God will shake the foundations of the world and thousands will be cast into the fire like weeds."

"Yes, I have heard him say such things."

"Do you believe him?"

Noah was forced to smile, for Little Joseph, who was the least gifted of Miriam's sons, actually seemed frightened.

"I do not know if I believe him," Noah answered. "Probably I do not. But I am not in the habit of thinking every man I disagree with is possessed by demons.

"Little Joseph, take your mother home. Nothing is going to be settled here tonight."

They left, and Noah returned to the banquet, where dinner was at last being served.

When it was over, Noah and Joshua left together.

"Can Uncle Benjamin find room for me tonight?" Joshua asked.

"I would think so. Why?"

"I can't return to my father's house. I don't think I can ever return there." Joshua looked down and shook his head. It was identical to the gesture his mother had used. "A prophet is not without honor, except in his own place and among his own family."

33

The next morning Noah rose early and had breakfast with Joshua and his disciples, who had gathered at Benjamin's house two hours before dawn.

"I will never return to this place," Joshua told him. "I now have no father but God, and no family except these companions."

When they were gone, Benjamin came out of his bedroom.

"You were awake?" Noah asked him.

"Yes."

"Why didn't you join us?"

"I am too old to enjoy good-byes." He looked at the remains of breakfast with distaste and poured himself a cup of wine. "They will be on the main road before Joseph realizes that he will never see his eldest son again."

"It was all unnecessary."

Benjamin seemed not to hear. He sat with his hands cradling the wine cup, his gaze fixed on nothing. Finally he turned to his grandson and smiled.

"I suspect it was necessary," he said quietly. "Joshua is preparing himself for whatever destiny God has chosen for him, and God whispers to him that he must face it alone. What is necessity but the will of God?"

"If it is God's will."

"The point is that he believes it is, and therefore he can do no other."

———

The next day Noah claimed his bride, and if, in the ensuing celebration, anyone in Nazareth gave thought to Joshua's absence, it was not evident.

Because the bride was a widow, the formal evidence that the marriage had been consummated could be dispensed with. No friend needed to wait outside Benjamin's door. It was kindly taken for granted that Noah had gone into Deborah and made her his wife. The couple were allowed to remain alone together while the whole village ate and drank and danced and made the customary jokes.

The next morning, husband and wife quietly slipped away and walked back to Noah's house in Sepphoris. No one seemed to notice their absence.

Sarah was staying with her grandfather, to be out of the way, so it was two or three days before either Noah or Deborah had a thought to spare for anyone else.

However, as the first Sabbath of their marriage approached, and with it the idea of returning, however briefly, to Nazareth, they both began to think about the wider context of their life together. Deborah recalled that her servant Hannah was still waiting.

"Can you send your apprentice for her?" she asked. "She is alone, and by now she must be feeling like a prisoner in Capernaum. She has no dependence upon anyone except me."

They were at breakfast in the kitchen, where there was no window to let in even the faint gray light of dawn, and Noah was thinking how beautiful and mysterious his wife looked in the soft flicker of the oil lamp.

"I'll speak to Hiram today. He can leave after the Sabbath. I'll tell him to bring her down by water to Tiberias. The road from Tiberias is shorter and safer, and the enforced idleness of a boat trip will provide them with an opportunity to become acquainted."

Deborah, with a bride's sensitivity to these things, noticed a sudden change in his expression.

"What is it?" she asked.

"Nothing." He shrugged and forced himself to smile. "I was just thinking of another prisoner."

Then he told her of his conversation with the Lord Eleazar. In the rush of his private concerns, he had almost forgotten about it.

"A nameless prisoner?" she asked. "How can he expect you to find him out?"

"I have no idea, but he does."

"And why would Caleb, who is so evil a man, release a prisoner?"

"You are discounting, then, an act of personal clemency?" Noah smiled, a little more willingly. "I would imagine because he needed someone as a spy. Anyone who has been in the Tetrarch's prisons for any time will emerge a broken man, prepared to do anything if only he can avoid having to go back. Caleb needed someone who feared him."

An idea was beginning to form in Deborah's mind. It seemed incredible, but . . .

"How long ago was the prisoner released?" she asked, almost afraid to hear the answer.

"Two or three months ago—why?"

"Where does Caleb live?"

It struck Noah, not for the first time, that he had fallen in love with a very clever woman.

"Perhaps we could take a walk today," he said. "You could show me where you saw Judah."

Once she was in the district around the Tetrarch's palace, Deborah had no trouble locating the doorway in which she had seen Judah speaking with another man. It was on the western side of the street, which was broader than those in the lower part of the city. There were shops opposite, but they did not seem busy. For the people who lived in these grand houses, it was probably still early in the day.

At the end of the block, on a corner, there was a tavern where one could sit outside, with a view of the whole street. Noah ordered beer for them both.

The tavern owner asked if they wanted anything to eat. Noah shook his head and then placed three silver coins on the table. The tavern owner stood looking at them, as if he had never seen so much money together in one place, until Noah invited him to sit down.

"How long have you been here?" Noah asked. It was a harmless, friendly inquiry, such as one might make to pass the time.

The tavern owner, who was a shriveled, unhappy-looking man, utterly lacking in the pleasant openness which was usually the hallmark of his profession, held up his right hand, the finger splayed, and then pulled down the little finger and thumb so that the ends touched.

"Three years," he said, as if he lamented every hour of it.

"And is trade good?" Noah took a sip from his cup. "The beer, by the way, is excellent."

"My wife makes it."

"Then please convey my compliments to your wife. So, you are prospering?"

"We only just get by." The tavern owner turned his gaze resentfully to the houses on the opposite side of the street. "People who live hereabouts seem to prefer to eat at home. Of course, they all have their own cooks."

"But as I said, the beer is excellent. It seems such a pleasant spot. There is nothing like beer on a warm day, in the company of one's friends."

"As I said, we get by."

"And I suppose you know everyone in the neighborhood."

"Nearly everyone. Yes."

Noah placed a finger on each of the three silver coins and slowly pushed them across the table toward its owner.

"I wonder if you could tell me who owns the house just there." He lifted his hand from the coins and pointed to the doorway Deborah had indicated.

The tavern owner swept the coins off the table and into his hand.

"The man who lives there never comes here," he said, suddenly angry—or perhaps only frightened. "He is a powerful man, a man about whom it is safest not to inquire."

"Would you happen to know his name? Surely his name is not dangerous."

The tavern owner stood up, and seemed to weigh the silver in his hand.

"There was a man whom Moses sent into the Promised Land to spy it out. He was one of twelve. Of those twelve, only he and Joshua reported back that God would deliver the land into their hands."

"I understand you."

As they got up to leave, Noah leaned toward Deborah and whispered in her ear, "The spy's name was Caleb."

That evening was the beginning of the Sabbath, so in the middle of the afternoon Noah locked his shop and he and Deborah walked to Nazareth.

To Noah, Judah was no more than a face and a name, so Deborah had tried to remember every detail of his story. It wasn't much: he had been rich but lost his money, he had been baptized by John, he came from Tiberias.

"But he speaks with a Judean accent," Noah observed. "He is not a Galilean. Perhaps he has never been near Tiberias. How much of his story do you believe?"

"He was baptized—Joshua remembers him. And I believe he was rich because when he first came to Capernaum his hands were smooth. They were the hands of someone who had never worked. And I believe he has lived in Tiberias."

"Why?"

"Because he talks about it. If he had never lived there he wouldn't mention it, for fear of making a mistake."

"You are a shrewd woman. What are your other impressions of him?"

"I believe his devotion to Joshua is real. He is not pretending."

"Then one wonders what his devotion to Caleb is like."

When they were in sight of the village, Noah kissed his wife's hand and said, "I think it best we say nothing of this to anyone. I will ask Sarah to return with you to Sepphoris, and I will say I am going on to Tiberias. I do business there, so no one will remark on it. I will see what can be found out about our friend. Do you know how much I love you?"

Deborah smiled, in a way that suggested she knew a secret. "Am I going to find out?"

There was still an hour before sunset when Noah embraced his grandfather. When the Sabbath began, Benjamin would go into his bedroom to fetch one of the scrolls, and then he would sit outside and listen to Noah reading the Law. It was a ritual enacted almost every Sabbath since he had first taught his grandson how to read.

But first they all sat down to the dinner Sarah had prepared. It was a chance to catch up on the news.

"You won't see Joseph in the prayer house tomorrow," Benjamin said as he filled their cups with wine. "He is spitting up blood and hasn't left his bed in two days."

"Miriam says he has given up all hope of life," Sarah added.

"I suppose this business with Joshua has finished him," Noah said.

Benjamin looked at his grandson with surprise, which gradually slipped into something very like amusement. "Or it is simply the time God has set for him to die," he said. "Men do not die of disappointment. His lungs are not bleeding because of Joshua."

"Yet he might have faced death with an easier heart if not for this stupid quarrel."

"Or perhaps it makes no difference. Dying usually absorbs a man's full attention."

Noah found himself suddenly eager to change the subject, so he turned to his sister with a teasing grin.

"I think we had better get you married to Abijah quickly, before he ruins himself by sheer inattention."

"It cannot be soon enough for me. I hate this veil."

"Yes, aren't they dreadful?" Deborah agreed.

And so the last of the day slipped pleasantly away, and at sundown Noah and his grandfather sat outside, an oil lamp hanging from a stand above Noah's right shoulder as he read.

" 'You shall not hate your brother in your heart, but you shall reason with your neighbor, lest you bear sin because of him. You shall not take vengeance or bear any grudge against the sons of your own people, but you shall love your neighbor as yourself. I am the Lord.' "

" 'I am the Lord,' " the old man repeated. "I heard a story once of a famous teacher who was approached by a gentile who said he would become his student and embrace Israel if the teacher could tell him the essence of the Law while standing on one foot. The teacher lifted one foot from the ground and said, 'You shall love your neighbor as yourself. I am the Lord.' And the gentile became his student."

"I have heard that story," Noah replied, smiling as he experienced a surge of love for his grandfather. He hoped Benjamin lived long enough that his own children would have some memory of him. "They tell it of Hillel, and probably others. There are, I suspect, several variations."

"There are always stories about men famous for their piety," Benjamin said. "Some of them one believes, some not. Some, it doesn't matter if they are true or not."

———

The next morning, as Benjamin had predicted, Joseph was not in the prayer house. His sons sat together and were silent during the discussion of the reading. When it was over they returned to their father's house, without a word to anyone. It was as if Noah and his grandfather were somehow included in their anger against Joshua.

"'You shall not hate your brother in your heart,'" Noah repeated, as if to himself.

"'I am the Lord,'" his grandfather murmured.

On the following morning, before it was even light, Noah set out for Tiberias. It was late afternoon before he reached the door of his friend Priam.

"What are you doing here?" Priam asked, forgetting his manners in his surprise. "Usually you write that you are coming."

"There was no time. I apologize for the intrusion."

"It is not an intrusion, for I am always glad to see you. It is merely unexpected."

"For both of us."

Then he told Priam about Judah.

"And what is your interest in this man? Or is it better I do not know?"

"You do not want to know. Who in Tiberias would have managed his affairs?"

Priam shrugged and pulled thoughtfully at his beard.

"It would have to be someone of standing," he said finally. "In all, perhaps a score of merchants."

"Can you give me a list?"

"I will do better than that. I will go with you. Business is slow, and it will give me something to do." Looking his friend over from head to foot, Priam shook his head. "But you can't appear before these men looking like that. You are covered with dust."

"An inevitable consequence of walking for ten hours."

"Yes, but you must take a bath and have my servants attend to your clothes. There is nothing more to be done today."

Noah could only shrug with resignation.

"Besides," Priam continued, "you must drink some wine and tell me all your news. Are you married yet? I am eager to hear how this second experiment is turning out."

———

Priam was nearing forty, and there were rumors that he had come from Sardis to escape his wife. Whether this was true or not, he lived in Tiberias as a bachelor. His household servants were all women, some very pretty, so probably he did not lack for amusement.

He listened to Noah's praise of his bride with patient cynicism.

"And yet I notice, since here you are, that her charms could not hold you in place for even a week."

"It was an emergency. Trust me when I say I prefer her company even to yours."

Priam laughed. "I am insulted."

The next morning they began their inquiries. By noon they had been in the counting houses of six of the most prosperous merchant traders in the city, and none of them knew of a rich wastrel named Judah who had lost his money and disappeared. Noah was beginning to believe he was chasing a shadow, that Judah had simply concocted the whole story. He wondered if Judah was even his real name.

Noah felt horribly exposed, as if he were playing his part upon a stage, in view of the whole world. It was like Damascus all over again.

Was he being followed? Had Eleazar once again given him a minder?

It was the middle of the afternoon before they found what they were looking for.

"Judah bar Isaac? Where has he taken himself off to?"

The question, in response to Noah's, was posed by a certain Onesimus, a trader with offices on the Street of the Palms.

"Sepphoris," Noah answered, consoling himself with the reflection that it was no less true than a number of other locations he could have cited.

"Well, what is your interest in him?"

"He is employed by a relative of mine—in a confidential capacity. I was asked to inquire about him."

Onesimus considered this response, probably deciding it was too vague to be quite the truth, but he too was curious.

"Well," he replied cautiously, "he didn't lose his money, I can tell you. He is still on my books, and the profits from his investments have done nothing but increase."

"I wonder why he left, then."

After glancing about, as if afraid of being overheard, Onesimus leaned forward heavily against his desk.

"I can hazard a guess," he said, in a low voice. "He favored a certain prostitute. She was found in her room with her neck neatly broken, and after that no one ever saw Judah again. It might be a coincidence, but he also might have killed her and then fled."

"When was this?"

"Oh, six or seven months ago. I would have to check my records." Onesimus smiled indulgently. "You can tell him he is free to return whenever he likes. No one is looking for him. No one cares anything about a dead whore."

"It's an interesting story," Priam said that night, over dinner. "A young man, possessed of wealth and leisure, disappears one day, leaving a dead prostitute behind him. Do you think he killed her."

Noah, who was thinking of something else, did not immediately answer.

"Do you remember the way he put it?" He looked up, and the expression on his face suggested he had a bitter taste in his mouth. "'No one cares anything about a dead whore.' She was probably some poor farmer's daughter, sold to a brothel keeper when she was ten years old. And after that her fate is of interest to no one."

"Your heart is too tender for your own good." When he didn't receive a response, Priam repeated his initial question. "Do you think he killed her?"

"I doubt it. He doesn't seem capable of it."

Then Noah seemed to disappear inside himself. He was concerned with quite a different mystery.

"Judah bar Isaac disappears six months ago," he began at last, "and then two months ago, he attaches himself to my cousin Joshua. That leaves four empty months."

"Where do you think he was?"

"I don't know," Noah answered.

It was the truth. He didn't know. But he could hazard a guess.

34

On the long, winding way back from Nazareth, Joshua seemed a different person, as if the break with his family marked the beginning of some shift in the way he saw himself and his work. Everyone noticed it, even Simon, who was not a very acute man.

Those who deceive, and thus live in dread of discovery, are perhaps quicker to discover changes in others, to anguish over their meaning, and to find the truth. It is the burden of such men to see clearly.

Thus Judah was probably the first to understand that Joshua was struggling to accept his own isolation. Now, it seemed, he belonged only to God.

The route they followed took them first east, as far as Beth Yerah, at the southern end of the Sea of Kinneret, and then north along the western shore. When they reached Tiberias, Joshua, to Judah's intense relief, refused to enter the city, so a fisherman who had been attracted by his message took them around by water.

Judah sat in the boat, gazing at the city that had once been his home, with a mingling of revulsion and nostalgia. Was Zebida still there, plying her trade? Had she forgotten him? Had she loved him, even a little? He could not disguise from himself that he missed her caresses.

Everywhere Joshua preached the coming of God's kingdom and the redemption of the land. God would soon set everything right for those who stood before Him with contrite hearts. Joshua made the world as it was seem like a prison. Soon, he said, soon all would be set free.

Yet one could not avoid the impression that Joshua was growing impatient. Why did God stay His hand? What was He waiting for?

And more and more—in private conversation, for it was not something at which he even hinted to the crowds that collected around him—the answer seemed to be, for Jerusalem during the Passover.

But if the heavens opened, Judah often wondered, and God's messenger came to judge the children of the earth, would he be cast into the fire like the nettles and weeds of Joshua's parables? Judah seemed never to have a moment when he was free of fear. Fear of God, fear of Caleb, fear of not knowing where to find the truth.

More than once he had made up his mind to go to Joshua and confess everything. He would tell him the whole story and beseech his mercy. But always his courage failed him.

Did he really believe in Joshua's message? He didn't know. He believed in Joshua, in his goodness and his love of God, but he did not know if he could believe in the Kingdom. Perhaps he was just too empty a man to have faith in anything.

And Caleb was real. Caleb was waiting—Caleb with his prison and his cross and his relentless conviction that he was the true servant of heaven's will.

So, with his divided heart, Judah could see quite clearly that the worm of doubt had found its home in Joshua. Doubt not about God or about the Kingdom, but about himself.

The message was true, but was he, Joshua bar Joseph, the carpenter from Nazareth, really the messenger?

When Judah first met him, he had rarely used the word *prophet*, and never applied it to himself. The Baptist was a "prophet" who spoke with an authority that was God's gift to him. Joshua revered the Baptist and quoted him constantly: "John said" and "John taught us"—these words were always on his lips.

Now he spoke less of John, although still with vast respect, and now openly referred to himself as a prophet. Often he would begin a teaching with "The Pharisees say thus, but *I* say . . ." Did he believe that he had assumed the Baptist's mantle?

Or was it more that he needed to believe it?

Judah, the deceiver, understood that need, and felt compassion for Joshua.

Perhaps only men like Caleb did not doubt.

"I will be glad to see Capernaum again," Simon told him, smiling companionably as they ate their dinner, leaning back against the hull of a damaged boat. "I haven't seen my wife in two weeks and three days."

After an initial hostility to the Judean man from the city—the man who had once been rich—Simon appeared to have accepted Judah. That mattered, because Simon was closer to Joshua than anyone else. Joshua would sometimes laugh at Simon, and even mock him, but he trusted and confided in him. Simon had been the first to follow Joshua.

Simon also did not doubt. He was a simple, straightforward Galilean, little given to subtlety. He was also, after Joshua, the leader, not only by seniority but by temperament. He would have been a good soldier, but God had made him a fisherman with a window in his heart open to heaven.

"I wish Deborah was still there," Judah answered. "She would feed us. We would eat meat."

"Well, now she is feeding the ironsmith." Simon laughed, appreciating his own joke, if that was what it was. "At least we will eat lamb in Jerusalem," he went on. "It's something to look forward to. I always like the Passover in Jerusalem. What a place!"

"I know," said Judah. "I was born there. My father is a Levite in the Temple."

Simon looked at him as if dumbfounded, and Judah could only laugh.

"Don't worry, I'm not bragging. He cast me off, and with good reason."

"All men are sinful," Simon told him, putting a thick hand on his shoulder. "God forgives us."

He was not sure why, but suddenly Judah found it necessary to close his eyes and struggle against the temptation to weep.

He recovered, however, before Simon noticed anything.

"I could use a jug of wine," Judah said, glad there seemed to be no thickness in his voice.

"A whole jug? Would you share it?" Simon laughed again, and his hand pounded on Judah's shoulder good-naturedly.

———

What would his father think? Who would he choose, Joshua or Caleb? It was a question that haunted Judah's mind like an evil spirit.

For his father would be aware of Caleb's history. He was a friend of Old Jacob and had doubtless heard all the circumstances of his son's banishment. But would he say that Caleb had redeemed himself in the service of God?

And what would he think of the peasant preacher, Joshua? Would he see a prophet or merely a carpenter turned agitator? *Could* he see the prophet, or would he be blinded by the calloused hands and the Galilean accent?

In a nameless village less than a day's walk from Tiberias, a woman who was subject to convulsions, so that she could hardly speak or walk, approached Joshua one morning, begging to be healed. Joshua knelt with her for almost two hours, his hand caressing the back of her head, their faces almost touching while she whispered her story to him and he told her of God's limitless forgiveness if she truly repented her sins.

She stayed close to him all the rest of the day, and her convulsions seemed to have left her. She was smiling and happy and at peace with herself. Whether, after they were gone, she was once more seized by her illness, Judah could not say, but for that day Joshua seemed to have worked a miracle.

"I have seen him do such things before," Simon told him. "He can drive away demons. It is a power he has from God."

But was it demons or simply grief that he drove away? Was it from God or merely in Joshua? And was it any less a wonder either way?

Judah came to think that it was the power of Joshua's goodness, an aura that seemed to surround him, and of his belief. Joshua had faith, and said himself that faith could do all things.

If others had faith in him, anything was possible.

And Judah could not help but conclude that it was some flaw in himself, a weakness of character, a moral cowardliness, that held him back from faith.

I will believe when the heavens open and one like the son of man appears in power, but not before, he thought. *Then it will be too late.*

On the evening when they at last reached Capernaum, Joshua decided that he wished to withdraw for a few days of prayer and fasting. He struck out for an area north of the village, where there were thick stands of trees too far away to be worth the trouble of felling and where therefore he was sure of being alone.

Thus the disciples were left to themselves and resumed their old patterns of life. Simon went fishing, and took Judah with him.

For the next three days they rose before dawn and were on the water long before the sun showed itself over the eastern mountains. Fishing, it turned out, was hard work, and once there was a storm that nearly swamped their boat. They would come back in the late afternoon and gut their catch. Then Simon would haggle with the fish merchants and they would go back to Simon's house for a hot meal and bed.

These were perhaps the happiest three days of Judah's life. He was busy all day long, and when the work was over he was too tired to think.

Then, on the evening of the third day, Joshua returned. He gathered the disciples and they ate a meal together, and there was wine.

And he explained to them everything that would happen.

"God has made all things plain to me," he said. "None of us will taste new wine before we have seen the coming of the Kingdom. Oh, how I long to be free of this wicked world!"

John, ever the practical one, was counting on his fingers.

"The grape harvest is in four months," he said. He seemed disappointed.

"I cannot believe God will wait so long," Joshua replied, raising his hands with the palm outward, as if praying for deliverance. "Where would God reveal His will except in Jerusalem? When, if not during the Passover?"

"Then He has revealed to you the time?" Simon asked.

But Joshua shook his head.

"The time is known only to the Father. But He will make His will known, and He will send His messenger. The dead will rise from their tombs and all mankind will be judged. The righteous will be gathered to God and the world will be returned to what it was before the first man learned sin."

No one seemed satisfied with this, but it was obvious that further questioning would be in vain. Joshua was in one of his ecstatic moods, when the only voice he heard was God's.

He disappeared again the next day, and his disciples, after waiting a few hours, once again went fishing. But the water was calm and the catch poor, so there was plenty of time, and nothing to think about except Joshua.

"He has said as much before," John said. "He expects this Passover to bring on the Kingdom. But he doesn't know."

"Yet he believes," Simon answered. "And that is enough for me."

"But is it enough for him?"

John wiped the sweat from his face and stared up at the sun as if it had insulted him.

"It is what makes him what he is, this belief in the mercy of God," he went on. "That is why we follow and love him, because to be with him is to believe it, too. But he *must* believe it. He has no choice."

35

"In accord with your orders, I had men watching the roads in and out of Nazareth. He left early the morning after the Sabbath, and a few hours later his wife and sister returned to the city. He was followed into Tiberias, where our agent turned him over to another and came back to Sepphoris to report."

Caleb's confidential clerk, a thin, unhappy-looking man of about forty, stood before his master's desk in the palace at Sepphoris.

"And he is in Tiberias now?"

"No. He and another man visited several merchants, and then the next day he came home. As soon as he was inside his door, our man came to me to report."

"And what did he discuss with these merchants?"

"We don't know that yet, but it is under investigation." The clerk, whose name was Bildad, cocked his head a little to one side in a dismissive gesture. "It probably is innocent. He is frequently in Tiberias on business."

"How is his marriage faring?"

Bildad, who had probably never had a sexual thought in his life, managed a condescending smile.

"The reports indicate they seem to be very much in love."

"And less than a week after his wedding he travels to Tiberias, alone. It must have been very pressing business." Caleb, whose instincts told him something dangerous had just occurred, shifted uncomfortably in his chair. "How soon do you expect the report on his activities?"

"In the regular weekly dispatch, if the results seem unimportant. Anything worthy of attention will be sent by runner."

"Notify me as soon as there is anything."

Caleb made a dismissing gesture with his left hand and the clerk bowed his way out.

Ever since the Tetrarch's amnesty, Caleb had maintained a loose watch on Noah. He could not arrest him, yet neither could he afford to ignore him. Noah was a clever man—a dangerous man. A man like Noah, a man with a network of business contacts, with whom he carried on an energetic correspondence, was a natural spy. Caleb even suspected that he might have been the source of the information which Eleazar had used to frighten Antipas into submission.

Fortunately he was also just a tradesman, with a tradesman's view of the world. Probably it would never occur to him that his movements were being followed.

It was the early afternoon and Caleb decided to leave his office and go visit the baths. With the new policy of peace, tranquility, and fatherly affection for the Tetrarch's subjects, there was very little for him to do, and he was, consequently, bored. If he went home, his wife, who was also bored, would subject him to one of her temper tantrums, which at the moment he did not feel up to facing. It was far pleasanter to go to the baths.

He had by then half persuaded himself that Bildad was right and that his suspicions about Noah were groundless. The man's journey to Tiberias probably was just business—or perhaps, like so many others, he had discovered that marriage as a steady diet was intolerable. Boredom again. Caleb suspected he was inventing things with which to distract himself.

He was just on the point of rising from his chair when his clerk returned.

"The report from Tiberias came in," Bildad said, flourishing a scroll. "I suspect it means nothing, but it is always best to err on the side of caution. He was making inquiries about a certain Judah bar Isaac."

Bildad handed him the scroll and, with admirable self-possession, Caleb managed to accept it without betraying his sense of shock. His hands did not even shake as he opened it.

"Probably he was looking into the man's credit," Bildad said

"Yes. Probably."

Caleb set the scroll down on his desk, as if dismissing it from existence, and forced himself to smile as he waved away his clerk.

He might have continued in his chair for as long as a quarter of an hour without once moving. He hardly knew what he felt. He seemed to feel nothing. It was as if his mind had frozen shut.

Finally he became aware of something like a tear on the side of his nose. He reached up to wipe it away and discovered that he was sweating profusely. It was at that moment that he gave way to a rising panic.

How had Noah ever guessed? Well, there was still nothing to connect Judah to himself.

He was deceiving himself. *Of course* Noah had made the connection. He had made inquiries about one of Joshua bar Joseph's disciples, and suspected . . . what? That the man was a spy. And who in Galilee would wish to spy on Joshua bar Joseph except the man who had originally recruited Noah to do just that?

And if Noah knew, then by now, or very soon, Eleazar would know.

There were individuals who were exempt from torture and arbitrary arrest, and certainly members of the Temple aristocracy were among them. Now Eleazar would know that he, Caleb bar Jacob, had kidnapped and held in prison a son of one of the three or four most important Levite families and then turned him loose to spy on a peasant agitator.

At the time, when he had felt sure he could get away with it—when he had thought he could get away with anything—it had seemed like a bold stroke, but now Caleb could see it for what it was and always had been. Stupidly, insanely rash.

He had provided Eleazar with the means to destroy him. He could almost feel the knife at his throat.

He would run. He would find a horse and ride for Caesarea. He would take ship for . . . anywhere. He would make his way to Gaul or Spain. The world was a big place, and he would lose himself in it.

How much money could he have in his hands within half an hour?

His plans for escape were almost complete before he realized that they were pointless—and probably unnecessary. He was watched, even now. He had spies on Eleazar, so it followed that he, too, was being followed and observed. Eleazar could have him arrested at any time.

Running was futile.

And why? Why throw away everything he had so labored to build? All Noah had was the name of a young wastrel who might have left Tiberias for any number of reasons. It was like a moment of inspiration when Caleb remembered the whore Matthias had killed to insure her silence. Perhaps—probably—everyone assumed that Judah had murdered her and then fled.

At this moment, all Eleazar would know or care about was that Judah had attached himself to Joshua bar Joseph and was probably an agent of his loyal servant Caleb bar Jacob.

The plan could still work.

So, instead of escaping, Caleb resumed his intention of visiting the baths. He had to regain his composure, and he had to think. All he really needed was a little steam to clear his head.

An hour later, lying on a marble slab, sweating profusely into the linen sheet he had wrapped around him, Caleb was able to feel some satisfaction with himself for not having yielded to panic. The situation was not so hopeless after all.

A servant girl brought him a tray bearing a jug of ice water and a cup. She was pretty, and the steam made her tunic cling to her body so as to hint strongly at the delights it covered. In a Greek bath she would have been naked. For a few moments Caleb amused himself with the idea of moving somewhere east of the Jordan when he retired, to one of the Greek cities, where people knew how to enjoy themselves.

But first he had to deal with this current problem.

Of course, he could always arrange for Judah to meet with an accident. Judah could never be allowed to tell his story to Eleazar.

But Eleazar was too subtle a man to want to hear it. As far as he knew, Judah was merely another of Caleb's spies, and a spy one knows about is most usefully left undisturbed. Eleazar would wait until the opportunity presented itself to turn Caleb's asset into one of his own.

The Passover was only four weeks distant. In another two weeks everyone who mattered would be in Jerusalem. There, when the trap was closed around Joshua bar Joseph, Judah would be irrelevant.

But something had to be done about Noah, and soon.

Noah's first thought would be for his cousin. Luckily, his new wife had drawn him back to Sepphoris—otherwise he might have gone straight to wherever Joshua was hiding himself, to tell him about the traitor in his midst. In any case, he would not wait long.

Suddenly Caleb felt no temptation to linger in the baths. He took a cold plunge to stop the sweating and then dressed hurriedly. He was back in his office faster than he would have thought possible.

"Send for the officer of the watch. Immediately."

Fortunately, today it was Lamech.

"Where is Matthias?" Caleb asked, rather more harshly than he intended. Lamech, who knew his place, stood at attention, seeming to look at nothing.

"Not on duty, my lord."

"Find him, and bring him to my house."

Lamech seemed fixed in place. One could see the question forming in his mind, but Caleb had no patience to wait.

"I don't care what condition he is in. Find him, throw a little cold water in his face, and bring him. You are responsible for getting him to my front door. After that, I will manage the situation."

"Yes, my lord."

It was just over an hour later that Lamech and his charge presented themselves. Having dismissed his servants to the kitchen, Caleb personally opened the door to them.

Matthias had trouble negotiating the stairs up to the roof, but it was the only place in the house where Caleb could be assured of not being spied on.

"You look terrible."

Had the man even heard? Wine made Matthias sullen and impenetrable. He sat down without being asked, and looked out over the Galilean countryside as if he hated it.

"Are you trying to kill yourself?"

This somehow registered, and Matthias turned his gaze and seemed to try hard to focus it on the Lord Caleb. The effort made him frown morosely.

He appeared to be trying to say something, but finally abandoned the effort.

"This is hopeless," Caleb said out loud. There was little chance Matthias would take offense, since he seemed about to collapse out of his chair.

If he falls, Caleb realized, he might break something. Then he would be useless.

He stood up and took Matthias by the arms, pulling him up and then letting him sink quietly to the floor. Then he went down to his own room and brought up a blanket for him.

The sun was already setting. There was nothing more to be done that day.

Caleb sat in the gathering darkness, drinking wine while he watched Matthias sleep. There was a slight breeze, just enough to render it uncomfortably cool, but that kept him awake. He spent the time planning what he would have happen in Jerusalem.

Shortly after midnight, Matthias started awake. Caleb could hear rather than see that he was trying to sit up, so he lit an oil lamp. The breeze had dropped and the air was still. Matthias stared at the little point of light as if trying to remember how he had come to be here.

Caleb gave him water, and then a cup of unmixed wine.

"My lord," Matthias said at last—that was all, just those two words, to indicate that he had returned to life.

"Why do you drink so much?" Caleb asked him. He didn't really care, but he was curious.

"To forget."

"To forget what?"

"The things I have done."

"You have a conscience, then?"

Matthias glared at him, which meant at least that Caleb had his full attention.

"Do you remember Noah?" Caleb asked.

Matthias shook his head. The operation must have been painful, for he put his hand on the crown of his skull, apparently to keep it in place.

"You beat him, as a warning. That was almost three months ago. Do you remember now?"

"On the road, coming home from the Sabbath."

"Yes. That's him. Now I want you to kill him."

He explained it all carefully. Noah would be leaving soon to find his cousin in the north. He must die somewhere on the journey, preferably in such a way that his body would not be discovered for some time. It would be inconvenient if he were killed in Sepphoris. It must be made to look like anything except what it was. An accident, suicide, a simple robbery, these were all perfectly acceptable.

"Do you understand? He must not be allowed to speak to his cousin. He knows about Judah, the man you kidnapped from Tiberias. It will be very dangerous if the cousin finds out."

"Shall I kill the cousin as well, then?"

"Preferably not. It would raise too many questions."

"Who is the cousin?"

Caleb briefly considered not telling him, but decided that he might need to know.

"His name is Joshua bar Joseph. He fancies himself a prophet. Have you heard of him?"

"No."

36

During that same night, Joseph was gathered to his fathers. He woke up, sat on the edge of his bed, and began to cough, spitting up blood. Soon, almost before the noise woke up his wife, he had collapsed. He was dead before Miriam could call for help.

When he was laid out, and Miriam had wiped the blood from his mouth, the family gathered in the kitchen. Miriam was the first to break the silence.

"Joshua must be told," she said. It was clear from the expression of her voice that she would brook no contradiction.

For a long, thoughtful moment no one replied.

"We don't even know where he is," Little Joseph said at last.

"Noah does."

Miriam looked at her second son, her dark eyes burning.

"Jacob, you must go to Sepphoris at first light."

"Yes, Mother."

Thus, when the sun first broke over the eastern mountains, Jacob was on his way. He had never been to the city, so he had had to wake up Uncle Benjamin and ask him for directions to Noah's house.

He found it easily enough. It was made of stone and was, to his eyes, huge. He had never realized that his cousin was so rich.

Noah was having breakfast and heard him knock. As soon as he saw

Jacob's face, he knew someone had died. His first thought was that it must be his grandfather.

"My father . . ." Jacob began, and then seemed unable to go on.

Noah's initial reaction was relief, of which he was instantly ashamed. He put his hand on Jacob's shoulder. He had to reach up to do it, because Jacob, like all of Joseph's sons, was tall.

"Come in. I don't suppose you have eaten. Come in."

They went into the kitchen, where Deborah and Sarah were waiting. Noah told them what had happened and Deborah stepped forward to kiss Jacob on the cheek. Sarah cried briefly.

They all ate in silence, until Jacob said, "My mother wants you to tell Joshua."

"I will tell him," Noah agreed. "I was leaving this morning to see him. I will walk back with you to Nazareth."

Matthias watched the two men leave Noah's house. He thought at first that he might already be too late, that the taller man might be the cousin, but then he dismissed the idea. The cousin was in the north. The Lord Caleb always knew about such details.

There were many travelers on the Jerusalem road, so Matthias was able to conceal himself. He stayed well back and out of sight, even after he saw Noah and his companion branch off from the road.

"They are going to Nazareth," he thought. "Good. Perhaps he will stay there for the day and return this evening. That would make it easier."

But the Lord Caleb had said soon—"soon he will be traveling to the north." It seemed possible, therefore, even likely, that Nazareth was the first stage of Noah's journey.

Thus, he would not be returning to Sepphoris.

And if he went north, what route would he take? East onto the plain, and then north and east to Tiberias, where he would perhaps take a boat up to Capernaum. The Lord Caleb had said that the cousin seemed to regard Capernaum as his base. That would be the easiest way.

So now, Matthias told himself, his problem was to find a spot from which he could watch both directions, east and west.

He found it north of Nazareth, in the line of hills covered with grape arbors. There he could sit comfortably in the shade, concealed by the arbors. The grapes were not yet ripe, which was a pity, but he had water and dried meat. All he needed was patience.

"It is kind of you to take the trouble about Joshua," Jacob said, as they made their way up the trail to Nazareth.

"*Kind?*" It struck Noah as an odd way to put it.

"Joshua is my kinsman and my friend. It is a duty. You would go yourself, but you must bury your father."

"When Uncle Benjamin dies, I suppose we shall see no more of you."

"What are you trying to say, Jacob?"

But Jacob did not answer. The only sound he made was that of his sandals scraping against the pebbles on the trail.

"I see. You intend some reproach."

"No."

"What then?"

Jacob was clearly embarrassed. They passed a bush and he stopped to wipe his hands on the leaves. He did not want to look at Noah.

"What then?"

"It's just that I had not realized you were so rich," he said finally. "You live in a stone house that could hold five families."

"So that's it. You think I fancy myself above my relatives? You and I played together as children, Jacob. I have not deserved this."

Jacob turned around and smiled, apparently a little ashamed of himself and in need of self-justification.

"It's just that I saw the house, and it's so different from the way I have always thought about you. When you come to Nazareth, you seem no different from us."

"Nor am I. As I appear to my family, as I am in the prayer house, standing before God, thus I am. The house was something my father bought before I was born—to please my mother."

Jacob could laugh at this. The moment of estrangement had passed off.

By the time they reached the village, Noah was thinking of something else.

He wondered sometimes if the strain of the past few months wasn't beginning to tell on him. He had gone through his whole life without making any enemies, and now he had the sense of being surrounded by them. Suddenly someone is there. The man in Damascus, the man who came out of the darkness to attack him while he was on his way home. He kept thinking he was being watched. Not all the time, but now and then.

Right now, for instance.

It had been growing on him all the way from Sepphoris. Had he seen something or heard something? There had been dozens of people on the road.

Or perhaps it was simply his mind playing tricks. Fear sometimes did that, and lately fear had been a regular presence in his life.

But still, even here, in the village where he had grown up, where every house and tree and living thing was familiar to him, he could not shake this feeling of unfriendly eyes on him.

Assuming it was true, what would a stranger watch for? For Noah to leave the village, of course. And where would this stranger place himself?

The answer was just as obvious. Had he not played such games countless times as a child?

Just before they reached Joseph's door, through which Noah would pass to pay his respects, he touched Jacob on the arm.

"Do something for me," he said. "You are more farsighted than I. Go out to Old Shomer's house and look through the window opposite the door, where you will have a clear view of the hills. Take your time. See if you can spot anyone in the grape arbors."

Jacob looked surprised. Shomer's house had been empty for six months, ever since the old man died. Why go inside to look out a window?

"I have an idea we were followed. You don't want to know about it, but it has to do with Joshua."

Jacob shrugged. "If you say so."

Noah entered the house and saw Miriam and her two daughters sitting around the kitchen table. He bent down to kiss each of them in turn. It seemed only then that Miriam realized he was there. She lifted her hand and touched him on the face.

"I knew you would come," she said. Then she told him how Joseph had died.

"Last night, when he came to bed, he lay there for a little time and then, suddenly, speaking into the darkness, he said, 'May God protect my son Joshua.' He never uttered another word. Joshua's father loved him, Noah. You must tell him that."

"I will."

After a time, Noah went back outside. He looked about him and everything seemed strange. Its very familiarity made this place seem dreamlike.

Then he saw Jacob.

"You were right," Jacob said, shaking his head with astonishment. "I didn't notice him at first, but then he moved. He brushed something off his sleeve. A big man, unknown to me."

"That presents a problem."

Matthias watched throughout the day, and he had many glimpses of Noah moving about the village. It was about midday when he discovered Noah's purpose in coming. Someone had died. Matthias had a clear view of the burial, and he could see Noah walking arm in arm with a very old man. It was Noah who stood at the foot of the grave and recited the prayers for the dead.

Matthias wished he had not seen this. He would have to kill Noah, and he preferred not to be on an intimate footing with his victims. To see him like this, one end of his shawl draped over his head as he prayed, made him too human.

The Lord Caleb seemed to hate him, which only meant that the Lord Caleb had lost control of him. That in itself was a kind of recommendation.

It had been a long time since Matthias first realized that he hated the Lord Caleb, who was as bad a man as God suffered to live. God had turned His back on them both, the difference being only that Matthias knew it and the Lord Caleb did not—or didn't care.

It hurt Matthias to watch Noah pray. He envied him. Noah had a family and was not afraid to beseech God's mercy. Probably he was a good man.

But that would not save him.

During it all, as the body was carried to the grave, while he prayed, when he took the old man's arm and they walked back to the village, Noah never glanced in Matthias' direction. His gaze never wandered from his immediate surroundings. He gave no indication he suspected he had been followed. If he had, the temptation to search with his eyes would have been irresistible.

The question was, would he spend the night in Nazareth or would he return to the city? It was too late to start for Tiberias.

Matthias could only wait and see.

The afternoon wore itself out, and in the evening, families ate their dinners outside. Matthias could see Noah walking from one house to another, still arm in arm with the old man. Since it would be dark in two hours, Noah probably did not intend to return to Sepphoris, and his constant attendance on the old man indicated where he would be spending the night.

Matthias considered slipping into the village after dark and killing Noah while he slept, but he decided it would be too dangerous. He would have to kill both Noah and the old man, and the chances were good that one of them would live long enough to raise the alarm. He did not have a horse, so rapid escape was impossible. He could not fight a whole village.

Sure enough, just before it became too dark to see, Noah and the old man headed back. In Nazareth it was time for bed.

The heat of the day was lost in a cold night. Matthias slept only fitfully and was awake long before the sun rose.

Shortly after dawn the old man came out and sat down on a stool beside his doorway. A few minutes later a girl came, greeted him, and went inside. Perhaps a quarter of an hour later she came back out with a bowl, the old man's breakfast. He sat eating it in that slow, contemplative way old men have, stopping from time to time to lift his head and warm his face in the sun.

Noah did not come outside. It was not long before Matthias realized that he had been tricked.

Matthias could not stand against a certain grudging admiration. Noah had somehow known that he was being watched and had arranged the whole performance. Why else walk back to the old man's house while it was still light? Not to see but to be seen. The performance at the gravesite—what a feat of self-control.

He had probably been gone for hours.

But in truth Noah was still in Nazareth. It had occurred to him that his nameless adversary might use the night to come into the village, so as soon as it was full dark he had brought his grandfather back to Joseph's house and had himself slept in the carpenters' workshop. Then, an hour before dawn, when he judged it safe, he had brought Grandfather back to his own house to make a show of eating his breakfast alone, and then Noah returned to the workshop.

It was about two hours past dawn when Jacob showed up to report.

"He's gone." Jacob smiled broadly. He seemed to be enjoying himself. "He's half an hour down the road to Tiberias."

"He didn't see you?"

Jacob shook his head. "No. I was careful. And he was in too much of a hurry to look back."

"Then I had best leave before other possibilities occur to him. And, Jacob . . ." He took hold of his cousin's arm. "In case he comes back, keep a watch on Grandfather. These people are capable of anything."

Half an hour later, Noah was in the village of Japha, south of Nazareth. As he was a stranger there, people noticed him, and noticed that, after passing through Japha, he continued south. But as soon as he judged himself out of sight, he started east, hoping to reach the city of Philoteria, at the southern end of the Sea of Kinneret, before nightfall.

Not long after reaching the main road, Matthias encountered a man riding a horse. He reached up and grabbed the man's arm, pulling him off the horse and dumping him on the ground. When the man objected, Matthias showed him the point of his sword, which ended the discussion.

He drove the animal without mercy for two hours, until he realized that he was not going to catch up with Noah because Noah was not on that road. He then cursed himself for having been tricked twice in one day by the same man.

But his respect for Noah, already high, increased.

He considered backtracking to Nazareth, but decided against it. Noah, he reasoned, was not fool enough to let anyone know what route he intended to follow, so terrorizing his relations would yield nothing. The man could be anywhere.

But Matthias consoled himself with the thought that his quarry's journey, no matter how full of turnings, would end in Capernaum. That was where Noah would expect to find his cousin, the prophet.

And death would be waiting for him.

————

Noah spent the night in Philoteria. He had hardly slept the night before, so he went to bed early, after a heavy dinner, during which his host, a tavern keeper who understood his trade, kept refilling his wine cup. So he slept late the next morning and awoke with a headache.

The headache yielded to breakfast and several cups of cold water, and thus Noah was left free to consider his situation.

He could not be sure that the man in the grape arbor was not from the Lord Eleazar, who might be keeping a friendly eye on him, as he had on the way back from Damascus. Noah had not had time to apprise him of his recent discoveries. Perhaps he was growing impatient.

It was also possible that Caleb was having him watched. Had he been watching in Tiberias? Did he know that Noah had been inquiring about Judah? Jacob had described the occupant of the grape arbor as a big man. Could it be the same big man who had attacked Noah on the road, sent now to finish the job?

If this line of conjecture was anywhere near the truth, then Caleb would know—or perhaps only fear—that Noah was intending to warn Joshua. Caleb would certainly regard another murder on his conscience as a small price to pay for protecting his spy.

Noah would have to wait until Capernaum to find out, and once there, he might not live long enough to rejoice in the accuracy of his assessment.

Nevertheless, an hour after breakfast he went down to the docks with the intention of finding a ride north. He discovered a freight boat that was just preparing to depart, and a meager exchange of silver bought him a seat on a crate of pottery destined for the bazaars of Hippos.

It suited Noah's purpose to travel up the eastern shore, skirting along the edge of Philip's domain and thus beyond Caleb's easy reach. He would get off at Bethsaida and thus approach Capernaum on foot from the north.

But before then, he had two days on the water. He enjoyed the sun in his face, and it was amusing to listen to the captain swearing at his men in Greek. He would have perhaps an hour in each port while cargo was unloaded, which would give him time to buy a meal. He reminded himself that at the next stop he should buy wine for the crew.

————

Matthias sold his stolen horse in Tiberias, since arriving in Capernaum with a horse would only make him more conspicuous. He spent an hour at the harbor questioning the boat crews, but he really didn't expect to learn anything of Noah and he didn't. Noah was far too clever to come anywhere near Tiberias.

With the money in his hand, Matthias seriously considered getting drunk. This job was beginning to oppress him. He felt himself overmatched, but more to the point, he could not keep out of his mind the image of Noah standing beside his kinsman's grave, his head covered with his prayer shawl, reciting the prayers for the dead. It filled him with self-loathing, an emotion he could usually keep at bay while working, when he was able to focus on the operational steps of his task.

To kill someone, it is first necessary to deprive them of humanity, to make them somehow deserving of death. The worst had been the little whore in Tiberias, whom he had bribed to betray her customer and then had strangled as a precaution. He had liked her, liked her flirtatiousness. She had been reluctant about Judah bar Isaac, but the silver Matthias had spread out on the table before her was perhaps more than she had ever seen in her life. She had yielded to the temptation, but in the end had bought herself nothing except Matthias's hands around her throat.

The men had always been easier—particularly men who were simply there, in the way, with no other purpose but to die. How much pity does a farmer have for the wheat beneath his scythe?

Remorse came after, in the darkness, in one's dreams. Then their faces haunted him.

Noah's face haunted him already. He could not lie to himself this time. There was no escape from the consciousness of what he was preparing to do.

Except, of course, in wine. If he drank enough he could achieve a certain detachment. Oh yes, I am an evil fellow, and God has turned His back on me, but I cannot care. And sleep became like death, dreamless and serene.

But even wine was beginning to be not enough. Only a week ago, so he was told by a woman he sometimes slept with, he had begun sobbing and had taken out his sword, swearing he would cut his own head off.

She said she believed he would have done it, but he was too drunk, and she took the sword from his hands, grown as strengthless as a child's.

Would that be how it ended one day? Would he slay himself, the final act of a man damned by God?

Matthias pushed these reflections from his mind and poured the money into his purse. He would drink himself into oblivion only after he had killed Noah.

37

Noah thoroughly enjoyed himself throughout the voyage. At first the crew thought he was no more than another soft merchant hitching a ride, but then, as the morning began wind-still, one of them asked, as a joke, if Noah might care to take his turn on an oar. When he pulled off his tunic, and they saw the muscles in his arms and chest, they stopped laughing. He was in the oar pits for over an hour, until there was breeze enough to fill the sail. By then the sailors seemed to regard him as one of themselves.

In the afternoon he made himself useful by rehinging the cargo door, and at night, when they dropped anchor outside Gergesa, they all held high revel with the wine Noah had bought in Hippos. At a certain point in the festivities, everyone went swimming. Afterwards, the captain was so drunk that he couldn't negotiate the rope ladder and had to be hoisted back aboard like a waterlogged bail of wool.

When finally they unrolled their sleeping mats on the deck, Noah was too tired to think or even to dream.

The next day, shortly after noon, they were in sight of Bethsaida, and for the first time since being on the water Noah remembered the man in the grape arbor.

Simply to put off making any decisions, he stayed to help the crew unload. Then he said his good-byes and found an inn in the harbor district. Capernaum was only a short walk down the coast, but he did not care to come into the town with only a few hours of daylight remaining. Joshua might not even be there, and he wanted time to find him before nightfall.

He wondered if, when the ship pulled into the dock at Capernaum, there would be a big man waiting to see who got off of it.

Matthias spent the night at Ezra's tavern. He knew that Ezra was one of the Lord Caleb's informers, but he did not make inquiries until after dinner. He sat outside in the failing light, and Ezra came around to ask if he would like something stronger than the weak beer he was drinking.

"Where is Joshua of Nazareth?" Matthias asked, without preamble.

"I . . . I don't know of any such person," Ezra stuttered out.

He was lying, of course—one could see that in his face. So Matthias grabbed him by the testicles and squeezed. Ezra doubled over in pain.

"I'll ask you once more, and if I don't like the answer, I'll rip these off and toss them out into the street for the dogs to eat. Where is Joshua of Nazareth?"

He tightened his grip and Ezra gasped.

"He's in Ginnesar. It's about an hour and a half down the coast. Oh, please!"

Matthias opened his hand and let go. Ezra sank to his knees.

"That's better. The Lord Caleb told me you were a man who could be trusted to know everyone else's business. Now go inside and bring me another jar of your disgusting beer."

While Ezra was gone, Matthias peered down at the beer that just covered the bottom of his jar. The beer was a compromise, since it did not cloud his mind but seemed to keep at bay his darker thoughts. Yet it was also the abandonment of his own rule about work, and it frightened him. He would have one more jar, which he would drink slowly, and then no more.

What would happen tomorrow? How many days before he couldn't stop himself? He would have to finish this job quickly.

But he had made Ezra afraid, and that eased his despair a little. Ezra feared his wrath the way Matthias feared God's, and somehow that made God's seem just a shade less terrible. What would happen, he wondered, if he ever met a man he couldn't make afraid?

Noah woke before sunrise and, since no one at the inn was awake, did not wait for breakfast. When he went outside he found there was just enough light to allow him to see, and thus he reached Capernaum only a little after full daybreak.

He did not go into the center of the village, but left the road to follow the shoreline. The fishermen were just preparing to launch their boats. He found Simon's house and knocked on the door. Simon's wife stared at him, apparently trying to recall his face, and then she smiled.

"You're the Master's cousin," she announced, as if she expected Noah would be grateful for this information.

"Can you tell me where I might find Joshua?"

"Gone—he and my man both. Left day before yesterday."

"Do you know where they were headed?"

"Down the coast, and then inland." She smiled again, seemingly pleased with the thought. "Spreading the Word. They'll be in Ginnesar for the next few days. Lots of friends in Ginnesar. But they need to be fortified from time to time, or they'll slide back into sin."

Simon's wife, like her husband, was solidly framed, but unlike him, she seemed gifted with perfect confidence in herself. Noah guessed she would have made the better apostle.

"Thank you."

Ginnesar, he knew, was just a walk down the beach. But he was hungry. He decided to go into town and buy breakfast.

Noah did not go to Ezra because he knew from Deborah that Ezra was not to be trusted. But there was no shortage of stalls open to sell a workman some bread and fennel. Noah did a little better and managed a piece of fish as well.

He was across the square from Ezra's tavern, just inside one of the streets that led back down to the shore, and that accident of positioning probably saved his life. For a man came out through Ezra's door, a big man, who glanced about with the bored expression that meant he had just awakened, walked about a little, and then threw himself into a chair. He had a face that looked as if it had been chiseled from iron, but Noah had never seen it before. It was, rather, something in the way he moved that made him instantly recognizable. Noah could recall the

shadowy figure walking away from him as he lay bleeding and breath-
less that night on the road to Sepphoris.

"You are Noah, the ironsmith?" He would remember the sound of that
voice to his last day.

Leaving Capernaum suddenly seemed an excellent idea.

He followed the shoreline for over an hour, staying on the bluffs
above the beaches, hardly noticing anything except the twenty or thirty
feet of trail in front of him. Fear concentrated his attention wonderfully.

He would find Joshua, tell him what he had come to tell him, and
then disappear. He would hire the first boat he could find and sail for
Tiberias, where he could lose himself in the crowds on the road to
Sepphoris.

But then what? In Sepphoris he would be easier to find. Deborah was
there. He could not lead this brute to his wife.

Where could he go? Damascus? The Greek islands? Spain? And do
what there? Spend the remainder of his life waiting for someone to come?

Could he somehow contrive to kill this man? Noah remembered the
precision with which he had been beaten—enough to insure that the
message was understood, but not enough to maim him. Just bruises, no
broken bones. This was a man who understood violence, the way Noah
himself understood iron and fire. What chance would he have against
such a man?

Could he bring himself to kill anyone, even in self-defense? He was
by no means sure, and it seemed the wrong time to put the question to
a practical test.

So, by the time he reached Ginnesar he had resolved nothing. He
stumbled into the village like a man in a trance.

Fortunately, he had no trouble finding Joshua. He simply asked the
first person he met and was directed to a house at the western edge of
the village. Joshua was in the front yard, crouched over, surrounded by
five or six little children.

When he came nearer, he saw that Joshua had a stick in his hand and
was drawing figures in the dirt. He could hear his voice. He was nam-
ing the letters of the Hebrew alphabet.

Then Joshua glanced up and saw Noah.

"That is enough for today, children," he said, and straightened up.

The children remained, clinging to his robes.

"Go and play," he told them. "God loves you."

Reluctantly, they departed. Joshua stepped forward and embraced his cousin.

"Has Deborah forgiven me?" he asked, only half in jest.

"For what?"

"For missing your wedding."

"There is very little Deborah would not forgive you. She sends you her love."

The expression on Joshua's face darkened just a shade.

"You bring bad news," he said.

"Yes."

"Then tell it to me."

"Your father is dead."

"When?"

"Four days ago."

"Four days . . ." Joshua seemed to consider the length of time significant.

For a moment Noah thought Joshua would weep, but then his mood shifted, as if he had withdrawn into some secret place in his soul.

"The chosen of God are my family. Father rejected both my message and me."

"Your mother told me that the last words he uttered were a prayer that God might keep you safe."

This was too much, even for God's prophet. Joshua began to say something. He opened his mouth, but the words died on his tongue. All at once he raised his hands, as if fending off a blow.

Then he simply turned and walked away.

"There is more that you must know," Noah called after him, but, without turning around, Joshua raised his arm and made a gesture like swatting at a fly.

"Not now," he said, in a choked voice.

Noah found himself alone in the empty yard of an empty house.

"I found you, ironsmith!"

Suddenly he was on his knees, even before he realized that he had been struck from behind. His kidney felt as if it would burst.

Slowly the man circled around to face him, staying just beyond Noah's reach. He was bigger up close. Noah forced himself to raise his eyes to the man's face, but he had to arch his back painfully. The eyes that stared down at him were ferocious.

"You ran a good race, but it ends here," the man said.

"Who are you and what do you want of me?"

"Only your life."

The man drew his sword, which came out of its scabbard with a slow hiss. Noah, sure that his last moment was upon him, began to whisper the Prayer for the Dead.

"Only his life?"

The voice was Joshua's. Something had brought him back. He stood not two paces behind Noah's attacker.

The man turned to face him. But Joshua merely smiled and raised his arms to shoulder height, as if to say, *Strike where you will.*

"Joshua, get out of here, or he will kill us both," Noah cried, his voice hardly more than a croak. But Joshua seemed not to hear. He never took his eyes from the big man's face.

"Do you imagine you are safe to do these things?" Joshua asked, almost mockingly. "Do you think that your Father, Who hears every beat of your heart, is too blind to see the blood you would spill?"

"My father is dead," the man growled. But he did not strike.

"Your Father is alive, and always has lived, and will live forever. For your Father is God, Who sees you now and weeps for the evil in your heart. Do you not feel His sorrow? Can you not feel His urging? Turn aside from your intent, and be forgiven."

"There is no forgiveness."

The man raised his sword, as if in warning. Noah saw that the point, which was no more than a span from Joshua's face, seemed to tremble slightly in the air.

"There is always forgiveness," Joshua said calmly. "No man is beyond God's mercy. You have turned away from Him, but He has not turned away from you. You are still His son. He still loves you and yearns for your return to righteousness. His heart is open to receive you."

Then, slowly but deliberately, he reached up with his right hand and touched the point of the sword with his finger. The big man, who was even taller than Joshua, seemed frozen.

Slowly, Joshua lowered his hand, and his finger carried the point of the sword down with it. The arm that held the sword, raised to do murder, sank as if of its own weight.

"Do not be afraid, my son. God loves you and will redeem you. Your sins are forgiven."

The murderer's hand opened, and the sword dropped to the ground.

By then Noah had managed to find his feet, but, like one in the presence of a mystery, he too had lost the will to action. He could only watch in awed fascination.

This man who, only a moment before, had been about to steal his life from him, now lowered his eyes and stared at his sword lying useless on the ground. Then he turned to Noah, his face mirroring his confusion of mind, as if begging him for some explanation.

The strength seemed to ebb from him and he sank to his knees. He covered his face with his hands and began to sob.

Joshua calmly picked up the fallen sword and, still holding it, he walked around and knelt before the weeping murderer. He put his left hand on the man's head.

"Kill me," the man said. "My life is a burden to me."

Joshua drove the point of the sword into the ground. Then he took the man's hands in his own and gently pulled them away from his face.

"God has forsaken me."

"God does not forsake us," Joshua answered, his voice low, as if speaking to a frightened child. "We forsake ourselves. We lose our way and wander into evil, but the path back to God is always open to us. We have only to repent, to cast off sin like a soiled cloak, and God welcomes us back. A father forgives his son, and God is our Father."

"God will not forgive me. I killed my father."

"God forgives all sins. We have but to ask."

"I have killed many times. I have done terrible things. I cannot sleep at night. The things I have done haunt my dreams."

"Your sins trouble you. Cast them off. God will cleanse your heart and set you free."

"God has cursed me for my crimes."

"You have cursed yourself. Now lift the curse. What is your name?"

"Matthias."

" 'Gift of God.' Now, accept God's gift of your life. Do you repent of your sins?"

"I repent. I do repent."

"Then pray with me."

"I cannot pray." Matthias's voice was like a cry of pain. "God has made the words die in my throat."

"Then repeat my words, and God will hear us both. 'Father who is in heaven.'"

"Father who is in heaven."

"Sacred is the name of God."

"Sacred is the name of God."

"May Your will be done on earth."

"May Your will be done on earth."

"Forgive us our sins."

"Forgive—I can't." With a child's feeling of helplessness, Matthias shook his head. "I can't."

"You can. You have merely to repeat my words. 'Forgive us our sins.'"

"Forgive us our sins."

"As we forgive those who sin against us."

"Please, God . . ." And then, slowly, haltingly, "As we forgive those who sin against us."

Noah, who was witness to it all, could only shake his head in wonder. He remembered Joshua's dead father, who had despaired of his son, saying, *How can he be a prophet? The prophets of old performed miracles.*

Now, Joseph, you have your answer, Noah thought. *Is it not miracle enough to turn a heart of stone back into living flesh?*

It was as if Matthias had been born all over again, and as a mother tends her newborn child, so Joshua stayed crouched on the ground beside Matthias, who seemed as helpless as any infant and was in a state of confusion the newly born are hopefully spared.

Repentance led to hope, and hope, it seemed, was the parent of fear. Matthias wept and prayed and was in terror of God's just wrath as he struggled to accept the idea that he could ever find forgiveness. All the time, Joshua remained with him, speaking to him in a low voice, his hand on the huge man's shoulder that he might not feel himself abandoned.

And as a woman may labor for hours giving birth, so Joshua slowly helped this murderer, this worst of men, to be reconciled with God and with himself.

In the late afternoon Matthias, exhausted by his struggle, curled up on the bare ground and went to sleep. Then Joshua, his knees stiff, stood up and stretched like a man just waking.

"I need to piss," he said to Noah, the only witness to this act of God's grace. "And then I think I'll take a walk. Will you watch him for me?"

"Of course."

Joshua stooped over to pick up Matthias's sword from where it lay in the dirt, and handed it to Noah.

"Best kept out of the hands of children," he said, and walked away.

Out of professional curiosity, Noah examined the blade and decided it was a fine piece of work. He found the maker's mark on the inside of the guard and was pleased to discover that he recognized it. "Suhis of Damascus," he murmured to himself. "Well, the Syrians have always made excellent weapons."

Not knowing what else to do with it, he was still holding the sword two hours later, when Matthias woke up.

"Where is he?" he asked, addressing no one in particular—he seemed unaware of Noah's presence. He seemed frightened.

"He has gone for a walk," Noah answered. "He'll be back."

Matthias's eyes came to rest on the sword in Noah's hand.

"If you mean to kill me, I wouldn't blame you," he said.

At first Noah didn't know what he was talking about, and then he remembered. He looked down at the sword blade, and then set it down on a bench beside the door to the house.

"I wouldn't know how," he said, surprised at his own anger. Then it occurred to him that his reaction was more one of fear than of anger.

"Then you are blessed," Matthias answered, and then shook his head. "You take a man's life, it changes everything. I will never be innocent again."

His sincerity was so obvious that Noah could not restrain a feeling of pity.

"I'll get you something to eat."

He picked up the sword again and carried it with him into the house, where he hid it under a pile of kindling.

The house was empty, but Noah found a pot of cold beans that only needed heating up, and there was bread and a few jars of beer. He made a fire, and in a few minutes he was able to go back outside carrying two plates of food and one of the jars.

They sat together on a bench beside the door. Matthias did the food justice, but he would not touch the beer.

"Why not?" Noah asked him.

"Because when I drink it is to kill thought. I drink until I am too drunk even to dream."

"A man can choose how much he drinks," Noah explained patiently, as if such an idea might never have occurred to this man. "Besides, in this instance you are perfectly safe, as there are only two jars of beer and I mean to claim my share."

Matthias laughed and, after a moment's hesitation, raised the jar to his lips.

"I won't be tempted," he said. "It's not very good beer."

Probably it had been meant as a jest, but Noah could not bring himself to laugh. It seemed so odd to be sharing a meal with someone who, only hours before, had intended to kill him.

They ate in silence for a time, and then Matthias said, "I am sorry I hit you."

"Which time?"

Matthias seemed confused.

"Which time that you hit me are you sorry for? Today, or on the road from Nazareth? In the dark."

"Both times. And I am sorry I tried to kill you."

"Well then, we'll forget about it. What are you going to do about Caleb?"

"You know about him?"

"Yes. He becomes vindictive when people don't do what he wants."

Matthias stared into the distance, considering this. He did not seem stupid, and no one would know better than he what Caleb was capable of.

Finally, he shrugged.

"If he has me killed, so be it. I will stay with the Master."

"His name is Joshua."

"I know."

Joshua came back from his walk and, seeing the two of them sitting together, raised his eyebrows in mock astonishment.

"Then all is well between you?"

"So it would seem." Noah stood up. "We must talk."

"About my father?"

"No. About something else."

"Then come inside." Joshua glanced at Matthias. "You come as well. We have no secrets here."

Noah nodded his agreement. "I think it likely he is intimately concerned."

They went into the house and sat down around a rough wooden table. Joshua found a lamp and lit it.

"Well then, what is it?" he asked.

"You have a spy in your midst. Judah bar Isaac."

Both of them observed the sudden change in Matthias's face but pretended to ignore it.

Noah then described his interview with the Lord Eleazar, and all that he had learned in Tiberias. "How Judah got into Caleb's hands, I have no idea. He is suspected of having fled after killing a prostitute."

"I did that," Matthias said suddenly. "I kidnapped Judah, on the Lord Caleb's orders. The girl drugged his wine, and I killed her to keep her from talking."

For a moment no one could say anything, and then Joshua touched him on the hand.

"Even for this you have been forgiven, my son. Now tell us what you know of this matter."

Matthias described everything he had done. "Judah was asleep the whole way to Sepphoris. He must have awakened in his cell. The Lord Caleb has a taste for such things. He likes to put a man's mind in chains."

"And then, after a few months in Caleb's hands," Noah said, glancing at Joshua, "Judah comes to you, claiming to have lost all his money and to have taken this as a sign from God."

Joshua listened to all this and then, finally, shook his head.

"I have no doubt that what you say is true. But a man can change."

"Deborah saw him in Sepphoris, talking to Caleb," said Noah. "He fears Caleb more than death."

"What would you have me do?" Joshua asked.

"Send him away." Noah could hardly believe that the suggestion needed to be made. "Part with him, or the day will come when he will betray you."

"If I do that, if I turn my back to him, what chance will he have?"

"What chance will you have if you do not?"

"God has sent me to bring His children back to Him." Joshua made a gesture with his left hand, which suggested his helplessness in the face of this obligation. "I cannot save Judah by abandoning him. I have no choice but to help him work out his salvation."

Noah could only sigh with exasperation. It seemed that reasoning with God's prophet was a hopeless business.

"Then you are a dead man."

35

On this trip to Jerusalem, Eleazar could not hide from himself the fact that he had brought the politician in him along. He had no choice.

Almost the last person he had seen in Sepphoris was the ironsmith, who had left a note at the house of Kenan bar Dathan requesting an audience. They had met there the next day, and Noah had astonished him by revealing not only the identity of Caleb's released prisoner but also a precise history of his kidnapping and of his movements since being set free.

"I will not inquire how you discovered all this," Eleazar had told him, "but from the nature of your information, you clearly have a source very close to my servant Caleb."

Unless he was mistaken, Noah managed an almost imperceptible nod.

"But I will ask if you know anything of this Judah's background," Eleazar continued.

"He seems to be of a Levite family. He had been amply provided for, but he is in disgrace."

"And naturally you do not know what his motives might be."

"My lord, I have no window into the man's heart," Noah told him, with perhaps just a touch of asperity. "But you would know better than I what pressures can be brought to bear on one in the Tetrarch's prisons. Caleb, whom you are pleased to call your servant, had several months in which to bend Judah to his will."

"And your cousin the prophet is aware of what you have told me?"

"Oh yes. But he seeks the man's redemption."

"Is he stupid, this cousin of yours?"

"No, my lord. His views on the matter are not so narrow as yours or mine. He is a true servant of God."

"And you have come to believe that?"

"Yes, my lord. I have seen things the sight of which you have been spared."

Eleazar had long since observed that Noah's deference was a mask for what, in another man, the Tetrarch's First Minister would have regarded as insolence. It was one of the reasons he both liked and trusted the ironsmith and was inclined to give him his way.

The Lord Eleazar smiled thinly.

"And what would you recommend I do about this Judah bar Isaac?"

"Recommend?" Noah shrugged his powerful shoulders. "I would not dream of such a presumption."

In other words, he would leave the First Minister to ponder the matter out for himself.

Eleazar's initial impulse was to have Judah bar Isaac arrested, but he quickly dismissed the idea. If Caleb had some dark design, it was better to leave things as they were and hope the fool would overstep himself.

Noah's information about the mysterious prisoner was interesting, but its real usefulness lay in the future.

It was to prepare that future that Eleazar had come to Jerusalem a full two weeks before the Passover. Because Caleb's wife had family in Jerusalem—family who seemed more forgiving of scandal than Caleb's had proved to be. Or perhaps they were merely indifferent. From his knowledge of them, Eleazar was inclined to that view. In any case, Michal had been much with them of late.

By comparison with Tiberias, or even Sepphoris, Jerusalem was not a place in which a woman alone could find much amusement. The priesthood dominated social life, and everyone knew about Michal's divorce and almost instant remarriage—and could be counted on to draw the obvious conclusions. Michal would be an outcast in Jerusalem.

Yet here she was. She spent almost as much time in Jerusalem and she had previously in Tiberias. One could not help but wonder why.

Except, of course, that one knew.

There had long been rumors, the accuracy of which Eleazar had gone to some trouble to establish, about Michal and a certain Nahshon bar Elhanan, a handsome, wealthy, and not very bright young man who spoke Greek as his first language and whose family, all conveniently dead, came from Caesarea. He had arrived in Tiberias on a visit of pleasure two years previous and had never returned home. After Michal's dismissal from court, he had suddenly moved to Jerusalem.

They had not been discreet. Eleazar had witnesses to their meetings. He had the testimony of Nahshon's servants that Michal had, on several occasions, spent the night in his house.

He wondered if Caleb didn't possess a similar collection of evidence. Nahshon had to be stupid to lay with the wife of so dangerous a man.

Thus, his first morning in Jerusalem, before he began his customary round of social calls, even before he saw his son, Eleazar bar Zadok waited in the reception hall of the house of Michal's mother.

"I regret that the mistress is not yet awake," a servant told him—a perfumed, prancing young man with an elegantly cut beard, who smiled and smirked as if privy to all the family secrets, which was possibly the case.

"I see no occasion to disturb the Lady Rahab," Eleazar told him, "particularly since it is her daughter, the Lady Michal, I wish to see."

The servant glanced aside, as if astonished that anyone could be so boorish, and then smiled.

"I am afraid the Lady Michal is also still asleep."

"Then wake her."

"Alas, it would prove impossible. . . ."

"Hardly impossible. Wake her. Be good enough to inform her that the Lord Eleazar wishes a private word."

For a moment the servant seemed confused. Then he appeared to be preparing to say something, but exactly what would forever remain a mystery.

"Be about your business, boy."

Eleazar wandered into one of the sitting rooms and found a chair. He anticipated a long wait, since, in his experience, women of questionable reputations tended to be most particular about their appearance.

He was happily disappointed, however. Not even a quarter of an hour had passed when the Lady Michal swept into the room. Her hair was a trifle disarrayed, which only added a becoming suggestion of voluptuousness to her face.

For an instant, Eleazar wondered what it must be like to make love to such a woman. Rather like handling a viper with a pretty skin, he decided.

"My lord," she said breathlessly, "you do me honor."

Eleazar did not rise from his chair. Neither did he smile.

"Fortunately, my lady, your honor is not my concern. I am here on business, so please be seated."

The change in her expression was instantaneous, but she said nothing. Instead, she sat down in the chair to which Eleazar directed her with a languid gesture.

Was she frightened? It was difficult to know. Her emotions, perhaps, were in a state of precarious balance, capable of being tipped in any direction.

"How may I serve you, my lord?" she asked.

Good, Eleazar thought. *She is assuming an air of humility, which only means that she has decided to wait and see.*

"I have made up my mind to destroy your husband, Lady. The only question left is whether you will go down with him."

Now, for the first time, Eleazar allowed himself to smile. The smile was almost kindly.

A moment passed, a silence that lasted through five or six beats of the heart, and then Michal moved uncomfortably in her chair.

"Are you threatening me, my lord?" she asked finally.

"Yes. With death. Do I have your attention, Lady?"

From the way she nodded, one could have imagined that the joints in her neck had frozen shut.

"You have been careless, Lady. I have more than sufficient evidence to bring an accusation of adultery against you, and you will recall that the penalty for adultery is death by stoning."

He paused and waited for some reaction. There was none. Good. That could only mean that she was thoroughly frightened.

"Have you ever seen someone stoned to death?" he went on. "A crowd surrounds the victim. There is no escape. I *have* seen it. Afterwards, the woman's head looked like pulp. And here in Jerusalem the crowd would be huge and probably more than a little hysterical. When they have finished, I doubt if you would be even recognizably human."

Michal did not move, and she made no sound. But tears were trickling down her face.

Eleazar was prepared to give her time.

"My husband . . ." she began at last. "My husband would never . . ."

"Your husband, if confronted with irrefutable evidence—evidence which, in the event of his refusal to act, will be made public—would have no choice but to accuse you. The Tetrarch will not be pleased, but that serves my purpose. It will weaken your husband and bring him another few steps closer to his ruin. So, as they lead you out to the execution ground, you can comfort yourself that your death will not have been in vain."

She began to sob. Eleazar was disgusted by the performance. He merely waited for it to subside.

"Can you save me?" she asked finally. She had the cunning, at least, not to raise her eyes.

"Of course I can save you. That is not the question. The question is whether you would be more useful to me alive or dead. What do you think?"

She straightened herself up and tried to assume something like a dignified attitude.

"What can I expect if I help you?"

Their eyes met, and they found they understood each other perfectly.

"When your husband is dead, you will be a widow and I will have no interest in pursuing any accusations against you. And I will see to it that you inherit some part of Caleb's estate. You can marry Nahshon bar Elhanan, provided he is fool enough, and you can live anywhere you want. Jerusalem, Caesarea, anywhere. Except in Galilee. You would do well, I think, to take yourself off to the gentile lands. You might like Alexandria. I'm told it's charming."

"What do I have to do?"

Eleazar smiled, not very nicely.

"First, I think it would be wise if, when your husband arrives in Jerusalem . . . which you expect, when?"

"Tonight."

"Then tonight I think you should have a touching reunion. He will be staying at the Tetrarch's palace. You should join him there, and soften his heart to you as best you can."

"That will not be difficult," she said, obviously regaining her confidence.

"I'm delighted of hear it, because I want to know everything you can discover about where he goes, whom he sees, and what he does. I want to know what he thinks, if you can find that out as well. There is a woman named Talitha who will be part of your household. You may speak to her in Greek and she will understand nothing, but she will remember everything. Anything you tell her, I will know before you are many hours older. Do you understand?"

"Yes. I understand."

"Do you also understand that if I fail to find your information useful, or if you attempt to deceive me in any way, you will die under a shower of stones?"

"Yes."

"Then our business is finished."

Eleazar rose and, without even glancing at her, left the room.

Once he was outside, he was able to consider the interview with some satisfaction. Michal would certainly betray her husband, so the only remaining question was whether Caleb was sufficiently blinded by love or passion or whatever held him to that woman not to guess that she was now his bitterest enemy.

As he walked along, and as his steps took him into a more fashionable quarter of the city, Eleazar decided he might as well go on and visit his dead wife's mother, whom he detested but who lived close by. It was a necessary courtesy, best gotten through as quickly as possible.

Then he would have dinner with his son.

39

Even as Eleazar left Michal, her husband was entering Jerusalem's northern gate. Caleb had arrived as one more anonymous pilgrim in the vast crowds that clogged the roads into the city.

Eight years before, he had left through the same gate, and in that time he had never been back. The city was at once utterly strange and painfully familiar.

But it was always thus during the great feasts. Jerusalem became a different place as the mobs took possession of it. Every street was transformed into a remorseless current of strangers that dragged one helplessly along with it. And the noise was inhuman, like the rumblings of a storm.

But still, it was where Caleb had been born, where he had expected to live until he died, a servant of the Temple and of God.

After all these years, the sight of the place tormented him, like the recollection of lost love. Even the Greek-speaking tourists from cities too distant to be named, who came to the Holy City for the only time in their lives, were more welcome than he. He was the uninvited guest for whom there was no room at the table.

Later, when he had attended to business and was settled in the Tetrarch's palace, he would send a note to his wife, but he would not go to her family's house, because it was in the Levite district, where his own extensive family had their homes. There was always the chance that he would meet someone he had known from the old days, and that would be awkward. He did not want his father to know of his return.

Caleb was a wealthy man and a high officer of the Tetrarch's government, and yet to his father he was dead, cast off, as if he had never been born. He did not even know if the old man was still alive.

And why? Because Caleb had grown uncomfortable in the straitened life of a Levite and had wanted to breathe the air of a more spacious world. Because he was attracted to the Greeks, who understood that a man might make mistakes but who recognized few sins. Because he had not kept to the Law with sufficient scrupulousness. And because of Michal.

His father had called her a wicked woman, and Caleb had of course known that he was right. But what did that matter? His father had been perhaps too old to understand passion, or even to remember its existence.

Jerusalem was his father's world. Aside from the Temple, what was Jerusalem but an overcrowded village on a hill? The Temple was its excuse for being, the center of everything, the throne of God. It was also a slaughterhouse, stinking of blood.

Caleb made his way along streets he had known since boyhood. The houses on either side were made of stones as old as the world. Strangers jostled him, and he was surrounded by a babble of foreign voices.

Prostitutes and gentiles were welcome, but he was not.

It took him almost an hour to reach the Tetrarch's palace, where the chamberlain was expecting him. He immersed himself in the ritual bath and then went to the steam room for an hour. When he felt himself restored, he scribbled a note and had it sent round to a certain office in the Temple.

The Temple might be the seat of God, but He occupied only a single room and He had little company. On the Day of Atonement the high priest, and only he, entered the Holy of Holies to offer sacrifice for Israel's sins. The rest of the year the King of the Universe was left in solitude.

But all around that quiet center, the Temple was a busy place. All priests were members of one of twenty-four divisions, each of which served for one week. The members of each week's division divided the work among themselves in twelve-hour shifts, since the work of placating God's wrath allowed for no rest. Through the day and through the night, doves, pigeons, goats, heifers, kids, lambs and, on special occasions, even bulls were slaughtered on the altars in the Court of Priests. The spilling of blood was endless. At any given moment more than a hundred priests—and vastly more during the four great festivals—would be on duty, offering sacrifice. Following these were the Levites, who acted as singers, musicians, gatekeepers, guards, guides, inspectors, and messengers. And then, of course, there were the priests, who functioned as the Temple's government.

For, indeed, the Temple was like a small city unto itself. Its ever-changing population could range from several hundred to a few thousand, and priests and Levites all had to be fed and housed, their clothes and their bodies washed, and the thousands of visitors had to be kept in order.

Order was essential. The Temple was constantly filled with people. During the festivals, the crowds were massive and excitable. As had happened many times, the most trivial incident could occasion a riot, which would cause the Roman soldiers to come down from the walls and "restore order" with their swords. Hundreds might be killed. If the disturbances spilled out into the city, thousands.

With the single exception of the sacrificial offerings themselves, since these were rendered to God, nothing was more important than that order be kept. And the man upon whose shoulders this burden rested was a priest named Meshach.

Caleb had never met him. Outside of the Temple itself, priests and Levites inhabited different worlds and, besides, Meshach's appointment had been recent. When he went to the offices of the guards and sent in his note requesting an appointment, Caleb had no idea what to expect.

The answer came back that the Lord Meshach was currently at liberty and would be happy to receive the Lord Caleb at once, should that prove convenient.

When Caleb entered the room, he found a man standing over a table, his attention focused on a document, the pages of which were spread out before him. The priest glanced up at Caleb and his face contracted in a slight frown.

The table was the only article of furniture in the room, so the two men stood facing one another.

Meshach was probably between thirty and forty. This could be no more than a guess, however, as his hair was already beginning to go gray at the temples, but his face was young. His eyes had an anxious quality, as well they might.

Caleb made a slight bow. He understood the deference a Levite owed to a priest, so he remained silent.

"Your reputation has preceded you," Meshach said at last. "One hears that you were responsible for the Baptist's arrest. Is that so?"

"It is so."

The priest merely shrugged. "Well, I suppose we shall all survive his loss. I imagine your master was glad to be rid of him."

He did not seem to be inviting a reply, so Caleb made none.

Meshach let his gaze drop back to the surface of the table. With his left hand he drew one of the sheets of papyrus toward him, studied it for a moment, and then seemed to lose interest.

"And how may I be of service to you now?" he asked, without looking up. "Are you here on the Tetrarch's business?"

He smiled, not at all pleasantly.

But Caleb was not put off. It did not surprise him that a priest might think he had risen higher than was appropriate for a mere Levite. He refused to take offense—or, at least, to let it show.

Instead he told Meshach about Joshua bar Joseph, former disciple of the Baptist, preacher of sedition and self-styled prophet of the end of Roman rule.

Meshach listened with attention, betraying no reaction. When the recital was over he looked down once more at the table, moved another sheet of papyrus a few finger widths to the right, and then raised his eyes, carefully looking at nothing.

"He is known to me," he said, as if the fact depressed him. "He is a carpenter or something of the sort, is he not?"

"Yes."

"He spoke in the courtyard last year. During the Passover. I remember him. He was possessed of a certain natural eloquence, but his accent was as thick as goat cheese."

Caleb smiled, pretending to be amused.

"Well, yes, my lord. He is a Galilean."

"He seemed harmless enough."

"He is not harmless, my lord. He has a following. He is capable of creating a disturbance."

"But there is no evidence that that is his intention."

Meshach stepped back from the table and clasped his hands behind his back. It was only then that he looked Caleb full in the face.

"If I arrested every village preacher who collected an audience, I would have little enough time for anything else. Providing he does not cause a riot, the Temple is a place where every Jew may speak his mind."

"And if he does cause a riot?"

"As I said, there is no evidence that he plans to. And as you said, he is a Galilean. Your master Herod Antipas, I notice, has not seen fit to arrest him."

"Galilee is not Jerusalem, my lord. In Galilee he confines himself to the villages. There are no Roman soldiers in Galilee, my lord."

"On the basis of what you have told me, not even Pilatus would arrest him. But trust me, My Lord Caleb. If this Joshua bar Joseph becomes troublesome I will see to it that he receives a sound thrashing and is sent home—to Galilee."

When Caleb returned to the Tetrarch's palace, he wrote his wife a note, merely advising her that he was in the city, and told the chamberlain to send a messenger, but he thought it might be days before they saw one another.

That priest. Caleb's resentment seemed to burn his throat. He hated them, all of them. He was a Levite, so they thought they had a right to think meanly of him. Their contempt they regarded as a birthright.

And his hatred burned the brighter because he was afraid. Resentment, he knew, was a luxury he could not afford. He had to find a way to destroy this peasant preacher or he would be destroyed himself.

He needed to stop thinking about it. He needed to clear his mind. The answer would come if he simply stopped thinking about it.

He had a light dinner, after which he read dispatches for an hour. Then he decided he might as well go to bed.

He was almost asleep when the bedroom door opened and he saw a light. It was a few seconds before he realized that it was Michal, holding an oil lamp.

She put the lamp down on a table and snuffed out the wick. Then she undressed in the dark and crawled into bed beside him.

"Did I wake you?" she asked, her voice soft and caressing, her lips close enough that he could feel her warm breath on his face.

"I hardly know, but if you did I'm glad."

He reached across his own body to touch her, and his hand came to rest on her rib cage. She drew herself closer to him, close enough that he could feel her breasts against him.

"I've missed you," she said. "You've been away from me a long time."

It didn't seem the moment to point out that she was the one who went off to Jerusalem to visit her family—that had been the stated reason, and if there was another he did not wish to know about it—so he said nothing. He merely turned his head a little and let her lips find his.

She straddled him with her legs and guided him into her. Her passion was intense and lasted even after he was spent, so that she went on covering his mouth with hot, panting kisses. After the second time, she grew quiet, huddling next to him.

"I'm going to win it all back," he said. The words just seemed to speak themselves, without his intending anything. He might have said, *"I love you. I cannot bear to be without you,"* and perhaps that was what he meant.

"Yes . . . ?" she answered, seemingly half asleep.

"Within a week or two, the Tetrarch will see how much he needs me. He will listen only to me."

He didn't know if he believed it himself, but somehow he needed to say it.

And perhaps, for this moment, it didn't matter, because by then her breathing was long and even, which meant she hadn't heard.

The next morning, as she lay in bed, watching her husband wash himself, Michal wondered if his promise that he would "win it all back" changed anything. It was obvious that, if Caleb really did manage to regain his position with the Tetrarch, he would have to destroy the Lord Eleazar. Only one of them would survive. That was clear.

But the Tetrarch could not bring down his First Minister during the Passover, while they were all still in Jerusalem. That would have to wait until they all returned to Galilee, where Antipas was the master. Until then, Eleazar was safe.

But Michal was not. Eleazar could charge her with adultery whenever it suited him and, if he did so in Jerusalem, his destruction in Tiberias would not save her.

Michal did not believe that Caleb would succeed. Caleb was finished. He was like a man pushed from a cliff, clutching at the air as he falls.

Thus, the safest side was Eleazar's. Besides, Caleb was beginning to bore her.

"I will be in the city all day on business," he told her as he wiped his armpits with a damp cloth. "I'll see you at dinner."

"*All* day?" she asked, drawing aside the sheet to display her naked body. "Then perhaps you could spare me a quarter of an hour?"

After he was gone, Michal lay in bed for a long time, waiting for the heat of passion to leave her. She told herself that, now, any suspicions he might have had of her would be lulled, and it might even be true. But she knew that was not the real reason she had offered herself. She did not quite understand it, but that she was about to betray him only heightened her appetite. It excited her to think of him inside her, his muscles tightening as he spent his seed, with her knowing all the while that he was doomed.

Eventually she washed and dressed. As she was not sated, she was tempted to go visit her lover—soon to be her third husband—but she decided against it. At this stage, there was no point in taking unnecessary risks. She would remain in the palace today and pretend to be her lord's devoted wife.

The idea made her laugh. All at once she felt quite gay. She wanted to dance, and actually took a few steps before she heard a knock on the door.

It was one of the pages, a boy of perhaps fourteen, and still frightened. He bowed very low and seemed on the verge of running away, until she smiled at him.

"Pardon me, my lady, but there is a man at the front gate. He looks like a beggar, but he insists he must see the Lord Caleb. I thought it best . . ."

"And you were right." She smiled again. It was like teasing a kitten. "The Lord Caleb is out for the day, but I will see him."

Why not? she thought. It would give her something to do.

The beggar at the gate was indeed unkempt and dirty, but his sandals gave evidence of once having been quite elegant and, indeed, he was no worse than many of the pilgrims one saw in the streets.

His eyes, though, as he huddled beside one of the gateway pillars, had a haunted look, as if he lived under sentence of death.

"The Lord Caleb is not here," she said, her voice sweetly understanding. "I am his wife. Will you tell me your name."

"My name?" He made a sound like despairing laughter, which it was not quite. "I am as nameless as the dead."

"But even the dead had names once. What was yours?"

"Judah. Judah bar Isaac. But I am not he now."

Michal was beginning to suspect that this man was a little mad, and the mad were capable of anything. Nevertheless, as courage was her only virtue, she knelt down beside him and touched his hair.

She knew the effect she had on men, and this one was no different.

"What is your business with my husband?" she asked. "You may speak freely. He has no secrets from me."

"He is himself the most terrible of secrets."

"But not from me."

He shook his head. Yes, this man had his secrets too. But he was not mad, only terrified of what he carried in his heart. He wanted to tell her everything—she knew this by instinct. And she suspected that what he had to say would be worth the trouble of finding out.

"We will talk later," she told him, making the words like a caress.

Then she stood up and turned to the page who had accompanied her.

"Clean him up and feed him," she said. "Be sure that he has some wine, and then bring him to me. Speak of this to no one. Do you understand?"

She gave the page three silver coins and let her fingers linger on his open palm as she gave them. She would have nothing to fear from him.

Fortunately, the Tetrarch had not yet arrived from Tiberias, so, except for servants, the palace was almost deserted. Michal waited in the garden, kept company by the tinkling of a fountain. It was more private there than inside, where someone could be listening behind any door.

In a little less than an hour, the page brought Judah bar Isaac to where she was sitting on a marble bench. She smiled at him, and the page left.

"Please, sit down here beside me."

Judah hesitated and then sat down. His hair was still wet from the bath, and his damp tunic clung to his arms. The calluses on his hands, she noticed, looked as if they had only recently been acquired. She was sure he was no peasant.

It was a small bench, and their knees were almost touching.

"Now. Tell me, what you would have of my husband?"

"I want nothing of him. He told me to find him when I reached Jerusalem. I have done that. I have done everything he has asked of me."

"Are you afraid of him?"

"Yes."

"Why? Why are you afraid?"

"Because he is God's terrible vengeance."

She could see it in his eyes, a fear that went beyond the fear of death. It was almost past belief, but it was true. Her husband, who in the privacy of her heart she had always despised, had so filled this man with terror that there was hardly anything else in him.

"The Lord Caleb has been cruel to you," she said. "He is an evil man."

"You are his wife and you understand nothing?" His eyes were wild, and he reached up to run his fingers through his hair, as if to keep his head from separating itself from his neck. "He is God's instrument, and no man may judge God. God has chosen to destroy His own prophet, to still His own voice in the world, and men cannot say it is good or evil. Men can only close their eyes and wish for death."

"You need to sleep."

"I dread sleep. I dread my dreams."

Michal stood up and held out her hand, which Judah bar Isaac, forsaken by God, instinctively took.

"I will give you something," she said. "You will sleep and you will not dream."

"Is it death?" he asked her, in a voice that mingled dread and hope.

"No, it is not death. But you will sleep."

She summoned the page, who had been waiting in a hallway, and told him to take their visitor to an unused bedroom and to wait there with him until she came.

She would give this Judah a cup of wine into which would be mixed a few drops of a drug she used sometimes herself, an extract from the leaves of the blue lotus. It was a lie that he would not dream. He would have strange and wonderful dreams, and when he awoke, their conversation in the garden would have become so confused with those dreams that he would not know where the dreams ended and waking began.

And then she would have a story for the Lord Eleazar that would make him wonder.

40

"I'm going to win it all back." Caleb's own words haunted him. He could say what he liked to Michal—no man is under oath in bed—but in the bright light of day he didn't know if he believed it.

That priest, with his anxious eyes, had been his best hope. He could not go to the Romans without the Temple's at least tacit consent, and Joshua was unlikely to attract their attention on his own. Besides, it would be dangerous to arrest a preacher, even a Galilean one, in public. That by itself might start a riot. It had to be done quietly.

And the Romans did not know the city. Besides, they were barbarians, intoxicated with their own power. They would turn Joshua's capture into a spectacle.

There was no escaping it. Caleb could see no other way. He needed the Temple and the Temple refused to listen.

That priest, that wretched priest . . .

He had left the Tetrarch's palace just after first light and had wandered aimlessly through the streets. But in Jerusalem all streets seemed to lead to the Temple, so by midmorning he found himself on the edge of the vast plaza south of the Temple gates. He had only to glance up to see the soldiers patrolling the walls.

Roman soldiers, constantly reminding everyone of their power, their absolute authority over a subject people. Roman soldiers, not even Temple guards. . . .

Then Caleb remembered something. He had a cousin, a childhood friend, in the Temple guards. Gideon had always been a troublemaker.

And a troublemaker was precisely what he needed.

Caleb had sent a note. Gideon bar Josiah was the only member of his family with whom Caleb had remained in even sporadic contact over the years of his exile. Yet, as he sat in a tavern nervously sipping at a cup of mediocre wine, he wondered if Gideon might not find it inconvenient to appear.

He need not have worried. At the appointed time, a strongly built, rather swaggering figure came through the door. He glanced about and, seeing Caleb, grinned. His one concession to his cousin's outcast status was that he wore ordinary clothes rather than his uniform as a captain of the Temple guard.

Caleb stood and the two men embraced.

"It has been so long since I've been here, I had trouble remembering the way," Gideon said, after he had sat down. He looked around him expectantly, and then laughed. "It's just another wineshop now, but the times we had here!"

"It was always 'just another wineshop' at this hour. The whores never showed up until after sunset."

"That's right. I remember now."

Gideon smiled, flashing his large, white teeth. He had the arrogant confidence of an athlete, and he was handsome, with a strong face set off by glistening, curly black hair, which he wore long, and eyes of almost feminine softness. The women had always loved him, and he had always returned the compliment.

"You look prosperous," he went on. "How is that bitch you married?"

Caleb lifted his hand in a dismissive gesture. "Still exactly the same. How is Edna?"

"She's pregnant again. This will make five."

It was obviously not a subject which held much interest for Gideon, so he tasted his wine and made a face.

"Some things never change," he said, his expression implying that the observation could be applied to more than the questionable quality of the wine.

"And some things do."

They could both laugh. They had not seen each other in eight years, but time seemed to have stopped. In each other's company, they were young again, hardly out of boyhood, and filled with mischief.

Their conversation wandered comfortably over their shared past and then drifted into the present, by way of Caleb's exile.

"What have you been doing with yourself in Galilee?" Gideon asked him. "I can't imagine you turning farmer."

"Well, I never actually saw the farm. I sold it as soon as I reached Tiberias."

It was a great joke, and their laughter was loud enough that a few people turned their heads.

"Then what did you do to keep from starving?"

"I entered the service of the Tetrarch. Antipas is not a bad old fellow, and he likes me. I keep his enemies frightened."

"And would those enemies possibly have included a certain lunatic known to the mob as John the Baptist?"

"I arrested him, and I ordered his execution."

Gideon was visibly impressed, but lest this be too obvious, he merely shrugged.

"Well, were that generally known, it would make you very popular in certain quarters. The Temple did not love him. The priests believe that only they can speak for God."

"He had disciples," Caleb said casually, his attention apparently absorbed by a close study of the rim of his wine cup. "They preach his message of sedition. One of them is presently on his way to Jerusalem."

"Is that why you are here, after all this time?"

"Yes." Caleb smiled thinly. "I was wondering if you could help me deal with him."

"And how do I benefit from helping an old friend?"

"You make the arrest. If I know you, your reputation with the Temple authorities could probably use a little polishing."

"That always."

"Good. Then you get the credit while I supply the money and the witness. The priests will turn him over to the Romans, and the Romans will crucify him. The Romans won't mind one more—I hear they crucify people by the score, all over the country."

"But the Romans won't crucify him just for following the Baptist. They won't care."

"Then the charge will have to be insurrection. During the Passover, when the city is bursting with people, they won't be fussy. What would do?"

Gideon had to think. His was not an agile mind, but his conclusions were generally sound.

"If he claimed to be king of the Jews. If he claimed Davidic descent. That sort of thing. And, of course, the mob cheering him, ready to riot at his merest word. It would take a public demonstration to get the Romans to notice."

"And perhaps not even that would be enough?"

"Perhaps not. It is always wise to prepare them for these things."

"And how would we do that?"

Gideon leaned back in his chair and let his eyes wander up to the ceiling.

"I have a friend—an acquaintance, really—a centurion in one of the legions. He likes to live beyond his means, so he's always sniffing for money. He can arrange for certain events to be witnessed and properly reported."

"What about Pilatus? Will he be a problem?"

"Oh, no." The idea struck Gideon as so ludicrous that he laughed. "Pilatus can be counted on to condemn anyone brought before him. He's a great believer in crucifixions as a remedy for public discontent. That one is a brute, even by Roman standards."

"Is your centurion in the city?"

"Unless he's died or been transferred, yes. The legions have been in barracks for two days."

"Then I would like to meet him."

"You will."

"How will we manage the demonstration?"

"Nothing could be easier."

Gideon smiled in an unpleasant way. He also was a brute. When they were children, it was always Gideon who earned the cruelest thrashings, which perhaps had only made a bad nature worse.

"All that is required," he went on, "is to position twenty or thirty men in the crowd. When your holy man enters the city, they will begin

to shout, 'The anointed one! The anointed one! Our king! Our king!'
The mob, which during the Passover is always half mad with excitement, will take up the cry. Do you know when he will arrive and what
gate he will use?"

"I am having him watched."

"By the way, what is his name?"

"Joshua bar Joseph."

Gideon shook his head. "I have never heard of him."

It was almost evening before they parted. Gideon had wanted to go
prowling, just for old times' sake, but Caleb hadn't been in the mood.

In the most offhand way, Caleb had learned that his father had died
four months before.

"Didn't anyone write you?" Gideon had asked.

"No. They wouldn't have known where to send the letter. Besides . . ."

Gideon had shrugged and changed the subject.

So Caleb was in a reflective and faintly melancholy mood when he
returned to his rooms in the Tetrarch's palace. He briefly considered a
letter to his mother, and even wrote a few lines, before remembering
that he had never liked his mother and felt no temptation to see her
again.

It occurred to Caleb that Michal, who lately was much in the city,
must also have heard that his father was dead and had not seen fit to tell
him. Perhaps she hadn't wanted to upset him. More likely, she hadn't
thought it important enough to mention, or it had slipped her mind.

41

At midday there was an almost inaudible tapping on the door of the Lord Eleazar's study.

"Come."

The door opened and a small, middle-aged woman named Talitha stepped over the threshold. She seemed hesitant to come further into the room.

Eleazar smiled and made a gesture with his right hand, as if drawing her toward him.

"My lord," she said quietly, making a low bow, "the Lady Michal sent me."

"Then perhaps you should shut the door."

Talitha was a remarkable woman. When Eleazar had discovered her, she was in rags, sitting outside the Temple reciting Torah for copper coins.

"And the people complained in the hearing of the Lord about their misfortunes; and when the Lord heard it, His anger was kindled, and the fire of the Lord burned among them. . . ."

Eleazar had found her performance fascinating. She seemed to have all five scrolls committed to memory, plus the Prophets and many of the Psalms. She was then in her middle twenties, quite plain, and trying to nurse a baby with breasts that had long since dried up. The child's father was unknown, even to her.

"Where did you learn this?" he had asked her.

"In the prayer house, my lord, when I was a girl."

"When did you leave home?"

"When I was sixteen, my lord. My father lost his farm and could not keep me."

"Can you read?"

"No, my lord."

How had she lived all those years? As a beggar at first, then as a prostitute. She was one of those for whom the world had no place, so naturally her wanderings had led her to Jerusalem. Finally, after she had found herself with child, and her pitiful condition rendered her beneath the attention of even the poorest of men, she had settled herself by the Temple gate and returned to begging. Each morning she would begin with God's creation of the world and recite as long as anyone would listen. The pious would give her a few gerah and pass on.

Eleazar had her brought to his house, where she and her infant son were fed and washed. Then he listened to her recite, which she did for four hours, stopping only now and then for a sip of water. If she made a mistake, Eleazar did not catch it.

"Was your father a scholar?"

"No, my lord. He was a poor farmer."

"Then how is it you can do this?"

"I just remember things."

Finally he took down a scroll, a history of the Maccabees, which he was quite sure could not have been known to her, and read her a long passage, after which he invited her to recall what she could. She repeated it all faithfully.

But when he asked her a question about its content, she could not answer. Then he asked her, in Hebrew, "In what village were you born?" and again she could not answer.

Then he recited to her part of an oration of Isocrates he had memorized as a schoolboy, deliberately transposing the first two sentences. She repeated it, including the error.

She could reproduce faithfully anything she heard, even if she did not understand the tongue in which it was spoken. It was becoming clear to Eleazar that a woman possessing such a talent would not be without her uses.

That had been ten years ago. Eleazar took her into his household and

had her trained as a housemaid, and he saw to it that her son was edu-
cated. Talitha was happy. To be a servant in a rich man's house was
more than she had ever dreamed of. She had her son, and one day he
would be a scribe. She worshipped her master and would have done
anything he asked.

All that he ever did ask of her was to listen, and repeat what she
heard.

In the present situation, since the Lady Michal was as unlettered as a
sparrow and it would hardly have been prudent to meet her again, Talitha once again proved her worth. Servants go largely unnoticed. A lady
may speak to her waiting woman without incurring the least suspicion.

The Lord Eleazar's house was only a short distance from the Tetrarch's
palace. Servants were engaged and dismissed so frequently that no one
thought anything of the fact that a woman they probably never noticed
in one place was now working in another. Talitha passed back and forth
a few times a day, a fact which would not strike anyone as remarkable,
since her son was being trained by the Lord Eleazar's secretary.

It was like having a private window into Caleb's domestic life.

Eleazar rose from his desk. "Speak," he said, and smiled encourag-
ingly.

"I have a message for the Lord Eleazar," Talitha said, in Aramaic—it
was her voice, but it was the Lady Michal speaking, even down to the
peculiarities of accent. And then, in Greek: "A man came to see Caleb.
His name was Judah bar Isaac, and I thought he was crazy at first, but he
was only very afraid. He said Caleb was God's instrument and God
would destroy His prophet. What did he mean? I don't know. *Are you
listening to me, you stupid sheep?*"

This last was again in Aramaic, and Talitha shouted the words, but
without emotion. She seemed to be in a sort of trance.

She continued, in Greek. "But he brought his cousin for dinner, and
they joked about arranging a triumphal entrance for the 'Son of David.'
His cousin is something in the Temple guard. The cousin, whose name
is Gideon—I didn't like him—mentioned a Roman named Gaius.

"Caleb says he will win everything back. He is like a coiled spring.
Whatever he is planning will happen, I gather, in the next few days.

"I am keeping to my bargain, my lord. I am betraying my husband.
I am telling you what he says and does. I am holding nothing back. I beg
you to be merciful to me."

And then, once more in Aramaic, "Leave me. Go away."

Talitha closed her eyes and then opened them again and smiled.

"Have I done well, my lord?" she asked.

"You have done very well. The Lady Michal has bad manners, but I ask you to be patient with her."

He reached into his purse and took out three silver coins and held them out to her. She took them and then kissed his hand.

"When did she tell you all this?" he asked.

"This morning, not an hour ago."

"And is there a stranger in the house? One who seems a little mad?"

"There was. He saw the Lord Caleb and then left, around noon yesterday."

"Go now, and spend time with your son. He misses you. You will soon be back in my household."

She bowed and withdrew, leaving the Lord Eleazar to ponder all she had told him.

Since first discovering the identity of Caleb's mysterious prisoner, he had learned a great deal about Judah bar Isaac, including the interesting fact of his relationship with his tormenter. Had Caleb chosen him, at least in part, as an act of revenge against his family? It was not un-imaginable.

Judah, the Lord Eleazar now knew, had been a disappointment to his father, a man of strict principles who occupied a position of importance in Levite society. At nineteen Judah had been involved in some scrape, the details of which were unclear but which involved his relationship with certain young gentile wastrels living in the city, and his father had seized on this to banish him to Tiberias, where he had lived a comfort-able and amusing life.

His involvement with John the Baptist was difficult to explain. Per-haps he saw the emptiness of the life he was leading. Perhaps, by being baptized, he felt he had reentered the community of the godly. It was impossible to know. Perhaps it was merely an impulse.

Now he seemed torn. He spoke of Joshua bar Joseph as God's prophet and of Caleb as His instrument. The one inspired devotion and the other fear. His allegiance was divided between them and, whichever triumphed, the consequences for him would be dreadful.

Then there was the problem of what to do.

Eleazar found himself almost wishing he knew nothing of the

matter. He considered warning Noah of the peril in which his cousin stood. After all, he owed the man. And Joshua was, apparently, innocent.

But what then? What would be gained by unraveling Caleb's carefully constructed plot? The man thought he had hit upon the perfect stratagem to regain his position, while in fact he was busily destroying himself. One peasant preacher seemed a small price to pay for relieving Galilee of such a monster.

Eleazar did not want innocent blood on his hands, but how many more would die if Caleb succeeded? And were *they* not innocent?

It was an unpleasant choice, but unpleasant choices were the business of government. Not to choose was to fail in one's duty. Not to choose was cowardice.

Therefore, he decided, the wisest course was to let events unfold as they would.

42

The pilgrimage routes within two days' walk of Jerusalem were clogged, and the villages along the way were hard pressed to accommodate so many people. Every night, the floors of every room were covered with sleeping mats, while the poor slept on roofs or pitched tents in the open. Food was expensive and sometimes not available at any price, so most carried their provisions with them. Occasionally—inevitably—there were arguments, some boiling over into violence, but the mood of the crowds was generally hopeful and joyous. After all, the Passover was a feast of deliverance.

Noah's party included six: himself and Deborah, Sarah and Abijah, who had only been married a week, Deborah's servant Hannah, and Noah's apprentice Hiram, who had begged to come, principally to be near Hannah, who flirted with him and teased him without mercy.

They had spent the night in a village not two hours' walk from Jerusalem, and might end by spending another night there, because Joshua and his party were late.

It was inconvenient. In Jerusalem they would be staying in the home of a relative, where there was privacy, but a man with any pretentions to decency could hardly go into his wife while twenty other people were sleeping around them. Four nights of this was enough.

Surprisingly, it seemed hardest on Sarah, who complained pitifully to Deborah and sometimes cried.

"What can be the matter with her?" Noah had asked, genuinely worried.

"Don't concern yourself," his wife replied. "It is a problem which will solve itself the first night we spend in your cousin Baruch's house."

When this answer did not seem to satisfy him, she could only smile and shake her head, implying her disbelief that he could be so stupid.

"Oh, that."

"Yes, 'oh, that.' She misses being with her husband, as I do."

"I never would have suspected Sarah of having so sensual a nature."

"She is only just a bride. It is too early. They would have done better to stay at home."

"Abijah would not miss a Passover in Jerusalem."

"Nevertheless, Joshua had better arrive today, lest both your sister and I greet him with a shower of stones."

In this answer, Noah discovered yet another reason to be pleased with his wife.

It was just after noon when Joshua finally did appear, leading about fifteen people. The first thing Noah observed was that Judah was not among them.

"I sent him ahead to make arrangements for our arrival," Joshua announced. "He knows the city better than any of us."

"No doubt."

For a moment Joshua seemed not to understand, and then he raised his hand in a dismissive gesture.

"You are too suspicious, Noah. This is not Galilee. We are beyond the Tetrarch's reach. Besides, there is nothing to fear from Judah. Although he may not yet know it himself, his heart belongs to God."

"I have every confidence you are right. Now, may we go? My womenfolk are weary of traveling."

Within five minutes they were on the road. Noah was walking arm in arm with his wife when he felt a hand on his shoulder. He turned his head and saw that it was Matthias, whom he then introduced to Deborah.

"My dear, this is the man who, two weeks ago, wanted to kill me. But God has forgiven him, and so have I."

Matthias looked abashed, and Noah was instantly ashamed of his jest.

"I have repented, Lady. The Lord has softened my heart."

"I rejoice in it," Deborah answered. "We are all friends here." She took the huge man's hand in both of hers and kissed it.

"I am jealous," Noah announced, and then everyone could laugh.

They walked on together, talking of trifles, and the change that two weeks had worked in Matthias was striking. He was relaxed and had even learned to smile. He seemed capable of happiness. For one, like Noah, who knew the horrifying story of his life, it was hard to believe this could be the same man.

Then he grew silent. He kept glancing from Noah to Deborah and back again. He seemed to be nerving himself up to say something, and it was possible to guess what.

"She knows about Judah," Noah said quietly. "There is nothing I know that she does not."

"I have not the Master's strength of faith," Matthias said, shaking his head in self-reproach. "I fear Judah. I always see the Lord Caleb standing behind him."

"Does he know of your association with Caleb?"

"No. None of them do. To them it is as if I was born the day the Master found me. They seem to think that to inquire further would be a discourtesy."

"And has your life changed so much then?" Deborah asked.

"Yes. I can drink a cup of wine without wanting another. I can sleep at night without fearing my dreams. I feel remorse for the evil I have done, but I know forgiveness. I have submitted myself to God's will."

"Which still leaves us with the problem of Judah," Noah said. "I do not wish to appear cynical, but I share your misgivings."

"It must be left in the Master's hands."

A few minutes later, the Master joined them. He was in a festive mood.

"I wanted to apologize," Joshua said, smiling broadly.

"For what?"

"For not staying with you this year. But I could not impose such a large party on your cousin. We will find other lodging. Yet we will all break the bread of the Passover together, as we always have, won't we?"

"I am sure Baruch won't mind a few extra guests," Noah answered, as he quickly tried to calculate how much extra food and wine would be required to take care of Joshua's followers. "He loves to play the host."

"I am very hopeful this Passover." Joshua laid his hand on Noah's shoulder, who thought it likely Joshua hadn't heard a word. "I think we will see great wonders."

The first of these was announced by a young man leading a colt. The colt was white and only just broken to the halter, and the swirling crowds of pilgrims, through which it was being led, made it skittish.

The colt held everyone's attention, and when the young man stopped before Joshua, the scene was witnessed by a multitude.

"You are he," the young man announced. "You are Joshua of Nazareth."

"Do you know me?" Joshua asked, perplexed. "Have we met?"

"No, but I was told I would know you when I saw you."

He held out the lead rope, offering it to Joshua.

"The colt is yours. Ride it into the city."

Instinctively, Joshua took the rope, and the young man melted into the crowd. Joshua hardly seemed to notice. He ran his hand along the colt's neck, speaking to it in a low voice, and instantly it began to grow calm. All his life, Joshua had had an affinity with animals, and now, as they stood together, colt and man seemed to have no attention except for each other.

"Well, why not?" Joshua said, smiling.

He took off his cloak and covered the colt's back with it. Then he climbed on. At first the colt tried to step away from the unaccustomed weight, but then seemed to accept it and grew quiet.

"I will enter the city like some great lord," he said, and laughed. "Or at least a bandit, which is even more honorable."

Noah found himself wondering who could have sent such a gift.

They were perhaps two hundred paces from the city gates when the tumult started.

Here and there people began to shout. At first Noah couldn't make out the words, but gradually, as the shouting grew, he heard "anointed one" and "Son of David."

Soon, many in the crowd of pilgrims took up the cry. Joshua, riding in the middle of the road, clearly visible to everyone, looked around him with astonishment.

People surged forward to touch him. Some wept. Joshua bar Joseph, the carpenter from Nazareth, was suddenly their hero. Israel had found her deliverer. "Anointed one! *Anointed one! Son of David!*"

It was a scene of madness, a riot of joy. The colt was on the verge of panic, and Joshua had so much to do to keep it from bolting that he hardly seemed to notice the swirling chaos around him.

Noah happened to glance at Matthias, who was standing beside him, and saw that tears were streaming down his face.

"They love him," he said, his voice choked with emotion. "He is their king."

Deborah held her husband's arm tight. "What does it mean?" she asked him.

"I fear this may be the beginning of a tragedy."

The Roman centurion Gaius Raetius, who was watching from the top of the wall near the north gate, had a different impression.

"It's more comic than a play by Plautus," he said, laughing and slapping his knee. "You Jews are a queer lot."

Caleb and his cousin Gideon exchanged a glance. The centurion was from Germania, a place of bogs and dark forests where the inhabitants worshipped trees. He was tall and broad, with a broken nose, scars on his face, and long, straw-colored hair that stank of rancid butter. And he thought the Jews were "a queer lot."

Standing a little to one side was the priest Meshach, whom Gideon had persuaded to come. He seemed determined to ignore the Roman's presence. His attention was fixed on the man riding the colt.

"Don't worry," Gideon whispered. "Gaius will report what he's paid to report."

Caleb nodded but, like the priest, he seemed wholly absorbed in the spectacle below him.

"It's odd, since for weeks he's been at the center of my plans, but this is the first time I've ever even seen this Joshua bar Joseph." He shook his head. "Somehow I had expected him to be taller."

"He *is* tall. It's just hard to judge from this height."

"The colt was a good thought," Caleb said, turning to Gideon and smiling his approval. "It increases his visibility and somehow makes him seem more like a king in the making."

"Has he ever claimed Davidic descent?"

"No, not that I am aware of. But what difference does it make?"

Gideon could not help but wonder what made his cousin so eager to destroy this village preacher. Of course, it hardly mattered. Self-styled peasant prophets were as common as finches—one more or less would not make any difference.

"Well, in any case, we'll need someone to stand before Pilatus and *say* the fellow has claimed it," Gideon said, complacently. "The forms of the law have to be observed, although I don't suppose anyone, least of all Pilatus, will care whether it's true or not."

"Never fear. There will be a witness."

Gaius Raetius turned to them, grinning and rubbing his hands together.

"I've seen enough to arrest him right now," he said, in the most vulgar Greek imaginable. "I can have him on a cross by nightfall, if you like."

"I think we'll just wait a bit," Caleb answered dryly, wondering if the man was really fool enough to contemplate arresting a man while he was being hailed by the mob as king of the Jews. "There's plenty of time."

43

Jerusalem was less a city than a miracle. God ruled the whole earth, and His presence was everywhere, rendering the meanest patch of wasteland holy. But Jerusalem was the most holy place where a man could draw breath, and the Temple was God's home. When God first spoke to Moses, on Mount Sinai, He told him to take off his sandals, for the place where he stood was holy ground. Thus, Joshua always removed his sandals and walked barefoot when he entered Jerusalem, for here he was in the presence of the living God.

In Jerusalem one felt the nearness of God as one felt the sunshine. God warmed the heart and illuminated the mind. Joshua could not be in Jerusalem without experiencing a joy he could hardly describe. It was incomprehensible to him that anyone could enter the city without feeling God's closeness. It was as real as the experience of the senses. How could anyone feel envy or anger, or break the Law or remain an unbeliever, when under the very eyes of God? It seemed impossible.

Yet all these things happened. The city belonged to God but was inhabited by men, and men—most, in Joshua's experience—were blinded by sin. Perhaps that was the nature of sin, to be a kind of blindness. An inability to see the obvious.

On the morning of his first day in Jerusalem, Joshua joined the crowds awaiting immersion in one of the many ritual baths surrounding the Temple Mount. The Passover meal must be eaten in purity, and the process of purification would take seven days.

As he stood near the immersion pool gate with a handful of his disciples, waiting for the sun to dry his clothes, all he could really see of the Temple was a long stretch of wall beyond the Antonia Fortress, where the Roman garrison was quartered. Along the top of the wall, soldiers were standing guard.

"Look at them," Simon said, with a bitterness unusual for him. "How the Romans mock us. I do not understand why the high priest tolerates it."

Joshua could only shake his head.

"He tolerates it because he holds his office at the pleasure of the Roman prefect. He tolerates it because he has no choice."

Suddenly he laughed.

"Probably those soldiers will be privileged to be the first to witness the coming of the Kingdom. Think how surprised they will be to hear the trumpet blast and see the messenger of God's judgment descending from the clouds."

"Will it be soon, Master?"

"Soon, Matthias. Soon enough. I am filled with hope that this Passover will see great changes. But the time is known only to the Father."

All the while they spoke, their steps carried them further from the fortress, which they all would have preferred to ignore, and in an arc along the outer wall. The Temple was a vast structure, best appreciated at a distance.

All at once Joshua stopped, crossed his arms over his chest, and smiled. There, over the heads of the crowd, he could see the thing whole. Over the inner wall he could even see the upper half of the Holy of Holies.

"Old Herod was a black-hearted rogue, but this one thing he did right. It took him thirty years, but he came as close as a man can to building a house worthy of the living God."

For a long while he stood there, letting the sight of it delight his heart. Then, as if something important had just occurred to him, he glanced about.

"Where is Judah?" he asked impatiently. "He was supposed to meet us here, and he is late."

"Here I am."

They heard his voice before they saw him, and then he emerged through the crowd. He smiled uncertainly, like someone unsure of his welcome.

Where had he been? It was the inevitable question, if only because he seemed not himself. Under any circumstances, Judah always appeared ill at ease and out of place, but that was ascribable to the social chasm between a son of the Levites and a crowd of Galilean workmen—Judah always tried a little too earnestly to forget that he wasn't a peasant. But today he looked unwell. His eyes had an unnatural glitter and his temples appeared hollowed out.

"Are you ill?" Joshua asked him, staring into his face. "Did you eat something that didn't agree with you?"

"No. I'm fine."

"Then, did you find us a place to sleep?"

"Yes. An upper room near the fuller's tower. We can have it for the week for two silver shekels."

"And where did you get the two silver shekels?"

"I borrowed them. A friend loaned them to me." He glanced about, as if to judge how the explanation was accepted. "I still have friends in Jerusalem."

Joshua threw his arm across Judah's shoulders.

"Very well then. Have you immersed yourself?"

"Yes. Yesterday."

"Good. Then we can go look at this upper room."

Beyond the eastern wall was a ridge covered with olive trees, and at its base a patch of wilderness called Gethsemane, an old word for "olive press." There may have been an olive press there once, but now it was deserted, given over to wildflowers and ancient trees. The place had a certain beauty and, though only a ten minute walk from the Temple gate, was very peaceful and quiet. Joshua had discovered it when he was still a boy, and he liked to go there to pray.

The next day was the Sabbath, and he spent most of it there, alone with his thoughts and with God. When he returned after sundown he was told that his cousin Noah had been looking for him.

"I will see him tomorrow, near the Temple," he said.

The next morning the final rite of purification took place. Joshua stood with a crowd of pilgrims as a priest sprinkled them with water mixed with the ashes of a red heifer. The following day they would enter the Temple to offer sacrifice for their sins.

He was still wiping the water from his beard when Noah turned up.

"Come away with me," he said. "I need to talk to you."

"Then you can buy me breakfast," Joshua replied cheerfully.

Just beyond the main Temple stairway they found a stall, where Noah bought two cups of beer, along with lentils wrapped in flat bread. The beer was weak and the lentils had been left in the pot too long, but one couldn't expect better in Jerusalem during a festival.

They sat in a doorway and ate.

"I have been making inquiries," Noah said, staring down into his cup. "I found the owner of your colt. After an exchange of silver, he told me it had been rented for the day by a man with whom he regularly does business and whom he knows to be an officer in the Temple guard. He would not give me his name."

"Someone had to provide the colt," Joshua answered. "Why not someone from the Temple?"

"Because the Temple guards are supposed to maintain order, and yet this one procures you a colt so that you may ride into the city."

"It was kind of him."

"It was part of a performance, in which you were the principal actor. You mount the colt, and almost immediately you are hailed, 'Anointed one. Son of David.'"

"I have never claimed to be either—well, at least not since we were boys."

"Does it matter what you have claimed? It is enough that you have been made to *appear* to claim these titles. How do you think the Romans will interpret all this?"

Joshua had by this time finished eating. He wiped his hands on his tunic and looked about him as if trying to remember where he was.

"The Romans? What have they to do with it?"

Noah could only shake his head.

"The Romans, for better or worse, are our masters. They don't like it when the mob becomes excited, and they particularly don't like it when someone claims to be king of the Jews. You don't even have to claim it—it's enough if the mob claims it for you. Did you know that Caleb is in Jerusalem?"

"It's the Passover, Noah. Everyone is in Jerusalem."

"I've looked into it. Caleb hasn't been here in years."

Now it was Joshua's turn to shake his head.

"You amaze me," he said, as if he meant it. "How did you find all this out?"

"I am told I have a talent for bad news."

"Apparently. And you think Caleb is behind all this?"

"Who else would go to the trouble? In Galilee you are safe because you cannot be arrested without the Tetrarch's approval, but in Judea you are under Roman authority, and the Romans are very sensitive about anything or anyone who might cause a riot during the festivals. I believe Caleb is working to convince the Romans that you are a threat. I don't pretend to understand his motives, but he means to have you killed."

Joshua grew very quiet as, apparently, he tried to absorb the idea that he was the object of a murder conspiracy, and Noah took advantage of the interval to get up and have their cups refilled. It was very bad beer, but it was at least something.

He sat down again and put the cup in Joshua's hand. Joshua looked at it for a moment and then drank it off.

"What do you think I should do?" he asked.

"Leave the city as quietly and as quickly as possible. Once you are beyond the city gates, the Romans will lose interest. Go back to Galilee, where you will be safe."

"We have had this conversation before. I can't run away." Joshua made a despairing gesture with his hands. "If it was your object to frighten me, then you have succeeded, but I can't run away."

"If you stay, you may be dead before the end of the week. The Romans will not tolerate a threat to their authority."

As if with a single impulse, the two men turned their heads to look into each other's faces. Then, quite suddenly, Joshua began to laugh.

"What of God's authority?" The laughter died away. "What of God's authority, Noah? We are in Jerusalem, within sight of the Holy of Holies, where on the Day of Atonement the high priest stands in the very presence of God. What is the authority of Caesar compared to that? I cannot leave. God demands my presence in this place, at this time. I have no choice."

"That is what I was afraid you would say."

"Yes, well . . . You tried."

"Yes."

For a long time the two of them sat together in the doorway, their arms across each other's shoulders, silently saying farewell.

That afternoon Joshua was in the Temple courtyard, preaching to the crowd.

"At long last God will redeem His creation and cleanse the world of sin. Those who live by the Law will inherit the earth and will live forever. There will be no poverty, no injustice, no death. And what is the Law? Is the Law so hard? It asks merely that you love God with your whole heart and you love His creation, your brothers, your fellow men. Are our hearts made of stone that this is so difficult? Love your enemies and pray for them. Treat others as you would be treated. Divide what you have with the poor. Open your hearts to God and know the joy of His forgiveness."

There was a large audience gathered around him, and they seemed receptive—more receptive than the villagers in Galilee.

"When will it happen, Master? When?"

"Soon, my friend. One like the son of man will come, sent from heaven to judge the world. The sky will open and we will behold the bright day of God's love. Prepare yourselves. Live as if the day had already come. Live in fellowship with all. Set aside your anger and jealousy. Know now that God loves his creation."

There was a priest among them. The crowd made way for him, and when he stood before Joshua they all fell silent.

"By what authority do you presume to teach?" the priest asked. "You appear to be a villager, and your accent betrays that you are a Galilean. Are you a learned student of Torah? What good ever came out of Galilee?"

The crowd laughed, but the priest ignored them.

"By what authority do you presume to teach?" he repeated.

"I will answer you if you will answer me," Joshua replied. He found it possible to pity the man. "By what authority did the Baptist teach? By God's or his own?"

One could almost see the priest's confidence draining away. They were in Jerusalem, in the Temple itself, and yet John had been much loved and respected by the people, who now revered him as a martyr. What could this priest say? What was his own authority compared to John's?

"I—I don't know."

"Then you cannot hope to understand my answer, so I will make none. But I will tell you this. Whether of our own will or not, we are all merely the servants of God."

Without a word, the priest turned and walked away. And Joshua raised his eyes to heaven and remembered Noah and his fears.

Am I not safe in my Father's house? he thought.

The priest, Meshach, walked back into the Temple precincts, which were closed to the common people. Caleb was waiting for him, leaning against a pillar.

"What was your impression, my lord?" Caleb asked, with just that degree of deference a Levite owes to one of priestly office.

Meshach smiled mirthlessly, as if to imply that the question was naïve.

"Except for that display at the city gate a few days ago, I would describe him as merely a nuisance," he answered, with a slight shrug. "The crowds are amused by such as him."

"Yet he allowed himself to be hailed as the Son of David."

"The mob hailed him as such. Yet he is here, preaching as usual."

"Preaching the end of Roman rule, my lord."

"Possibly." The priest glanced about him, seeming bored. "A return to Eden might be thought to presuppose an end to Roman rule. Personally, I think it sounds delightful."

Meshach had only to look at Caleb to realize the irony was lost on him, so he raised his hands in a gesture of surrender.

"It is not a violation of the Law to preach that God will redeem the world. It is not even a violation to claim to be the seed of David."

"Yet the Romans would think so, my lord."

"Then let the Romans deal with him. As you see, he is popular. I don't want the Temple authorities involved."

"Yet he is dangerous."

"Possibly. I would have said so a few days ago."

"And now?"

"Possibly." Meshach looked down at the stone floor beneath his feet. He seemed to be preparing to make a decision he found distasteful. "I am like you, my Lord Caleb. I don't want to see a riot. I am responsible for order in the Temple and therefore, indirectly, for the safety of the people who come here. I don't want the Romans coming in, because then there will be blood."

"Then, my lord, you would be prepared to recommend that the case be referred to the Romans?"

"Possibly." The priest looked up. He decided he didn't like Caleb very much. The man would himself have done very well as a Roman. "Yes, I suppose so."

44

Joshua prayed and God was silent. There was no quiet in his heart. Thus does a man know that he is abandoned to death.

For four days he preached in the Temple. Many gathered to hear him. Some mocked, some listened for a while and then wandered away, but some came back the next day, and the next. A few believed.

The priests left him alone.

Yet even in the Temple, God seemed deaf to him. He could not feel His presence. The house of the Lord seemed deserted by its master.

In the mornings Joshua wandered through Gethsemane, seeking in its wilderness solitude some way to make God listen, and in the afternoons he preached. In the evenings, in the upper room near the fuller's tower, he taught his disciples. They had to be prepared to continue his work, as he had continued John's, for he was coming to believe he would not be with them long.

"He means to have you killed," Noah had said of Caleb. Noah understood the world.

What would motivate such a man? Had Caleb grown so estranged from God that he had forgotten the commandments? Thou shalt not bear false witness. Thou shalt do no murder. Could a man be so blind? It seemed incomprehensible.

The fear of death was never absent from Joshua's prayers. "Father, if I may be spared this, if I may continue to do Your work . . . But if not, give me the strength to accept Your will."

But God's voice was stilled. In his heart Joshua heard only silence.

He could not help but think about going home. In a week he could be back in Nazareth, in his father's workshop, with the smell of freshly cut wood in his nostrils. If he simply admitted to himself that he was a carpenter and not a prophet, his family would welcome his return and he could resume the life he had known before the Baptist. He could survive into old age.

He tried to picture all that to himself, but it seemed like someone else's life, not his.

People believed in him. He had brought Matthias back to life simply by convincing him that God had offered forgiveness. Had he been wrong about that?

In memory, he kept returning to John and those days beside the Jordan when he himself had been a disciple. John had realized that he would soon face death. Either Antipas or the Romans would arrest him, and he would be executed.

"To die is nothing," he had said. "We suffer for a little time and then sleep. And then at the coming of the Lord we awaken and we live forever. What is there to fear in this?"

John had had no doubts. He knew that the end time was near, that the power of the mighty was a shadow. One had merely to trust in God.

"So I will trust in God," Joshua told him. "I will school myself to trust. It must be as God wills."

So, on the seventh night after his arrival in Jerusalem, while he gathered with his closest disciples, he spoke for the first time of the possibility that he might not live to see the coming of God's kingdom.

It was time for dinner. After prayers, when they were all seated, he took a loaf of bread and broke it.

"Thus you see," he told them. "Bread must be broken before it can be eaten. We even speak of eating as 'breaking bread.' That is what bread is for, to be broken and eaten.

"Men, too, sometimes are broken. When God wills it, men kill other men. Men die, and this too can serve a purpose—a purpose which God does not reveal to us. It is well to remember that all things happen through the will of God."

Joshua looked around him, and it was clear to him that they did not understand.

"Yet there is one difference between men and bread," he went on. "Bread, when it is broken and consumed, is no more. But the dead will rise again in God's kingdom. For those who believe, death is no more than a little sleep. If I am taken from you, you will have but a short time to wait until you see me again. For such is the mercy of God."

They ate in silence. They seemed depressed and confused. It did not matter, Joshua decided. In a little while he would take them with him to Gethsemane and teach them to pray for understanding.

Noah's cousin Baruch was the grandson of the man to whom his own grandfather had been apprenticed, who in turn had been a cousin of Benjamin's mother. Thus the tie was one more of affection than of blood. Baruch was nearly seventy, and he and his wife had had no children who survived beyond infancy. Noah was a great favorite, almost a son.

And now they could welcome Noah's new wife, whom it was impossible not to love.

"But what of your cousin Joshua?" Baruch had asked, as if to reassure himself of some future pleasure. "Will he be joining us again?"

"Yes, and I fear he will bring a mob of his followers." Noah threw up his hands, as if the thing were no more in his power to stop than the wheeling of the sun.

"The more the better," Baruch answered, puffing out his chest. "For the Passover, I like a house full of friends."

At dinner that night, Noah was like an actor playing a role. He laughed and told jokes, but a part of him was somewhere else. He had to force himself to attend to the conversation.

He was full of dread.

Joshua, he was quite sure, would never again sit in this room and break the unleavened bread of the Passover. He felt as if he were attending a funeral banquet.

After the meal, he and Baruch stayed a long time over the wine.

"What is troubling you?" Baruch asked him at last. "There isn't . . . some problem with you and your wife?"

"Oh no!" Noah actually laughed, it seemed so ludicrous. "A man would have to be far more fastidious than I not to be happy with Deborah."

"That was my impression. Then, is it business? Do you need money?"

"No. I am prospering."

"Then, what?"

It seemed impossible to explain. Noah gestured, as if waving away a fly, and said, "It is nothing. I think I am merely still tired from the journey."

They were all about to go to bed, when a servant entered the room.

"There is a man here," he said. "He says he must see the Lord Noah."

"Did he give his name?"

"Yes. He said his name was Simon."

Noah felt as if his bowels had turned to ice.

"I will see him," he said.

He followed the servant down to the entrance of the house, where he found Simon. He had only to look at the man to know that something was terribly wrong.

"What is it?"

For a moment Simon seemed unable to bring himself to speak, and then he opened his arms in despair.

"Joshua has been arrested."

45

From his first entrance into the city, Joshua had been watched. In the crowds at the Temple there was always someone who listened attentively and reported to Caleb everything Joshua said. When Joshua left, he was followed. When he was in the upper room near the fuller's tower, someone watched the door. His every move was observed.

Caleb knew it was necessary to acquire an understanding of Joshua's habits, but time was running short. The Passover would be celebrated in only two days, and this business had to be over by then or it might be too late. After the Passover, Joshua could easily melt into the crowds and disappear.

The crowds were what Caleb feared most. Joshua's teachings were making an impact. People listened to him. He was popular. If he were arrested in public, there might be a riot. The whole matter had to be handled with discretion, so that he was up on his cross and safely dead before anyone missed him.

The best time, Caleb decided, was after the last sundown before the Passover. People's attention would be directed toward the feast. On that night, men did not go into their wives, so as to maintain ritual purity when they went to the Temple for the sacrifice of the lambs. The wineshops were closed. People stayed home and prayed.

There would be no one about to take an interest in what happened to Joshua of Nazareth.

And the best place was the wilderness of Gethsemane. In the evenings, after dinner, Joshua went there to pray, and he was usually alone, although sometimes two or three of his disciples would accompany him. Gethsemane was outside the city walls. A dozen men could close off all avenues of escape. The arrest could take place with a minimum of disturbance.

Caleb knew Gethsemane well, having played there as a child.

He had decided on a mixed force of Temple guards and Roman soldiers. The Romans would be there mainly to be seen. The Temple guards knew the area, but the presence of the Romans would be what everyone remembered.

Gideon was just as content. He had observed Joshua in the Temple, and the man's popularity worried him. "Let the Romans take the blame," was the way he had put it.

Gaius Raetius was happy to oblige. For a little silver, some of which he parceled out to his men, he was quite willing to risk the mob's hatred.

"We will get him to the fortress, and then he's your worry," he had said. "Just be sure you have him in front of Pilatus at first light. The prefect likes to deal with this sort of business before breakfast."

They reached Gethsemane and took up their positions before it became dark. A trail no wider than a goat path threaded its way through the trees, which were dense and would impede flight. They had merely to close off both ends to trap anyone within. The first group went a few dozen paces up the Mount of Olives to wait. Concealment was easy, provided they kept silent.

Shortly after dark, Caleb saw a glimmer of light coming from the northern end of the trail. Gradually the light began to fragment into separate little points, the flames of oil lamps carried by perhaps as many as twelve or fifteen people, the flames dancing with every step they took. He heard the sounds of voices and laughter.

Finally the group stopped, and then Caleb heard only one voice. He could not make out the words, but it was clear from the cadence of sound that someone was explaining something. He did not have to ask himself who that someone was.

"Give them a few minutes," he murmured to Raetius, who was crouched beside him. Caleb did not understand precisely what, but there was something about the voice that made him reluctant to silence it.

Raetius did not look pleased. After a moment he shook his head.

"We need to close them off before they even know what is happening," he said in a hoarse, insistent whisper. "Every moment we wait increases the chances of discovery. Do you want him to get away?"

"No. Of course not. You are right. Go."

Raetius drew his sword and slapped it against his body armor. That was the signal. Within a quarter of a minute the soldiers were at either end of the trail and closing toward the center.

Joshua and his followers were taken completely by surprise. No one even tried to escape. They simply stood there, holding their flickering oil lamps as if afraid they would drop them.

Raetius made a sign with his hand, and four of his men lit torches. Suddenly their little patch of bare ground was awash in lurid yellow light.

Caleb looked over his catch. He saw Judah, who avoided his eyes, and then suddenly realized that the disciple standing beside Judah was his own man, Matthias.

"Bind those two," Caleb ordered. "Be careful of the big one."

There was a pause, just long enough to make him glance back at Raetius, who then nodded to one of his men. When Matthias was secure, Caleb walked up to him and smiled.

"I wondered what had happened to you," he said quietly, almost confidentially. "I was worried they might have succeeded somehow in killing you. Before we're finished, you'll wish they had."

He looked up into Matthias's face and his nerve almost failed him. He was confronted not with fear or hatred but with an almost pitying serenity.

He quickly turned away and directed his gaze at Joshua, who was calmly snuffing out his oil lamp. When he was finished, he rubbed his fingers together to wipe away the soot and then handed the lamp to the disciple standing beside him.

"So you are he, Joshua of Nazareth," Caleb announced, perhaps with more force than he had intended. "King of the Jews."

He allowed himself to laugh.

"You have said so, not I."

"But you have prophesied that God will sweep away the rulers of the earth. And who better to take their place than you?"

"God. There will be no king but God."

Caleb did not immediately respond. For a moment he merely stood there, one hand at his waist, as if admiring Joshua like a work of art.

"It is an interesting idea," he replied at last, "but it involves a distinction I doubt the Romans will understand."

Joshua said nothing. He seemed to have lost interest in the conversation.

"Bind this one as well," Caleb almost shouted.

"What about the others?" Raetius asked, as one of his men roped Joshua's hands together behind his back.

"I care nothing about the others. Let them go."

A big, square-looking man, who seemed to be a leader of the other disciples, looked at Joshua appealingly. Joshua nodded and said only the single word "Go."

They all quickly vanished into the darkness.

"We can't wait around here," Raetius said. "Let's take him to the fortress. We can hold them there until everyone is asleep."

"An excellent idea."

During the march back, the prisoners were kept surrounded by their escort of soldiers. It was unlikely that anyone in the streets even noticed them.

When they were inside the fortress walls, Joshua and Matthias were taken to a long, narrow, windowless room on the first floor. It contained no furniture and had iron rings fastened to the walls.

At the doorway, Caleb took Judah by the arm and held him back. He then drew a knife and cut Judah's bonds, after which he courteously offered him a cup of water.

Judah hardly seemed to hear him. He merely sank to the floor.

"You must forgive the little pantomime," Caleb said, crouching beside him. "After tomorrow, if you play your part, you can go back to Tiberias, pick up your old life, and forget any of this ever happened. You can tell people you suddenly decided on a trip to Athens."

"What is my part tomorrow?"

"Nothing much. You will simply tell the prefect that you heard Joshua bar Joseph claim to be the rightful king of the Jews."

"I can't do that. It isn't true. He is a good man, beloved of God. I can't."

Caleb shook his head.

"You can't? Of course you can. The Roman will crucify him anyway, and if you don't do as I tell you, you'll be right up there next to him. You've seen what it's like. Do you really want to die that way?"

"No."

"I didn't think so."

Caleb patted him on the shoulder and stood up. He then went over the where Raetius was drinking a cup of wine.

"Keep the big one here for now," he said. "Be careful with him. He'll go back with me to Galilee."

"For special treatment?"

"That's right."

Raetius grinned.

"Don't underestimate him," Caleb warned. "He's done worse things than you ever will, and he's clever."

"You don't need to worry. We know how to handle his type."

They waited two hours, during which they were joined by the priest Meshach, who did not seem pleased to be there.

"I thank you, my lord," Caleb said to him. "It is a—"

"Never fear, my Lord Caleb," the priest answered from behind his masklike face. "I shall do what is required."

He then walked away and stood by himself, gazing at the bare stone walls in a way that suggested he wished to be alone with his thoughts.

When Joshua was brought back out, his hands were no longer bound.

"I would feel better if we used the Romans for this," Gideon murmured to Caleb, glancing about nervously.

Caleb allowed himself to laugh.

"Oh, certainly. And how would the Lord Anas feel if, after we wake him up, he found a crowd of legionnaires standing around in front of his door? You want the credit for the arrest, don't you?"

Gideon looked as if he were no longer sure.

"Come along. It has to be done."

Gideon formed up his squad of Temple guards around the prisoner, and the gates of the Antonia Fortress were opened. For most of the way they kept close to the Temple's outer wall. It was only a short walk to that section of the city where dwelled the upper orders of the priesthood, and the streets were deserted.

Meshach knocked at one of the grander houses. He had to knock several times before an elderly servant answered.

The old man opened the door, saw the uniforms of the guards, and said nothing.

"We must see the Lord Anas," Meshach told him. "It is important."

"The high priest is asleep," came the answer.

"Then you must wake him."

The servant shut the door, and they stood waiting for almost a quarter of an hour. The priest was about to knock again, when the door reopened.

"Be pleased to come in."

Meshach, Caleb, Gideon, and Joshua went inside. The rest waited without.

The Lord Anas stood in the center of his reception hall, still in his night tunic, with a long shawl thrown over his shoulders. He was over seventy, heavy, and his hair and beard were startlingly white. He had once been the high priest, a title by which his servants still called him, and he was the father-in-law of the current high priest. He did not look at all pleased to have been disturbed.

"What is it, Meshach?" he asked crossly. "What couldn't wait until the morning?"

"We have arrested a village preacher, my lord. I thought it best to deal with the problem in a way that will attract the least attention."

"Ah." The former high priest nodded and turned his eyes to Joshua. "You were right, then. In daylight you might have precipitated a riot."

"Precisely, my lord. He is preaching that God will exalt the poor and bring low the mighty, and he has been hailed by the mob as a son of David."

Anas began absentmindedly stroking his beard, which reached down to his breastbone.

"Has he?"

"Yes, my lord. The Romans are aware of him and, needless to say, they are concerned."

"And what have you to say about all this?" Anas asked, directing his question to Joshua.

Joshua let his gaze rest on the old priest, as if noticing him for the first time.

"I teach that men should turn their hearts to repentance," he said at last. "I teach that God will redeem His creation, that we should love God and love and forgive all His children. My message is the same as that of my master, John."

"He means the Baptist, my lord," Meshach interjected.

"I know who he means," Anas replied, not without asperity. He put his hand on Meshach's arm and pulled him a little aside.

"Why have you brought him here?" Anas whispered. "We are priests. We can only judge this man in accordance with Mosaic law, and in that light he is guilty of nothing. It is not against the Law to claim Davidic descent."

"You did not see how the mob reacted when he entered the city, my lord. We are responsible for the safety of our people. This man preaches rebellion—at least, so it is interpreted."

"Nevertheless, *we* cannot take responsibility. I agree with you that we can't risk the Romans coming in to quell a disturbance, but if, as you say, they are concerned about his activities, let *them* deal with him." The old priest patted Meshach's arm, as if to console him.

"If they have any wisdom," Anas continued, "they will hold him until after the festival, then give him a good thrashing and send him home. That would be Galilee, by his accent, and what good ever came out of Galilee?" He laughed, not ill naturedly.

"Then I have your authorization to refer this case to the prefect, my lord?"

"Yes. Yes, of course."

All at once the former high priest stiffened, as if his heart had turned to ice.

"Pilatus is an evil brute," he said, "but I suppose we have no choice."

"None, my lord."

They turned back to the others, and Anas looked into Joshua's face with something like pity.

"Well, my lords," he said, seeming to address the room itself rather than its occupants, "you have my opinion. Now good night, and let an old man go back to bed."

When they were back out on the street, Caleb fell in beside Joshua, taking his arm in the most friendly fashion.

"Do you see how swiftly they dismiss you to the Romans?" he said. "The last time there was a riot during the Passover, some five thousand people were killed. The soldiers entered the city, and by the time they left, the cobblestones were thick with blood. Compared to that, what is the life of a peasant preacher, particularly one from Galilee?"

"So it is settled? I am to be put to death by the Romans?"

Joshua raised his eyes to the night sky, as if he could see through it to the face of God.

"Of course. You preach sedition and you claim to be king of the Jews. We have witnesses."

"Witnesses? More than one? I thought it would be only poor Judah, whom you kidnapped and terrified into submission."

Caleb shook his head and laughed. "Yes, of course, you would know about that. From Matthias. Well, he will pay for his treachery."

"Is it treachery that he found himself unable to kill an innocent man? Yes, I suppose to one such as you it must seem so. You murdered the Baptist and now you will murder me."

"It was not murder. The Baptist died by the Tetrarch's warrant. And you will die because the Romans will judge you guilty of rebellion."

"On the basis of perjured testimony."

"The testimony concerning your entry into the city will not be perjured."

"No, but you invented that episode, didn't you." Joshua turned to look into Caleb's face and smiled. "The guard commander, he is your intimate friend, is he not? Or, perhaps, your kinsman? One can see these things. And a certain high-ranking officer of the Temple guard hired the colt I was unwise enough to ride through the city gate. Doubtless you witnessed the whole scene yourself, or had witnesses present."

"You are very clever, Joshua bar Joseph. I admit I have underestimated you."

"It is not I who am clever, my lord."

It took Caleb a moment to understand what he meant.

"Then your cousin is clever. But I have long known that."

They walked on in silence for a time. The only sound was the *clap, clap, clap* of so many sandals against the stone street.

"I hope someday you will look back on all this," Joshua said at last, almost as if to himself. "I hope that you will see it for what it is, and that you will repent and open your heart to God."

"Like Matthias?"

"Yes, like Matthias. God has forgiven him, and would forgive you, if you would but allow it. Your heart is full of darkness. I pity you."

"*You* pity *me?*"

"Yes. I will suffer and die, and sleep for a time, and then arise to everlasting life. You are already dead. But God will forgive you. You have only to ask. I hope someday you will remember what I have said."

46

"When?"

Simon's face went blank—perhaps less because he didn't understand the question than because he couldn't imagine how it could matter.

Noah decided to restate the question.

"When was he arrested?"

"About three hours ago." Simon looked down at his feet, as if suddenly ashamed. "We all ran away. Then I had trouble finding this house."

"Who arrested him?"

"Soldiers."

"What sort of soldiers? Romans or Temple guards?"

"I don't know. Just soldiers."

Yes, of course. Why should the distinction even occur to him? The Romans did not occupy Galilee.

"You have seen the soldiers who stand guard on the Temple roof? Were they wearing helmets like those?"

"Yes, some of them. But not all."

"And they let the rest of you go?"

"Yes. Except for Matthias and Judah. They arrested them too."

All at once Simon looked very tired, as if he would slump to the floor.

"Come upstairs," Noah told him. "You can spend the night here. It's probably not safe for you to return to your own quarters. Have you had anything to eat?"

"I couldn't."

"Well then, a cup of wine to settle your nerves. Perhaps two cups."

When he had seen to Simon, Noah told Deborah what had happened.

"What will you do?" she asked. "What *can* you do?"

"Try to find Joshua. Then perhaps I can buy him out of this." He smiled wanly. "I don't have much hope, but at least I can try. I'll talk to Baruch and see how much coin he has in the house."

Deborah put her arms around him, pressing her cheek against his chest.

"Come back to me," she said, her voice hardly above a whisper. "Just come back to me."

Five minutes later, Noah was out on the street, heading for the Antonia Fortress. If the Romans had Joshua, they would be holding him there.

Baruch lived in a prosperous quarter, so all the houses were dark, with their doors barred. Respectable people were asleep—particularly tonight, the last night before the Passover. Tomorrow would be full of preparations, and then, at sundown, the feast itself would begin.

It occurred to Noah, simply as a random thought, how disappointed Joshua would be if he missed the Passover. Of course, he would probably be dead by then. Caleb certainly planned to have him die a rebel's death.

Because it never entered Noah's mind that the Romans had acted on their own. Caleb had arranged all this. Its purpose was difficult to imagine, but the plot was clear.

Noah had been walking perhaps a quarter of an hour when suddenly he turned a corner and saw the fortress in front of him. The sight of it made him stop. It was a grim, forbidding structure, tall and narrow, its few windows high up and unreachable. The long south wall was flush with and overtopped the outer wall of the Temple compound.

The gate was heavily fortified, and perhaps for that reason it was felt unnecessary to mount much of a guard. There were only two soldiers outside, and at the slightest hint of trouble they could retreat into an impregnable outbuilding, which was probably connected somehow to the fortress itself. The soldiers were crouched around a small iron brazier, for it was an unseasonably cold night.

As soon as they saw Noah, they stood up.

"What do you want?" one asked, almost shouting.

"Only information." Noah opened his hand, on the palm of which rested two silver coins. "Do you have a prisoner inside named Joshua bar Joseph? He was arrested tonight."

The soldier took the coins and gave one to his comrade.

"We have many prisoners," he said. "We don't know their names."

"Would it be possible to speak to someone who might know?"

"Not tonight. The garrison is locked down. During the festivals they don't take any chances."

"Perhaps in the morning?"

"You could talk to the duty officer."

"I see. Then I am sorry to have disturbed you both."

And to have wasted my money, Noah thought as he walked away, along the long outer wall of the Temple.

What to do now? Joshua might or might not be inside, but it was impossible to find out until the morning, by which time he might be already judged and condemned. The Romans were known for their efficiency in dispensing death sentences.

What to do now?

It was a question Noah had been pondering ever since he left Baruch's house. For all that it was necessary to try, he had no real expectation of seeing Joshua or anyone else in the Antonia Fortress. Occupying armies are rarely given to such displays of hospitality.

So the problem had been, from the beginning, to find some way to breach the wall of silence. They would not listen to him, so much was certain. Noah was neither powerful nor rich. To the men who ruled in this little pocket of the vast Roman Empire, he did not exist.

With one possible exception.

The Lord Eleazar owed him, and now seemed a good time to try to collect.

That the First Minister was in Jerusalem for the Passover it had never occurred to him to doubt. He was a priest and a pious man, so where else would he be? The point was to find him.

It was after midnight when Noah reached the starting point of his search, the Tetrarch's Jerusalem palace.

The guards, as guards do, at first tried to drive him away. But a modest bribe quickly had them calling Noah "Your Honor" and "My Lord" and very willing to be of help. No, the Lord Eleazar did not have rooms in the palace, but he did own a house close by, to which—for a small additional gratuity, since it involved a neglect of duty—one of their number would be happy to conduct him.

There were no guards in front of the Lord Eleazar's door, so Noah had to pound on it in hopes of waking the porter. He was quite insistent, and after several minutes he was rewarded by hearing a click as a peephole opened, though which emerged the faint, sluggish light of an oil lamp.

"What do you want?" a voice asked. "It's late. Everyone is asleep." The voice was male and had taken on the gravelly quality of middle age.

"I wish to speak to your master."

"I told you, he is asleep."

"Then I will stand out here, beating on your door, until you wake him."

"I will wake up a few of the servants instead, and they will beat you senseless."

"I have a better idea. Look down at your feet."

There was a space beneath the door, less than the width of one's little finger, but it was enough to allow Noah to slide some silver coins through to the other side. He could hear them scraping against the stone as someone knelt to pick them up.

"Who shall I say you are? My lord will not be pleased to be awakened. He probably will refuse to see you."

"Tell him it is Noah the ironsmith. He will not refuse."

"Wait here."

The peephole closed and Noah was once more in darkness.

A short time later the door opened.

"Follow me."

The porter, made no less resentful by more money than he could have earned in a year, led Noah up a flight of stairs and through a series of hallways until they reached a small room containing only a desk, two chairs, a lamp stand, a shelf full of scrolls, and the Lord Eleazar, tall and thin as a pillar in a robe of blue silk that shimmered in the dancing light.

The Tetrarch's First Minister did not quite manage a smile.

"It is always a pleasure to see you, Noah," he said. "Although the hour suggests that this is not a social call."

"No, my lord. My cousin Joshua has been arrested."

The Lord Eleazar was not a man whose face betrayed much, but in that first moment Noah had the impression he was trying to decide not what such news might mean but how to receive it. Did he already know, or had he simply been expecting it?

Finally he raised his eyebrows slightly. No, he was not surprised.

"And this happened . . . when?"

"This evening, just after dark."

Eleazar sat down in one of the two chairs and gestured for Noah to take the other. Then he turned to his servant.

"Jabez, bring us some water," he said, and then directed his attention back to Noah. "Or would you prefer some wine?"

"No. Thank you. My lord."

"Tell me everything you know."

Noah described Joshua's entrance into the city and what he had discovered about the colt. Then he related what he had been told by Simon about the arrest.

To all this Eleazar listened without discernible reaction.

"Caleb has a cousin who is a captain in the Temple guard," Eleazar said finally. "It was probably he to whom the stable owner was referring. He is a scoundrel, but that seems to run in the family."

He smiled, as if he had made a jest.

"Judah is also Caleb's cousin," he said. "Did you know that?"

"No, my lord."

"Have you any idea what his role in this might be?"

"Both Judah and Matthias were arrested with Joshua. Everyone else was let go. Matthias's arrest demands no explanation. Judah, I suspect, will be required to give evidence."

"You are a perceptive man, Noah. No doubt you are correct."

For a moment the Lord Eleazar sat very still, staring at the blank wall above Noah's head. Then he lowered his gaze and smiled coldly.

"But I suspect you did not wake me up simply to report these interesting events. What is it you would have of me?"

"I don't know." Noah shrugged. His face perfectly conveyed his sense of helplessness. "I am only an ironsmith from Galilee. I can think of nothing I might do that stands any chance of saving my cousin's life. But you are a powerful man, and Caleb is your servant. If you were to intervene . . ."

"I am a powerful man, as you say, but only in Galilee. This is Judea, where I am no more than another Jew under the heel of our Roman masters. As for Caleb, he has slipped beyond my control."

"Perhaps you could speak to the Tetrarch."

"The Tetrarch?" The First Minister allowed himself a spasm of bitter laughter. "The Tetrarch has a great fear of insurrection. Forget about the Tetrarch. You will receive no aid from him."

"Then you could go to the Roman prefect."

Noah was aware of a strain of hysteria in his voice. He could hear it, and he could see it in the way the Lord Eleazar looked at him in reproving silence. He struggled to calm himself, but he succeeded only imperfectly.

"Pilatus is worse than Antipas."

"You could explain to him that Caleb has concocted this whole plot."

"Pilatus will not believe me."

"You can try!"

"Pilatus will not listen to me. There is nothing I can do to save your cousin."

Suddenly Noah could endure no more. He rose out of his chair and stamped his foot against the floor in pure vexation. The anger boiled in him so that he no longer cared what he said.

"Remember, my lord, that Caleb is your creation," he shouted. "You turned this monster loose on the world. I might also recall to you that you are a priest, a servant of God, and that God hates injustice. How can you tell me there is nothing you can do?"

Eleazar also stood up, as if he had been jerked from his seat. His face was white.

"You forget yourself, Noah! You are impertinent! You are . . ."

Word failed him, he was so choked with wrath. His fists were clenched and shaking, until he looked down at them and, by an act of will, forced his hands to open.

At the sight of them, wrath seemed to yield to astonishment. And then, abruptly, he sat down again.

"You are also right," he went on, almost in sorrow. "I bear a responsibility here."

For a moment the First Minister seemed to retreat inside himself. Noah stared at him in something like disbelief. Finally, not knowing what else to do, he himself sat down again.

"I have had no dealings with the prefect," the First Minister began, his eyes fixed on Noah's face. "His administration is unconnected with Galilee and, if we must deal with the Romans, it is through the provincial governor in Damascus. I know Pilatus only by reputation, and what I have heard is not encouraging."

"Will you speak to him about Joshua?"

"Yes. But don't expect very much."

Eleazar dropped his gaze. The sight of Noah seemed to distress him.

"We had best be there early tomorrow. I will have the servants make up a bed for you here."

47

An hour before dawn, the Lord Eleazar entered Noah's room and found him awake, sitting in a chair, staring into the darkness.

"Did you sleep at all last night?" he asked.

"No."

"Neither did I."

Eleazar was carrying a tray that held bread and wine. He was a considerate master and had himself fetched these from the kitchen, letting his servants sleep. He set the tray down on a table.

"Eat. Even if you have no appetite. Today will be a hard day."

So the ironsmith and the Tetrarch's great minister sat sharing out bread and wine, as if such had been the habit of a lifetime.

"I want you to understand one thing," Eleazar said finally. "I will need to see the prefect alone. He is a Roman knight, not a senator, and therefore all the more sensitive about his social position. He will take it as an insult if he is asked to receive you."

"I will wait outside."

"You will trust me with this?"

"Yes."

"I have little hope."

"Without your help, I would have none."

———

The prefect's palace was a few steps beyond the great stairway leading from the Temple. It had been built by Old Herod and, like the Antonia Fortress, which he also built, was grim and unwelcoming. Its windows were high up, and the stone walls could have defied an invading army— or an angry mob, which Herod doubtless feared even more.

The sun's rim was just visible over the eastern horizon when they entered the courtyard, where a handful of supplicants were already hoping to be admitted to an audience.

There was a chamberlain, holding his staff of office and standing in front of the main door. His gaze swept disdainfully over the courtyard, seeming to dare anyone to approach him. But the Lord Eleazar was not intimidated by servants.

"I wish a few moments with the prefect," he said, first in Latin and then, when he received no response, in Greek. "I am Eleazar bar Zadok, servant and First Minister to the Lord Herod Antipas, Tetrarch of Galilee and Perea."

"The prefect is engaged. You will have to wait," the chamberlain replied, and then he turned his eyes away, as if dismissing one more petitioner from existence.

"He is hearing criminal cases this morning?" Eleazar asked, refusing to notice the man's impertinence. "I am in possession of evidence regarding one of them."

"He *is* hearing criminal cases this morning. He will see no one until they are dispatched."

"Nevertheless, I wish you to inform him of my presence."

There was a gold coin pinched between Eleazar's first finger and thumb. The chamberlain glanced down at it and then opened his hand slightly to receive it.

"I will inquire," he said.

A few minutes later he returned.

"The prefect will see you," he reported, as if it were a personal triumph, "but not until he has done justice for the morning."

Eleazar returned to where Noah was waiting for him.

"He will see me," he told him, "but after he has judged the case."

"That is better than not at all."

"Perhaps a little."

Raetius understood how Roman justice worked. It might be different in Rome, but in the provinces there were only three parties to a trial: the judge, the accuser, and the accused. He personally had witnessed Joshua's triumphal entry into the city, and the rogue's follower, this fellow Judah, would testify the right way. Caleb, who was hard enough to be a Roman himself, had given instructions: "If he doesn't confirm that Joshua bar Joseph claimed to be of the seed of David and therefore the rightful king of the Jews, denounce him. Let him be crucified next to his master." He had said it with his hand on Judah's shoulder, just so there wouldn't be any misunderstanding.

Fortunately there was a short list that morning—only Joshua and a couple of bandits. And the prefect wasn't going to waste much time on bandits. The officer in charge had but to recount the circumstances of their arrest. "Crucify them." That was the sentence, and they were taken out.

"Now, what's this?" Pilatus asked, looking at Joshua the way a butcher looks at a lamb.

"A preacher, my lord," Raetius answered. "Made a disturbance coming into the city. He claims he's king of this lot. The mob believed him, and there was almost a riot."

"Well, what about it?" Pilatus took a step toward Joshua and looked him square in the face. "Are you king of the Jews."

"No. Nor have I ever claimed to be. God is my king."

"He's lying, my lord. Trying to save his skin. Here's one of his followers, ready to tell the truth." Raetius pushed Judah forward. You could almost feel sorry for Judah, he was so scared. "Tell his lordship, now. This one says he's a king, right?"

There was a pause, a breathing space maybe, and then, very quietly, Judah said, "Yes."

"I'm not sure his lordship heard you. Say it again."

"Yes. Yes. He said he was of the seed of David."

And then Joshua said something to him, in their tongue, and the poor fellow looked as if he might burst into tears.

"Is that the end of it?" Pilatus asked.

"Yes, my lord."

"Then he's guilty. Crucify him." He turned to his secretary. "Is there any more business?"

"Yes, my lord. Someone wishes an audience. He's Herod's man. Probably best to see him."

"One supposes so. Bring him to my study."

The prefect turned back to Raetius. "You know what to do, centurion," he said. "Do it."

That was Roman justice. It worked well enough.

A servant came out through the palace door and whispered something to the chamberlain, who then caught the Lord Eleazar's eye and, raising his hand, made a curt gesture summoning him forward.

"The prefect will see you now," he said, in a tone that suggested he felt himself imposed upon.

Eleazar glanced back at Noah, as if to say, *"I will do my best,"* and then followed the servant inside.

The prefect was seated in a room probably reserved for such meetings. He did not rise to greet his guest but merely gestured at another chair, which, Eleazar gathered, was all the invitation he was likely to receive, so he sat down in it.

"I have agreed to see you out of respect for your master," Pontius Pilatus announced. "I have heard of you, of course, but I gather your visit here today is unrelated to the Tetrarch's business."

Pilatus smiled thinly. He was a man of about forty, tall and languid. As a knight, he had probably reached the pinnacle of his official career, and the cast of his face suggested that he knew it. Judea was not a posting much coveted by ambitious men, and Pilatus therefore resented his subjects and made no attempt to disguise the fact. He was regarded by them as cruel and insensitive.

"You are correct in assuming I am here as a private person," Eleazar began, returning the smile. "My visit concerns one Joshua bar Joseph, who was arrested last night."

At first Pilatus seemed mildly puzzled and then, apparently, remembered where he had heard the name before.

"He appeared before me just now." The prefect smiled again, as if the recollection pleased him. "He claims, it seems, to be your king. I condemned him."

"Did he admit the charge?" Eleazar asked, giving the impression that the question was of purely theoretical interest.

"No. He denied it. They always deny everything. But there was proof, and a witness."

"I have reason to believe that he was telling the truth, that the evidence against him was fabricated, and that your lordship has been imposed upon."

There was a slight shift in the prefect's attitude. Suddenly he seemed on the verge of becoming angry.

"He was hailed as king by the mob," Pilatus replied, his voice unnaturally calm. "It was witnessed by one of my centurions. Are you questioning the testimony of a Roman officer?"

Eleazar shook his head, suggesting that such an enormity would never have occurred to him.

"No, I am not. The event took place. However, it was staged. Joshua bar Joseph is a preacher, a religious figure, without political pretensions of any sort. My master knows of him and regards him as harmless. Yet he has powerful enemies, who have hit upon this means of destroying him."

"One of his own followers gave evidence that he claimed to be king of the Jews."

"The man has perjured himself."

The prefect stared at the wall for a moment, and then he returned his gaze to Eleazar, his eyes narrowing.

"Why do you care?" he asked, giving the question the full weight of his suspicion. "This Joshua is a peasant. We can take it for granted that in his heart he hates us both. Why do you, a man of position and wealth, concern yourself with what happens to him?"

"Because I have been reminded that I am a priest, and that the God I serve hates injustice."

"Injustice."

Pilatus repeated the word as if it were the answer to a riddle. He seemed on the verge of laughing.

"Injustice, you call it," he went on, his amusement drifting over into anger. "It is never unjust to execute a peasant. They are all traitors—or would be if they dared. The only excuse for not killing every one of them is that we need their work. So we kill them selectively, as an example to the others. This morning I have sent three of them to the cross, and I rejoice in it."

"And I am asking you to spare only one. I give you my word that he is innocent of the charges against him. I would be in your debt for this act of clemency."

Without compromising his dignity, Eleazar tried hard to appear as a supplicant. He himself had been the object of hundreds of entreaties, and he tried to sort through his memory for the faces that had moved him most. It was a demeaning exercise, and probably useless, but it was necessary to try.

"I would be grateful," he added, purely for emphasis.

But the prefect appeared unmoved.

"The city is full of people," Pilatus said finally. "Exactly what feast is it this time?"

It was a calculated insult, but Eleazar ignored it.

"The Passover," he said quietly.

"That's right." Pilatus looked pleased—he had made his point. "Passover. The city is swarming with pilgrims. It is always dangerous when the lower classes don't have enough to keep them busy. They become excited over trifles and there is a riot. Then the soldiers have to restore order and more people die than I would condemn in a lifetime. You see, when people like you, the leaders of this country, can't quiet things down, the emperor expects me to do it for you. He doesn't care how I do it. He just wants it done.

"Beyond this, the emperor is the only person on earth whose gratitude concerns me."

He was refusing. That was substance of it. Eleazar had expected as much, but he felt he had to make one final attempt.

"An act of clemency would do much to soothe the people," he said. "Many believe that Joshua is God's prophet."

"Prophet or king makes no difference. I don't care if he's innocent or guilty. The mob misunderstands clemency, taking it for weakness. But a man dying on the cross is a clear message."

The prefect smiled.

"Now, you must excuse me," he said, abruptly standing up and obliging Eleazar to do the same. "I have much to do, and this business has detained me too long."

Noah had been alone in the courtyard for only a few minutes before the door opened again and Judah came out into the morning sunlight. He was alone. He looked as if he expected to be that way for the rest of his life.

He looked directly at Noah without, apparently, seeing him. But Noah did nothing to call attention to himself. He didn't have to. There were no questions for which he needed Judah's answers. Judah was free, which meant that Joshua was condemned.

What was it that Joshua had said? *"I cannot save Judah by abandoning him. I have no choice but to help him work out his salvation."* But Judah had abandoned Joshua. And now, from the look of him, he was in the process of abandoning himself.

In a moment, he was gone.

Shortly thereafter the Lord Eleazar came out through the same door.

"There was nothing I could do," he said, shaking his head. "I offered him my gratitude, which is worth something in this world, and he spurned it. He does not care if your cousin is innocent. He is determined to make an example of him for the mob."

Without realizing what he was doing, Noah covered his face with his hands. It was really going to happen. It was appalling, unthinkable, but it was really true. His cousin Joshua, his friend since childhood, was going to be nailed to a wooden cross and left to die.

His mind felt as if it had been frozen shut, but he forced himself to think. Was there nothing he could do?

"I can be with him," he said, half to himself. "At least, if he must suffer and die, someone, some friend, should be with him."

"Come away." Eleazar put his arm over Noah's shoulders. "Come back to my house with me. We cannot save his life, but perhaps there is yet something we can do to help him."

"I have to find him," Noah said almost defiantly. "I have to find him."

"You will not find him. The Romans are holding him close now, and they will not let anyone near him. Come away."

The walk did him some good. The first shock had been followed by a terrible numbness, which gradually wore off as they made their way through the narrow streets. By the time they reached the Lord Eleazar's door, Noah had recovered enough to grasp his own helplessness.

They went to Eleazar's study and sat down. A servant brought a jar of wine and two stone cups. Eleazar poured out the wine, and at first Noah simply stared at it.

"Drink. You need it. We both do."

Noah picked up the cup and drained it in one swallow. Eleazar instantly refilled it.

"What is happening to him now?" Noah asked, with reasonable detachment. "Do you know? Can you guess?"

"I know. Have you ever seen a crucifixion?"

"No."

"I have."

For a moment the Lord Eleazar's eyes closed, as if he wished to blot out some ghastly recollection. Then he poured himself a cup of wine. He did not speak again until he had drunk it.

"You are not old enough to have lived through it, but when Great Herod died I was seven years old. There was a rebellion in Galilee. The Romans came in force. They burned Sepphoris and there was a great slaughter. Many of the survivors were sold into slavery. My father was warden of the city—Herod's man—and so we were allowed to leave. We went to Jerusalem, and we returned when the rebellion was over. My father was reappointed to his post by Antipas, Old Herod's son, and he helped rebuild the city.

"I remember the journey home. I will never forget it. The Romans crucified all the captured rebels. They started at the eastern gate of Sepphoris, and the crosses extended for miles along both sides of the road to Jerusalem. My father and mother and I rode in our cart along that road, under the shadows of crucified men.

"It takes a long time for someone to die like that. Sometimes three or four days, sometimes a week. The first ones I saw called down to us, begging for water. Later they were mute—alive, it seemed, only to their own suffering. Finally, within sight of the city, they were all dead."

"Why are you telling me this?" Noah asked, his voice thick with grief.

"To prepare you for what you will see if you are fool enough to search out your cousin's place of execution. It will be terrible beyond my poor powers to describe it."

The Lord Eleazar drew a deep breath and let it out slowly. The subject, clearly, was painful to him.

"Right now your cousin is probably being scourged. They use leather whips with pieces of bone and sharp metal woven into the lashes. They will not stop until he is covered with wounds, until he is half dead. When you see him next he will look like nothing human."

"You said there was something we could still do to help him."

"Yes. One thing."

45

Gaius Raetius did not like Jerusalem. He liked Caesarea, which was on the sea and where the food was better. There wasn't much going on in Caesarea, which was another advantage.

But in Jerusalem there was always trouble. The legions came up here four times a year, for the festivals, and the crowds were always getting excited about something. Soldiers had to stay in their barracks to avoid "incidents," because the Jews hated them.

And then there were the executions.

In Caesarea there weren't more than five or six crucifixions in a month, but in Jerusalem there were sometimes that many in a day. Crucifixions were boring duty. If you flogged a man to death or cut off his head, the thing was done in a few minutes, or maybe half an hour, but crucifixions took a long time, and you had to post a guard while the bastards died and then after they were dead, to keep relatives from stealing the bodies.

The only thing good about crucifixions in Jerusalem was the site. In Caesarea, criminals would be left on the cross until they rotted off, and then the dogs got them. But in Jerusalem there were just too many, so you had to take them down and dispose of them. And Golgotha, which someone had told him meant Place of Skulls, had been a stone quarry, so there were lots of deep holes in the rock. You dropped the corpse into one of the holes, dumped in a little quicklime, and that took care of it.

Still, it was boring duty. You stayed busy until the day's batch was nailed up but, after that, there was nothing to do except sit around and play dice.

At least this time Raetius was getting paid. Gideon, who wasn't a bad fellow, said his cousin wanted to be sure the execution was properly carried out, and the fifty silver pieces they had agreed on would be paid as soon as this Joshua was dead.

Raetius didn't care anything about reasons. One Jew wanted another killed, and who cared why. But if he had to take sides he would have preferred it the other way around, because he didn't much like Gideon's cousin. Joshua, though, would have made a good soldier.

Put a man under sentence of death and you find out fast enough what he's got inside him. Joshua didn't beg or cry or piss himself. He kept his dignity, which was a thing one had to respect. Of course, he would scream like all the others when the nails bit into him, but that didn't count.

He took the scourging pretty well.

In Caesarea the scourgings were carried out in public. It was entertainment for the crowds, who were mainly Greek and felt no kinship with the condemned. But in Jerusalem a public scourging might cause a riot, so they were done in the garrison, where there was no audience in front of whom a man might feel he had to display courage.

This morning there were three: two bandits and Joshua. Each man got a quarter of an hour by the water clock—if he collapsed, the clock was stopped until he was back on his feet, and then it started again. A quarter of an hour, not a minute less.

A quarter of an hour under the scourge was a long time. It ripped a man apart. The very air grew pink with blood. By the end, his whole body was covered with open, bleeding tears, and the wounds were sometimes deep enough to leave the bone exposed. It was not uncommon for the lash to take out a man's eyes.

Raetius ordered that Joshua go first. He was really doing him a favor, because scourging a man for a quarter of an hour is hard work, and the first man always got the worst of it. The worse the scourging, the weaker they were and the less time they had to spend dying on the cross.

Joshua was pretty good. He only went down once, not on his face but only on one knee, and he got back up on his own. He groaned a lot, but they all did. Who could help it?

Then came the hard part. Golgotha was less than half a mile from the garrison, but that was a long way for half-dead men who had to carry their crosspieces the whole distance. It was an ordeal.

Some men had to drag them, but Joshua simply picked his up, balanced it across his shoulders, and carried it. He did it as if he had been bearing such burdens all his life. Perhaps he had.

The whole route was outside the city walls, but there were always crowds and they were always hostile. It took at least thirty men to guard the prisoners and overawe the crowds. Any less and there was a good chance of a disturbance.

Less than half a mile, and it usually took at least an hour.

But it also served its purpose. Sometimes a man died before he ever reached the execution grounds, and the ones who didn't were worn down all the more. It just meant less time on the cross, which was better for everyone.

Once they reached Golgotha, it was time for the actual crucifixion.

Raetius had fought in scores of battles and had killed more men than he could remember. He was hardened to suffering—his own as well as others'. It did not bother him to drive nails into men's flesh and leave them to die. He could listen to them sob and beg for water or for death and feel no pity. His world was full of horrors, and he was accustomed to them.

Golgotha was a little hill, and it really did look like a skull. There was a path to the top, where the uprights were already in place, and the prisoners carried their crosspieces up that path and then threw the crosspieces to the ground and sat down on them.

For most of the soldiers, their job was done. They collected in little groups and had their midday meal. Some had wine in their canteens.

And while the others ate, a crew of four men, who had been especially trained, got to work crucifying the prisoners.

One after the other, the condemned were made to lie down on the ground, their shoulders resting against the crosspiece. Then their arms were roped to it, from about the center of the upper arm to the elbow. When all three were secure, a soldier with a bag of nails and a hammer went from one to the next.

The nails were driven into their forearms, about three fingers' width above their wrists. First a small piece of wood was positioned over the spot, which would prevent the condemned from pulling loose from the nail. Then the nail was driven through the piece of wood, through the arm, and into the crosspiece. First the right arm and then the left.

Everyone screamed. Everyone. Raetius was not sure why. He had seen men have a hand hacked off in battle without making a sound. But everyone screamed when their arms were nailed. With every stroke of the hammer, they screamed. They couldn't seem to help it.

The two bandits were done first, the younger one and then the older. The younger one wasn't even twenty, and he couldn't seem to grasp what was happening to him. He begged and pleaded and wept, and when the nails went in he screamed with that mingling of fear and pain one hears in children.

Then the older one, who took it better, and then Joshua. Joshua was good. He was a strong man. If he screamed, no one could hold that against him.

Then, on either side of the upright, wooden tripods were set up, each with a pulley dangling just beneath the apex. Ropes were run through the pulleys and tied to the ends of the crosspieces. The uprights were tapered at the top, and the crosspieces had holes at the center. A man would work each rope, hoisting up the crosspiece, with the prisoner dangling from it by his arms, and then a third man on a ladder would position the hole in the crosspiece over the top of the upright. Then the crosspiece was lowered into place.

Finally, the prisoners' feet were nailed to the sides of the upright. The nails went through the heels, and again were held in place by pieces of wood. Somehow that didn't seem to bother them as much. Perhaps there was some limit to how much pain can make itself felt.

Once the work was done, the crew could clean up and eat their meal. There was always extra wine for the crew.

When everything was finished, Raetius always took a little tour of inspection. He liked to look the condemned over and form some idea of how long they were likely to last. In Caesarea the men would lay bets on it, but in Jerusalem there were too many executions to leave a man hanging until he died. Tomorrow there would be another batch, and this lot would have to be thrown into a hole to make room.

So sometime before nightfall one of the crew would take a hammer and break their legs. They would die quick enough after that and, except for a small guard, everyone could go back to barracks.

The crosses weren't high. If a prisoner could somehow have gotten a

foot free, he probably could have touched the ground with his toe. Raetius would look each of them straight in the face, just to see how they
reacted. Then he would know.

The young bandit just whispered, "Please, please, please," over and
over. He seemed to be out of his head—that happened sometimes. The
older bandit was conscious, but little more. Raetius thought that one
wouldn't last very long.

Joshua was another matter. When Raetius spoke to him, Joshua
licked his lips, which were caked with blood, and said, in Greek, "I forgive you."

Raetius smiled.

"Don't forgive me yet," he replied, his face no more than a span from
Joshua's. "See how you feel about it in three or four hours."

Joshua used his arms to push himself up and fill his lungs. A little cry
of pain escaped him as his nailed wrists and feet took the weight. From
now until he died, every breath would be agony.

"I forgive you," he repeated. "I will pray for you."

Raetius only shook his head and walked away. That one was strong,
he thought to himself. In Caesarea, where the thing would have been
done right, that one would last for days.

Noah came within sight of Golgotha just in time to see Joshua dragging
himself up the little hill, carrying a large piece of lumber across his
shoulders. At least he thought it was Joshua. The man was taller than
the other two prisoners, but it was difficult to know for certain. He was
covered in blood, even his face. At the sight, Noah could feel his eyes
filling with tears. The Lord Eleazar had warned him, but it was still a
shock.

Noah stopped and leaned against the city wall, struggling to recover
himself. He could be of no use to Joshua if he could not mask his feelings.

In truth, he did not know if he could be of use—if he could bring
himself to do the one thing that would spare Joshua from the full ex-
tremity of his suffering.

Tied to his belt was a small leather water pouch, which the Lord
Eleazar had given him.

"I have mixed something in," he had said. "It is slow to take hold, but
it will ease the pain and, eventually, after a few hours, end his life. It is

common for a man to die suddenly on the cross. The Romans will have no idea that you drugged him."

"Thou shalt not kill," said the commandment. It was not wrong to kill in war or in defense of one's own life, but would it be wrong to kill Joshua to end his ordeal?

May God guide me to the right choice, he thought.

The consciousness of his dilemma helped to sober him. It was like ice in his heart.

Noah had had few dealings with Romans, and none with Roman soldiers. But he assumed that they were like other men—hardened, no doubt, by the brutal discipline of military life, a life inseparable from cruelty and death, but still subject to the customary human weaknesses.

So Noah, as a practical man, realized that he would have to appeal to those weaknesses. He would have to befriend these murderers and wheedle favors from them.

He began with the guard posted at the bottom of the little trail leading up to the execution ground.

"You can't go up there."

The soldier scrambled to his feet. He was about sixteen, with copper-colored skin, tall and slender as a reed. From the way he barred the path, planting the butt of his spear in the dirt and holding it out at arm's length in front of him, he gave the impression that he thought he was protecting the whole Roman Empire.

"Why can't I?" Noah asked, careful to keep any hint of a challenge out of his voice. He spoke in Greek, since the boy's Latin was as imperfect as his own.

He thought he detected the hint of a smile, before Caesar's legionnaire remembered his dignity.

"You just can't." The answer was also in Greek. "They don't allow anybody up there until they've finished."

"Finished what?"

"The crucifixion. It takes a while. Once the prisoners are in place, then maybe."

In place. It was an interesting way to put it.

"Then I'll have to wait," Noah said. He sat down. He had been carrying a large jar, which he placed ostentatiously before him on the ground.

After a minute, the guard sat down too. He couldn't take his eyes off the jar.

"What's inside?" he asked finally.

"Wine. Would you like some?"

Noah had supplied himself with a dipper. Without waiting for a response, he broke the seal on the wine jar, lowered the dipper inside, and then offered it to the guard.

They drank to the accompaniment of inhuman screaming from the top of the hill. Noah fought hard to appear not to notice.

"They squeal like pigs, don't they," the guard said, grinning. One could see that it affected him, but he was a soldier, and very young, and he wanted to appear callous.

"One of them is my cousin," Noah answered, as if stating a neutral fact. He offered the guard another dipperful of wine. "Where are you from?"

"Alexandria." The guard seemed grateful for the change of subject. He drained the wine and then added, "That's in Egypt."

"I know. I've never been there, but I hear it's a beautiful city."

"Not the part of it I come from." He kept glancing up the trail. The top of the hill was not visible, but the screams of the condemned were an immediate presence.

"I wish they'd finish," he said, almost desperately.

Finally they did, and there was silence again.

They waited another half hour. The guard drank all the wine that was offered to him, but hardly a word passed between them.

Finally, Noah reached into his purse and took out five silver coins.

"Perhaps you could go up and have a look," he said, putting the coins in the guard's hand. "Just see if they're finished. I'll wait here."

Sober, the guard might have said no. But he was drunk enough to have forgotten his orders, and he obliged willingly enough.

He came back down the trail a minute later.

"Yes, they're done." There was a haunted look in his eyes. And then, as if suddenly aware of his lapse in courtesy, he said, "My name is Anubis. I'm sorry about your cousin."

"I know you are, my son."

Noah rose to his feet, picked up his wine jar, and started walking slowly up the path, his heart like lead.

When he reached the top he tried not to look at the three crosses. He tried to make himself believe that these Roman soldiers, lounging about on the ground, were not responsible for Joshua's fate but were merely its instruments.

He had almost managed to convince himself when one of them, presumably an officer, from his attitude of command, rose up and approached him.

"How did you get up here?" he demanded.

"The trail," Noah replied. He smiled, to indicate he was jesting.

"The guard should have stopped you."

"He's a good boy and thought you might be thirsty."

The officer had been glancing speculatively at Noah's wine jar almost from the first, but he was suspicious.

"Have you tasted it?"

"Oh yes." Noah set the jar down and then held up the dipper, full to the brim, as an offering. "Your good health, sir."

"You taste it first."

Noah drank, and then smiled with what he hoped would appear to be satisfaction. In truth, the wine reminded him of blood.

"Please." He held out the dipper. "It's from Crete, and less than two years old."

The officer consented to taste it.

"It's not bad," he admitted. "I prefer Falernian, but you can't get it out here."

"I apologize, sir."

"It's all right."

"A gift for you and your men."

The officer looked around him. He was a large, broad man with long blond hair and a scarred face. He picked up the jar and held it against his breastplate with one hand.

"Good thing for you the escort has returned to barracks." He laughed shortly, and then immediately stopped. "What do you want here?"

"One of the prisoners is a relative."

"Well, you can't save him. His punishment was decreed by the prefect."

"I know. It's just . . . We grew up together."

"Umm. Well, just don't interfere."

"I won't. May I speak to him?"

The officer made a gesture with his free hand, expressing his indifference.

It was only then that Noah turned and really looked at the three crosses. Simply by his size, he instantly recognized the man in the center as Joshua. Then he found himself wondering how, otherwise, he could have known. All he saw was blood. All three men had been scourged until they were covered with wounds.

Noah recognized that it was cowardly of him, and he reproached himself for it, but he could not immediately bring himself to face his cousin. He could not bear to be confronted with Joshua's suffering, not in that first instant, so he turned his attention to the other two.

What had they done to bring them here? Did it matter? One, the older, seemed already to be sinking into death, but the younger had eyes filled with fear and the longing to live.

Suddenly Noah realized that the younger one was Samson.

So this was the end of his "kindness." He felt like a murderer.

It is too much, he thought. *It is past bearing.* And then he reproached himself as a weakling and a coward. *These three are suffering through a slow and painful death and, because I happen to know two of them, I think my own pain beyond endurance.*

He forced himself to turn to his cousin.

"Joshua."

They were face-to-face, and yet, at first, Joshua seemed unable to focus enough to recognize who it was.

Then he smiled.

"I was wondering when you would get here," he said, in hardly more than a whisper. The effort of that one sentence seemed to exhaust him.

"Are you in terrible pain?" Noah asked him.

"Yes, but it was worse before."

Joshua pushed himself up to take a breath, and the sound that came from him was like the squeak of an ungreased wheel. It was a long moment before he could speak again.

"God will deliver me," he said, "even from this. You will be a witness."

Noah could see it in his eyes, that flicker of doubt. The first worm had entered his heart.

"Yes."

Noah wanted to touch him, to let him feel that he was not deserted, but he was afraid of inflicting yet more pain.

"I will sit at the right hand of God."

"Yes."

Joshua nodded. He was worn down and exhausted, yet he still had many hours left to suffer.

How can men do this to one another? Noah found himself wondering. *How can they do this and still be men?*

But all he said was, "Can I do anything?"

He received no answer. Joshua had drifted away into some terrible world of his own. He did not even seem to know that Noah was there.

Noah waited awhile for him to come back, but he did not.

"Come away."

There was a hand on his shoulder, and it belonged to the Roman officer.

"They go in and out. It is the only mercy the gods allow them. Come away and drink a little of your own wine, before it is all gone."

They sat down together, and the officer, who had his own little bronze cup, filled it from the jug and then offered the dipper to Noah. He was trying, it was obvious, to be kind.

"My name is Gaius Raetius," he said. "At least, that was the name I was given when I joined the legions. I've almost forgotten the name I was born with."

"I am Noah bar Barachel."

"And Joshua is your relation?"

"Our grandfathers were brothers."

"Tell me, for I am curious, was he ever a soldier?"

"No. He is a carpenter."

"Well, he could have been a soldier," Raetius said, not attempting to disguise his admiration. "He's tough."

Noah took a tentative sip of his wine, even though it smelled like death.

"What will happen to him when he is dead?" he asked.

Raetius looked at Noah as if he thought him mad.

"He will be thrown into the pit, with all the others," he answered, calmly. "The crows will get him."

"I would like to buy back his body for proper burial," Noah said, raising his eyes to the man's face, almost making a challenge of it. "I am prepared to pay a great deal of money."

The Roman officer sighed, perhaps thinking of all he could have done with Noah's money.

"You aren't rich enough," he said finally. "Your cousin Joshua goes into the pit and he rots. If I gave you his body, I and every one of my men would get twenty stripes. Under another prefect, maybe. But Pilatus

means every condemned man to suffer the last measure of his punishment. No exceptions."

As he listened, Noah's resolve hardened. Coming here, he had not
known if he could bring himself to use the Lord Eleazar's gift, but now
there were no more doubts.

"Then at least can I give him a drink of water?"

The price was twenty pieces of silver. Gaius Raetius was not fool enough
to let such an opportunity pass. Noah counted out the coins for him,
and even pretended to be grateful.

"Are you thirsty?" he murmured, his face close to Joshua's. "Do you
want some water?"

At first there was no response. Joshua knew he was there, but he did
not seem to know what the words meant. Then Noah put his hand on
Joshua's face to support his head. His touch seemed to cause no pain,
but it brought Joshua back to himself.

"Do you want some water?" Noah repeated.

"Yes."

The one desiccated syllable was a sound like someone scraping inside
a dried gourd. Joshua opened his mouth, and his tongue looked gray.

"Here, drink."

Noah gave him the water, a sip at a time, careful not to waste any.
When he had drunk about half, Joshua seemed to recover.

"That's enough," he said. "Will you stay with me?"

"Yes. Of course."

"Until the end?"

"Yes."

"Good. I didn't want to die among strangers."

"You won't. I will stay with you."

Noah wanted to say so much more, but his voice failed him. He was
afraid even to have Joshua see his face, sorrow and despair had so robbed
him of all disguise.

After a long time Joshua managed a rusty laugh. "I will miss the
Passover," he said.

"I think we both will."

"Deborah will be angry."

"No, she won't."

Noah had sat down on the ground to make it easier for Joshua to see him. Joshua was having trouble keeping his head up.

"The Baptist died, I will die. It will still come."

For an instant Noah couldn't grasp what he was talking about, and then he remembered.

"The kingdom of God?"

"Yes."

"We will share the Passover feast, then." Noah's eyes felt as if they were burning.

"Yes."

Joshua pushed himself up with his arms, filling his lungs. This time he did not cry out.

For a long time neither of them spoke. For much of it, Noah could not even be sure that Joshua was conscious.

"Let me have some more water," Joshua said finally. Noah got up and gave him what was left.

"I can get more if you want it."

But Joshua shook his head. "No. Don't leave me. Stay with me."

"Of course."

It was nearly an hour before Joshua spoke again.

"I don't feel the pain anymore," he said, almost as if he missed it. "I mean, it's there, but it's like the buzzing of flies. I feel almost as if I can wave it away whenever I like. Do you think that means that I'm dying?"

"I don't know."

Then, for a long time, Joshua seemed to drift away. Sometimes his eyes would come to rest on Noah's face, and he might smile, but for the rest he seemed far off.

"I will never see the Kingdom."

Noah's head snapped up, and he realized that he had fallen into a doze.

"What? What did you say?"

"I will never see the Kingdom." Joshua's face was a mask of agony. "I will die and I will never see it. It is God's judgment upon me—upon my failure. I will never see Rachel's face."

"Yes you will. You will see it. You have not failed. You will be with Rachel again."

Noah had no idea if he believed what he was saying. Some things were more important than the truth.

But Joshua might not even have heard him. He forced himself up again to fill his lungs, twisting his head so that he could see the sky.

"My God, my God," he shouted, with a power one would not have thought in him. "Why have You forsaken me?"

And then he slumped down. After that he hardly stirred, and he never spoke again.

About an hour before sundown, Noah felt a hand on his shoulder.

"He's dead," Raetius told him. "Quite a while, from the look of him."

"Yes, I know."

"Well, we have to start taking them down now. Just the young one's alive, but we'll soon fix that."

"What will you do?"

"Break his legs. He won't last long after that."

Noah scrambled to his feet and took out his purse of silver. He put it in Raetius's hands.

"Take it all," he said. "But don't break his legs."

"He has to die," Raetius said. He felt the purse with his fingers and shook his head. "It's the law."

"Then kill him quickly, so that he doesn't suffer. You're a soldier, so you must know how."

"Nothing to it."

He drew his sword and walked the few steps over to where Samson was hanging, still conscious, but very little more. Raetius positioned the point of his sword just inside the boy's left collarbone and then drove it quickly down. Samson opened his eyes as if surprised, and blood poured out of his mouth.

Raetius pulled his sword free and hunted around until he found a piece of cloth he could use to wipe it dry.

"I shall have to give it a good cleaning when I get back to barracks," he said, studying the blade, turning it this way and that in the late afternoon sun. "By the way, what was he to you, the young one?"

"Nothing. Only a son of man, like you or I."

Raetius laughed. "You Jews are a queer lot."

The crew finally had all three dead prisoners down. They cleaned the nails and put them away and tied the three crosspieces together with rope. They carried the bodies over to a great, gaping hole in the stone and threw them in.

The smell from the hole was terrible. Noah stood on the edge, his eyes on Joshua's corpse as it lay, about twenty feet down, among uncounted others in various stages of putrefaction.

He began to recite the Prayer for the Dead. "In the world which will be renewed, He will give life to the dead and raise them to eternal life. . . ."

It was simply impossible to go on. The words stuck in his throat. And he knew, in that moment, that Joshua had spoken the truth—that God truly had forsaken him.

The sun was down, which meant that the Passover had begun. He had no idea when or how he left the Hill of Skulls, or where he went after that.

It had long been dark when he found himself standing in front of the door to his cousin Baruch's house. He could not go in, so he sat down outside. The memories of this terrible day clutched at his heart.

This was where Deborah found him the next morning.

"Don't touch me," he said, glancing at her and then quickly looking away. "I am defiled."

49

"You have served God. Now your life is your own again. Go."

The words kept echoing in Judah's head. Thus Caleb had dismissed him, as casually as he might have brushed the dust from his sleeve.

"You have served God." How? By destroying His prophet?

The truth was, Judah no longer knew what to do with a life that was his own. He could have returned to Tiberias, but it never occurred to him to do so. He was now trapped in his own future, while everything that meant anything to him existed in an irretrievably lost past. And every moment of that future was and always would be stained by his betrayal.

Of what value was such a life? Every hour was a burden.

So he stayed in Jerusalem, simply because he could not summon the will to leave. He had money in his purse, but he slept in doorways. For a few days he drank wine, but he gave it up when he found it changed nothing. He ate only when the pangs of hunger began to distract him from the one idea that had come to fill his mind: atonement.

"I know what they have done to you," Joshua had said to him, even as they condemned him. "I forgive you."

But Judah knew he had committed a sin for which there was no forgiveness. When God's kingdom came at last, there would be no place in it for him. All that was left was to confess his guilt and accept the punishment and the release of a shameful death.

"A hanged man is accursed by God." So it was written in Torah. So let it be.

The Passover had ended and the city soon emptied of pilgrims. With their departure, Judah's mind seemed to clarify. He took a room over a wineshop and began to compose a letter to his father.

"I have come to understand that you were wise and just to discard me. I have turned away from my duty to God and to you. I have broken the commandments and have borne false witness against an innocent man and a servant of God, and thus have I turned my life into filth. All that remains to me is to accept my punishment as just. Yet I feel I must render some account to you of the trail of events which has led me to this. . . ."

When he had finished the letter, he went to the house where he had been born and knocked on the door. A chamberlain answered, an old servant who knew him at once.

"Put this into my father's hands," Judah told him, giving him the letter.

Afterwards, his steps carried him to Gethsemane, where Joshua had prayed and where he had been arrested. Along the way, Judah passed through a marketplace, where he bought a coil of rope.

Joshua's death ended many things. For some of his followers it ended all hope. Some did not wait for the end of the Passover but, escaping like thieves, set out on the road back to Galilee. Many drifted away soon after. Only Simon and John stayed in Jerusalem.

Noah could not bring himself to see them. It was not out of anger. He simply could not bring himself to do it. So they turned to Deborah.

"I ran away," Simon told her. "I was afraid and hid myself."

"You could not have saved him." She placed her hand on his head, and it was like a mother's caress. "He would have understood your fear."

"He understood everything," John said. "He foresaw his end. Do you remember what he said about men being broken like bread, and that it was all the will of God? If God brought him to the cross, it had to be for some purpose."

"But what purpose?" Simon shook his head. "If he knew he was soon to know death, he must have known why. I think we were unworthy of him. We heard him but we didn't understand. It was all a riddle to which only he had the answer."

When they had left, Deborah went up to the room in Baruch's house where Noah hid himself. He had not left it since the end of the Passover, when he had finally come in from the street. He sat on the floor, in a corner, as if trying to make himself as small as possible.

"What did they say?" he asked her.

"That Joshua's death was for some reason that only he and God knew. It is all a riddle to them."

"A riddle?" Noah's laughter was the bitterest sound she had ever heard. "God is the riddle. If He has some purpose or if He is merely toying with us, we can never know. Joshua thought he understood God's purposes, and that error—that arrogance, that presumption—is why he died. This is all the lesson I can draw from it, that the only wisdom is to understand that we understand nothing."

"Joshua loved God," Deborah said, she sat down beside him and took Noah's hand in both of her own. "He trusted God. He called God his Father."

"Every Jew calls God his Father. It is simply part of the ritual of prayer."

"But Joshua truly believed it."

"I know."

Noah brought her hand up to his mouth and kissed it. It was the first time he had done that since coming back.

"Joshua loved and trusted God," he said quietly, his voice hoarse with emotion. "And that love and trust ended in the worst death a man can die."

"Tell me what happened."

But Noah only shook his head.

"I could swear I saw him," Simon told her. "It was near the Temple. He looked at me and smiled, and then he was gone."

Deborah made no reply. She merely poured him a cup of wine.

"Is it possible he never died?"

"Noah says he died. He was there."

"But men have been raised from the dead before. Elisha brought the Shunammite woman's son back to life. Joshua once said that the coming of the Kingdom would be heralded by miracles, that the graves would give up their dead."

" 'One like the son of man will come, sent from heaven to judge the world.' Isn't that what he said?" John suddenly raised his hands, like someone who has finally seen the obvious. "How many times did he tell us that?"

"We did not understand him while he was among us. But now he will reveal the truth to us."

They had come to say good-bye. It was the last morning before Noah and Deborah were to begin the journey back to Galilee. Hannah and Hiram would accompany them and would be married as quickly as Hiram could establish a household. Abijah and Sarah had left the week before.

Deborah was anxious to be at home. She had tried in vain to persuade Simon and John to come with them.

"No." Simon smiled and shook his head. "I've already sent for my wife. The answer, whatever it is, will only be revealed to us here in Jerusalem."

They still had never talked to Noah.

"Why wouldn't you see them?" Deborah asked him, once the walls of Jerusalem were no longer in sight. "They came every day, and what they really wanted was to see you."

"What they really wanted was to have you feed them breakfast and comfort them," Noah answered. "It's what *I* really want. It's what every man who knows you really wants."

He could smile now, and make his loving little jokes. He still hadn't gone into her since before Joshua was arrested, but Noah appeared to be mending.

"They seem to think he's come back."

"Come back?"

"Yes. Simon told me he saw him."

"Whatever he saw, it wasn't Joshua. Joshua is in a pit at Golgotha. By now there are probably twenty or thirty more corpses on top of him, but if you could pull him out, you wouldn't recognize him."

"It's terrible the way you say it."

"The reality was much more terrible."

They walked in silence for a time. Deborah did not need to look at her husband's face to know that in his mind he was back there, seeing it all again. She could feel it in the tension of his arm.

50

The Lord Eleazar was also on his way home, to Sepphoris, having been detained in Jerusalem by business. Three days after the Passover he had received a brief note requesting an interview that afternoon. The note was from one Isaac bar Zedekiah, head of one of the more important Levite families. His name was known to Eleazar, having appeared in a number of recent reports which had attracted his attention. He was the father of Judah bar Isaac.

Eleazar had written back, stating that he would be pleased to receive Isaac bar Zedekiah at the time indicated.

Isaac was approaching seventy, Judah having been the last child of his second marriage. He was thin, with small, fretful eyes, and his hair and beard were iron gray. A servant showed him into Eleazar's study, and Isaac sat down without waiting to be invited. In his hand was a sheet of papyrus. He could not seem to keep his feet still. It was obvious that he was in a state of considerable agitation.

He refused the wine that was offered to him.

"Then how may I serve you?" Eleazar inquired.

"My son Judah's body was discovered this morning at Gethsemane," Isaac answered, his voice cracking, whether from grief or anger it was impossible to know. "He had hanged himself. I received this letter from him yesterday. I suggest you read it."

He thrust out the hand that held Judah's letter. Eleazar accepted it and read.

"My son was kidnapped, threatened with death, and abused," the old man shouted, unable, it seemed, to wait upon Eleazar's examination of the letter. "He was made to live among peasants and outlaws. His wits were turned. And all by this fellow Caleb. Your servant!"

Eleazar refrained from replying, *"and your kinsman."* Isaac was too important a man to be trifled with. Besides, Judah's written confession was a sudden and unexpected gift from God.

"Caleb has been of use to the Tetrarch," Eleazar answered, without looking up from the letter. "I had no foreknowledge of this, and neither did the Lord Antipas."

"My son hanged himself! He embraced the most shameful of deaths. He must have been driven mad."

There were tears in the old man's eyes. His hands were trembling. His grief was bitter.

"He killed himself out of remorse," Eleazar announced, looking up from the papyrus. "By his account he felt guilt over the execution of this Joshua, this prophet. As you say, the balance of his mind was probably disturbed, but there is a certain nobility in his death. He did not try to evade responsibility for what he had done. He passed sentence on himself."

"Yes. That is true." Isaac bar Zedekiah closed his eyes for a moment, perhaps taking some comfort in the reflection. "And what he wrote to me was loving. If he did wrong, he was driven to it. Others are more guilty than he."

"I will see to it that they are punished." Eleazar refolded the letter and held it up. "May I keep this, just for a time? I think the Tetrarch should see it. It shall be returned to you when justice is done."

The letter was in Eleazar's possession when he passed under the gates of Tiberias. He held it in his hand when he entered the palace garden for his audience with Antipas.

The Tetrarch was sitting on a white marble bench, scattering bread crumbs on the gravel walkway for little brown birds, which fled at Eleazar's approach.

"What is it, Minister?" he said. "You look grim as death."

"I think you should read this, my lord."

He held the papyrus out to his master, who took it, unfolded it and, after the most cursory of inspections, handed it back.

"My eyes are not what they were. Tell me what it says."

Yes, of course. The letter was in Hebrew, which Antipas knew only haltingly. "Tell me what it says," not "read it to me." Naturally he would blame his eyesight.

"It is a letter from a certain Judah bar Isaac to his father, written just before Judah took his own life. He hanged himself in Jerusalem."

"And what has any of this to do with us?" the Tetrarch inquired, with just a hint of suspicion in his voice.

Eleazar told him the whole story, what the letter said, and what he had learned from his own inquiries, including the evidence of Michal. For once he had the Tetrarch's full attention.

"Caleb plotted the arrest and execution of this Joshua bar Joseph, a peasant preacher, using perjured testimony," Eleazar concluded, "and for no other reason, my lord, except to ingratiate himself with you, to convince you that the Baptist's followers really are a threat, that you therefore need his protection.

"But this is nothing. It is a measure of his desperation, nothing more. But to achieve all this, he kidnapped and drove to suicide the son of an important Levite family. We are fortunate, my lord, that Isaac bar Zedekiah brought this letter to me and not to the high priest."

Antipas, who had sat motionless for some time, finally nodded.

"Yes," he said, laying emphasis on the word. "We want no trouble from that quarter."

Eleazar, who appeared at first not to have heard, was studying the pattern of the bread crumbs at his feet.

"Precisely, my lord."

"What do you suggest should be done?"

"What can be done?" Eleazar raised his head and smiled bleakly. "Isaac bar Zedekiah demands justice for his son. A life for a life."

Antipas shrugged. It was a heavy, ponderous gesture. Then he rose from the bench.

"Minister, I leave this matter with you. I expect I will not hear the name of Caleb bar Jacob again."

"As you see fit, my lord."

———

As this conversation was concluding, its subject was on the road from Jerusalem, just out of sight of the city walls. Caleb had been enjoying himself in the city, renewing acquaintances with people who acted as if he had never been away.

He traveled with an escort of cavalry and Matthias, who walked behind Caleb's wagon, his hands chained to an oxbow that he carried across his shoulders. Matthias would be detained in Sepphoris, there to await his death, and Caleb would then go on to Tiberias. He was looking forward to his conversation with the Tetrarch.

And, to keep himself amused on the journey, Caleb sat in the back of his wagon, the curtains drawn aside, and taunted his prisoner.

"Are you aware of the punishment for desertion? No? It is crucifixion. That is how your friend Joshua died."

The weight of the oxbow on his neck meant that it required a special effort for Matthias to raise his head and look at his tormenter. He made the effort now. He wanted Caleb to see his face.

"What do I not deserve, my lord, for the things I have done in your service? But God in His mercy has forgiven me, has spared me His wrath, so I have little enough to fear from you."

"'Little enough'? You think so?"

"Yes, my lord. Death and pain are little enough, for I will pass through them to everlasting life. God has redeemed me."

It was enough for the time being. Caleb drew the curtains closed, having decided he would take a nap. He would dream of his wife, who had been very affectionate of late and who had promised to join him in Tiberias.

At walking pace, the road from Jerusalem to Sepphoris took seven days, with six nights in one or another of the villages along the way, which did a good business in accommodating pilgrims. It was an agreeable journey, particularly after one left the highlands, where the nights were cold.

A man in chains, especially one as big as Matthias, excited a great deal of curiosity. Little children, sometimes accompanied by their parents, would approach him, sometimes with food and water, and ask him questions. At first the soldiers of Caleb's escort shooed them away, but in the end they grew tired of it and left them alone.

The common people did not assume, simply from the fact that a man was a prisoner, that he was evil, or had done anything really wrong, or was any different from themselves. Bandits were often popular heroes, and no one thought any less of Matthias when they were told he was a deserter.

At night, Matthias was chained to a wagon axle and left outside, and the villagers would build a fire to keep off the cold and bear him company. He would tell them about his life and his many crimes and about how he had found forgiveness. He told them about Joshua and God's kingdom. He told them about the mercy of God. He was not gifted as a preacher, but the fact that he had been condemned to death, and did not seem to be afraid, carried great weight.

The soldiers sometimes came and listened, too. They liked Matthias, and Caleb was not a favorite. No one told Caleb what was going on.

Nevertheless, after the fourth night he found out and ordered a stop to it. A guard would be posted wherever they stayed overnight, just to keep people away from Matthias.

"I'm told your master Joshua lasted only a few hours on the cross," Caleb said, that morning, while Matthias was being unchained from the wagon axle. "Perhaps his heart gave out, or perhaps the Romans are going soft. In either case, I've decided that you won't be so fortunate. I've decided that you'll be spared the scourging and be crucified just as you are. And they won't come and break your leg bones either. You'll have to die all on your own. A strong man like you might last a week. We'll see."

Matthias made no response. He did not appear even to have heard.

For the rest of the day, Caleb was in a filthy mood.

In Sepphoris there was a gated courtyard through which soldiers always entered and left the palace, because it was adjacent to the barracks and the stables. It also served as a receiving point for prisoners. The walls were windowless up to about twice a man's height and, once the gate was down, there was no escape. Until a few days before, the Lord Eleazar had not known about a prisoner, but he knew that, because of his escort, Caleb would enter through this gateway.

He had had Caleb watched since the end of the Passover. On the day Caleb left Jerusalem, a rider on a fast horse had carried word of it to Sepphoris. The Lord Eleazar had had plenty of time to prepare his servant's reception.

When he knew that Caleb was only half a day from the city, he summoned the captain of the watch to his office, where he handed him a papyrus scroll.

"This is a warrant, signed by me, for the arrest and execution of the Lord Caleb," he said. "You will speak of this to no one. No soldier of the guard is to be allowed to leave the palace until the arrest has been effected. Do I make myself understood?"

"Yes, my lord."

The watch captain was careful to keep his own face impassive. Yet, was there just a hint of satisfaction around the corners of his mouth?

"Will the men feel any compunction about obeying this order?" Eleazar asked.

"No, my lord."

"I thought not."

For the next half an hour, they went over plans for the arrest. While they talked, the Lord Eleazar sat at his marble desk, sketching an outline of the courtyard on a wax tablet.

"What can be done about the escort?" he asked, without looking up.

"They won't cause any trouble," the watch captain answered. He hooked his right thumb into his sword belt, a gesture which somehow conveyed his vast contempt for cavalrymen. "All they'll care about is looking after their horses and then getting drunk."

"Nevertheless, the best thing would be to draw them off somehow. I'd prefer it if they went back to Jerusalem without even knowing that anything had happened."

"Then we'll get them into the stables before we make the arrest. By the time they come back out, Caleb will be gone."

Eleazar nodded agreement.

"How many men will you need?"

"No more than four."

"Choose ones you can trust, then." The Tetrarch's First Minister made a despairing gesture with his left hand. "There is no chance of keeping the arrest a secret, but I would prefer that Caleb be dead before it becomes widely known. The prisoner, of course, is a complication. I will decide about that when we have established his identity."

"What do you want done with Caleb?"

"I will leave the palace as soon as he is in custody. Bring me his head in the morning."

The watch captain smiled. "Perhaps you could send it to his wife as a wedding present," he said pleasantly.

"You knew about that?"

"My lord, everyone knew about it, except perhaps her husband."

Two hours later, when the gate was raised for the arrival of Caleb's party, everything was in place. A small knot of soldiers were playing dice. The Lord Eleazar and the watch captain were standing in shadow. First the wagon entered, then the prisoner, then six men on horses. Then the gate closed.

The watch captain swore under his breath and then plucked at Eleazar's sleeve.

"The prisoner's name is Matthias, my lord. He is one of ours—or was, until he disappeared a few months ago."

"I am familiar with his history, Captain."

The arrest went as planned. The cavalrymen dismounted and, under the direction of a palace groom, led their horses into the stable, where they were offered wine to clear the dust from their throats. The watch captain went over to the wagon and opened its door.

"My lord," he said, smiling and offering his hand. "Welcome back."

Caleb of course took the offered hand, and was about to say something, when he was unceremoniously yanked off balance. He tumbled out of the wagon and onto the stone floor.

"Lamech," he shouted, "are you out of your mind? I'll have you . . ."

The threat died in his throat when the felt the point of the watch captain's sword resting just under his right eye.

The dice players, by this time, had abandoned their game. Three of them took up positions around the prostrate Caleb, and the fourth attended to the wagon driver.

"Come on down," he said. "We have a nice cell for you, where you can stay drunk for two or three days, and then go home to the wife."

"But, but . . . What about the horses?"

"They'll be attended to. Don't worry about that."

The watch captain lifted his sword away from Caleb's face and slipped it back into his scabbard.

"Get up."

Two soldiers grabbed Caleb by the arms and pulled him to his feet. At that moment the Lord Eleazar stepped forward out of the shadows.

"My lord . . . !"

But Eleazar ignored him. His attention was fixed on Matthias.

"Unshackle this man," he ordered. "Who has a key?"

A search of Caleb's pockets turned it up, and in another moment Matthias was flexing his arms and shoulders, for the first time in a week, free of the oxbow.

"Come with me," Eleazar said quietly, gesturing to him with his hand. "You have nothing to fear."

"My lord," Caleb shouted, "what have I done?"

Eleazar stopped and turned to him, as if he had just noticed his existence.

"What have you done?" He shook his head in dismay. "Captain, you have your orders. Remove him."

"Yes, my lord."

With Matthias following behind, Eleazar returned to his office. Matthias slumped into a chair, only looking up to accept a cup of wine.

"Have you eaten?" Eleazar inquired gently.

"Not since this morning."

"Shall I order you some food?"

"No. I am too tired to eat." Matthias looked around him, apparently unable to comprehend where he was. "What will you do with me?"

"Nothing. You are free." Eleazar cocked his head a little to one side. "Do you have somewhere to go?"

"If I'm not to be crucified, I'll go back to Jerusalem."

"What will you do there?"

"Try to pick up the threads." Matthias set his wine cup down on the floor. "Try to find my master's disciples and see what can be done. I don't know. I'll have to see."

Eleazar opened a small wooden box on his desk and took out a leather pouch containing silver. He tossed it to Matthias, who snatched it out of the air by reflex.

"You will need money for the journey, and for when you get there. Consider it your retirement pay."

He smiled. He had decided that he liked Matthias.

"You will need a place to spend the night," he continued. "Why don't you look in at Noah's house? I'm sure he'll give you a bed. I'm sure he'll be very glad to see you. Do you know the way?"

"Yes."

"I thought so."

"What will happen to Caleb?"

"By now he's probably already dead."

"May the Lord God have mercy on him."

"I'm inclined to think it unlikely."

"What shall we do with him?"

The question was directed at the watch captain, who stood close in front of the prisoner, smiling into his face.

"The Lord Eleazar wants his head by morning," he said, speaking mainly for Caleb's benefit. "Beyond that, he doesn't seem to care."

"What was he going to do to Matthias?"

"You can imagine."

If Matthias had had a friend among the guard, it was Lamech. And, in any case, the men hated "Little Ahab."

"Are there any volunteers to take his head off?" Lamech directed his gaze from one to the next of the four men who had been detailed for the arrest. "No one wants to do it? Are you afraid of getting your uniforms dirty?"

The men laughed nervously.

"Then I suppose it will have to be Uriah."

The name was like a splash of cold water.

Up to that point, Caleb had been able to preserve his dignity. He knew how these games were played, and he had accepted the idea that his life was over. He thought he could face death, provided it was quick and he didn't have to wait too long.

But Uriah was another matter. He felt the panic rising in his throat as they hustled him down the stairs to the lower prison.

Uriah was sitting on his bench. He looked up when the door opened. He saw Caleb, and immediately noted that his hands were tied behind his back.

Uriah stood up, but without hurry. There was no one before whom he needed to grovel.

"Death sentence," Lamech announced. "Order of the First Minister, the Lord Eleazar. Cut off his head."

The soldiers on either side of Caleb forced him to his knees.

"When?"

It was the only question Uriah asked, and he waited for the answer as expectantly as a child waits for a treat.

Lamech had to think. There was still an hour to dusk. What would be a just punishment?

"I'll be back in twelve hours," he said. "The Lord Eleazar wants the head, and it would be better if it were left unmarked—the lord might have a weak stomach."

The men departed. The prison door closed. There was no one left behind except Caleb and his executioner.

Uriah walked around his new victim in a slow circle, as if he wanted to appreciate the sight of him from every angle.

"I was always your friend, Uriah."

"No one is my friend."

"Make it quick."

But Uriah didn't answer. He merely stepped behind Caleb, grabbed him by the rope that bound his hands, and dragged him over to the wall, to which an iron ring was bolted, about four feet above the floor. Uriah took a chain, threaded it around Caleb's chest and then fastened it to the ring.

Then he crouched in front of Caleb. A small knife appeared in his hand. He lifted up the hem of Caleb's tunic and cut away his loin cloth. The point of the knife went against Caleb's scrotum, and with a quick backwards movement he tore it open.

Caleb was too astonished even to cry out, as the blood slowly leaked out onto his leg.

"You want to die quickly?" Uriah shook his head. "We have a long time. You will beg for death, but it will not come. You will suffer as you would not have thought it possible to suffer, but a man does not die of suffering. When at last you feel the blade against your throat, you will bless me for it."

Then he stood up and walked back to his bench. He would give his victim time to think.

But Caleb could not think. He could not even catch his breath. He tried to remember something—anything—that would help him now, but all he could think of was Joshua on the way to the Antonia Fortress. *"I hope someday you will look back,"* he had said. *"God will forgive you."*

"God forgive me," he whispered. But all he meant was "God save me from this."

"God forgive me!" he repeated, screaming now. And then, as his heart filled with fear, leaving room for nothing else, the screams became merely screams, incoherent and meaningless.

All the while, Uriah sat on his bench, rocking with obscene laughter.

51

It was the spring, and the grass was long and green around the city walls. The children were running ahead and Deborah was calling something to them. He couldn't hear what she said because there was no sound in her voice. Young Joshua, their third son, looked back at her and laughed.

What was Deborah calling? Why couldn't he hear it?

"Uncle Noah. Wake up."

He opened his eyes and was back in the present, where he was an old man, sitting beside his doorway in the morning sunlight, and Deborah had been dead for two years.

"Don't you want your breakfast?"

It was Merab, Hannah's girl. She had married one of Hiram's apprentices and they had moved to Nazareth. Nazareth was getting to be a town now, not a village, and there was plenty of work for an ironsmith.

Thus everything goes around and around. Benjamin comes back home to Nazareth and sets up his forge. He teaches his son Barachel, who moves to Sepphoris. Then Barachel's son Noah, when his father dies, comes back to Nazareth and learns his trade from his grandfather. Then he moves back to Sepphoris and teaches Hiram, who teaches Jediael, who moves to Nazareth and sets up his forge.

"No, I won't want any breakfast. I want a cup of wine."

"It's too early for wine, Uncle Noah. Have your breakfast instead."

"Oh very well."

Around and around. And now Noah had come back to Nazareth to live out his last years in his grandfather's house, where he had been raised. After Deborah's death, the house in Sepphoris was haunted for him and, besides, his eldest son Berachel's family was growing and they needed the room.

But they all came to visit him—even widowed Sarah, still spry enough to walk the five miles to Nazareth. Family was the last remaining consolation.

Merab brought out a little tray and set it on the table to the left of his chair. She kept house and cooked for him. She and her husband were still struggling, and the money was welcome, but she was three months with child now, so other arrangements would soon have to be made.

Or perhaps not. Noah was an old man and gave very little thought to the future.

Breakfast was bread and lentils and beer. Noah ate slowly, drinking the beer, which was foul stuff, in little sips. When his breakfast was finished, he would pretend to fall asleep again so that Merab could slip back to her own house for a few hours. By these little stratagems does an old man hope to avoid becoming more of a nuisance than absolutely necessary.

Except that he actually did fall asleep again. He was awakened not my Merab but by a man making a noise as if to clear his throat.

"I apologize," the man said first. "Did I awaken you?"

He was young, not much over twenty. He was also tall, with light brown hair, and he was speaking Greek, which meant that he was a stranger.

"It doesn't matter," Noah answered, in Greek, which he had not even heard in ten years. He tried not to scowl—the young are so sensitive. "Very soon I will sleep forever. Do I know you?"

"No. I am from Antioch. But when I was a boy I met a friend of yours. Do you remember Matthias?"

"Yes."

He had not seen Matthias since the year of Joshua's death. The sound of his name brought everything back, as if it had happened yesterday. It was very unpleasant.

"From the way you speak of him, I assume he is dead. How did he die?"

The young man from Antioch seemed taken aback.

"In his sleep. He was old."

"Not as old as I am now." Noah smiled. "But I am glad his death was gentle. Is that where he died, in Antioch?"

"Yes. But he will rise again when Jesus Christ returns."

Noah sat quietly, his eyes cast down, as he tried to understand what this lad was talking about. Then it struck him. *Jesus* was the Greek for "Joshua." Joshua the Anointed One. Was that still going on?

"So Matthias was a preacher?"

"Yes. He was our elder, the only one who had actually known our Lord in the flesh."

"And your 'Lord' was, I take it, this Jesus?"

"Yes. Our Savior, the Son of God."

Noah could only shake his head. Then it occurred to him that Merab was nowhere about, and there was a jar of wine in the kitchen. Company was the perfect excuse.

"But I have forgotten my manners," he said, standing up. "Please be good enough to sit down and I will bring us some refreshment."

The wine was reasonably cool, and she hadn't cut it with more than three measures of water. Noah could hardly believe his luck.

He sat down again and poured two cups. The young man tasted the wine, apparently just to be polite, and then set his cup down again.

"Matthias spoke of you often," he said. "He told us you were with the Lord Jesus when he died."

"Joshua. His name was Joshua. By the way, what is your name?"

"Marcus. I am a Roman," he answered, not without a hint of pride. "My father was posted to Antioch, and there my mother received the true faith."

"I am pleased to meet you. I am Noah, as you know. And my cousin's name was Joshua. Say it."

But Marcus the Roman knew not a syllable of Aramaic and could not get his tongue around it.

"I suppose I shall have to be content with 'Jesus'," Noah said at last.

"I feel that I am on sacred ground," Marcus said, giving the impression that he had not heard, "to be in the place where he grew to manhood."

"We both did."

Noah raised his arm and pointed to the house just opposite, across an open space of perhaps twenty paces.

"He was born in that house," he said, as if the fact proved something important. "His younger brother's grandchildren live there still. Of course, none of them remember him."

"But you remember him."

"Oh yes."

"Were you really with him when he died?"

"Yes. That day has lived in my memory ever since."

"Then you will be able to tell me. What were his last words?"

For a moment Noah was silent. He had never revealed to anyone the despair that had gripped Joshua in his final moments. It would have seemed a betrayal.

" 'My God, my God, why have You forsaken me?' " he answered, in Aramaic.

"What does that mean?"

"He was asking for a drink of water."

Marcus's disappointment was palpable. He didn't know what to say, so he changed the subject.

"What was he like when you knew him?"

"When I knew him?" Noah shrugged, and poured himself another cup of wine. "That would be his whole life, for we were born only a few days apart. We learned our letters together—he was cleverer than I. He loved God. It was a love that left little room for anyone else."

Except for Rachel, he could have added, but he did not. It seemed to him that these people who called his childhood companion the Son of God had no claim to know the man of flesh and blood that Joshua had been, with his infirmities and his private sorrows.

Instead, Noah pointed to a line of hills, visible to the west over the rooftops of Nazareth. "Those hills are terraced, and covered with grape arbors," he said. "On a dare, when we were seven years old, Joshua jumped down from one, and broke his arm. He thought God would hold him up. He was mistaken."

But Marcus the Roman, the follower of Jesus the Christ, did not want to hear about broken arms. He wanted to hear about wondrous signs and miracles.

Noah was not able to satisfy him. "I saw him convert Matthias, which saved my life, but I suppose that was not, strictly speaking, a miracle. I heard stories from his disciples of miraculous cures, but I never witnessed one. I think he was a man like other men."

"Then you did not accept his ministry?"

"In the end, no. We only know a true prophet by the truth of his prophecies. It has been more than forty years since Joshua died, and God's kingdom has never come."

"Yet forty years is not so long."

Noah smiled. "Joshua was not as patient as you seem to be."

"Yet are we not living in the end times? Doesn't the destruction of the Temple prove that?"

For a long time Noah was not able to speak. His youngest boy, also named Joshua, had gone up to Jerusalem that Passover and had never returned. Noah could only assume that he had been trapped when the Romans laid siege to the city and had perished like so many others. *Please God,* he had prayed, so many times. *Please God I did not curse him when I named him after Joshua. Please God he died a quick death and did not suffer on the cross.*

"The Temple was destroyed once before," Noah said at last, fixing his gaze on this son of conquerors. "By the Babylonians. And now again by the Romans. God is silent."

"And yet He raised His son from the dead, as a sign to us."

"Did he?" Noah inquired, as in his mind he saw the fetid pit into which the Romans had thrown Joshua's corpse. "Did he indeed?"

"Many saw him, so it is said. He appeared to many."

"He did not appear to me."

"Why should he?" Marcus was almost angry now. "Why would he have appeared to one who denied him?"

All at once, in memory, Noah was a little boy just able to see the top of the Passover table, and his cousin Joshua grinned at him and then, suddenly, stole a fig and ran away.

Then, an old man again, he began to laugh. It was a hollow, scratchy sound, like coins being rattled in a wooden box. He had to wait until the fit was over before he could answer.

"Why, you ask? Because he would not have been able to resist it."

Marcus left unsatisfied. He was on his way to Jerusalem, although it was impossible to say what he expected to find there. Jerusalem was a graveyard.

And Noah was left alone once more, with his wine and his memories.

All he had to do was close his eyes, and Deborah lived again. He could hear the sound of her voice. He could turn over the days of their life together like the pages of a book. He could remember passion, but love was stronger. Love did not die. Love was with him still.

His memories of his wife were a refuge. Better to remember her, a woman full of light, than all the darkness.

"That damned boy!"

Noah couldn't keep it at bay. It all came flooding back over him—Joshua's cruel death, his own dead son, the war.

Some things were at a remove. He could remember the feelings they had stirred, but not the things themselves. They were outside his experience.

The war, for instance, had not much touched Galilee. The war had been something far away. After the Romans tired of Antipas and sent him into exile, Galilee was ruled from Caesarea. But the prefects had confidence in the Lord Eleazar, and the people listened to him. He sided with the Romans, and Galilee remained quiet.

Eleazar had died in his bed before the siege of Jerusalem began. He was spared that, at least. And Galilee knew peace.

And now the Temple was a ruin.

But Noah did not have to imagine what had happened to Joshua those forty years ago. He had seen it. He had witnessed the intolerable suffering of that death. And now, whenever he thought of it, he saw Joshua with his son's face—the son who had been named for him.

Yet, through it all, God had remained silent.

Oh God, Noah had asked, in the privacy of his heart, *Why did You not spare Joshua, who loved You as a child loves his father? Why did You not spare Your people? Why did You not spare my son? Why?*

But there was never an answer. There was only silence. God had turned His face away.

There was nothing left to do but weep. In his old age, it was God's silence he could not forgive.

Then suddenly, though his tears, Noah realized that he was praying. The words came to his lips unbidden, almost against his will, for there was no choice. In all of blind creation, it was only to God that men could turn, in the fading hope that He might listen.

"Blessed art Thou, O Lord our God, King of the Universe . . ."